COVENANT

Daniel Martin

Energion Publications
Gonzalez, Florida
2012

Most Scripture taken from the THE KING JAMES VERSION OF
THE BIBLE.

Scripture references are frequently quoted loosely in dialog in this
novel. These are cited as they would be naturally in conversation.

This is a work of fiction. All persons, events, and organizations are
products of the author's imagination.

Cover Illustration: Christian Wetzel; preliminary design by Bob Mytch.
Additional graphics by Jeb Hunt.

ISBN10: 1-938434-00-5
ISBN13: 978-1-938434-00-6
Library of Congress Control Number: 2012935884

Energion Publications
P. O. Box 841
Gonzalez, FL 32560

850-525-3916
www.energionpubs.com

I'd like to dedicate this book to those who are hurt and lonely
and feel there is no hope.
Don't let yourself be lied to, there is hope.

To those who can't hear the music anymore,
Let yourself get quiet and listen closely. His song is still in
the air.

Many people have helped me in my life, Thank you, I will
never forget you.

This novel reminds me of my weakness and His strength.
(2 Corinthians 12:9)
If I could do many things again in life I would, and would
hope to love you more. To be there for you.

But no one can go back, only forward.
His victory is that I can see clearly now,
and now I see his likeness in you,
and the very best I can do for anyone is to live to present Him,
to you and to the world. His strength will never fail you.

God told Abraham that his descendants would be as the stars
of the Heaven (Genesis 22:17)
If you trust in Jesus the Messiah you are one of those stars
and your future is bright and shining.

So thank you to all who have rescued, reached and loved me.
Thank you to all the workers in the fields of God who keep
loving others.
Soon we will sit down at the table with the King who still
takes a little, and makes much of it.

Thank you Lord, look what God is doing in us!

Let your light shine!

ACKNOWLEDGEMENTS

I sincerely thank Rosemary Otzman of the Belleville Area Independent Newspaper who allowed me the space and time to develop my skills.

Ellen Stewart who helped with early edits and making my sloppy style somewhat readable.

Tina who always believed.

Darlene Prox and the reading group who helped me keep it real.

Pastor Larry Owens of Living Word Worship Center who first inspired and encouraged me to be a Minister. I will always be your friend.

Energion Publications, who were brave enough to take a chance on a first time novel author. May we all be granted the fruit of our expectations.

TABLE OF CONTENTS

1
HOLIDAY BEACH

Like a fish washed up on the shore, Sam McBride lay deadly still in the sand. Bright sunlight brutally attacked his bloodshot eyes causing him to squint. He was recovering from the self-induced poison in his system. He actually thought he'd like it here on Holiday Beach; beautiful sunshine, boardwalk and all.

Along the beachfront people peppered the shoreline. He watched with mild amusement as couples and families laughed and played in the water together. Sam lay back in his sand shifting a little to avoid a wet spot. His hazy memories recalled the simpler times in his life. He had been here many years ago on a family vacation with his mom and dad.

He was four then. His parents were expecting another baby and Sam's dad, Bill McBride, had been so excited he'd brought them here on vacation to celebrate. The smell of fresh roasted peanuts and the warm sea air seemed to blow a little peace into his anxious mind. He could see it all like it was yesterday, his family, all three of them together walking on the beach, collecting shells, swimming, playing. He half-smiled remembering how his dad had helped him build a sand castle. His thoughts drifted back with the sound of the waves.

"Look Dad," Sam joyfully exclaimed," here's you and me and Mom in the castle, right here in the tower. Wait! I'm gonna' put another shell right here for the new baby." Little Sam, knowing his dad was hoping for a girl ran to the water's edge till he found the right pearly pink shell. He carefully added it to the castle in her honor, and then he looked up for his Dad's approval.

"That's great, Sam, good job," Bill McBride smiled and said as he looked down at his son affectionately and ruffled his hair.

Sam was red as a beet from the sun and had sand all over him. He ran to catch up with his parents as his dad looked behind him and motioned for Sam to come along as they walked. They all peered out together over the ocean watching the spectacular orange sun retire for the night. It was one of the most beautiful days Sam had ever known. Even the pelicans and gulls seemed to celebrate as they danced in the air and dived for their food, all the while calling out their love songs.

The steady harmony of the waves washing against the shore seemed to inspire Sam's dad, his smile said it all. Bill McBride was tall and pencil thin with jet black hair and just a bit of gray around the edges. Sam watched intently as his dad leaned in whispering in his wife's ear, "Annie McBride, you are truly the most beautiful woman in the world." She blushed so much you could almost hear it. She was wearing a one piece bathing suit that really accentuated her athletic figure. It was black with gold striping and went well with her golden brown eyes and chestnut hair. Little Sam overflowing with curiosity saw how his dad couldn't take his eyes off her.

Bill McBride drew his wife to himself and kissed her with a long passionate kiss. Sammy giggled as he watched his mother playfully push his dad away from her. She laughed and taunted him, "Catch me if you can, you scrawny weasel." Bill McBride ran after her and then Sam joined in.

Sam stopped and giggled, studying his parents flirting with each other. Quickly he ran and skipped a stone at the beach's shallow water." "Whoa!" He exclaimed at the top of his voice. The stone made five long skips.

"Good throw, Sammy." His mother had seen him and loudly clapped her hands together. Sam glowed with pride at her encouragement. He owned the world at that moment. Everything was just perfect. But that would soon change.

Months later back in Michigan on a blistering hot day, "Bill! Bill, come quick, something's wrong!" a horrendous scream came from inside the house. Annie was in her bedroom crouched up in a ball on the floor holding her stomach. Bill McBride terrified, grabbed Annie and Sam and swiftly put them in the back of their black

Ford Galaxy 500. The drive to the hospital was a blur. In the fifteen minutes it took to arrive at the E.R. Annie's pain had become completely unbearable, she screamed in desperation.

Little Sam was petrified as they ran inside. His mom looked pale. "Help, help, someone please help me!" His dad had a contorted look on his face as he carried Annie past the E.R. desk.

"What's wrong, Daddy?" Sam frantically pleaded and hung on to his dad's trousers. "Mommy, what's wrong with you?" There was no response. The orderlies put Annie on a gurney and rushed her through two green swinging doors. "What's wrong Daddy, please?" Little Sam cried out frantically, running after his dad.

"Not now, Sam. Not now!" His dad intently watched the concerned look on the face of the head nurse. She turned beet red when the doctor came over and whispered something to her. Bill McBride tried but couldn't hear a word. She nodded to the doctor and then walked over to Bill and told him, "I'm sorry, sir, but you and your son will have to wait in the waiting room now."

"Why? Tell me what's wrong." Bill demanded, his voice cracking.

"Sir, we don't know anything yet." She said firmly, and then whispered something to an orderly who quickly escorted Sam and his dad to the waiting room. They reluctantly sat down in two green plastic chairs.

Moments later the intercom crackled, then blared. "Dr. Roberts to the E.R. Code Red!" and again. "Dr. Roberts to the E.R. Code Red!"

Hearing this, Sam's dad shot down the hall like a rocket. He pushed away an orderly attempting to force his way through the doors. Another larger orderly blocked him from entering. "I've got to see my wife. Get out of my way!" Bill screamed at the top of his lungs. "I've got to see my wife, dammit!" He shouted and cried at the same time, "let ... me ... in ... there!" His knees gave way as he imagined the worst.

The burly orderly held him and firmly said, "You can't go in there right now, Mr. McBride. Please, we're doing all that we can. Please!"

The orderly helped Bill turn around and head back toward the waiting room. Worried and frustrated he continued to pace the hallway, pleading, "Please God, please! She's all I have!" Sam just watched, not understanding one bit of what was happening. Seeing his father cry scared him and he started to cry, too. He curled up in a ball on the hard chair and cried himself to sleep.

Minutes seemed like hours. Suddenly loud footsteps forced Sam awake. A tall man in a white coat stood in front of them. He hesitantly walked up to Bill McBride. "I'm sorry," he whispered with disappointment written across his face. He said some other things that Sam couldn't quite make out. Sam's dad literally fell to the floor.

"No! Oh no! Please, God! Please, God! No! Damn you! No! Why? Why?" Sam could only watch as his father wept bitterly. Sam had gone over to comfort him, but it was as if his dad didn't even know he was there. Sam stood beside his father with tears streaming down his face, his tiny hand on his dad's knee. He felt invisible, forgotten, cold and alone.

Days later, two silvery gray caskets had been set up on metal stands under a burgundy canopy. One was full length and the other only about a foot long. People couldn't even bring their eyes to look at the smaller one. The sky was dense with dark clouds threatening to burst open at any second. Tears abounded through the handful of family & friends, but Bill McBride was a stone. He didn't want to talk to anyone and was completely abrupt to any who tried to comfort him.

When the service had concluded and the bodies of Annie McBride and little Sarah were being lowered into the earth, Sam cried out and ran and grasped the handles on his mom's casket. "No, Mommy! Don't leave me." It was as if he was being lowered into the ground with them. His heart sank. The funeral director looked over at Bill McBride who then coldly pried his son's small hands from the casket. "I don't want you to go!" Sam cried violently. The straps were lowered and the caskets disappeared from sight into the dark cold ground.

"Come on, Sam. She's gone." Bill McBride said gruffly. "There's nothing we can do about it now." He practically dragged Sam up the hill toward the black Ford. Bill McBride put Sam in the back seat, and locked the door. Sam was looking back screaming for his mother as the car pulled away. He couldn't believe she was gone.

Sam's dad never fully recovered from the death of Annie and Sarah, his early gray hair bore witness to that. And he was never really nice to Sam again either. Little Sam McBride learned early what it was like to be all alone in the world.

Days, months and years sailed by. Sam's dad became a shell of a man. It often seemed to Sam that he was the one taking care of his dad, instead of the other way around. Those days were far behind him now though and Sam was all grown up. Now he had his own responsibilities, and he neglected them consistently. Life, his life anyway, was full of requirements that he never felt qualified to carry out.

Awakening from his dreams, Sam hazily rose up from the sand. He ran his hands through his unwashed matted hair and slowly looked around him. *"How did I ever wind up here? Where am I gonna go now?"* He had only come back here after being thrown out of his house for being an idiot, an alcoholic. And this wasn't the first time. He wasn't sure exactly why he'd come here, maybe for the memory of a better time in his life. Sam was now 34-years-old. He was still that same child in many ways. He still felt like little Sam.

An unusually strange song echoed in the distance. Sam thought he heard his name. He looked out over the ocean and saw what looked like a huge white bird. Was it a seagull? It appeared to have some kind of a golden thread wrapped around it. It quickly flew out of sight. *"That is strange,"* Sam thought, then lay back down in the sand and closed his eyes.

Just then a strong morning breeze washed up from the ocean stirring the leaves of a tall palm tree.

"Wake up, Sam, it's time to live."

Sam rose up. *"What was that? Did I hear a voice?"* Sam thought it was just his conscience. He ignored it like he usually did and washed the thought away with another drink of cheap whiskey.

"Ah, this place has changed," he thought. Looking around he could see the beach was now littered and a little dirty. Everything seemed more aged, worn out. He fit right in. Sam watched a beach bum going through a trash can a few yards away from him. The old man pulled a half eaten burger out of a bag and devoured it without hesitation. Sam gasped. *"Oh my God! How gross!"*

"That's you, Sam." a voice whispered. "That's where you're headed, maybe worse, if you don't let me help you." Sam glanced down the beach front at the sound of the voice. Two children were building something in the sand. No one else was near him.

"Sam," the soft voice spoke again.

Sam shook his head and tried to ignore it. *"I've got to be hearing things. This stuff's pickling my brain."* He glanced down at the bottle concealed in the brown bag and grunted out half a laugh at the thought.

"You're not hearing things, Sam." the voice became a little louder.

"Did I say that out loud?" Quickly Sam spun around in the sand to catch a glimpse of the source. He angrily rose from the ground. "OK who are you? If this is some kind of joke or something, it's not funny!"

"Thud!" Sam tripped on his feet and fell into the sand face first. Opening his eyes wide, he slowly lifted his head and looked around. Still no one. He wiped himself off and crawled on his knees to a wooden bench and leaned back against it.

After a few seconds, the wind came again.

"It's no joke, Sam, and I don't find it funny either. I've been waiting, watching. Your life's been like a bad novel, one chapter to the next. If you'd let Me, I'd turn it into a story filled with joy, instead of the train wreck it's been so far. What do you say?"

Sobering a little, yet still confused, Sam replied, "Who are you? Part of a bad hangover or something?"

"You know who I Am. I knew you before you were even born. That ocean over there, that blue sky, I did that. You say you don't need anyone, but Sam, I think you know how much you need Me. But it has to be your decision. I Am here for you."

"Sure, OK. You're trying to tell me that you're ..., that you're God, right?" Sam laughed and took another deliberate drink of his whiskey. "Like I'm really supposed to think that hmmm, God is talking to some drunk on the beach at 9:00 in the morning?"

A jogger overhearing Sam's voice ran by and gave Sam a dirty look. Sam, ashamed, turned away.

Again the wind came, "So you admit it then?"

"That you're God? And that you're talking to me? No way." Sam's voice cracked now. He looked up angrily. "You're just a figment of my imagination. A bad joke someone's playing on me or somethin'."

"No. I mean you admit you're a drunk?"

"I didn't say that!"

"Yes, you did."

Sam realized whatever was happening, this was not just his imagination. He was becoming more angry and defensive with each passing moment.

"Well, alright! If you are who you say you are, where have you been?" Sam's face darkened with rage as he shook his fist in the air and shouted, "Where were you when I really needed you? Where were you when my mom needed you? Where were you then? Dammit. You took away the only person who ever really cared about me." Sam was trembling now. "If that's what God's all about, I don't want nothing to do with you!"

"You can't blame me for that, Sam. Did you know your mom believed in Me and is here with Me, right now?"

This peaked Sam's curiosity. His mind raced back to a day only a few months before she died. He had just turned four. Her bedroom door was open, barely a crack. The sun had just come up, and was boldly beaming through the old wood framed windows. He had just walked down the hallway and heard his mom's voice.

"Who was she talking to?" he wondered. He quietly peeked in and watched in wonder as she knelt down by her bed. Her hands were folded in front of her and her head was bowed. What was she doing? No one else was in the room. All this just confused him now. Sam had never been to a church.

"Is it all true?" Sam asked aloud looking up to the sky.

Another jogger ran by, "Yeah, you're a bum. Get a job!" The jogger had gone out of his way to avoid Sam. To the outside world he probably just seemed like another unshaven, unloved, homeless man who seemed to be in the throes of a nervous breakdown.

"My God!" Sam thought, *"I'm hearing things and talking to myself."* Sam looked down at his pants and noticed that he had wet himself. A tear escaped from his eye. *"I am a bum! I'm going crazy."* He struggled to comprehend what was happening to him. He cried out, "OK, I am .... I am a bum. God, I don't wanna be like this. I don't wanna wind up like that man!" Sam pointed and shouted as the bum nearby dug deeper in the trash can.

The bum turned around and gave him the finger. "Screw you, buddy!"

The ocean breeze swept Sam's matted hair from his face revealing another tear. Like a drive-in movie, memories of better times with his family flashed in his mind. One summer they were all washing the family minivan together.

"Dad, can I spray off the soap?" his daughter, Amanda, asked.

"Only if you wash your mother off at the same time," Sam teased and quickly got out of the way.

"No!" Denise screamed as her daughter chased after her totally drenching her with the hose. They all laughed hysterically

"What am I doing here?" Sam said to himself.

The voice from nowhere answered again.

"Destiny brought you here, Sam. It was time for some changes. I Am your Father if you want Me to be. You are my son if you want to be. And you're not hearing things. You're hearing Me. You don't have to end up like that. Ever since you were a child I've called you, waited for you."

"When? When did you ever call out to me?" Sam asked, meekly now, letting down his guard a little.

"I tried to get you to come to a Bible study after your mother died. An old friend of hers, Rosemary, gave you a Bible and invited you to come. You almost did, but you went to be with your friends instead."

"How did you know about that?" Sam asked." *"Are you really Him? Man, I thought I heard you then, but I wasn't sure. But even if you really are talking to me, I don't think you can help me now. I'm too far gone and I don't care anymore. I don't have anyone that cares about me. My wife threw me out. I've got nothing."*

"I care, Sam. You're not too far gone. Denise still loves you and there are others who care, too. But you're gonna have to step up. It's time to be lifted up now. I have plans for you." The voice trailed off as a whisper. "You know what to do." The wind blew against his face again. All that could be heard was the gentle harmony of the waves washing in. Instinctively, Sam turned around and folded his hands together leaning his elbows on the seat of the bench.

"Oh God, please, help me." He was openly weeping. A downpour of emotion rose up in him. He collapsed on the bench with his head in his arms. "Forgive me for how I've lived. How I treated You and for what I said." His nose was running all over his face, but he didn't care. "I don't have any right, but, please help me. Denise hates me. I don't even know my own kid. I ..." His words trailed off into a muffled cry. "I don't know what to say. I don't know what to do anymore. I'm sorry. I'm really sorry. Please?"

Sam groaned inwardly, a purging that went far beyond words made his whole body shake. An ocean of tears washed the sand from his face, as a Father's love washed the pain from his heart. Sam was being renewed in a way he didn't even know or believe was possible. The toxic contents of his stomach began to erupt. He ran over to the trash can and threw up. A moment later he dragged himself back and sat down Indian style in front of the bench. He put his hands together, bowed his head and prayed. "Lord, please help me. I do want You to be my God. I do want to be your son." He waited for seconds. Then minutes. It was so quiet. An inner peace enveloped him. He slowly lay down in the sand and fell asleep.

Sam dreamed a beautiful dream that his mom was alive. She was talking to him. *"Wake up, Sammy! Wake up and live. I'll always love you, Sam. I want you to know, you were meant for so much more. It's time to wake up now."*

Then strangely her voice seemed deep, masculine sounding. Everything became dark. "Wake up. Come on wake up, buddy."

Sam confused, opened his eyes and grimaced. A police officer dressed in a blue uniform, knee-high black motorcycle boots and a white helmet loomed over him. A silver badge on his shirt read, 'Holiday Highway Patrol.' Sam squinted again when he noticed a holstered gun at the officer's side. It made him extremely nervous.

"How are you doing there, sir?" the officer asked in a deep voice, looking down at Sam in his mirrored teardrop sunglasses. Sam thought he sounded like Johnny Cash.

"Weird" he thought. Sam did his best to pull the hair out of his eyes and straighten his shirt as he lifted himself from the sand.

The officer waited patiently.

"Good sir, I think I'll be all right." Sam said meekly. He could see how bad he looked though the reflection in the officer's sunglasses. "Umm, am I under arrest?"

"I don't know. Are you doing something wrong?"

"Sir, to be honest, ahh …" Sam stuttered. "I … uh, was drinking. But I'll … umm … I'll just pour it out if you let me. I really am fed up with it anyway." Sam bit his lip apprehensively.

To Sam's surprise, the officer nodded and smiled. Sam leaned down, picked up the bottle and poured the whiskey out on the ground. The officer motioned with his head toward the trash can. Sam got up, walked over and dropped in the bottle, then slowly walked back to the bench. They both just looked at each other for a moment. Sam was waiting for the officer to say something, but he just stood there. Finally, Sam looked down the shoreline and said, "Well, I'll just go now if you let me."

"Where are you going?" the officer asked. "You have a place to go?" This policeman seemed to have a real cool demeanor about him.

"Not anymore," Sam uttered under his breath. He looked down at the ground ashamed. The thought of being homeless was overwhelming him. It was not something he thought he'd ever have to face.

The officer kindly asked, "Do you want to tell me about it?"

"You really want to know?" Sam asked guardedly, although curiosity was biting at his ankle. He thought to himself, *"Could this guy really care?"*

"Sure." The officer said, sitting down on the bench. He took off his helmet, then his sunglasses, revealing jet black hair above kind amber eyes.

"Strange," Sam thought, *"he must be Italian or something. I've never seen eyes that color before."*

Sam began his story. "Well to be honest, I, ah, got thrown out of my house. My wife, she got fed up. You know, the drinking and all. See, I'm an alcoholic and I've never been able to hold down a job for too long." Sam paced as he talked. "And usually when I did get a little money, I always seemed to be able to find an excuse to totally shipwreck everything. I'd blow all our money on booze or dope." Sam cocked his head. "You've heard all this before right?" Sam waited, yet the officer said nothing. "You're not going to arrest me, are you?"

"I don't think so." the officer replied with squinted eyes, a gruff whisper and a grin. He sounded like Clint Eastwood this time.

"I must be losing my mind," Sam thought, but he nervously continued.

"Well Denise, my wife, finally got fed up with it all and threw me out. But not before my kid, Mandy, started drinking and getting high too, following in her old man's footsteps." Sam paused at the thought of Amanda, a tear escaped making a trail down his cheek. "What right have I got to say anything to her when I can't even stop myself?" Sam placed one hand on top of the other to keep them from shaking. Expecting a harsh answer, he nervously asked, "So, what do you think?"

The officer chose his words carefully.

"You know, Sam, it's not really a new story around here. But you seem a little different from the normal drifter that blows in here. You somehow seem like you still care." The officer hesitated, and leaning in, he looked Sam in the eye. "That shows hope." He lowered his voice and crossed his arms.

"And you know that's the gold a lot of people around here ran out of a long time ago. You know I knew of a man who struggled through addictions once. He was a terrible drunk and a thief, too. But he eventually turned around through the help of someone who loved him. And, believe it or not, later in his life he took in thousands of orphans and taught them all about what he learned through his own faith. And most of them turned out really great. And there was another man, he struggled terribly with lust, amongst other things. But through the unfailing love of a close friend, he eventually became a great teacher. Some today even call him a saint."

"Who …? I mean, are they on T.V.? Would I have heard of them?"

"The first one you might have heard of. His name was George Mueller, a famous minister that helped thousands of orphans. They've written books about him and everything. The second you might know as St. Augustine."

Sam raised his eyes. He had heard of St. Augustine.

"The point is, Sam, either one of them could have gone the other way, but they turned to the One who could really help them. A Friend they say, that is closer than a brother." The officer smiled his Clint Eastwood smile again.

"God, right!?" Sam exclaimed like he was on a game show. The officer just continued to smile. "Wow, I never heard of a cop talking about God before! If I told you about the conversation I had with Him a few minutes ago, you'd be carting me off to the mental hospital."

"Yet here we are, aren't we?" the officer asked modestly. "So which way do you want to go? Do you want to stay here and lose what's left? Or do you want to try again? Maybe with God's help this time?" This all seemed so surreal to Sam. He thought for a second maybe someone was setting him up for a reality show prank. But he had to find out where this was going, not to mention he was extremely desperate.

Finally, Sam replied, "I want to go home. But I don't think she'll take me back this time." Sam shook his head slightly, looking down at the ground. "And I don't have any way to get there either."

"Do you really want to go home?" the officer asked, a fire in his eyes.

"Yes sir, more than anything," Sam said, hope rising in him. The officer pulled out his wallet, took out $200, and handed it to Sam. "Go home, Sam. Go home to your wife and daughter. Put your trust in God. He'll change your life." The officer said this in a low tone, sounding a lot like John Wayne. It almost made Sam laugh, but he decided he'd better not.

"Are you really allowed to do all this?" Sam asked. He looked at the officer and then stared in amazement at the money in his hand.

"It's my job," the officer replied calmly.

"The cops back home aren't anything like you," Sam laughed. "Thank you. Thank you so much. Will you … Could I ask you to … maybe, pray for me?"

"You bet I will." the officer replied.

"So, what's your name, sir, if you don't mind me asking?"

"Steven. But my friends call me Steve." the officer paused and smiled. "You can call me Steve."

Together they walked to the place where the sand and pavement met. The officer put on his helmet and glasses then climbed on his exceptionally chromed, super shiny Harley-Davidson motorcycle. "Sam, it's really been a pleasure meeting you." He started the bike. It sputtered and gave its usual Harley roar.

"I think you're going to do great!" Officer Steve said loudly over the sound of the bike. He extended his hand and shook Sam's. "If you're ever out this way again, look me up and give me a call. We'll be praying for you. Hey! God Bless you, Sam."

Sam, astounded with the gift, almost speechless, turned and walked back toward the beach. Suddenly, he realized that he had never told the officer his name. Mystified, Sam asked out loud, "How did he know my …?" Sam, turning around quickly shouted, "Hey, how did you know …?" Steve was gone. There was no motorcycle, no noise or anything. Sam looked down the ocean walk, to the left, to the right. He scanned the horizon, but there was no sign of him. He thought to himself, *"There's no way he could have gotten away that fast. And he said 'We will be praying for you.' Who's we?"*

2
A FRIEND IN NEED

Completely amazed at what just happened, Sam grabbed up his green army duffel and made his way downtown to get his bus ticket home. Something in him had awakened. Surprisingly he didn't feel the effects of the alcohol at all anymore. As he walked to the bus stop his mind raced, pondering all the times he'd heard God speak to him but never realized it. He had real hope now, a joyful anticipation greater than any he'd ever experienced before.

Looking down at the sidewalk he talked as he walked, "Lord, I'm sorry I treated you real bad. You're the best friend I ever had. I just never knew it. You never gave up on me."

Hope burned brighter in his mind as he wondered what his life might have been like had he only known what he'd just found out. He shook his head at his own blindness, now able to see that he was loved, really loved. Sam looked up at the sky. "Thank you for loving me, Lord!"

A tattooed teen-age girl on a skateboard rolled by. Hearing Sam's conversation, she circled him looking to see if he was talking on a blue tooth cell phone. When she realized he wasn't, she shook her head and mumbled, "Freak! Friggin' town's full of people talking to themselves."

Sam overheard her but it didn't bother him. He just laughed to himself. *"I wonder if I will be like one of those Jesus freaks? They always seemed a little brainwashed, like they were from another planet or something."* But as he thought about it now, he realized that they mostly seemed like they were … just happy.

He remembered how impressed he had been when he met a man back home at a job center that told him that God had rescued him from drug and alcohol addiction, and that he never used again. The man got all emotional when he told Sam his story.

Thinking back further, Sam recalled it wasn't until his little girl was born that he had really started to drink heavily.

"Dave, I don't feel like I'm ready to be a dad." he had told his best friend at a Tigers' baseball game.

"Don't worry, Sam, it'll get easier. Just give it some time," Dave had replied encouragingly. But it never did. Sam just felt lost and inadequate as he held her tiny little life in his hands.

Sam attracted flies and repelled people as he walked up to the bus station ticket counter. His lack of hygiene wasn't winning him any friends. "How much for a one-way ticket to Detroit, sir?" he asked the seated clerk.

"One hundred seventy-five bucks. Bus number eight leaves in about ten minutes," the man replied in a monotone not even looking up from his paper.

Sam gave the clerk the wrinkled cash from his hand and waited, then took his change and sat down on an old wooden bench.

Across from him a little girl in pink coveralls quickly devoured a melting ice cream cone. She smiled and waved over at Sam, who waved back, touched by the gesture. She reminded him of his own daughter, Amanda. She had always craved his affection but he never was really there for her. Sam had held these emotions at arm's length for years, but something inside was breaking free.

As seagulls cried out their songs in the distance, Sam cried inside. He never really knew how to get very close to anyone, not even his own family. Growing up an only child in his father's strict home, affection was practically forbidden. But now, with a new expectation rising in him, all he wanted was a chance to make it up to her, to hold her and tell her how beautiful she was, how much he loved her. She definitely deserved that.

"What will I say to her?" Sam wondered as he lifted up his legs planting his feet on the bench. He bowed his face into his knees, covered his head with his arms, and prayed softly, *"Help me, Lord, to love her and be a good father."* Filled with mixed emotions, he subconsciously rocked a little on the bench. He was anxious to get

home and try to begin a new start with his family, but not sure he'd have that chance.

Sam was completely unaware of the fact that he was being watched. A large African American woman, waiting for the exact same bus, had been studying him carefully. Marguerite Amaya Ashton was her name. She was vastly overdressed, adorned with a floppy purple hat with a bright red scarf wrapped around her neck. She was especially careful not to get caught watching him. She waited, listening intently for instructions. A stiff warm breeze blew her scarf to the other side of her shoulder. She felt the presence of the One that comes with the wind. A still small voice spoke, *"I've got a job for you to do, my dear lady."*

Knowing the voice well, she whispered, "Be with me Lord." Then she opened her purse, twisted the lid off of a small decorative glass bottle and poured something on a handkerchief.

"Now boarding number eight," a shrill voice cried out. All sorts of passengers quickly made their way up and onto the bus. Sam slowly got up and climbed the steps. With his dirty sleeve he tiredly wiped the most recent in a series of tears from his sunburnt face.

The bus driver gave him a nasty look as he passed to take his seat, emphasizing his disgust by quickly spraying air freshener in Sam's wake.

Marge was right behind Sam though and purposely gave the driver a stern glare that said, *"Go ahead, and try that one more time!"* The driver smirked and deliberately turned his head to the left, looking out the side window.

Marge plopped down all 300 pounds right next to Sam. She quickly extracted the handkerchief she had prepared from her bag of treasures.

"Here honey, you have this. My name is Marge and it's a pleasure to meet you," she said lovingly.

Sam, surprised at the unexpected kindness, looked at Marge cautiously. He paused for a second, and then with half a smile took the handkerchief and wiped his face and his eyes.

"That smells really nice. Thanks." his voice barely a whisper. "I'm…I'm Sam." He offered her his dirty hand, which she shook without hesitation.

"You're welcome, honey. My friends, they sometimes call me 'Large Marge,' or 'Marge at Large,'" she boldly laughed, "'cause I'm a big woman if you hadn't noticed, and I like to share large joy wherever I go. You look like you could use a little. Now that's special anointin' oil on there. I made it myself." She looked down at the hanky and smiled wide. "Well, I'll leave ya' alone now." She softened her voice and continued, "But if you need a shoulder, honey, I got some wide ones ya' know, and I've been there, too. So you just let me know."

Sam looked up curiously, a tiny bit skeptical at her kindness. But when he looked into her eyes, he could see nothing but love. "Thanks. Thanks a lot," he said genuinely.

With the effects of the alcohol somehow gone, Sam was fighting mixed emotions. On one hand he was definitely alive with anticipation, yet on the other, he was terrified. He looked out the window, his mind replaying the last conversation he had with his wife, Denise. He had just dragged himself in at 9:00 in the morning after an all night binge. He walked through the foyer into the living room. His wife was standing there with her hands on her hips, in battle position. She glared at Sam and then looked down.

"*Uh-oh,*" Sam thought.

The atmosphere in the room became thick as she waited then took a deep breathe.

Sam froze in place like a deer caught in headlights.

"This is the last time, Sam." She couldn't look up at him again. "I can't keep doing this and it's not fair to Mandy either." she paused. "You can't stay here anymore."

Sam gasped. Denise had his duffle bag leaning against the wall, packed and ready to go.

He sobered quickly and went into survival mode.

"I'm sorry, 'Neesi!" (That was her nickname.) "I'm gonna try, babe. Please don't do this. I'll change Denise. I ... I," he stuttered looking at the floor. "I got no where else to go! This is my home. I'll get some help, OK? Really."

Denise chose her words carefully.

"You've had help and it's not helped!" She raised her voice increasingly. "You just keep dragging us down with you. Why? Why again? Dammit, Sam! How much do you think I can take?" With that she picked up the duffle bag and hurled it at him, then turned and walked away into the kitchen leaning over the sink.

"Just go, Sam. If you want to be a bum, you can go out there and live like one."

Sam couldn't see her tears streaming down her face, falling into the dishwater. All he saw was her back and then the note on the bag that read, "Don't bother coming back, I've had it!" The note was signed, "YOUR DOORMAT NO MORE!"

That was the day Sam hitchhiked out of Michigan, heading for warmer weather. But as warm as it got as he hitched west, he only had grown colder and lonelier deep inside.

It had really hurt his wife to write that note, but she was worn out and needed refuge from this adult child. Sam knew now she was right. He had taken advantage of her strength ever since they met, but had never really been there for her. Even those times when she'd let down her guard and let him know that she'd needed him, he couldn't see past his own selfishness. He'd often tell the guys at the Eagle's Nest that she was putting the pressure on, but everything was fine as far as he was concerned. So he had a few drinks now and then. So what?

Now, on the way back home, with the road stretched out before him, he was seeing everything behind him clearly. He sighed a little, hoping for the chance to make it right.

"It will get better, mister. It always gets better eventually," Marge said.

"What makes you so sure?" asked Sam.

She tried to be encouraging, "Son, there's an ebb and flow to everything. The Master has made things that way. People get second chances. It's kind of almost built in."

"And the Master would be?" Sam asked.

"The Lord, of course!" said Marge, like she'd just struck gold.

Sam laughed deeply. So genuinely that Marge laughed with him. She was just really glad to see a smile on his face.

Finally, with curiosity etching her eyes and brows, she asked, "So what are we laughing about anyway?"

Sam replied, "Oh you wouldn't believe me if I told you. It just seems like the Master's running a special on Christian advice today and I seem to be His biggest customer. You might not believe this, but I woke up on the beach this morning about seven and …" Sam related the conversation with God and with the motorcycle officer.

Marge looked at Sam with the affectionate smile of a mother for her own son and said slowly, "Well, I know one thing, young man. The Good Lord put you on my heart when you were on the bench waiting for the bus, and I said to myself, 'Marguerite, that man over there is in desperate need of a love transfusion.' I began to pray for you then and there. I was hoping we could be friends. And mister, I don't really know who you are, what you've been going through or where you've been, but I do sense the Lord's hand in your life and His light on your soul."

"Now I don't wanna be 'Barging in Marge,' but if you need an ear, I've raised four boys, three girls, and I've got thirteen grandkids. So, I can definitely handle it. Now that's all I'm saying for now. You just rest a while, OK? I'm here if you need me."

"Thanks," Sam replied. "You're nice." Exhausted, he leaned over, pulled up his duffel bag and rested his head on it. He fell asleep quickly and dreamed of how life could have been if he would have just stayed away from the alcohol and how much he'd missed all these years caught up in his own drudgery. He stirred and awoke briefly as the sun warmed his face. He smiled and faded quietly to sleep again, grateful for the possibility of a second chance. As he slept, Sam recognized that the hum of the bus on the road seemed to have a melody all its own. It was a song about going home. A peace greater than Sam had ever known came over him.

As he slept, Marge prayed quietly. Opening her eyes she looked over and saw Sam's face finally relax, as he gave in to a gentle slumber like that of a peaceful child.

Marge smiled closed her eyes and went to a beautiful place.

The sun was setting in the Colorado Rockies when Sam awoke. He had gotten a few hours of much needed rest. The bus had just pulled up at a country store for a bathroom and snack break. Shhhhishh! The brakes hissed noisily as they brought the huge wheels to a stop. As Sam stepped off the bus a beautiful sight overwhelmed his senses. The mountains seemed alive, majestically covered in blue and white, purple and green, the sun highlighting them with an orange-like tint. He drew in the clean crisp air as he looked around at the surrounding splendor.

"I've missed so much all these years trapped in my own stuff, but not anymore," he thought. Looking up at the sun disappearing behind a mountain peak, he smiled extra wide, grateful for a second chance, extremely grateful.

After a few minutes everyone was climbing back on the bus. Sam walked quietly toward his seat, quickly noticing Marge was still asleep. He stole a long look at this unusual new friend. To him, she looked like an angel sitting there. She held her knitting project in one hand, still sitting straight up, her head bent slightly to the left. Her Bible was open in her lap. Her hair had braids adorned with various multi-colored beads. She wore a beautiful handmade African-style red and yellow dress. It had colored silhouettes representing African people working the land sewn throughout the fabric.

Sam carefully moved past her into his seat. Seeing her fast asleep like that reminded him of how much he still missed his mother. He remembered after she and the baby had died, his dad had told him, "There is no God, Sam. Just remember you are all you've got in this world. Everyone else will just let you down."

He believed his father for the longest time, but now after his experience on the beach, Sam knew his dad was wrong. He wished he could tell him that God was real, and that God loved him, too.

His memories drove him back to that dark old house. It always had a foul musty smell to it. Leaning back in his chair he was now half asleep again. He daydreamed uncomfortably of the plastic tape over the cracked windows, liquor bottles lying empty on the floor, others partly full, hidden in strategic places. There were cigarette butts all over the place and burns in the second hand furniture from when his dad had fallen asleep with lit cigarettes. He had almost burned down the house once. Sam swore he'd never become like that. But yet, he was bitten by the same bug.

"Like father like son," he thought. The last time he'd seen and spoken to his dad he'd said some things he wished he hadn't, like "When are you going to climb out of your shell and start living again? I can't stand being around you, you make me sick!"

His dad had shouted back, "Get out of my house, you **@*! You can't talk to me like that. This is my house. Who do you think you are?"

He knew he had really offended his dad that day.

"If I could only take it back," he reflected.

Sam could still see his dad's cold stare as he walked away. He had almost turned around and apologized, but pride had stopped him, blinded him. Now he wished he had, knowing what he knew now. But it was too late. His father had died years ago and very few people attended that funeral.

Marge stirred in her chair, startling Sam back to the present. Opening her eyes, she smiled sleepily and said, "Hey there, young man, did you get some good rest?"

"Yes, Ma'am. How about you?" Sam replied, grateful for the interruption.

"You bet," she stretched in her seat. "Whew, look at that sunset. Oh my Lord, You do good work!"

Others on the bus were looking out the windows and enjoying the spectacle as well.

There was fresh snow on the tree line and in the mountain tops.

"I always keep a lookout for eagles," Sam said, looking toward the trees.

"Have you seen one before?" Marge asked.

"Not in the wild, no, only like in a zoo." Sam replied turning to face her. "They really don't belong in a zoo, you know? They need their freedom too much."

"Don't we all, son. Don't we all."

Sam looked back up at the snow caps. Beautiful as they were, they reminded him of cold Michigan winters, one thing he was not looking forward to back home. His face grew long.

"What will I say to her? Will she take me back?" Sam squirmed uneasily in his seat.

Marge picked up on his troubled expression and asked him, "Something bothering you, young man?"

He tried to find the words, "I, well, I guess I, I am a little worried," he finally spit out. "I really don't know if I have a place to stay. If my wife doesn't let me back in, the only friends I have, are, well, they drink a lot. I don't want to go back to that. I don't have a job any more, and I'm not …"

"Wait, son." She scolded. "Just hold on there, just a second. Have you entrusted all this to the Lord or did you pray to a cartoon cat or something? 'Cause if you gave it all to the Lord out there by the ocean, like you said, then you gotta let Him shoulder the load. You got to know He's gonna open the door. Here, look at this." she opened her Bible to Matthew and read, "In Matthew 11:28-30 Jesus says, 'Come unto me, all ye that labor and are heavy laden, and I will give you rest. Take my yoke upon you, and learn of me; for I am meek and lowly in heart and ye shall find rest for your souls. For my yoke is easy, and my burden is light.'" She set the Bible back down in her lap.

"Son, He walks with you in this! And sure you have to do your part, but remember He gives you the rest. It's now His yoke and His burden. All you have to do child is what He's sayin' today. If He wanted you to be all stuffed up with what's behind, He'd have given you eyes in the back of your head. And If He wanted you to see into the future, He'd have given you a third eye right in the middle of your head," she gently poked him in the middle of his forehead to emphasize the point.

Sam laughed. Marge continued, "But the fact is He said to take care of today. Here read this out loud so we both can hear it. It'll be our soul food." She placed her finger at the text.

Sam smiled and began to read out loud. As he did the last beams of the sun shone in on the page almost like a spotlight from heaven. He was so amazed at that, he did a double take and looked out the window. "'Therefore I say unto you, take no thought for your life, what ye shall eat, or what ye shall drink, nor yet for your body,'" he continued to the end of her finger. "That is pretty good," Sam smiled and said.

"Oh, you know it is. It's real good, thank you, Lord." Marge said, smiling and looking up.

"Now young man, listen to me good. There is an enemy out there. And he is called the devil. If we let him, he would steal, kill and destroy every good thing that we have, so we have to trust in the Lord everyday, and as we do, He gives us the strength to take steps to make things right.

As Marge continued, Sam's thoughts turned to his daughter again, how he wished he would have really been there for her. He wondered where she was right now.

Back in Michigan, a teenager with a pierced lip, leather jacket and jet black hair sat with a friend on a bar stool. Pinball machines, video games and coin changers made their music and flashed their lights as she text messaged one of her friends from school, even though she was sitting right next to her.

Suddenly Joey Osborn, the local teen-aged oppressor interrupted them. "Hey Mandy, your runaway bum of an old man come beggin' to come home yet?" His gang of followers all laughed with him while digging for quarters in the change returns.

"Oh look," Amanda said to her friend, "a single cell, bottom feeding parasite, trying to evolutionize himself with the help of his grunting, cave dweller friends."

All the boys were speechless, trying to figure out what she had just said.

"Not even going to respond?" Amanda looked to her friend Laura who said, "I'm not sure if they even speak English yet."

The two girls got up and took a shortcut home through the woods. Amanda had heard it all before. And even though she had begun to drink and actually smoke pot herself, which she and her friend were about to do, there was a part of her that really hated it. But the pain her family was going through was too much for her to bear. Amanda had no idea her dad was on his way home. She missed him terribly.

Marge, knowing she had precious little time, continued to encourage Sam. She leaned toward him in her seat. "Now young man, God doesn't want us walking around in clouds of fear and doubt. He wants us to get up and get out, and do what's right. And He promises to fight for us, but we've got to show up for the fight. Son, it appears to me, if I may be so bold …" Sam smiled his approval. "… the first thing you've got to do is ask your wife and your child to forgive you, for not being the man that you were supposed to be." Marge looked Sam square in the eye.

"But what if she doesn't take me back?" he asked.

"You're asking for forgiveness, not so you can get something, but because it's the right thing to do. Even if she doesn't take you back, you have to trust the Lord will help you, when you do right. You can only do your part and trust God with the rest. And then you will be blessed."

"It's weird but I do believe that now. Something in me does feel different." He reached up and turned on their personal lights as it was dark.

"That's the Holy Ghost shedding hope in your heart, Sam. Glory to God!" she said out loud, smiling from ear to ear, her hands raised in the air.

Sam, amused, asked, "So, who is this Holy Ghost? I know I feel different, but how do I keep this feeling, or whatever it is?"

"Well son, you do and you don't. It, or I should say *He* really keeps you if you let Him. The Lord stays with you and will always stay with you, if you want Him to, but He won't force you. It's so important that you pray and read His Word and don't grieve the Holy Ghost by giving in to sin or living in fear or doubt. And He'll never leave you. That's His promise."

"Yeah, but who exactly *is* the Holy Ghost?" Sam pressed.

"The Holy Ghost is God's Spirit who fills us with His presence, His life."

Marge reached into her bag and handed Sam a fruit bar, and then a sandwich and a diet soda. It was a huge bag with red swirl designs. It looked to Sam to be custom made for her, maybe as a gift or something.

She continued, "The Holy Ghost teaches us all about Jesus. He wakes up our minds to think like God's mind thinks." She searched deep into the bag. "Now where is that? Oh good." She pulled out a brick of cheddar cheese. "Pray for me, Sam. This is my weakness. Oooh, how I love cheese." She broke a piece for each of them and handed one to Sam.

"Lord, thank you for this food. Amen. Isn't God good?" she exclaimed while looking up as if to heaven. Sam smiled. They continued to talk while they enjoyed their food.

"Now, He lets us see further than our old eyes ever could. He lets our ears hear and know about real truth and love. He raises up hope in our hearts, as big as an Iowa cornfield. And He gives us love for people like He has for us. The Holy Ghost is the fuel that gets this granny out of bed in the morning and sets my path straight."

"Did you ever think about being a preacher?" Sam asked, impressed by Marge's way with words.

She replied, "Oh son, I do my share. I don't need no pulpit to get the job done."

Sam paused for a few seconds. "How do you know if you've got the Holy Ghost?" asked Sam looking at Marge earnestly.

"Well that depends on which camp your in, son. In my camp they call us Pentecostals. We speak in tongues and prophesy and operate in the gifts of the Spirit, and, oh, how I enjoy a good old-fashioned revival." She smiled broadly.

A neatly dressed passenger in the seat ahead turned around to stare at them through his round metal glasses. Looking down his pointed nose at them, he rudely interrupted, "Are you two going to carry on like this the whole trip? If so, why don't you take it to the back of the bus where you won't be bothering everybody?"

"Now look, Mister Eavesdropper sir," Marge spoke with a quiet confidence, "I don't go to the back of the bus for anyone, unless I have to use the facilities, and the last time I looked it was still the American flag flying in this country. Now you would be more than welcome to join in and talk, and share with us, but if not would you be so kind as to turn around and please mind your own business so that we can continue our conversation. And either way, God bless you, sir."

The man was speechless. For seconds he stared dumbfounded into Marge's eyes. She calmly returned his stare. Then losing the standoff he turned around without further protest and continued to look at his magazine. Sam tried to conceal his smile.

"I really like this lady," he said to himself looking at her.

"You're a gift from Heaven," he told her. She smiled.

"Anyway, Sam," Marge cleared her throat, "it's quite simple. No matter what side of the tracks you're from, Jesus said 'Ask and you'll receive'." She handed Sam her Bible and said, "Look up Luke Chapter 11 verses 9-13, and you'll see it's as simple as asking, and then believe you've received what God has for you, and in time you'll know."

There were a few minutes of silence as Sam looked down and read the passage. It was now so quiet on the bus you could hear the steady hum of the tires on the road. They were in Iowa. There were cornfields for miles. It was a clear sky and it seemed all the stars were out.

"Wow, it's that simple?" Sam asked after reading the verses.

"God is often really not that complicated, young man. We're the ones that complicate things. Now for each person it's the same and different at the same time. Our Father knows each of His kids and often ministers to them according to their uniqueness, you know? For example, some folks dance with joy in the presence of the Lord, other people they shout and some get quiet. Some have certain gifts and some have others. And if there's one thing I know for sure, if you'll pray in the name of Jesus to the Father, He'll open this book up to you and the Holy Spirit will teach you all about Jesus."

Marge knew she would be home soon and that she was giving him a whole lot of information at once, but she wanted to leave Sam with all the help she could. She continued. "If we let Him, the Holy Spirit comforts, fills, speaks in our hearts and mind, and helps us to get God's work done here on earth. And it's all for the asking, Sam. The smart ones are always asking for the right things, for the right reasons."

Marge grabbed Sam's hand in a motherly way. "Ask the Lord what that means and He'll show you, son. Anyways, I've got some knitting to do. But if you want to borrow that," she looked at the Bible in his hands, "feel free to read to your heart's content." After about ten minutes, Marge's knitting slowed as did Sam's reading. Soon they were both fast asleep as well as most of the others on the bus. The driver was wide awake though. He had a box of No-Doze on his bench and a two-liter of cola. You could hear a portable radio with the news talk radio on.

Shhhhishh! They awoke to the sound of the brakes. Hours had passed and dawn had come but the sun was hidden by gray clouds. The radio blared out snow reports. "All off for Lincoln!" the driver loudly proclaimed though the P.A.

"Well, young man," Marge exclaimed, wiping sleep from her eyes, "this is my stop." She put the Bible into his hands and folded his hands around it. "I want you to have this now, and as you read it, ask the Lord's help and He'll help you to understand." She teared up a bit like a mom leaving her son.

"Wow, I can really have this? Thank you so much, Marge. Are you sure you don't want to come to Detroit?" Sam said, half joking.

Marge smiled lovingly as she gathered her things and replied,

"Don't ever forget how much He loves you, Sam. I'll be praying for you."

Sam looked at Marge thoughtfully. "You know, I just met you but I feel I've known you my whole life. Thanks for showing me everything about, you know, the Bible and all." Sam hugged her neck with such force, she gasped for air. "Thank you so much, Marge. And I'll pray for you, too. I'm really gonna miss you."

"Oh, son, stop now, or you'll have me bawlin' like a little child," she said, lovingly. "Here, you take this and don't tell me 'no'." She put $40 in his hand as well as the rest of the food she had in her red bag. "I want you to take your wife out to dinner and do your best just to bless her. Don't worry about yourself. The Lord will take care of you. Just be a blessing to your wife, expecting nothing back, and you'll see His hand working. I really believe that. And Sam, if you don't mind I'd like to adopt you in a sense. I'm always gonna be like a prayer momma in your life, if that's all right with you? You know, to be praying for you like I would my own son, and be there for you if you need me. Here's my phone number and address." She handed him a piece of paper.

"Is that all right?" Sam laughed, overcome with love. "You've got to be one of the nicest people I've ever met. I'd be honored to be your adopted son, and don't worry, Marge, I plan on making you proud. You'll see … with the Lord's help, of course." Sam hugged Marge's neck again. She had touched a part of him that had been hidden for a long time.

"OK, easy now, big boy. Old Marge ain't got the strength she used to. And if you don't stop you'll have me bawlin' in a minute. I know we'll meet up again some day." She walked down the aisle, turned and waved to Sam as she exited the bus. Sam watched out the window as her family greeted her.

The bus pulled away and Sam began to read and read as if he couldn't get enough. He ate some fruit bars that Marge had left. Then he got up and cleaned up a little in the bathroom.

Later in the evening, Sam faded off as he wondered if any one of the people on the bus were pondering the question of eternity or thinking about God. In his dream he heard God speak to him.

"I love them too, Sam, and I will use you to touch their lives."

He stirred a little, half awake and thought, *"Me? I don't know anything. How could I possibly touch their lives?"*

Drifting off at the steady hum of the wheels on the road, Sam slept peacefully for hours. As the sun came up, he read some more until a little girl asked, "Do you want to see some pictures of angels I drew in my art book?"

Sam was flattered she chose him to share her artwork. "Those are really nice," Sam said, surprised at how good they were.

A baby cried and was suckled by its mother.

Sam read and prayed to himself till he fell asleep. In his dream someone called out, *"Detroit."* He dreamed of people walking down the street, shaking his hand.

"Hi, Sam, heard you quit drinking! Way to go."

"Way to go Sam," another stranger would say, slapping him on the back in congratulations.

Suddenly awakened to the sound of people shuffling by him hurrying to meet their families, Sam realized it wasn't totally a dream. The bus had stopped and all the inside lights were on.

The driver was calling out, "Detroit! All off for Detroit!" Sam adjusted his eyes and looked out the right side window through the fogged glass and quickly recognized the area. He was in his hometown. He rose from his seat and gathered the Bible Marge gave him and his green duffle.

He approached the front of the bus and slowly stepped off, taking in the familiar surroundings. It looked very different now. Now that he was sober. Arriving families greeted their loved ones and helped take their luggage to their vehicles, chattering cheerfully on the way to the parking lot. Sam stood alone in the cold. He was only a few blocks away from his house, but he wasn't welcome there. He hoped, he longed, for a place called home, and knew there was still a long ways to go.

3
THE ROAD HOME

Dimly lit street lights looked like giant matchsticks in the road, spotlighting the night's snow flurries. A stiff breeze came through the window with a howl, reminding Sam of how little he missed the weather here. It was really cold for November.

He felt a little depressed as he stepped off the bus. There wasn't any family or friends to meet him like the other passengers. Although he expected as much, the truth of it still bit at his mind, just like the cold air outside bit at his flesh. He didn't have a jacket either. The snow salted his hair and he rubbed his arms and shivered.

"Where am I going to sleep tonight?" he asked himself. Sam took a few small steps in no particular direction. Most of the folks from the bus were gone now. He slowly walked west toward the street light ahead. He remembered what Marge had told him, "You're asking for forgiveness, not so you can get something, but because it's the right thing to do." Her words and image were as clear as if she was standing next to him. He wished she were. Uncertain as he was, Sam knew what he had to do.

"All right, Marge, here goes."

He knew he had to find a pay phone. Seeing a phone booth outside of a party store about 200 yards up, he threw his old army bag over his shoulder and walked to the store to get some change.

Walking in he saw that the owner was a unique creature. He had hair coming out of everywhere except his head. Sam gave him a dollar bill for some change.

"You want a bottle?" the man asked in a heavy Greek accent.

Sam looked at his old friends Jim Beam and Jack Daniels sitting on the shelf. Sinister voices seemed to call his name enticingly, "Sam, don't forget about the money in your pocket. Get a pint to take the edge off."

Sam heard a still small voice speak to him from within, *"Free man, you're a free man now. That was the old man. Go and call your wife. Live again. Take your life back, Sam!"*

In Lincoln, Nebraska in an old brick and wood home built in the thirties you could hear Mahalia Jackson singing strong in the background. And under the music, the familiar voice of another saint.

"Oh Lord, I thank you for savin' Sam! I lift him up to you, Lord. Watch over his life." Marge didn't have to know someone well to care for them. If God cared for them, then she cared.

"Let him know what you've done for him, Lord. Let him know. Oh, have your way, Lord." She was on her knees in front of a nicely made double bed. It was covered with a quilt that had cloth pictures of her family and scriptures sewn into it. She used it as a reminder to pray for each of them.

"And help Sam's wife, too, Lord. Soften her heart. Give 'em both a chance. Please give 'em a chance, Father. In Jesus name, Amen." Tears filled her eyes as she cried out from deep in her heart.

Sam, resisting the temptation to buy the alcohol, quickly walked out the door to the pay phone.

"Yes," he breathed out loud, "I am free, thank you! Thank you, Lord." He picked up the receiver and fed the phone, then dialed his home number. He didn't even know if his wife Denise was home or if she'd answer the phone for that matter. He waited anxiously. The phone rang once, twice, three times. "Come on, Denise." Another ring and then finally on the fifth ring someone picked up.

"Hello," a woman's sleepy voice answered.

Sam was scared and speechless. He opened his mouth but nothing came out.

"Hello!" she said a little louder this time.

Sam could barely breathe.

"Look you, frickin pervert or whoever you are, if you don't say something I'm hanging up!"

Sam remembered missing every thing about her, except that sharp tongue.

"Babe, it's me," he finally said, his voice noticeably trembling.

"Sam?" she asked curiously. "What do you want? I told you unless you were finished with the booze, I didn't even want to hear from you. I don't have any money, so what do you want?"

"Yeah, babe, I know," he replied softly. This was harder than he thought.

"I quit, Denise," he said meekly.

"You quit what?" she asked, agitation in her voice.

"I quit drinking," Sam replied nervously, expecting the outburst of sarcasm he knew was coming.

"For how long this time, Samuel?" Denise fired back. "One hour? Two hours? Since lunchtime?"

"It's been two days. God stopped me," he said awkwardly.

"Ha Ha Ha," she laughed mockingly. "Oh, that's good. You've found God now, have you? Do you think this will last a little longer than when you got hypnotized, Sam?" sarcasm and pain filled her voice. "I don't have time for these games, Samuel."

"No, babe, it's true. I'm done for good," he said, his voice rising.

"Hey," she said, her voice softening a little. "You do sound different. How come you're not making excuses or arguing with me? I just insulted you!" she asked curiously.

"I'm done fighting, babe," he said quietly. "I just want … I just …" Then like a volcano rising up in him, he said, "Denise, I just want to tell you how sorry I am. I've been such a disappointment to you and Amanda. You really don't deserve all I've put you through. Even if you never want to see me again, I pray you'll forgive me." There was an awkward silence and then, "I don't want to be that man anymore, Denise. I *can't* be that man anymore." He shivered involuntarily, some from the emotion and partly because he was freezing. Sam wiped the tears from his face as they began to form icicles.

"Sam? You're serious, aren't you?" her voice softened. "Where are you, honey? Are you okay? You're worrying me." She nervously ran her hand through her hair.

"I'm okay, babe. It's different now. I don't know how to explain it but something's changed. I'm different, Denise. I don't expect you to buy it all at once, but I'm not the same person anymore. I can't be that man anymore. Can we talk? Can I buy you dinner or something, babe? Just to talk with you a little?"

The rare treat of going out to eat really encouraged her. "You've got money, Sam? Where'd you get money?" Denise asked excitedly. *"If nothing else I'll get some fajitas out of this adventure,"* she thought.

"It's a long story," Sam replied. "If you'll meet me, I'll explain over dinner."

"Okay. Where are you?" she asked. "I'll come get you. Can we go to *Mexican Town*?" The excitement of having Mexican food was obvious in her voice. She was addicted to it.

"Sure, Denise. Wherever you want. I'm over in front of the party store by the bus stop."

"Don't you go in that store and blow this, Sam!"

"I won't, babe. I'll be right out front, Denise. Get here quick, okay? I don't have a coat on and its freezing." The Liquor Lottery sign at the market squeaked loudly as the bitter wind blew through the town. Sam stayed in the phone booth waiting for Denise to arrive.

After hanging up the phone, Denise threw on her coat and hat, grabbed her keys and walked over to the landing and yelled down into the basement, "Hey, Mandy, I gotta' go take care of something. I'll be back in a couple hours."

"Where you going, Mom?" Amanda called back up.

"I just gotta pick somethin' up. I won't be long." she half lied.

"OK, Mom!" Amanda yelled back.

Denise argued with herself as she ran out to her car. *"It can't be, can it? I just can't let Mandy go through this again. But what if it is true?"*

Denise jumped into the old Ford bondo mobile, started the car and spun out of the driveway. Fifteen minutes later she pulled up to the party store. Sam walked up trembling and quickly climbed in the car. He warmed his ice cold hands in front of the heater vents.

"Hi," Sam said. Denise blushed a little as Sam's eyes looked her over affectionately.

"Hi, yourself!" Denise got a quick whiff of him as he defrosted. *"This man smells! Did I marry this man?"* she said to herself, her nose wrinkling at the stench. She reached into her purse and pulled out a bottle of her favorite cheap perfume, then sprayed him with it.

"Hey, what the heck are you doing?" he protested.

"You stink, Sam! You think me and everyone else wants to sit there and smell you over my fajitas? Whatever God did for you, He sure didn't clean you up on the outside," she joked.

Sam just looked at her and rolled his eyes. "OK, I'll stop in the wash room before we sit down, all right? Do you have a comb?" She reached in her purse and handed him an old curved 70s style, hippie comb. "Just toss it when you're done, Caveman," she said with a half smile.

In spite of their problems, Sam and Denise still really did love and miss each other.

Sam, surprised at her teasing, gave her a hopeful glance.

Denise, still cautious yet curious, asked him, "Sam, is all this for real? You know this God thing? What you say happened to you? You seem different, you know, but Sammy, it's not the first time you said you've changed. So what's goin' on?"

"I'll tell you all about it when we sit down, OK?" he replied. They drove for several minutes. Turning on to Bagley Street, you could actually smell the Mexican food. There were several restaurants to choose from. Denise's eyes lit up like she'd stumbled onto a carnival.

She parked and they both got out of the car. Denise tried to walk a step behind, purposely studying Sam. *"He looks like he was hit by a train,"* she said to herself. *"And he stinks, but his eyes are as clear as glass."*

At the restaurant entrance, Sam opened the door for her, something he hadn't done since they were dating. She gave him a surprised glance. "Thank you, Samuel." With a deep breath, she took in the aroma of the place. "I'm home," she sighed. Sam laughed, adoring her. For the moment, he felt at home too. He stood tall because he was standing next to his wife.

A sombrero hung on the wall behind the hostess stand. "Hi! Welcome to *Tres Hombres!* Just two tonight?" a perky young blond girl asked. She was wearing a red bandanna around her neck and quickly came out from behind the counter with two menus in her hand.

"Yup, just two," Denise answered.

Seeing Sam's appearance the hostess decided to take them to a secluded table at the far left corner of the restaurant. The sound of recorded mariachi music and the smell of Spanish rice filled the place as they sat down at their table. A waiter came to get their drink order, but they both ordered everything right away.

Sam excused himself to clean up a bit in the restroom. As he ran the comb through his hair, he closely looked at himself in the mirror and contemplated what he was going to say to her. He was so nervous he was shaking.

"You can do this, Sam," he heard a quiet voice encourage him.

"All right Lord, here we go."

He walked backed to his table and began his story as they waited for their dinners.

"… and then he was gone just like that!" Sam said. "It was the weirdest thing, Denise. There's no way he could have gotten away that fast, and I swear, I never told him my name."

"Well, maybe it was just the shakes, Sam. Maybe you blacked out for a minute and you didn't realize that the cop had left! And that's why you didn't see him ride away."

They looked at each other for a moment, excitement shone in Sam's eyes but doubt filled Denise's.

"But I didn't have the shakes or anything after that. I felt like I never drank at all." They both held their conversation for a moment as the waiter and another waitress delivered their food. The assistant lit the plate on fire as the waiter held it up in the air. "Ole!'" they shouted. The waiter doused the flames with lemon juice and placed the dish in front of Denise. The fajitas sizzled and crackled. She inhaled and smiled wide.

"You have a smile that could change the world," Sam told her.

She ignored the compliment and prepared her food, quickly loading a tortilla with beef, green peppers, onions, spices, sour cream, cheese and guacamole. She took a huge bite. This was her favorite dish and she didn't have the chance to go out often. Sam watched with his chin resting on his hands, his untouched cheese enchilada's waiting for him.

"Amanda has your smile," he said. "Hey, how is Mandy, Denise? Man, I miss her."

"She's fine," Denise mumbled with a mouth full of food. She chewed quickly, holding up her index finger and then took a drink of water. "She's at home with one of her friends right now. I didn't tell her I was meeting you, Sam. I didn't know how all this would go." Denise lowered her voice looking directly at him,

"And Sam, you know we can't go through this anymore … honey, what you've put us through. We can't do it. I really don't want to make you feel bad, Samuel, but if you come back, and I say *if*, this better be *real*. This God thing, or whatever, I'm finished staying up all night, wondering if the police are going to call and tell me you've crashed a car or fallen off a bridge or something. And it's not fair to Amanda. Her grades have gone up a little, and she's been in on time at night, for the most part. She's doing better now that you've been gone, Sam." He looked away, wounded by this last statement.

Denise continued. "Tell me the truth, what do you want from us? Because I don't know anymore. Is this all so you just have a place to sleep? Please just be honest with me. I'll try to help you find a place, but I have to know that you won't hurt us anymore." She took another bite of her fajitas, then looked up, waiting for his response.

He hesitated for a moment and then looked down at the table. He chose his words carefully.

"I know I don't deserve anything, Denise, but I just want you to forgive me." His eyes moistened. He nervously looked around the restaurant, trying to muster up some courage.

"Like I told you on the phone, I am deeply sorry for how I've treated you and Amanda, and if I could take it all back I would." His lip quivered. "And whether you take me back or not, I want to thank you for always being strong, Denise, and for all the good times you gave me." Sam took in a deep breath and sighed. "And how you've taken care of Mandy. Either way, I hope I can be part of your lives. I know I haven't been a very good man, but I really do want to be now. I'm not going backwards anymore." He looked at her now with a confidence that came from an integrity he'd not known before.

"You've been a good wife and mother, Denise, and I love you, baby, very much, and I miss you both. It's your choice now, and if I can't be there I understand," he paused and bit his lip. "But I'll always love you and I'm really sorry. You deserved better."

Denise looked down at her plate for what seemed like an eternity. She didn't move or speak. She seemed frozen. Sam held his breath. Finally her eyes filled with tears. She looked up.

"Oh, Samuel! I do love you! You always were the only man for me and I don't think I could ever love anyone like I do you, except maybe George Clooney, but that's probably not going to happen," she kidded, now laughing and crying at the same time.

"But I have to think about it, baby. This isn't an easy decision. Too much has happened for me to jump right into this again." She wiped her face. "Can you let me think about it for a day or two?" She leaned forward. There was a hint of hope on her face. "But if we do work this out, we need to have a plan, Sam, and be like a family, and do things together; get out of debt, and get a decent car."

"I tell you what," Sam said smiling, "let's see if they can find me a room for a day or two at the Salvation Army and I'll call you okay, OK? Is it OK if I call you tomorrow?"

"Yeah Sam. And I'll talk to Mandy, and we'll figure this whole thing out. I … I just … I just need a little time, OK?" Sam nodded and they both sat quietly, contemplating where to go from here. They slowly finished their meal, occasionally looking up at each other. When their eyes did meet though, even for a moment, there was hope there.

As they got up to leave, Sam grabbed the bill. He left a $5.00 tip on the table for the waitress. This prompted a smile from Denise. Sam had always been a little on the cheapskate side of things. Sam walked over and quickly hugged Denise as they rose from the table. Denise, surprised and not quite trusting all this yet, guardedly yet gently pushed Sam away. Sam knew it would take time and gave her a reassuring smile.

Leaving the restaurant, they drove without conversation to the Salvation Army shelter. In their eyes shone mixed feelings of hope, doubt, faith, love, and fear. But mostly hope. Sam went inside after asking Denise to wait a minute to see if they would let him in. He appeared a moment later.

"They've got a room," he said excitedly. "Thank you, 'Neesi,'" he picked up his bag and leftover enchiladas. "I love you, babe," he said warmly. "Talk to you soon."

"I love you, too, Sam." Denise said softly under her breath. She couldn't look him directly in the eye. "We'll see, OK?" She put the car in gear and gave him a quick glance and drove away. Her debate started again, *Could this be real? Has he really changed?* A million memories crowded her mind as she drove home.

Inside the shelter, Sam put his bag down in the small room that the Lieutenant graciously let him use. There was a glowing space heater in the corner. He walked down the hall to the shower and looked around. He then walked down a narrow stairway to the greeting area to find Lieutenant Stewart.

A man with a white beard and military style uniform was sitting at a wooden desk that was way too small for him.

"Lieutenant Stewart? Is there a chance I could borrow a shaver?" Sam hollered down the stairs.

Sure," the Lieutenant replied, "but I'll do you better than that, Sam. I've got a voucher for a haircut and shave down at Rusty's Barber Shop. If you're interested, I could drop you first thing in the morning?"

"That sounds really good, thank you, sir." Sam said as he scratched his dirty head.

Sam showered and then came into his room and lay down. He tightly clutched the Bible Marge gave him against his chest. The glowing heater made the room toasty.

"Ah, it sure feels good to be clean," he thought, *"and to be almost home."* He looked over at a unique lighthouse night light that cast a soft glow in the room.

"Thank you for showing me the way, Lord," he whispered and then faded off to sleep. He dreamed of family conversations and healing embraces.

A warrior dressed all in white guarded the doorway to his room. Sam didn't wake once for several hours.

Bright sunshine flooded in through the large crystal cross window in the dining hall of the shelter. It was a brand new day. Sam woke early and quickly got dressed in a pair of blue jeans and a cotton T-shirt that Lieutenant Stewart had left for him on an old wooden chair.

"It sure felt good to be scrubbed up," he thought. Now he had to try and clean up his relationships with his wife and daughter.

Aware of the struggles that lie ahead Sam got down on his knees beside his bed and prayed, *"Oh God, I really don't know what's going to happen today. You've helped me this far, please help me to not give up no matter what, even if she doesn't take me back. Please help me to stay with you, and keep me from drinking. In Jesus name, Amen."*

Marge, in Nebraska, was also at the foot of her bed in prayer for Sam and his family.

Denise was arguing on the phone with her best friend, "He's my husband, Cathy! If he's coming home, then he's coming home. You know there's no half way with me," she paused. "Don't worry. If he drinks, he's gone …. Yes, I know."

Sam ate with 20 other men who had stayed at the shelter that night. A man named Jim treated each one like they were royalty. He greeted each person cordially and poured hot oatmeal into their bowls. Each had a box of raisins and an orange juice box. Sam didn't talk much to anyone really. He just smiled and returned the greeting if someone said good morning. He was taking it all in. *"We all need You,"* he thought to himself, thankful for another day.

Sam was just finishing his breakfast when Lieutenant Stewart sat down by him.

"Well, are you ready to get de-haired there, Sampson?" joked the Lieutenant. Sam smiled.

"It's actually Samuel, sir, but I could see being mistaken for a Sampson." They both laughed, got up and casually headed out the door.

Rusty gave Sam a fine looking hair-cut and a shave. Just as he was finishing up, the door opened and someone stuck their head in the doorway.

"That's one good lookin' man o' mine," Denise said flirtatiously as she walked in with their daughter, Amanda. Denise stood there dressed in a beautiful floral print dress. She had fixed herself up with her hair and make-up. Sam's face, wide with awe, was totally surprised by the visit. His heart was overjoyed.

"Daddy! Oh, Daddy!" Amanda ran to her father and wrapped her arms around him. "I missed you so much! I was so happy when mom told me you were coming home! Oh, Dad, please don't go away anymore. I was so worried about you."

Sam held Amanda close, his hand cradling her head. He trembled and kissed her face. "My baby girl," he said, voice cracking. He looked at Denise.

"I'm coming home?"

"I think it's worth another shot, don't you, babe?" she replied softly.

"I really do, 'Neesi. I missed you both so much." They all hugged each other, crying and laughing at the same time. Even Rusty had a little tear in his eye.

"Let's go home, Sam," Denise said, smiling. Sam never thought he'd hear those words again.

Later at the McBride dinner table, Sam said, "Well you guys, the first thing in the morning I'm going out looking for a job. And on Sunday, what do you think about the three of us going to church together?"

"That would be cool, Dad!" Amanda said and smiled.

"Hold on a minute. Let's take this one step at time," Denise said a little harshly, getting up from the table and clearing dirty plates. "Look, Sam. If God is keeping you from drinking, then I'm all for you going to church and meetings, whatever you need to do. But I don't need a big building and someone preaching down my throat to keep my head on straight. You go right on ahead. And Mandy, you can go too, if you want, but you make up your own mind." Denise began to walk to the sink.

"But ... I just thought ..." Sam began. Denise quickly turned and shot him a warning look. Sam backed down. He realized this was going to be an uphill battle. But he knew he owed her some patience. She had definitely showed him that much over the years.

4
THEY OVERCAME HIM?

Tuesday evening at 7:00 p.m., Sam made his way up a set of narrow creaking stairs. His heart was pounding, his mouth dry. A drop of cold sweat ran into his left eye and he wiped it away with his hand.

At the top of the stairs was a door with a sign that read, "Overcomers, you're at the right place!" Sam cautiously turned the brass doorknob as if he were expecting someone to jump out at him. He stuck his head into the room, took a deep breath and entered. The room was crowded. People of different shapes sizes and colors were talking, laughing and mingling. They all began to sit around a huge round wooden table.

A man stood up and shook Sam's hand, "I'm Jim Mullins. Welcome, brother. You're Sam, right?" Sam nodded. The six-foot-four giant of a man put his arms around Sam and embraced him with the strength of a sumo wrestler. "God bless you, brother. Glad you're here," Jim said genuinely. "They call me Hugs, for short."

"I can't see why," Sam joked smiling, feeling like he'd just been to the chiropractor and immediately at ease now.

"Sit down, Sam," Jim invited warmly as he pulled out a steel chair, and Sam gratefully occupied it. Jim had founded the group five years earlier to help people overcome addictions. There was a plain, glass framed plaque with black letters on white paper on the wall that read:

And they overcame him by the blood of the Lamb, and by the word of their testimony;
and they loved not their lives unto the death. — Revelation 12:11

Sam had heard that verse before but couldn't remember where.

"You're the same Jim that was helping at the Salvation Army shelter the other day, right?" Jim nodded and smiled. Sam, astonished, replied, "Wow, you really get around, don't you?"

Jim had long sandy brown hair and a full mustache and beard. He wore blue jeans, cowboy boots and a flannel shirt. He didn't look like at all like your average minister, nor did he care to. The world was his church and he just wanted to be known as Jim, or 'Hugs.'

Sam slowly took in the room, noticing a single bulb ceiling fan overhead and a small window open near the corner. This room was in the attic of the church. *"This is like the upper room,"* Sam thought thinking of what he'd been reading in the Bible Marge had given him.

There were various posters with Bible passages and encouraging sayings on the wall. One was a hand painted cross with a red robe draped across the beams which read *"For You."* Each member went around the room and introduced themselves and said why they were there until it came to Sam.

"Your turn, Sam," Jim said receptively looking in Sam's direction.

"Oh, I don't know if I can … I don't know if I'm ready …"

"We can't let you leave here if you don't share, Sam. You know all our secrets," Jim teased.

"Ha ha ha," Sam laughed heartily. "OK. Well my name is Sam, Sam McBride that is, and it's my first time here." Sam not sure what to say, wrung his hands nervously and looked down, focusing on the wood grain in the table.

"Hi, Sam!" everyone replied harmoniously.

"So why are you here, Sam?" the assistant leader, Dave Sturgis, asked warmly.

Looking up, Sam mustered up all the courage he could and spoke out, "I want to learn to live sober. I thank God that He set me free from drinking and all the crap that goes with it, and I want things to stay that way." He glanced over at Jim. "Oh, sorry. Can you say 'crap' here?"

"Yea, but just once, and that's twice now for you!"

The group laughed at that. Sam was feeling even more at ease.

Sam continued, leaning back in his chair, "You know I really can't believe I'm here. I always thought I didn't need anyone, not God, people, groups or anything. Man, was I wrong. Things are so good now. It's almost unbelievable and it's amazing to be to able to talk with you guys and pray together and everything. I never could see myself having friends that didn't drink or use. So anyway, thanks." Sam looked and smiled at everyone.

"Thanks, Sam," Dave smiled, nodding to the lady next to Sam. Jeanine Davis shared as did everyone in the group. Sam was encouraged as he listened to the stories of the others. He knew he wasn't alone.

When the meeting was over, Sam started the drive for home. It was a beautiful night out and on a whim he decided to stop and get Denise some flowers. Even though it was cold, the stars seemed to be shining more brilliantly than he had seen in a while. He decided to sit in the driveway for a minute before going inside. He looked at his house and thought about his family. Overcome with gratitude, Sam leaned his head on the steering wheel and prayed.

"I almost lost everything," he contemplated the thought, "but You found me and gave me back my family and so much more than I could ever have imagined. Thank you. Thank you, Lord."

At that very same moment, unbeknownst to Sam, someone was at work on his behalf.

"Yeah Frank, I think he'll do really well. Sure, 8:00 am. OK, I'll tell him," Lieutenant Stewart said. He hung up the phone and then picked it up again and dialed another number.

Sam walked into the house with his hand behind his back. "What do you have there?" Denise asked curiously as she stepped from the kitchen to the living room. Sam brought the roses out from behind his back and presented them to her.

"Thank you, baby," she said expressively with an appreciative grin.

Ringgg, the phone rang and Denise answered. Sam took off his coat.

"Phone's for you," she said handing the receiver to Sam.

"Hello," he answered. He listened for a few seconds and then shouted. "Really???!!! $12.00 an hour? Oh wow, thanks Lieutenant! Yes, yes, I'll be there. That is so great!" Sam hung up the phone and looked at Denise who was now wide-eyed with curiosity.

"Lieutenant Stewart said he got me a job at the docks, full time with benefits, making $12.00 an hour!"

"Woo hoo!" Denise shouted doing a little dance. She gave Sam a hero's embrace. Amanda quickly walked over from the kitchen table and wrapped her arms around her dad's waist. "That's great, Dad. You're gonna do great."

A brilliant shining white guardian stood in the corner. Invisible to the McBride's, laughing with them as he watched them celebrate the good news, his wings lifted toward the heavens in worship. Other unseen messengers were there laughing, talking, praying, "Glory to the Lamb who provided again ...." a faint song echoed in the distance. Two worlds were as one, even if only for a moment.

Later that night Sam lay next to his sleeping wife. He watched her breathe as she slept. He thought about his new life, how fortunate he was, everything was just falling into place. *'It's a good job. We can get out of debt. We'll be able to do things we could never do before."* He laid thinking of family outings and watching Mandy go off to college and eventually get married. Finally he fell into a deep, contented sleep.

A dark monstrous figure watched Sam from outside of his window. In his sleep, Sam heard a grumbling voice, full of rage, *"We'll see how long all this lasts, McBride,"* the demon prince hissed. A cold draft permeated the room. Sam pulled the covers up over himself. Then a stench like the smell of a putrefied rat or something filled the air causing Sam to unconsciously cover his nose and cough. In his dream he saw two fire-red glowing eyes glaring at him. Was it really a dream? Sam, startled, quickly awoke and sat up in bed. Sweating now, with his heart racing he looked around the room. No one was there. He laid back down and eventually faded to sleep.

The next day at the docks, Sam stopped by the office to show his appreciation for the new job.

"Thanks so much, Mr. Simmons. I really appreciate the work. Same time tomorrow?"

"Sure, that'll be fine, Sam. Good job today, by the way. I was watching you. You're a good worker."

"Thanks a lot, sir." Sam beamed at the compliment. He felt good, clean. Everything was falling into place.

On his way out the door, his boss called out to him, "Hey, Sam!" Sam walked back and listened.

"I was wondering, could you use a car until you can save some money up? I've got this old beige Delta 88 out back and it needs to be driven once in a while to keep the engine in shape. If you're interested, I could have you a set of keys by Friday. You'd really be doing me a favor just by keeping it on the road."

Sam stood speechless for a second. "Seriously? Wow. Are you sure? I mean, thank you, sir." Sam almost shouted, overjoyed at the prospect of not having to arrange rides or catch the bus. That night a co-worker dropped Sam off at home.

At the dinner table that evening, Sam began to give thanks for the meal. Amanda respectfully waited. Denise, however, was already halfway way through her drumstick when he began and just kept eating.

"Thank you, Lord, for this food, my beautiful wife and daughter, my job, and wow, now even a car? Amen."

Sam and Amanda both gave Denise a 'you could have waited' look.

"What?" Denise asked with fried chicken in her mouth and a defensive look on her face.

"So what kind of car do you want?" Sam asked Denise with a half smile and twinkle in his eye.

"What are you talking about?" Denise replied playfully.

"Well babe, I figure with this new job and with the free loaner car I've got now, we can save and get you a decent car for your work and our family trips."

"Are you serious?" Denise asked.

"Yeah, 'Neesi, you deserve it. I really do want to take care of you guys like I should, both of you." Denise could tell Sam was serious. Both she and Amanda gave Sam a lingering smile.

Denise folded her hands and bowed her head, acting like she was praying, "And Lord, thank you for this new man you brought home to us. He sure looks like the old one, but definitely new and improved. Amen."

Amanda laughed, waving her hands in the air. "Hallelujah to that!" They all laughed uncontrollably till tears came from their eyes.

Goodwill overflowed the McBride home that evening. If there was any unforgiveness or regret left for Sam's misgivings you couldn't tell. After dinner, they all played a board game and watched television. When Amanda had gone to bed, Sam told Denise all about his new job. She laid her head in his lap listening to his hopes for their future and soon drifted off to a deep sleep. Sam carried her up the stairs and put her to bed. He gently covered her with a blanket, kissed her head and watched her for a few moments.

"Thank you Lord, for my wife. She is beautiful," he whispered as he lay next to her, arms around her shoulders. He closed his eyes and faded off to sleep.

Friday's workday quickly came and went. Sam was on mid-shift today but the boss notified everyone he was closing up shop an hour early for his son's birthday. They could all go home early but would still be paid for eight hours. This prompted shouts and whistles from all the hard working dock hands. Earlier he had given Sam the keys to the Oldsmobile. Sam began the drive home after work in his boss's car feeling like a million bucks. Halfway home he spotted the familiar worn wooden sign of his old hangout, The Eagle's Nest.

The Eagle's Nest. *"People may go in like eagles,"* he thought, *"but they come out like buzzards."* He laughed to himself wondering if any of the old gang was there. Suddenly the taste of his favorite beer, and the jokes Betty the bartender came up with, were in his mouth and mind. "Betty," he laughed, "she always has new material." He smiled at the memory then slowly pulled up to the edge of the parking lot.

"You know it really wouldn't hurt just to have one, Sam," a familiar voice seduced him. *"You're off early and you have a little time to kill, and what could be wrong with having just one?"*

Sam thought about that for a moment and then slowly pulled the car into the parking lot turning the engine off. He got out of the car and stood up, the outside lights were just coming on. He paused for a second, thinking. He almost got back into the car, but then looked at the door of the bar. He'd opened that door so many times, so many memories in there. *"What could it really hurt? Just one,"* he said to himself and was drawn inside like a moth to a flame.

Smoke filled the dimly lit interior. The neon signs that advertised different brands of intoxicants were a familiar site, and the sad country music brought back mixed memories. Sam proceeded past the pool table and sat down on his favorite old bar stool.

"The usual, Sam?" Betty asked as if he had never been away. He nodded and took out a fresh five dollar bill.

"Hey there, Sam McBride!" George Pullman yelled out from a table to Sam's right. "Been a while, bud. Heard you got religion. Buy ya' a beer to celebrate?" George and his buddies all laughed.

"No, thanks, George. I got it. I can only stay a minute, thanks though." Sam, nervous and feeling surprisingly out of place, still didn't leave. He picked up the draft beer and suddenly felt a puff of air blow part of his hair out of place on the right side of his face. He turned to look but there was no one there. He straightened his hair, looking in the huge mirror behind the bar, when he heard the voice from the beach whisper in his ear,

"Sam, what are you doing? Don't throw it all away!"

"I'm only having one," Sam whispered to himself as if in some kind of trance.

"You're just having one," a different sinister voice hissed in agreement, "what could one hurt?"

The voice that came with the wind whispered again, *"Have you ever been able to just have one? I set you free, Sam. Don't put those chains back on! You're a free man. Be free!"*

Sam's head jerked up. "What am I doing?" He set the beer down without taking a drink. "I am a free man. I'm done with this!"

A boldness and power Sam had never experienced before came over him. He called out to the bartender, "Hey Betty, let me pay this out and keep the change, all right? I don't drink anymore. I shouldn't be here." He pushed the beer away from himself, adding, "I don't think you'll see me in here again, but thanks for everything." As he was speaking, a dark shadowy figure faded into the floor.

Just then Roxanne Perello, wife of notorious local trouble maker, Angelo Perello, walked by on her way back from the Unisex restroom. She was all decked out in her ostrich feather coat and knee-high brown leather boots. She had just snorted some cocaine with her husband Angelo. Seeing Sam, she stopped for a moment.

"Hey, Sam! What are you doing here?" she asked slurring her words, eyes glazed over. "I heard you quit the booze and got Jesus or something."

"Yea, I did." Sam said and then turned to the bartender.

"Take care, Betty." Sam turned and walked out the front door.

Roxanne strutted her way back over to her friends, their table filled with glasses and beer bottles, some full, some empty.

After Sam had left the bar, Angelo Perello, all clad in his usual black leather walked out of the restroom. He was sniffling from the cocaine he had snorted. He wiped his nose with a handkerchief, walked up to the table and asked George Pullman, "That was Sam McBride in here, wasn't it?"

"It sure was! Heard he got religion." George replied laughing.

"Sure!" Angelo fired back. "Him and God just stopped in for a beer." They both laughed mockingly. "That dude hasn't changed a bit, frickin' hypocrite," Angelo spewed out.

Angelo walked over to a dark corner that somehow seemed to get a bit darker when he stood there. He took out his cell phone and punched in some numbers. After three rings a female voice answered.

"Hello. This is Denise."

"Hey Denise! It's Angelo over at the Eagle's Nest." he said in a soft but gruff voice. "Guess who I just saw in here drinking a few minutes ago?" His lip snarled as he said it.

"No way!" Denise protested, her face getting red. "Are you messing with me, Angelo? Don't be trying to start something."

"Saw him with my own two eyes. George, Roxanne and Betty saw him too. Hey babe, when you get tired of messing with that bum and you want a real man, you know where I'm at." Angelo pressed the end button on his cell phone.

Denise's heart raced. Her anger was so intense she could barely breathe. Her face reddened more as she looked at the receiver still in her hand. She couldn't believe it. After what seemed an eternity, she exploded slamming down the phone so hard that it fell off the counter and crashed to the floor. She headed to the other side of the house, smashing everything that had anything to do with Sam on the way. Pictures flew off the walls. Gifts he'd given her off the mantle.

She stopped, her face red with rage. She looked up, pointed her finger and shouted at the ceiling, "Is that what You do? You get someone's hopes up and then You squash them into the ground? If that's the case, I don't want no part of You or that bum of Yours!" Her knees went weak as she slipped to the floor, hot angry tears fell from her eyes. "No! Not again," she pounded the floor with her hand. "This isn't happening. Not again!"

5
THE ACCUSER

Breathing hard with her fists and teeth clenched. Denise rose up off the floor.

"Why, why again?" she screamed and grabbed Sam's duffle bag from the downstairs closet and ran upstairs. She dumped his clothes from the dresser drawer onto the floor and ferociously kicked at them and then zealously stuffed them into his bag. With her eyes wild with fury, she grabbed their wedding picture off the dresser and smashed it against the wall. She then took the picture out and tore it in half, stuffing his half into the bag.

Sam was nearing the corner of their street. He was looking forward to spending time with his family. He had no idea of the firestorm he was walking into.

Angelo put away his cell phone and turned to see his wife Roxanne standing directly behind him.

"You're a pig, Angelo! A filthy rotten, stinking, cheating pig," she roared. She had overheard every word of his phone call with him hitting on Denise McBride.

Angelo turned around sadistically, "What did you just call me?" He grabbed her arm, and quickly forced her outside. The full moon cast a creepy glow over the parking lot, spotlighting Angelo as he pushed his wife up against the brick wall. He brutally grabbed her by the throat and cursed her. "I told you I'd kill you if you ever talked to me like that again! You had your fun with your boy toy in Texas and now I'm having mine." He let out a stream of profanities that would make Howard Stern blush. He looked around to see if anyone was watching, enraged he cocked his arm back.

An evil voice in his head whispered, "No one talks to Angelo Perello like that. Smack her! Put her in her place."

Inside the bar Betty asked George Pullman, "Do you think she's gonna be alright?"

"Yeah sure. They love each other," George replied drunkenly.

Back outside Angelo snarled, "You believe me now?" Roxanne was bleeding from her lip. Angelo had an inhuman look in his eyes, his hand was tightly gripped around her throat practically lifting her from the ground. She was choking.

Panic stricken and struggling to breathe, she begged, "Yes, Angelo! I'm sorry, baby! *Please* let me go!" she gagged and coughed. Trying to free herself from his grip, she forced a smile. "I'll just go and walk home if that's OK, baby. I'm really sorry." She was looking out the corner of her eye for a way of escape.

"Yeah, well you do that, and I think I'd better frickin' find something good to eat when I get there 'cause I'm kinda hungry." His black menacing eyes sent chills down her spine.

"OK Angelo, I'll have something for you when you get home. Please, honey let me go now. I know what you like. I'll give you whatever you want." She lied out of self preservation. She had no intention of going home. Angelo hesitantly released her and with a despising glare, he slithered back into the bar.

With the snow and the cold as her only companions, Roxanne disappeared into the night. The look in her tear-ravaged eyes asked, *"What did I ever do to deserve all this?"*

Black clouds blocked out the moon as they slid past its face. Strange cold shadows seemed to hover over the streets as Sam stopped at the last light near his home. Wet snow was beginning to fall and there was a chill in the air.

Denise took Sam's duffle bag and hurled it down the stairs. *"It's a good thing Amanda is at a friend's for the night,"* she thought.

Sam pulled up in the driveway and climbed out of the car. He made his way up the steps and was about to open the door when he thought he heard something. "Surprise, surprise, old drunk Sam McBride!" A raspy voice hissed at him. He looked toward the hedges and the sound but there was nothing there but shadows. He turned the key and opened the door. Denise was standing right there. She had something in her hand.

"Hey 'Neesi!" Sam barely got the words out when *CRASH!* Sam's eye began to bleed as the glass shards struck his head. She had hit him with the vase from the roses he'd bought her.

"Damn! Hey! What the hell, Denise?" Sam quickly put his hand up against his head pulling out the fragments.

"Get out!" she screamed in a loud shrill. "You sick, lame excuse for a man. Get out of my house and this time don't come back! Ever! Don't call, don't write. Get out!" She jumped at him and struck with the worn roses, the thorns scraped against his face. He stood there frozen in place. Sam never had and never would, hit a woman.

She pushed him toward the door. "Just leave, loser, and do us all a favor. Stay gone! Find someone else's life to mess up." Tears streamed from her eyes, causing her make-up to run, giving her an Alice Cooper-like appearance. Sam struggled to make sense of it all. Denise, quivering, began to pace. Sam had never seen her this upset in their whole life together.

"What did I ...?" He couldn't get a word out as she then she pounded on his chest with her fists.

Sam, bewildered, meekly asked, "Baby, what's going on? What's wrong? What did I do?" he pleaded as he used his shirt tail to try and stop the bleeding.

"You know what's going on!" She screamed. "Don't play games with me, Sam! Get out! Get out! Get out! Go back to your booze, you filthy drunk!" She was sobbing loudly now, then screaming, "They called me from the bar. I know what the hell you were doing!" Enraged she pointed her finger at him, "Why didn't your God stop you from going into that bar?"

"But babe! I didn't … I mean I was there, but please. Let me explain," he begged, trying to calm them both.

"No, Sam! I can't believe you're lying to me about it. I can't take it, Sam." Her eyes narrowed. She drew a deep rasping breath then bluntly told him. "Just go and let us get on with our life. You had your chance." Denise threw the duffel bag at his feet. "And you cared more for your damn booze than you did for us. I want a DIVORCE, Sam!" she screamed as she tore off her wedding ring and threw it at him. It bounced off his chest and rolled under their old green thrift store couch.

"Oh, my God!" Sam shook his head in unbelief. "Please, no." She had never used that word before. Divorce. The finality of what was happening was sinking in. Sam felt deep despair overtake him in a moment's time.

"I didn't do it, babe. Please believe me, please." He pleaded trying to hold back the sorrow that had suddenly come upon him. Denise shoved him out the door with both hands. In shock, he stood stunned on the front porch. She threw his bag out on the steps and slammed the door behind him. He heard the dead bolt and chain lock click into place, sealing his fate.

Sam hesitated. He just stared at the closed door in unbelief. His head dropped. He groaned. Overtaken by sadness he slowly sat down on the porch. The 'D' word played over and over again in his head like a looped tape recording. It crushed him.

"I must be dreaming," he thought. Not knowing what to do or where to go, he dragged himself and his bag to the car. He still could not believe what just happened. He was disorientated. He took a step back toward the house, and then to the car, then the house again.

"What? Where am I? What am I going to do?" he mumbled to himself, unable to think, able only to feel the pain of his wife's rejection. "What did I do? What did I do, Denise?!" he screamed to the whole neighborhood.

He put his duffle bag on the front seat, and got behind the wheel. Barely visible through the open zipper of his duffle was the edge of a torn picture. He pulled it out and looked at it. It was just him at the altar in his tuxedo alone. Her half of the photo was torn out. "No, Lord, no." he cried again, biting his lip and realizing the finality of the situation. He slammed his head into the steering wheel and shouted, "Why are you doing this to me? Why? Why? I didn't do anything. Please God, don't."

Distraught and upset, he started the car and jammed the gear shift into reverse. Squealing the tires, he raced out of the driveway taking out the mailbox in a 'thump'. He sped down Bemis Road, not knowing or caring where he was going. It was almost as if the weather was imitating his changing emotions as freezing rain replaced the snow and was clinging to the windshield. Faster and faster he recklessly rocketed down the road. Hail began to bounce off the car, then snow again. A fog rose.

"Your life is over now, McBride." a sinister voice taunted him. "Just crash into that pole up there and all the pain will be gone. It's easy Sam, just step on the gas and head for that light pole. They'll be sorry then. You'll show em', Sam. They'll all be sorry they didn't treat you better."

"No!" Sam cried. "Lord God, please help me! I feel like I'm going crazy."

He was struggling to see the road ahead as tears and sweat filled his eyes. Confused and wounded, he prayed and pleaded. "Lord, what's going on? I didn't drink. I didn't do it, but she wouldn't even let me say a word. Everything was going so good. I was doing really good and now...Is that it?" He cried out in pain to the God he had trusted. "What am I going to do? Where do I go now?" The tires began to slip on the road a little as the temperature dropped. Sam didn't even notice.

On the other side of town was a two-story brick house on top of a small hill. All the lights were on in the lower level. It was Delaney Duchovney's house, the usual place for the church's weekly prayer meeting. All the usual gang was there, gathered for prayer. Sam's name was on the top of the list.

"Come on, you guys, turn off the TV, please." Delaney asked for the third time.

"Yeah, we'll be there in a minute," Bill Simmons yelled, "only five minutes to go and it's over!" The basketball game had taken precedence over the prayer service. A couple of the ladies there drinking coffee discussed the upcoming church's rummage sale.

Delaney just waited at the kitchen table with the prayer list in her hand, frustrated.

Dark shadows engulfed Sam's car. "End it, Sam. Your life is over. No one cares!" a low voice growled. "You weren't meant for love. God hates you. Why is He doing this to you? Show them, Sam. End it all now!" Sam felt himself weakening as the seductive voices flooded him with thoughts of despair.

"Lord, help me!" he cried. "I don't like what I'm thinking right now." he pleaded.

Far above the stars, beyond all the familiar planets, a place of wonders was hidden behind reflective clouds. It was full of waterfalls, green pastures, mountains, valleys and streams as far as the eye could see. Soft white light cascaded across the country side and there were rainbows in every direction. There was no sun, but light seemed to come from everywhere, illuminating the whole place. Bald eagles, hawks, and a great variety of birds, some even unknown to man, flew around or were perched in the many trees that were there. Suddenly a multitude burst into flight from a huge oak tree. They all flew together as if one species. A long-necked full grown dinosaur lifted its head and pulled down a tree so a giraffe could more easily reach it.

Crickets, frogs and thousands of other animals echoed their songs throughout this Kingdom. There were elephants, tigers and every type of exotic animal in all creation. A lion could be seen playing lovingly with a baby lamb as a pterodactyl flew overhead. You could even hear the rumble of the earth as a herd of wild mustangs ran at a full gallop up a steep hill.

A strong, majestic looking creature stood on the banks of a running stream. He was resting in a valley of lush green grass and various multi-colored wildflowers. He had snow white wings, each five and a half feet long, tucked down by his side. His hair was shoulder length and golden brown. His name was Nathanael. He was a leader. There was a gold patch on his silver breastplate. It had the symbol of cross inside of a star with some unrecognizable writing on it. A gold sash was wrapped around his waste and brown laced leather boots came up to his knees. On his left side was a sharp double-edged sword with a golden handle.

He opened a scroll with a wax seal that was similar to the one on his chest. He broke the seal, unraveled and read the scroll. He looked up and opened his mouth, and proclaimed in the language of messengers, *"Leka hayosheb al-hakisse velaseh!"* being interpreted is: *"For You who sits on the throne and unto the Lamb."*

The words echoed off the purple and blue mountainsides and throughout the whole land as all the creatures roared and sang. Birds flew up and circled. The horses stopped for a moment, winnied and bowed their heads.

Suddenly a trumpet sounded. The creature placed the scroll in a pocket under his armored breastplate and then shot off like a bolt of lightning. He ran past tall cedars like a blur. He passed other messengers of different sizes, shapes and colors. Some were reading and praying, some singing. Others were exercising and sword playing; some were doing flying maneuvers.

Nathanael ran beside a river with steep banks. His speeds quickly reached seventy miles an hour. He passed a huge mountain, then a waterfall. He reached ninety, then one-thirty. Everything else became a blur. A flock of doves in his path burst into the sky.

In a split second he leaped into the air, wings extended like a majestic swan with the span like that of an albatross. A light beamed out from a glass temple-like structure and reflected onto his wings. Immediately, a tempest-like wind came from behind him and whipped the leaves that lay on the ground into the air. A voice like thunder echoed, "I am with you, Nathanael. Go and be victorious!" A sound like that of a trumpet or a ram's horn emanated through the air. He shouted, "Glory to you, O King, forever and ever!"

He broke through the expanse. His sword shimmered in the starlight as he traveled at speeds hundreds of miles per hour. Stars passed by him like bits of dust in a cosmic storm. He hummed an unknown tune, enjoying his journey when seconds later, out of nowhere, he was suddenly struck on the wing by a fiery red twisted blade. And again another CRASH! A sword struck against Nathanael's breastplate with a force like dynamite, making a huge dent. Nathanael was disoriented and bleeding. He turned to see the ugly ogre-like spirit of evil flying at him again. He pulled his sword, turned and blocked the next blow. The demon had a flaming sword in each hand.

Like eagles, they latched on to each other. Both intertwined as they struggled to land the next strike. They fell through the atmosphere, a blur of red and white, gold and silver, spinning together in a freefall. A shower of sparks flew as Nathanael repeatedly struck with his sword against the spine-like bony plating on the demon. But the creature was unharmed and wouldn't let go. Nathanael's light began to fade.

At the prayer meeting, the basketball game had gone into overtime. The guys were screaming at the TV and even the ladies watched now.

The King looked down through a portal in heaven.

The demon slashed with his left blade which Nathanael blocked with his sword. The cursed monster immediately thrust with his right, making a deep wound penetrating through the already wounded area into Nathanael's breastplate. Nathanael cried out weakly as his light faded even more, "My Lord Jesus!" he cried out.

His light went out. Unconscious he quickly fell to the earth. The demon, successful in his mission, flew off like black smoke into the night.

Nathanael's wings flapped in the dark windy night as drops of blood mixed with the snow falling into earth's atmosphere.

The earth was now coming closer and closer as Nathanael fell to the ground like a comet. In any second he would crash head first! Suddenly, the strong, yet gentle voice of the King called to him.

"Nathanael ... Awaken!"

Brought to life by The Master's voice, he opened his eyes wide. His wings shot out like a parachute. Light within him radiated and, with no time to spare, he turned right side up. His boots touched down on the wet asphalt of Bemis Road, making a soft landing.

As soon as he landed, he heard tires screeching, and in the blink of an eye saw two bright lights. They slammed into him, knocking him violently backwards into a large tree. The force of the blow knocked him unconscious again.

The car came to a stop and idled in the road, slightly angled in the direction where Nathanael lay against the tree.

"What did I just hit? What was that?" Sam fearfully muttered, as his heart almost climbed up into his throat. "No one was there a second ago." He quickly jumped out of the car and ran over by the tree. "Oh, my God." Sam said, not believing his eyes.

Across the street, an elderly woman had been watching her television while sitting near her living room window as she always did. She gasped when out of the corner of her eye she suddenly saw car lights collide with someone dressed all in white. She immediately realized someone had been hit by a car in front of her house. She grabbed her cell phone and coat, and dialed 911 as she hobbled to the door, eager to get a better look.

"Hello! Someone's just been hit by a car and I think it's pretty bad. Whoever it was – was thrown from the street into my tree. Oh my … No, no, I can't tell if he's alive or not. It's hard to see from here, there's so much snow. I'm going out right now to check. Oh yes, 413 Bemis Road, Belleville. Yes. My name is Janine Lee."She limped quickly out the side door, her half open coat flapping in the wind, her cane thumping. She called out in a strained voice, "I'm coming! I'm coming! I called the police."

Sam stunned, didn't even hear her. He was kneeling, staring, trying to make sense of this remarkable creature. Nathanael's wings were crumpled and blood was dripping from his chest. Sam saw the shiny golden star and cross-like emblem with strange writing on it.

Totally amazed and awed, Sam whispered, "Hey, are you okay? You're … no you're … Are you?" Sam, so nervous he could hardly speak, rubbed his eyes and then opened and closed them to make sure of what he was seeing.

Nathanael gradually opened the most unusual, crystal clear blue eyes Sam had ever seen. A literal, visible light was coming from within them. Suddenly another light emanated from the bottom of the three and a half inch wound in his chest working its way to the top, closing the wound as it went. Sam, speechless, watched in wonder as the messenger was being healed from the inside out. Nathanael's eyes shone even brighter. The wound healed until finally there was not even a scar left. It was as if the attack had never happened. His wrinkled wings straightened and then were brought into his side. He cocked his head upward and to the left. He gave Sam a curious look, smiled, and then disappeared right in front of Sam's eyes. Sam just continued to kneel, confounded, staring at the tree Nathanael had been leaning against.

Sam drew in a deep breath and stood up. He looked all around him and then to the sky. There was no sign of the creature. He had completely vanished. Sam turned around and looked at the car with its lights illuminating the falling snow. The only evidence he saw of the crash was the car's bent front end, some blood on the bumper and on the icy ground. He didn't notice the feather that was stuck in the grill just out of his eye shot. He looked down where Nathanael had been laying, unconscious. All that remained was an indentation left in the snow, and a small pool of blood. Sam's mind was spinning, trying to make sense of everything. He then heard a woman's voice and turned toward the source.

Mrs. Lee, now at the end of the road, was pointing her cane at him and screaming, "Where is he? What did you do to that man? You killed him, didn't you? What did you do with his body? You have blood on your face, mister." Sam still had blood on his face from the vase Denise had thrown at him. "The police are coming to arrest you. You better stay right there." She brought the cane down to steady herself and inched closer.

"What? What did she say?" Sam asked himself. *"I killed someone? No, no! I don't need this. This can't be happening, this isn't real."* Taking a couple steps forward with his hands in the air, he beckoned.

"Ma'am, please. It's not what you think. It was ... it was ...," he hesitated. "It wasn't a person. It was ..." he quickly realized if he told her what really happened they'd lock him up for sure.

"Stay away from me! The police are on their way, "she warned waving her cane in the air as if to defend herself.

Sam, in a panic, walked quickly toward the driver side door of the car, realizing no one would ever believe him. He had to get away from here. But to where?

The old lady began reading the car's license plate numbers into the phone as Sam got back in the car.

"Hey! You better stay right there!" her voice quivered as she wobbled closer to him.

Sam put the car in gear and sped away. There was no time to feel or think. He knew he had to get away, to sort things out. All that he knew was that in less than two hours time his whole life had completely crashed and burned.

She returned to her cell phone, "Officer? Yes, the man just left here driving very fast. Yes, I know I saw him hit someone, but there's no one here now. The driver had blood on his face and there's some blood on the road, and wait a minute, I think I see blood over by my oak tree." She walked closer to the tree, the moon was like a spotlight illuminating the crime scene. "It's dark, Officer. I'm not sure. I think he must have somehow taken the body with him. Oh my."

"Which way did he go, Ma'am?" the dispatcher asked.

"He was going west toward Rawsonville Road."

Sam, on the freeway heading east on I-94, was at speeds of seventy-five, then ninety miles per hour and climbing. He had no idea where he was going. The road was slippery and it was all he could do to keep the car on the road.

911 dispatch sent out a broadcast over the radio. "All available units we have an APB for a 94 Olds Cutlass, plates 7CS-R58. Suspect is wanted for possible Hit and Run/Manslaughter. Suspect may be armed and dangerous. The victim may be in the vehicle."

Two State Police cars that had been patrolling for speeders on the highway, moved closer to the exit ramps east of Sam's location when Trooper Greene of the State Police spotted Sam racing down the fast lane of the highway. He immediately picked up the handset on his radio.

"Forty-six to base. Suspect spotted on eastbound 94 at mile marker 193 exceeding approximately ninety-five miles per hour. In pursuit." Trooper Greene turned on his lights and siren and sped onto the pavement spraying gravel, ice and salt in the air. He approached Sam rapidly and about 100 yards behind him the other trooper also closed in fast. Sirens echoed off the houses on the service drive.

Metro Airport Police keyed the radio, "Metro 1 responding, we can head him off at the airport. I've got four available cars for a road-block. You want us to lay down spike mats?"

"Copy that," Officer Greene responded. "Let's get this guy quick."

Two Metro Airport Police cars pulled out immediately, waiting for Sam to pass. As soon as they saw the Olds fly by, they dropped flares behind him as he passed the exit. Two cars followed and two cars ahead temporarily closed the highway to keep oncoming traffic from entering. The highway was lit up with police lights and flares everywhere. Sam had reached ninety-seven miles per hour when he saw police cars in the road ahead of him, blocking him in. One of his tires blew out on the spikes. Frantically, his eyes searched the left and right sides of the road. He saw no way out as flashing lights came rapidly closer and closer; the police sirens screaming at him.

An evil voice spoke again, "There's no way out, McBride. Crash the barricade. You might as well take a few of 'em with you when you go." The rest of the blown out tire flew off making the rim shower the road with sparks.

Sam slammed on the brakes. He swerved off onto the gravel to the left side of the road and quickly jumped out of the car and ran into the grassy median. He ran across oncoming traffic into the opposing lanes, causing drivers to brake as they swerved to avoid him. An SUV slid by him barely missing him.

The officers, now in foot pursuit over the icy road shouted, "Stop right there, buddy! Show your hands. Get on the ground!" Two officers waved their hands in the air to stop traffic while other officers raced after Sam, guns drawn.

Terrified now, Sam turned and shouted back, "I didn't do anything! Leave me alone! I didn't hit anyone."

Sam, soaked from the rain and snow, was now across the west-bound lanes on the road's right shoulder. A chain link fence loomed 15 feet in front of him. He slipped on a patch of ice, tried to get up when he felt his whole body painfully convulse as electricity traveled through his body.

"I said stop, Mister." Trooper Greene was ten feet away with a taser in his hand, the dart was in Sam's back. Sam fell to his face on the shoulder of the road, his body violently shook and spasmed on the pavement. His already bloody face scraped into the gravel. Two officers walked cautiously toward Sam with guns drawn.

Another officer knelt on Sam's back, pulled his arms behind him and handcuffed him. They dragged him to his feet. Trooper

Greene grunted, "Come on, killer, you won't be running again anytime soon." He aggressively lifted Sam up and walked him back to the cruiser, patted him down and thrust him into the back of the car. Sam sat there exhausted, his arms cramped behind him from the hand-cuffs. "Oh Lord, please help me," he whispered.

The police searched Sam's car and quickly opened the trunk, but found nothing except a jack, a spare tire, an empty gas can and jumper cables. They collected a blood sample from the front bumper. One officer took pictures of the bent hood and bumper. Other officers looked under the seat, then the glove box and thoroughly searched every part of the vehicle for evidence.

Officer Kilpatrick found a white feather stuck in the lower part of the grill of the car. He looked at it for a moment, took a digital photo and then with a gloved hand carefully placed it in a plastic zippered bag. A tow truck arrived and hooked up Sam's boss's car. Sam dazed, looked back through the window from back seat of the police cruiser as it took him away.

"This has got to be a dream," he thought and wondered when he would wake up.

6
PRESSED, BUT NOT CRUSHED

Florescent lights buzzed throughout the long, decaying yellow hallway of the county jail. They seemed to match the buzzing in Sam's brain as he shook his head repeatedly from the effects of the taser. "Hey! You high or something?" An older officer jabbed Sam in the back with his stick as five of them pulled him down the hall and sat him on a blue steel bench. They secured his handcuffs to a steel bar built into the wall. Sam looked around apprehensively. He was terrified as he began to realize that this dark, clammy place was reality, not just a bad dream. One of the officers began to fill out a report. Sam, in kind of a stupor began to mutter something under his breath, "I'm not supposed to be here. Why you are doing this? I didn't do anything."

"Yeah, buddy," Blondie answered (his friends on the force nicknamed him Blondie), "Nobody we bring in here ever does anything." He then leaned in to within an inch of Sam's face. His breath stank. Sam gagging turned his head away. Blondie grabbed Sam's jaw and jerked his head back to make Sam look him in the eye.

"But somehow you've got someone's blood on your bumper and one hell of a dent in your car. So how do you explain that? I want to know what you did with the body!"

Sam nervously blurted out, "There is no body. I didn't kill anyone. It was an angel." Immediately he wished he could have put the words back in his mouth and he wasn't at all surprised when most of them laughed hysterically.

Sam continued awkwardly, "Really, I didn't kill anyone! I know it sounds crazy, but after I hit him, he healed right up and disappeared. It's the truth." They all looked at Sam and then at each other with smirks on their faces.

"Oh now that's different," Blondie said sarcastically. He circled the room like a ringmaster at a sold out show. "We didn't know it was an angel, did we guys? They do that disappearing stuff all the time, right guys?"

The other officers played along. "Sure," one said. Another on his right, slapped Sam's back playfully.

"All the time." he nodded, smiling broadly at Sam. The others nodded their heads in mock agreement.

"Should we let him go then, fellas?" Blondie joked.

"Sure, let him go." Trooper Reeves joined in. "I think we just misunderstood you, mister. We're sorry."

Sam actually had a small flicker of hope that they would let him go. He stared at the locked security door longing to be on the other side.

"Not!" Blondie suddenly screamed in Sam's face. Sam recoiled. All of them except Officer Kastansik broke into laughter.

Then Captain Ben Franks, who'd been watching the whole thing from a camera in his office, suddenly entered the room.

"That's enough guys, just keep it clean." They all became stone faced.

Captain Franks was dressed in his usual neatly pressed blue uniform. As the captain he could just wear slacks and a comfortable shirt if he chose to, but he wanted his staff to know that he was one of them, that he was for them. He was a formidable figure, six foot two inches tall and still in excellent shape despite that fact he was nearing 60. Ben Franks had piercing bold green eyes; neatly trimmed black hair, graying around the edges though, and reading glasses that forced him to realize, his better days were behind him.

He had been on the force for 19 years and was looking forward to retiring soon. Most would say he was the rock of the department. After reprimanding the men harassing Sam, he walked back up to his office. He stopped briefly to look at the wall of honor. It was adorned with pictures of friends, policemen who'd given their lives in the line of duty, as well as numerous awards and commendations. Ben had his share of good stories. He'd also seen his share of corruption in the department, and often, like tonight, had made a firm effort to stay away from the good ol' boy mentality. But his integrity had cost him dearly at times.

When he wasn't on duty Captain Benjamin Franks served as an elder in his church, New Covenant Assembly. He actively helped with the youth and with programs for the poor in his community. And whenever he had a chance he tried to share his testimony in the department. Some of the guys listened, others told him they weren't interested. A few heard him out of respect for his age and rank, because even if they didn't agree with everything he said, they did respect him, most of them anyway.

Ben sat at his desk and scratched out some notes on a piece of scrap paper. He was puzzled. He didn't know what to think about tonight. He pressed a button on the intercom and called, "Kastansik, come here for a minute, will you?"

Just then the phone rang. "She's missing?" Franks questioned. "Oh, no." he sighed and continued to listen and wrote notes on his pad of paper.

"OK. Thank you, Mr. Perrelo." Ben stood up as Sergeant Kirk Kastansik, young and adorned by his usual crew cut came into the room. "Kastansik, I want you to personally make sure that this man, Sam McBride, doesn't get harassed anymore. And after you've booked him and taken his statement, get a hold of me. Kirk, come over here." Ben whispered something in his ear and handed him the paper.

"Yes sir, Captain." Kastansik said, turned, and then left the office.

The phone rang and Ben picked it up. "Ben Franks."

"Captain Franks, this is Maria Espinosa from Channel 3. What can you tell me about Sam McBride? Have you found a body? Did he confess?"

"I don't really have any details right now. I'll call you back when I know something, Maria."

"But Captain ..." she tried to get him to say more but Ben abruptly hung up the phone.

Officer Kastansik proceeded to lead Sam into the fingerprint room.

Sam, quiet now, seemed tired and withdrawn. Kastansik felt a little sorry for him.

"This guy doesn't seem like your average criminal," he thought. There was a kind of innocence about him he couldn't quite put his finger on. Kastansik pondered all this as he electronically recorded Sam's prints.

Sam looked at the officer and asked in a whisper, "Can I make a call, sir?"

"Sure, Mr. McBride. First I have to get you booked, then your statement, and then you can make your call." Kastansik then took Sam into a brightly lit room equipped with only two blue steel chairs. There was duct tape holding the exposed padding together on one. After closing the door, he pulled the chair out for Sam and took off his handcuffs. He put a tape recorder on an old wooden table and set down his note pad. He informed Sam that he was being recorded. Then Kastansik sat down across from him. Sam, with his head hung low, just stared at the scratched up table.

"Samuel McBride, you are being charged with leaving the scene of a personal injury accident causing death and resisting arrest." The hairs on Sam's neck stood up. "Other charges may be pending as well depending on the evidence found. You have the right to remain silent. Anything you say can and will be used against you in a court of law. You have the right to consult with an attorney, and to have an attorney present during questioning. If you cannot afford an attorney, one will be provided for you." Sam cringed at the reality of what was happening to him. The room seemed to grow darker with each word that came out of Kastansik's mouth. "Mr. Mcbride, do you understand these rights as I've explained them to you?"

"Yes sir, but I ... I didn't kill anyone."

Without responding, Kastansik handed Sam an official looking paper.

"Please initial each line indicating that you understand your rights as I've read them to you." Sam did as he was told, his mind was moving in slow motion. He then slid the paper back to the officer.

"What happened tonight Mr. McBride?" Kastansik asked softly but intently, his eyes glued on Sam's.

Sam frowned and looked down at the table as his mind recalled the nightmarish events. He slowly related the details beginning with his stop at the bar after work and then about getting thrown out of his house. Kastansik showed surprise in his eyes that Sam was actually honest about the bar, everyone knew that Sam had a reputation of being an alcoholic.

"After I left the house I was just driving," Sam said. "The weather went crazy changing from rain to sleet to snow and fog everywhere ... and then it was like this huge ball of snow just landed in the road in front of me and I slammed on my brakes! But it was too late. I didn't know what it was I hit, so I got out of my car and there were these ..." Sam paused, looking down at the table again, he took a deep breath and said, "you're not going to believe this, but what I saw were crumpled up wings and a guy in a golden-like outfit and a sword. And suddenly I realized, it was an actual ... it was a real angel!

Kastansik had a slightly amused look on his face. "Just a second, McBride," he interrupted, leaning in. "You're saying you hit an angel with your car? You really want me to buy that? Come on, fella. Had you been drinking or using drugs, Sam?"

Sam just shook his head.

"Look we need a body." Kastansik got up and walked around the room first to the right and then to the left. "We know you hit someone and it just so happens that Roxanne Perello has gone missing, and if we can prove you did it on purpose, you could be charged with second degree murder."

Sam stood up wide-eyed, shuddering at what he'd heard. "Roxanne's dead?" his mind racing back to the bar scene and the brief dialogue he had had with her.

"Sit down! We think you know, McBride." Kastansik began writing on his legal pad. "How you hid the body so fast without a trace has got us all baffled, but I really need to let you know that if you just confess right now, it will go a lot easier for you. There's an eyewitness that saw the whole thing and we've got blood samples from the crime scene, from the car and from where the body was. Why don't you just save us all some time and tell us what you did with her. We will find her you know." (Kastansik was saving the feather they found in the grill for the grand finale.)

Sam's heart raced. Bewildered now, he nervously pressed his lips together, tightening his face. "Look I know you think I'm lying or crazy, but it really is the truth. See, I promised the Lord when He saved me, that from now on I would always try to do what's right. I know it's hard to believe, but it was like snowing and sleet and foggy and raining all at the same time, and I was upset, and all of a sudden this white angel with these huge wings landed right in front of me and I couldn't stop. When I hit him with the car he landed against a tree and when I got out to find out what happened, I saw he was bleeding, and then this light from inside him just healed him from the inside out! And he looked at me and his eyes, like ..." Sam again paused and tried to collect his thoughts and speak as openly as he could. "They were glowing, kind of with the same light, and then he just disappeared. I know you don't believe me, but that's exactly what happened!"

"He just disappeared? And he was bleeding?"

"Yes, sir." Sam swallowed hard, knowing how incredible his story sounded.

"Did you make a pass at Roxanne and she turned you down?" Kastansik asked.

"No, not at all. I would never do that. I love my wife and that's one thing I would never do is cheat on Denise. And it wasn't Roxanne, it was an angel! I really didn't do anything. I didn't drink,

I didn't do drugs, and I sure as heck didn't kill anybody." Sam was shaking, beginning to have some kind of a breakdown. Nervously he started to look around the room for a way out.

"Oh, if only I could wake up," he thought, "if only this was just a dream."

The sinister voice whispered, "They're gonna fry you, Sam. Where's your God now?"

Kastansik pressed on. "Look, we've got three witnesses that place you at The Eagle's Nest bar about an hour before the accident. Roxanne Perello is missing, her husband, Angelo, called and said that she was wearing an ostrich feather coat and had on brown boots which lines up with what Mrs. Lee says." Sam's heart sank as Kastansik described what Roxanne was wearing.

"Mrs. Lee said a car was speeding by her house and she heard brake noises. Then the car skidded and hit a person with a white coat on. We've got blood on the street and on the car and by a tree with an indentation in the snow. Sam, we've got a feather that was found in the grill and it's most likely from her coat. Confess, McBride! We've got way more than we need. Did you have words with Roxanne Perello?"

"No, I saw her and she made some crack about drinking and me finding Jesus, but I didn't really say anything to her and it wasn't a white coat, it was wings!" Sam's voice was sounding hysterical now. "What that lady saw was the angel I hit, and he just disappeared. It's the truth. Really."

"One more chance, McBride, okay?" Kastansik stood up, irritated. "If you come clean with me now, it will go better for you later. No one is going to buy all this angel crap, okay!" Kastansik had both hands on the table, leaning in a bit. He was trying hard to play the tough cop, but wasn't very convincing at it.

"It's the truth, sir. If I told you anything else, it would be a lie."

Kastansik, aggravated, took a deep breath, shook his head, and just glared at Sam. "OK, McBride, let's make that call."

Kastansik walked Sam over to a steel gray desk with a 70's style push button phone. "What's the number?"

"734-699-5483," Sam responded, a touch of eagerness in his voice.

Resting comfortably in an old Lazy Boy chair, a pair of bifocal glasses barely hanging on to his nose, sat an older, mostly bald, white-haired man. Sitting on his pot belly was a half-eaten peanut butter and jelly sandwich on a paper plate. An almost empty glass of chocolate milk was on the wooden oak table beside him. The volume on the TV set was almost deafening, even so his eyes were shutting as he was fading off to sleep.

"Channel 3 News live in Van Buren Township," blared from the television. "This is Steve Hinter bringing you breaking news! There has been a terrible accident and possibly even a murder near the Sumpter Township and Van Buren border tonight about a half mile behind where I'm standing. Police are there now at the scene collecting evidence and more importantly searching for the missing person, Roxanne Perello, whom they think may have been struck by an automobile and killed. Sam McBride of Belleville is being held for the hit and run and manslaughter after an eyewitness said that she saw Mr. McBride hit a person with the car he was driving outside of her home at about 6:30 p.m. this evening."

This shook Reverend Earl awake and he sat up and listened intently to the newscast, his half sandwich falling to the floor. His poodle quickly ate it up. He didn't even seem to notice.

"Once again, police believe the person who was struck to be Roxanne Perello who has been missing since leaving The Eagle's Nest bar in Ypsilanti earlier this evening. We go live now to Maria Espinosa at the home of Angelo & Roxanne Perello. Maria?"

A lovely Spanish-looking reporter in a fur lined beige coat stood in front of a small, brick ranch house. Maria Espinosa was well known in the area for her aggressive but professionally mannered style of journalism. Her dark complexion, long brown hair and deep brown eyes had opened many doors and even gained her many proposals for marriage. But for now at least, she had chosen career over romance.

Standing next to her was a black-haired Italian man dressed in a black leather coat and slacks and black leather shoes. Angelo fit the "Italian greaser" stereotype perfectly, and wasn't ashamed of it either.

"Thank you, Steven. This is Maria Espinosa reporting live for Channel 3 News. I'm here with Angelo Perello at his and his missing wife's home. Mr. Perello, you said your wife left a couple of hours ago to walk home from The Eagles Nest? What can you tell us? Please describe her, and what she was wearing?"

"Yeah, that's right we were at the bar." Angelo said with his usual Elvis-like curled lip. He looked Maria over with a smirk that made her feel uncomfortable. "She had on her favorite coat, a white ostrich feather jacket with white leather sleeves, you know. She always wears it when we go out."

"And you think the person Sam McBride hit with his car was your wife, correct?"

"Well, I hope not, but you know I don't know where she is and she was walking that way when she left the bar and no one's seen her since. She said she was gonna walk home, ya' know. But, see I called McBride's wife and told her he was in there drinking … 'cause she's a good lady you know, but I just heard she threw him out, so I'm thinking maybe he ran over my wife to get back at me … and let me tell you something, McBride! You better hope they never let you out, you son of a …" Angelo let out a stream of threats and profanities, which luckily the satellite operator was able to beep out in time.

"OK, thank you, Mr. Perello. This is Maria Espinosa for Channel 3 News. We'll keep you updated as the story advances."

The news feed was now back on reporter Steven Hinter near the hit and run scene. A photo of Roxanne Perello was on the screen along with the phone numbers of the police hotlines.

"If you have seen this person, or have any knowledge of her whereabouts, please contact the Belleville, Van Buren or Wayne County Sheriff's office at once. We will keep you updated as we receive new information on this tragic crime. This has been Steven Hinter for Channel 3 News Live."

The full moon helped to light the snow-covered woods as the camera cut to an area closed off with police tape on Bemis Road. Many police cars were there with their headlights and spotlights shining into the dark woods. Other officers were walking and searching using flash lights. In the distance you could hear the faint barking of police dogs. Many area residents watched the scene from their living room windows, with a few venturing out into their front yards.

Rev. Earl had known Sam since Sam returned and began attending his church. He was startled by the loud ringing of the phone. Sam waited for the Reverend, hoping he'd pick up.

"He knows I've stayed clean. He can help me out of this." Sam thought.

Slowly, stiff from sleeping in the chair, Rev. Earl made his way to the phone. One of his legs had fallen asleep and he was aggravated that he had to answer the phone at all. He seemed to step into a shadow as he picked up the phone.

"Hello." he answered more curtly than anyone would expect a preacher to answer.

"You have a collect call from the Wayne County Jail," a recording spoke. Just about to hang up, Earl heard "will you accept the charges from ..."

"Sam McBride" Sam said, when cued by the recording.

"Yes, all right, I'll accept." Rev. Earl said reluctantly.

"Hello? Pastor Earl? Oh, I'm so glad you're there. It's me, Sam McBride. I'm in jail. They think I ... they think I killed someone. Can you believe it?"

"Yes, I heard all about it on the news. Sam, I can't believe you've got the nerve to call me after all you've put me and this church through. You think you had us all fooled. I bet you were drinking the whole time and lied to everyone about it. Well, you'll not lie to us anymore, Sam. We're finished with you. You'll not find any help here, not for a liar. The best thing you can do for yourself is to confess, be a man and own up to what you've done. You hit and killed that man's wife, didn't you?" the pastor's voice raised. "Just admit it, Sam, and tell them what you did with her."

"But, but ... Pastor, I didn't ..." Sam sputtered.

Pastor Earl interrupted, "I said we're done, Sam! At least for now, if you're not going to own up to what you've done. I pray your jail time will teach you a lesson. Goodbye." The shadow dissipated through the paneled wall as the reverend hung up the receiver abruptly.

Sam's hope disappeared as he heard the dial tone.

"What do I do now? Will anyone believe me?" Sam laid his head on the desk, the receiver still in his hand.

"Hang up the phone and let's go, McBride." Officer Kastansik led Sam to a brightly lit room where he was handed a pair of green pants, a t-shirt, and a short sleeve pullover shirt and a pair of flip-flops.

"I need you strip down to your underwear and leave your clothes and shoes on the bench, and put these on." Kastansik pointed to the prison clothes on the chair.

Sam methodically did what the officer told him.

The officer then led Sam to his cell and bolted the heavy iron door behind him. It made a loud heavy metal sound that echoed through the jail.

He told Sam, "We'll see you, McBride. I think the Captain's coming to see you before the night's out, and then you'll be arraigned and probably held over for trial in the next day or so."

Sam looked at the steel commode, and the filth written on the wall. Someone had managed to scratch in "Welcome to hell" right above his bunk. His heart sank even deeper within him. He paced for a few minutes struggling to believe all this was real.

"Is this really happening? There must be something I can do." A thought came to him as he looked through the small plexiglass window. He slowly knelt down on the cell's cold pavement and prayed.

"Oh my God, my Lord, why did You let this happen to me? You know, only You know, I didn't do anything. Why did You let this happen? You promised me You'd never leave me or forsake me." he whispered sadly, "but I don't feel You with me anymore. I feel so alone. Please help me. You promised. You promised me!"

he said despairingly, "No one believes me. If You don't help me I don't know what I'm ..."

Moans and sobs began to wrack his body. To hide their sound, he put the skinny pillow over his face and curled into a ball on the dirty bunk.

An invisible wisp of vapor like powder floated up to the ceiling and then passed right through it. It cascaded through the atmosphere into the heavens, then into a wide blue expanse. It floated through what looked to be a huge shining curtain. Stars glimmered all around the place. Flashes of lightning could be seen through huge pillars and clouds. Voices could be heard as a figure was seen moving behind the curtain and drew near to the One.

7
ON EARTH AS IT IS IN HEAVEN

The vague outline of two iridescent figures could almost be seen behind an immense curtain. One, who appeared to be robed with a crown on his head, was standing nobly like a King. The other sat on what seemingly was a huge ornate throne that had a golden gleam to it that reflected out through the curtain. Light seemed to emanate from them both, or were they the source of light?

"I have heard him." said the One who sat on the throne. "He has touched our heart."

The temple shook as He spoke.

"*Ken*, Abba, he has. We must help him. We must keep covenant, as always." The King walked, pacing, planning.

Their eyes glowed like embers in a fire.

"You have authority, Son." The One on the throne spoke with tenderness, a Father's delight evident in his voice.

"Yes, Nathanael must return, but with assistance this time."

"Wisdom would enlist a church that would pray, one with our heart."

"There is one, and a good attorney. I've been watching a man who is ready to be restored from great losses."

The Father stood in response to the Son's words. Together they walked as the Father put his arm around his Son's shoulders.

A swift rushing wind blew through the great hall and lifted the curtain as He came in. "Jacob Luke." The three voices spoke in harmony as One, a sound like that of many waters.

"Great minds think alike." the Father said, hearty joy-filled laughter burst from Him and then the others and echoed through the temple.

"It is done!" the King shouted. The posts of the temple shook at the sound. Doves erupted in flight into the sky. A trumpet blast could be heard in the distance and a lightning branched off in the distance as a slow moving mist cascaded throughout the surrounding blue, gold and purple hills. A peaceful luminous quality could be felt in the air itself. The sweet smell of almonds came up as a Celtic-like voice in the distance began to sing a song in a beautiful, unknown language. And yet, though there was no sun or moon, it appeared as if someone had dimmed the lights, like that of a beautiful summer sunset.

At that moment on earth, in the little town of Belleville, Michigan, the cold winter rain that had been falling for days suddenly stopped. The sun shone brightly.

A little boy called out, "OK, Mom. God smiled on us just like you said and the rain stopped. I'm going to ride my bike." Intrigued, his mother looked, and sure enough the sun was beaming brightly through her kitchen window.

"Hmm," she mused, and walked outside as she watched her son take off down the street on his bike. "I'm glad I have soap," she laughed.

Again the wind swept through the temple courts. A soft voice clearly heard but unseen, whispered, "Heaven has prayed, even wept for him. It is his time. Now, I will go."

"We are with you." the two that were One said.

A little girl ran into the temple behind the veil. She came up and quickly hugged them both.

"I love you," she said, then laughed as she ran off to play again.

"We love you too, Darla." Heaven declared.

Outside, at the top of the stairs, on the second story of what used to be an old mill, a sign in Old English lettering engraved with faded gold leaf, hung on a weathered oak door. It read, "Jacob Luke Withers, Attorney at Law." Inside, sitting in an antique Victorian chair, an aging man dressed in a well-worn college sweater looked down at the fishing magazine in his lap. The television on top of his desk provided ambient noise as Jacob studied the magazine. Jacob looked up as his attention was drawn to the TV when a news reporter said something about a hit and run and possible manslaughter accident in Belleville.

"Captain Ben Franks, what can you tell us about the accused killer, Sam McBride?" Maria asked.

The captain replied, looking directly into the camera, "Well, only that he's just accused at this point. The blood found at the scene has been declared to be human blood, but no body has been found … yet. There is, however, an ongoing search for Roxanne Perello who, as you know, went missing around the same time that Sam McBride was in the accident."

"Do you think Sam McBride ran down Roxanne Perello in cold blood, Captain Franks?"

"What I think is really not the issue here. We intend on doing a thorough investigation. Mr. McBride insists he has not hurt anyone and that the alleged person he hit was actually … well … he says it was an angel."

Maria laughed mildly and then regained her composure. Captain Franks didn't even smile. He just gave her a cold stare.

Jacob, now captivated, continued to watch intently as he sat back in his favorite chair and stroked the orange fur of his best and only friend, his overfed cat, Candice.

Maria continued, "Captain Franks, has the accused seen a psychiatrist to determine whether or not he's sane? Also was Sam McBride drunk when you brought him in? We heard he was drinking at the Eagle's Nest just an hour before the hit and run and that he actually had words with Roxanne Perello. Is this true?" Maria shot the questions at him so forcefully he had to back away from her just to gather his thoughts.

"Well, in answer to your first questions, psychiatric interviews are really a matter for the court, and secondly, the blood alcohol levels have not been returned to us yet. I can say that the initial breathalyser came out negative, but that doesn't necessarily rule out the possibility of drug use. We should know more in a few days on that. However, I can't comment at this time on conversations leading up to the crime, for obvious reasons, as I'm sure you well know, Ms. Espinosa."

"Well, thank you, Captain. This is Maria Espinosa for Channel 3 News Live! We'll keep you updated on the Sam McBride case as the information comes in."

Denise McBride was just getting up from a stress nap. She decided to make herself a sandwich and heated up some soup and brought them both on a tray into the living room. Turning on the TV she heard the news about Sam. She gasped when she heard that the breathalyser test was negative and dropped her soup and sandwich on the floor. Her knees went weak as she barely made it to the couch to steady herself.

"*What?*" she thought. Her eyes grew wider and wider as she watched the newscast. She quickly cleaned up the mess on the floor.

Confused, worried and unsure what to believe, she grabbed the phone and immediately called Angelo Perello.

"Yeah?" Angelo answered in his usual hard guy demeanor.

"Angelo? It's me, Denise."

"Hey, Denise." he answered in a surly drunken tone.

"Angelo, you said Sam was drinking the night you called me, but on the news the police captain said the breath test was negative. Angelo, did you actually see him drinking?"

"Yeah, I saw him. We all saw him." Angelo lied.

Denise decided not to make an issue of it now, needing him to give her other information.

"Angelo, do you think Roxanne might have gone somewhere or …" she hesitated, "Look, I don't think Sam is capable of murder. Are you sure you don't know where Roxanne is?" her voice was shaking.

"I don't know, Denise. They got an eyewitness." A clanking of glasses, voices, and noises from the pool table could be heard in the background.

"Angelo, are you at the bar right now?"

"Yeah, I'm over at the Eagle's Nest. You wanna join me?"

"Your wife's missing, maybe even dead, and you're not out looking for her, and you're trying to hit on me?" Denise scolded him in unbelief and disgust.

Angelo replied, "Look I'm doin' everything I can I … I gotta go. I'll see ya' later."

Denise was completely shocked when she heard the dial tone. She had always thought Angelo was a little creepy, but now she was sickened, completely sure he was a total loser, maybe worse.

Angelo returned to his drink. Even the regulars and the bartender gave him a suspicious look.

A swift breeze blew the curtain in Jacob Luke's office into the air a bit. Jacob caught it out of the corner of his eye.

"What the heck," he thought. *"It's the middle of the winter!"* He looked again. He walked over to the window. Sure enough, the window was closed and locked. There was even a good deal of dust on the sill.

"Hmm, just my mind playing tricks on me," he thought out loud. He walked back over, shut off the TV and sat down in his chair. On the top of his desk he picked up an old faded picture of his wife and daughter. His eyes misted up a bit. They always did when he thought of them.

A still small voice that seemed to come from nowhere, and everywhere at once, spoke, "Jacob Luke." He looked and saw the stereo was off.

"What? Who is that?" He looked around.

"You know who it is, Jacob. You know My voice."

Jacob looked over at the television.

"*I'm hearing things,*" he thought to himself after he saw that the TV was undeniably off.

"You're not hearing things, Jacob. It's Me."

"Did I say that out loud?"

"You didn't have to, Jacob. I can hear your heart."

Jacob's heart ached and skipped a beat.

"Oh God." He hung his head and mumbled under his breath.

"I'm dying." He put his hand to his heart. There was no pain?

"You're not dying, Jacob. You wanted to talk to Me face to face, remember? Here I AM." At that statement a shock wave seemed to come through the air, Jacob's knees almost buckled. He steadied himself by grabbing the chair, then slowly sat down on his old blue couch.

"I've been waiting for you to call, Jacob. We used to be so close. What happened?"

Jacob, astounded, began to understand what was happening to him. He slowly answered.

"You … you know what happened." Jacob began trembling. "You took my family from me, the two people I loved most in this world. You took them from me, and now I'm … all alone."

"You are not alone, Jacob, and I didn't cause that accident. I don't cause car accidents but I did take them home with Me. I have been trying to reach out to you."

The scene suddenly played again in Jacob's mind: the screeching tires, the crunching metal.

"Daddy, help!" his daughter had cried out as she'd been flung out of the car. He could see her face as she lay curled up on the ground. He couldn't get to her, his leg was pinned under the dashboard of the crumpled car.

"Darla, hold on. Darla, Darla!" he had screamed again and again, but her light faded. Internal bleeding was the official cause of her death. His wife, Jennifer, had died instantly. He wished he had died with them. Part of him had.

"They're happy here, you know, and they love you very much.

And you will see them again. I will not let you be all alone, my friend."

Jacob, surprised and suddenly overcome at the full realization of who he was talking to, slid off the chair. He covered his face with his hands and knelt on the floor. He was filled with a glimmer of hope at the words of assurance that his family lived. Deep inside he had waited for this day; many had prayed for this day for him. He knew in his heart of hearts he had to start living again.

"I will see them again?" Jacob asked. "Will I really? Oh I miss them so much. Will you tell them how much I love them and I miss them?" He wept. "Tell them I'm so sorry. I was supposed to protect them! I'm sorry!" Jacob was lying face down on the floor now, with his head in his hands moaning from the heartache. This was good for him. He had held this in far too long.

"Jacob, they know it wasn't your fault. They hear you." the Lord wept. "They love you and know how much you love them. You couldn't have prevented it; it's time to heal and time to move on now. They miss you. I miss you too, Jacob. I've missed your prayers at night, and the gentle heart you showed people who had less than you." With each word the Lord spoke to Jacob, he melted a little more. He realized the time he'd wasted, how unhappy he'd been since he isolated himself from the life he'd known, his friends at church, people in town.

The Lord continued, "I've missed your singing to Me in the congregation."

"Oh, I've got a terrible voice, you know that." Jacob now humbled, replied with a much lightened heart. A smile of joy came to his face. He was being restored by a Father's love.

"It always sounded pleasing to My ear and to all of us up here. We listen more with the heart here, Jacob. "

"I have missed You too, Lord. I'm sorry I blamed You. I know it's not Your fault. I've just been so hurt, and I missed them so much."

Tears ran down his cheeks, as he remembered his daughter, Darla, on the swing set calling to him, "Daddy watch me, I'm going higher! Mom, look!" The memory was so real with sounds and colors, the smell of the air, just like it was yesterday. He sobbed loudly.

Then, he felt invisible arms wrap around him. Angels filled the room watching as the Lord embraced Jacob. Then, a whisper, "They're in the highest place now, Jacob, and their love for you hasn't changed one bit. Jennifer prays that you would be happy again, and Darla actually prays for you to marry again and have more children. She told me, 'He's the best Daddy ever, and he knows how to make kids smile alot.'"

Jacob could hear her voice in his mind, saying just that. He laughed through his tears. "Oh, I'm too old to have kids now."

"That's what Abraham and Sarah thought, but both Jennifer and Darla want that for you. They both pray that prayer for you. Is anything too hard for God, Jacob?"

"People really pray in Heaven?" Jacob asked.

"On Earth as it is in Heaven," the voice replied.

Jacob sat up. "Yeah right, I never thought about it that way. They pray for me? What else do they say?" Jacob asked, his face lighting with wonder.

Like a healing breeze, the voice whispered again, "When you weep, Jacob, they weep with you. They want you to move on and to be closer to Me. That's what they pray about, and I want that too, My friend."

"It was just hard for me to tell anyone; I've never felt so alone before. I didn't know how to tell You. I've been so angry at You. But, it's really not your fault, is it?"

"No, Jacob, it wasn't My fault. But I still want you to tell Me how you feel, even if you turn out to be wrong about something. I know the pain of loss, too. I've felt all you could ever feel. And Jacob, I hope you'll learn to trust Me more. When I paid for you, I knew what I was getting, and I am always willing to help you through anything. It hurts my heart when you don't come to Me with your pain. I was waiting for you to cry out to Me all these years. But it had to be by your choice. I only want your love, freely given as I freely gave you Mine. Do you understand?"

"Yes Lord, I think I do now. Thank You for not quitting on me. I've been a selfish old man."

"To Me you're My loving son, My good friend, as well as My brother, and I love you very much."

Jacob buried his face into the small pillow on the couch. He shook as a cry from deep inside him was brought out. A washing, a healing took place. A soul, a son, rejoined in harmony with his Father.

"Oh Father, forgive me for not loving You and following You. You've been so good to me and I just ignored You. Please forgive me and restore our relationship. I want to be close to you again, please Lord. In Jesus' name. Amen."

"It is done," whispered the voice. A great ocean of peace that he had not known in a long time came over Jacob. He just lay there, breathed deeply and basked in it.

In the highest place, messengers and men with golden crowns and white robes, as well as many creatures throughout Heaven all sang as if in one voice. Beautiful sounding instruments sounded slowly gaining in volume, all within Heaven's gates, they sang,

"Glory, Glory, Glory to the Lamb, and to him who sits on the throne!"

One of the elders walked forward, turned around to face the assembly and shouted

"Another son has come home!"

An angel flew overhead toward the elders and blew a golden trumpet and they all shouted, "Hallelujah, Hallelujah!"

Angels lifted their wings toward the throne where there were seven lamps burning. Then all the assembly bowed to one knee. As the song continued, a light streamed out from the Holy Place and emanated toward each living thing. This light filled all the Heavens. Every creature soaked and became fulfilled by it. There were Creatures flying with unusual faces that had six wings and they cried, "Holy, Holy, Holy, is the Lord God Almighty which is and was and is to come."

Suddenly a great silence came over Heaven as they carefully listened.

"Jacob?"

"Yes, Lord?"

"I would like you to do something for Me."

"Anything at all, Lord."

"Sam McBride needs a good lawyer and you're the best that I've got."

Jacob interrupted, "The best? I haven't won a decent case in years."

"Jacob?" the Lord said warmly.

"Yes, Lord?"

"You really shouldn't interrupt Me when I'm speaking and if I say you're the best, then you are."

"I'm the best, yes. Sorry about that, Lord," Jacob said, looking up.

"And I want you to return to your church and reunite with your family there. Ask them to pray for Sam, and then go visit Sam in prison and tell him I sent you to help him, and that he will bring glory to My name. Tell him to be of good courage and that I always keep covenant, and I won't leave him or forsake him. And also … that I've heard his prayers, he has touched My heart, and that I love him very much!"

"And Jacob?"

"Yes, Lord?"

"Tell him help is on the way!"

"What does that mean, Lord?"

"Never mind, Jacob, you'll see soon enough."

8
Help Is on the Way

It was early Sunday morning. Jacob awoke at 8:27 after one of the most peaceful sleeps he'd had in quite some time. Something red was in his windowsill, curiously, he got up to look. A bright red cardinal perched outside on the sill was enjoying the heat leaking through the old wooden window. Jacob was fascinated, not only by the cardinal being here in the winter, but by how he felt. Everything seemed new today. He felt like a brand new man.

After its brief rest, the cardinal took flight. Jacob decided to shave his beard.

"When had it become salt and pepper?" he wondered. He got stuck in the mirror when it dawned on him, *"It's Sunday."*

"You've got some fences to mend, Jacob Luke," he told himself. He put on his cleanest dirty shirt and slacks and drove to New Covenant Church. It was about 20 minutes away on the 1-94 service drive.

Many years had passed since he'd entered these doors. He wondered if his old church family would scold him for being gone too long. Jacob tried to keep a low profile. Walking in with his head low, he mustered all the courage he could and slid quietly into the pew where he had sat with his wife and daughter years before. He looked to the right at the empty spaces beside him. It made him a little lonely but he knew he had to get past this.

The worship team came out of the back room, where they'd been praying. Christy Bines, as if she had radar, saw Jacob and at once ran over and hugged him super tight.

"Oh Mister Withers, it's so good to see you! We've missed you so much. We never stopped praying for you." She took both his hands and practically dragged him to the front of the sanctuary.

Jacob was relieved that someone greeted him so warmly, and you could see it in his face as he walked with her. He wore an ear to ear grin.

Christy was just in 7th grade when he had been here last. She had become a beautiful young woman. She used to babysit for his daughter, Darla, when his wife, Jennifer and he went out for an evening.

"Look, everybody! Mr. Withers is back!" she said exuberantly.

"Jacob!" Bryan Snider exclaimed. "It's so good to see you; we've missed you very much." Bryan, an old friend and long time pillar of the church, hugged Jacob's shoulders, admonishing him, yet smiling as he did. "Even though you never called us back, we've never given up on you, Jacob."

Jacob was overwhelmed by the many familiar faces that came up to greet him, some with hugs, others with handshakes and even 98-year-old Great-Grandmother Winnie gave him a soft kiss on the cheek. They all told him how much they'd missed him. Jacob felt like an old fool, wondering why it took him so long to come back.

When Pastor David Owen came out of his office and saw the crowd, and then Jacob standing in the middle, he looked astonished for a second and had to do a double take.

"Jake, is that you?" as he walked up with his hand outstretched. "You old eagle you! Where the heck have you been? Good to see you, young man." Pastor Dave was the only person Jacob had ever allowed to call him Jake.

Pastor Dave shook his hand firmly, and then gave him a great big bear hug.

"We've missed you, Jake" he looked at Jacob affectionately for a moment, like a son to a father. "It's really good to see you. Now I've got to go and earn my keep, but we'll talk, OK?" Overcome with emotion and unable to speak, Jacob just smiled, nodded, and continued to grin. He really hadn't experienced anything resembling real love in a long time. Tears welled up in his eyes again, though these were definitely tears of joy, not sorrow. He rubbed his chin where his beard had been. He prayed quietly as he sat down in the pew.

The church had a beautiful time of worship. The song, *"Holy, Holy, Holy, Lord God Almighty"* was sung by the congregation with the words displayed on the huge screen in front of the church. Many ethnicities and colors made up the membership here. The voices were beautiful. Natural harmonies filled the air. Some raised their hands, others knelt. One lady waved beautiful flags in the air as the music played. Jacob thought he felt a faint breeze come up through the aisle. There was an evident freshness in the air. Maybe even a presence.

Many people began to kneel down where they were, some began to weep. Some prayed. Some even laughed, seemingly overcome with joy. Jacob thought he heard the fluttering sound of wings. He looked up to the ceiling to see if maybe there was a bird loose in the sanctuary. There were bright sunbeams coming through the stained glass window which had a likeness of Gabriel appearing to Mary to announce the birth of Jesus.

As Jacob worshiped, in his mind's eye he could see angels all over the place with their wings stretched up toward the heavens. He laughed at himself and his overactive imagination.

As he closed his eyes he imagined a warrior-like angel perched near the stained glass window. Its outstretched wings had different colored gemstone plates that changed colors according to the music. Jacob quickly opened his eyes, turned, and looked up. But there was nothing, just the stained glass. He laughed at himself again, but secretly wondered, *"Are we all surrounded by angels? Protecting us? Encouraging us?"*

Pastor David moved toward the stage. Overcome with gratitude, he knelt down at the altar and began to pray. A few people joined him there and offered thanks and prayers for themselves, their friends and loved ones.

"Help us to reach those that are lost, Lord," Grandma Winnie cried. Many more continued to worship where they were.

The pastor then walked up to the pulpit and as the congregation quieted, he greeted everyone. He took hold of the microphone,

"We have a special guest with us today who we are extremely blessed to have back worshiping with us," he looked over in Jacob's direction, "Jacob Luke Withers." Most people clapped. "Hi, Jake!" one yelled out. The pastor continued, "And we hope he'll stick around for a while. Jake, would you like to say anything?"

Jacob still taking it all in, slowly walked up the few stairs around the left side of the podium. Pastor Dave handed him the microphone and stepped back as Jacob, visibly overwhelmed, eventually spoke.

"Hi. I ..." he hesitated, "I really missed you guys." Nervously he cleared his throat. "I've been gone a long time," he paused. "Thank you for your prayers and for never giving up on me. For reminding me that there is a place that I can call..." he choked up a little bit, looked down at the podium and then at the people again. "A place that I can call home." Jacob looked over at Pastor Dave who smiled, and nodded for Jacob to continue. Tears of love and sounds of applause poured out of the congregation, encouraging Jacob as he continued.

"I was in my office the other day, and guess who came to visit me?" He looked around at the curious faces. "Have you ever had the Lord talk to you so plainly that there was no denying who it was?"

"Amen, Amen," came from more than a few of the worshipers. "Come on, brother, tell it." another said.

"For so long I was hiding from Him, from you, and just everything. And of course, He found me, but so much more than that. The other day the Lord spoke to me and restored me, and He loved me, and comforted me about missing Jennifer and Darla. It was so awesome! And I have to tell you, I'm really sorry. I have been a fool for many years. I can't believe I stayed away so long. I have missed you." Again the crowd applauded.

"We missed you Mr. Withers," one shouted and with it many "Amen's," were heard from the crowd.

"Thank you, thank you all so much." Jacob said earnestly. "Well, anyway, you might find this hard to believe, but I've got to obey

His voice, so hear goes." He again looked over at the Pastor who smiled his approval.

"After my 'God experience' yesterday, the Lord asked me to do something for Him. This may sound way out there, but He asked me to legally represent and to ask you to pray for a man that is in jail. His name is Sam McBride. You've probably heard the story by now. He's in jail for hit and run and he might be charged with murder. They're looking for a missing person, or her body. Her name is Roxanne Perello. Well, the police believe that he killed her with his car. Now according to what I saw on the news Mr. McBride told the police he hit ..." Jacob paused and scanned the peoples faces, wondering how well this was going to be received, "that he hit an angel, And I know how all this sounds," he said throwing his hands in the air with a shrug, "but I don't know? All I know is what happened to me the other day was real." He gripped the podium tightly now. "And if the Lord is telling me to go and talk to this man and represent him in court, then I'm going!"

"Amen, Mr. Withers!" a man in the front row encouraged him.

"But there is a very important part that involves you. The Lord told me to come back here and reunite with you, and to ask you to pray for Sam. So heck I'm asking. I'm not asking you to believe the story, or even me for that matter, but to just pray. Please? And seek Him on this." Jacob nodded to the pastor that he was finished.

Pastor Dave came up and embraced Jacob and took the microphone back. "I think we can do that, can't we, Church?"

A few parishioners of their own volition came and stood before the altar, then a few more after that. "We'll stand with you." One of the deacons said, "Yes, Jacob, we'll stand in prayer for your friend."

"I think you've got your answer, Jake." Pastor Dave said confidently shaking his hand.

A few of the men and women stepped up and put their hands on Jacob's shoulder, and just began to pray, "Father, in Jesus name, we stand in agreement with Jacob to help this man. We ask that You be glorified in his life, and bring honor to Your name. We agree to pray until You see it through. Amen." At that point most in the church within ear shot said in unison, "Amen!"

Jacob had a good meal at Pastor Dave's that afternoon and later back at his apartment, a great nap. He came out and sat at his old roll top desk. "He makes me lie down in green pastures," he thought out loud. "I think I understand that better than I ever did before." Jacob looked at the photo of Jennifer and Darla on his desk. For the first time in years, it didn't tempt him to tears. "I'm doin' it, sweetie. I'm living again. I'll never forget you though." He smiled.

Monday morning 9:00 a.m. Jacob slipped some coins into the meter, looked up at the huge building and then walked into the Wayne County Jail. His suit was still dusty and smelling of moth balls from hanging so long in his closet.

"I'd like to see Sam McBride, please," he said to the officer at the desk.

"And you are?" the officer asked.

"Attorney Jacob Luke Withers."

"Well okay, Attorney Jacob Luke Withers, I'm afraid you'll have to wait. You're about the fifth one here today and he hasn't wanted to use any of them. It's kind of foolish if you ask me, even if you all are in it for the fame. It's better than not having a lawyer at all. There's one in there right now."

"It's a mad-house out there," Jacob said looking through the mini-blinds. News crews representing television and radio stations, newspapers and Internet news sites from all over the country, and some even from other countries, had been lining up outside the jail, as well as spectators. There were canopies, satellite trucks, and campers. Boxes of water and food were brought in. It looked like a festival. Someone had a "I Believe in Angels" sign. This made Jacob cringe. He hoped this case wasn't going to turn into a circus.

"Yeah, they've been here for hours and interviewed a bunch of attorneys that tried to talk to this McBride fella," the officer divulged. "But like I said, he really didn't want to talk to any of 'em."

Jacob sat in a light blue padded chair and patiently waited his turn.

Inside the visiting area stood Joshua Stone, an overweight red-haired lawyer in a brown polyester suit. He was looking down, mumbling to Sam who was sitting with his head down in his hands.

"It's open and shut, Mr. McBride," Attorney Joshua Stone said. "We'll just plead insanity, and after a few years in a mental facility, you'll be free again. It's just that simple."

"I'm not insane!" Sam replied. "Thanks for coming, mister, but I think I'll wait."

"Well, you just think about it, McBride. Here's my card. Just call me and I'll come see ya' right away."

"That's alright." Sam said. "Thanks anyway." Sam handed him back the card.

One of the two guards there escorted Stone out of the area. The man smelled like stale cigar smoke and nachos. Sam didn't trust him.

News pit bull Maria Espinosa from Channel 3 News attacked Mr. Stone as he was leaving. "Are you Sam McBride's attorney?"

"Well, he's weighing his options," Joshua Stone replied stuffing a fat cigar in his mouth, "but it seems like it will be a 'yes'."

When he said that, the other news media moved in for a quote but Maria asked quickly, "What did he tell you? Did you discuss a defense?"

"I proposed an insanity plea."

"He didn't really hire you then, did he?" Maria pushed. "You're the fifth attorney to try that today and he turned all the others down."

"No, No, I believe he'll come around. You'll see."

"Thank you, Mr. Stone." Maria said perturbed, as she walked back to the satellite truck.

"Is there such a thing as an honest lawyer?" she shouted over to Don the cameraman. He just shrugged his shoulders. He knew better than to get into a heated discussion with Maria.

Jacob was escorted into the visiting area after being searched thoroughly and going through the metal detector. Sam McBride was in a prison-issued bright orange jump suit. He just wanted to go back to his cell. He'd had his fair share of lawyers today.

"Mr. McBride?" Jacob asked softly. Sam, with his head hung low, just nodded.

"I'm Jacob Luke Withers, an attorney from downriver. May I have a word with you?"

Sam slowly looked up. "Look, thanks alot for coming, mister," Sam whispered, "but there's been a bunch of lawyers here today, trying to make a name for themselves, wanting me to say I'm crazy. But I'm not. So if you're just more of the same, I'd just as well like to be left alone."

"Actually, Mr. McBride, I know this is going to sound crazy. But I was sent to represent you." Jacob told Sam about the amazing experience at his office. Sam was spellbound. He didn't say one word as Jacob spoke.

"He told me He wanted you to know that He sent me to help you and that you will bring glory to His name. And to tell you to be of good courage that He always keeps Covenant, and He won't leave you or forsake you, and also ..."

Jacob suddenly closed his eyes and his head dropped. Sam wasn't sure if he was meditating, praying or what. After a thirty second silence, Sam spoke up, "Mr. Withers, are you alright"? Still just silence. "Mr. Withers!" Sam shouted. The guard looked over. Jacob shook his head slightly and then opened his eyes.

"Did I ... did I fade out?"

"Yes, you did. Are you alright?"

"Yeah," Jacob replied. "I have a slight case of what they call narcolepsy, It's kind of an awake-sleeping disorder. I lost my wife and daughter some years back and I've had this ever since."

"Are you gonna be okay to represent me?" Sam asked, worry was written across his forehead.

"Oh, yes I'm sure. My case is really mild and I have medication that I take, so my bouts are infrequent and short usually. So, you want me to be your lawyer then?"

"Yeah, I think so. You were telling me something about a covenant, and not leaving me and you were about to say something else?"

"Oh right, yes! He wanted me to tell you that He's heard your prayers, and you have touched His heart, and that He loves you very much!"

Sam asked excitedly, "Really? He said all that? He really did?"

"Yes, and one more thing, I'm supposed to tell you that help is on the way, but He wouldn't explain what that meant. You believe me, right? You don't think I would just make something like that up, like I'm some kind of religious freak or something?" Jacob asked.

"The question is do you believe me?" Sam reiterated. "I mean you must know the story."

"Yes, it is kind of fantastic," Jacob said with a grin, "but I do believe angels on occasion appear to people. And I know God spoke to me about this, so, I guess I kind of do. We'll have to talk about it some more though. The question is, will a jury believe you?"

"I don't know but I believe what you're saying is true, too. It lines right up with what I've been praying. So, do you really think you can help me?" Sam looked up with hope reflecting in his eyes.

"I know He told me to represent you, so if you agree, we'll have to find this Roxanne person. Someone must know where she is. My church is praying, too. Now the arraignment is Wednesday morning. They're going to try to charge you with 'Leaving the Scene of a Personal Injury Accident Causing Death.' But Sam, there's more. If they think they can prove that you killed Roxanne, and did it on purpose, they will charge you with second degree murder, and you could get 10-30 years. It's unusual without a body, but it has happened before."

Sam shook his head. "But I didn't kill anyone. I didn't even hit anyone. Well, you know, it was a ..."

"I believe you, Mr. McBride." Jacob let out a sigh. "We'll ask for a jury trial and that will buy us some time to find her. And I'll find out exactly what evidence they have. But Sam, they've got a pretty strong case with this eye witness and the blood they found at the scene and on the car. And with Roxanne disappearing the same night and you talking with her in the bar ... well, we've just got to find her."

"Thank you, Mr. Withers. I appreciate all you're doing. I do have a question though. You said God wanted you to tell me that He always keeps covenant. What does that mean exactly?"

"He didn't explain it to me per se," Jacob said. "But a covenant basically is a pact or an agreement, like a marriage covenant. But with the Lord it's even more, because He's God. It's an unbreakable bond. He doesn't go back on His promises."

"That sure is good to know." Sam thought about all the things Marge had told him.

"Mr. Withers? Would you call my wife, and tell her that I love her and that I didn't do it? Will you tell her everything you've told me?"

"Yes, I'd be happy to do that," Jacob said standing up and gathering his things.

"And Mr. Withers? You know I don't have any money, right?"

"Oh really. Yeah, well, I assumed as much. I have sources though. There's a passage in the Bible that says that all the cattle on a thousand hills are His, and another one that you can look up in Philippians 4:19, *But my God shall supply all your need according to his riches in glory by Christ Jesus,* so not to worry. Let's get you free first and then maybe I'll take your first born child or something," Jacob smiled and said, "just kidding!"

"Thank you so much, Mr. Withers. You have no idea what your coming here has meant to me today. You brought me some hope."

"Not me, Mr. McBride. Someone greater than me, and please just call me Jacob."

"Could you, Jacob …?" Sam hesitated for a moment, "is there any chance you could bring me a Bible?"

"You bet, Sam. Next time I come." Jacob was touched by Sam's sincerity.

Both men smiled and shook hands. A guard then took Sam back to his cell while another escorted Jacob out of the room.

As soon as Jacob was through the front door, Maria Espinosa ran up and shoved a microphone into Jacob's face.

"Mr. Withers? Will you be representing Sam McBride?"

"I have no comment at this time. How did you know my name?"

"That's not really important." Maria replied.

"Where is the body, Mr. Withers? Did he tell you what happened to Roxanne Perello? Was it really just an accident, Mr. Withers? What are your defense options? He did hire you, didn't he?"

"Goodbye, Mrs. Espinosa." Jacob had seen Maria on TV many times and knew how pushy she could be. He made a beeline for his Old Chevy Impala in the parking lot. He quickly started the car and headed for home.

9
A Virtuous Woman

Jacob pulled up to a red light and glanced briefly at the piece of paper in his hand with Denise McBride's cell phone number on it.

"What am I going to say to her?" he asked himself, unsure of how to approach Sam's wife.

When he looked up he saw a little girl was crossing the intersection with her mother. She was in a cute blue and white dress and had a helium balloon in her hand. The words 'Happy Birthday!' were written in bold blue letters across the top. She turned slightly to the left and smiled at Jacob. He smiled back, touched by the gesture.

A gray cloud quickly moved in above and blocked out the already dim winter sun. Jacob hated gray skies. A seductive voice taunted him, "She reminds you of your little girl, doesn't she?" Jacob nervously watched as the mother and daughter mingled into the crowd. He sighed deeply gripping the steering wheel more tightly as the old familiar emotional pain of his family memories shot through his mind.

Dark shadows seemed to penetrate every bit of space in his car at that moment. Accusing voices whispered, "You don't have the capacity to handle a big trial like this, Jacob. You're still healing from losing Jennifer and Darla. Let the big shots take care of this, Jacob. They're better equipped than you. Don't embarrass yourself. Don't be a fool."

"It's true," Jacob groaned with a sinking look on his face. *"It is a big case."* He reminisced about his string of lost cases over the last few years. *"I'm so out of practice … I don't know, Lord, maybe I shouldn't*

do this." He rubbed his chin nervously as he often did when he was worried. In the back seat directly behind him, the evil spirit smirked, an expert in doubt and fear. Its black twisted finger was near Jacob's head and he was spinning it around like it was dialing an old phone. Jacob was becoming depressed. Lost in the taunts the spirit was planting in his mind, he didn't even notice when the light changed to green.

Freckled-faced messenger, Parakaleo, broke through the gray clouds, stretched out his wings and gracefully landed on the top of the car. He swiftly swung in the window like an acrobat and plopped down on the front seat next to Jacob who was completely unaware of his presence.

"You can do all things through Christ who gives you strength, Jacob," said the messenger.

Parakaleo was an angel gifted in encouragement. He was a very unusual looking warrior. He had red hair and green eyes and always seemed to be smiling. Also, and most unusually, he was adorned with freckles all over his face, arms and legs. They were even sprinkled on his off white wings. This 5 foot 4 inch messenger ultimately spread joy wherever he went, even by those who couldn't see him, which of course, was almost everyone. They often experienced joy rather than fear or alarm whenever he came on the scene.

The man in the car behind Jacob impatiently blasted the horn. Jacob, startled, looked up and saw the light had become green. He stepped on the gas.

"I can do all things through Christ who gives me strength." he proclaimed as the car sped through the intersection.

"Get behind me, Satan." Jacob ordered boldly as his confidence seemed to grow. The encouraging verse the messenger gave him was enough to bring him to his senses. "I've had enough of you, in Jesus' name. Get away from me." Darkness seemed to leave the car, the voices were gone. Jacob took a deep breath. Even the air smelled cleaner now.

"'Way to go, Jacob." Parakaleo said encouragingly as he quickly flew out the same way he'd come in.

"Thank you, Lord." Jacob said sensing the joy of the Lord.

Arriving home and filled with new enthusiasm, Jacob walked into his office, sat down and called Denise McBride.

"Hello," a young sounding voice on the other end answered.

"Hello. Is this Denise McBride?" he asked.

"No, this is her daughter, Amanda. Hold on, I'll go get her … Mom!" Amanda yelled loudly, "Phone!"

Jacob pulled the phone away from his ear and, with his finger, checked his hearing. "This girl has got a set of pipes on her," he thought out loud.

"See who it is, Amanda," Denise McBride shouted back. She was in the basement folding laundry.

"Can I ask who is calling?" Amanda tilted her head and listened. "Oh. Okay." She yelled back at her mother, "Its Dad's lawyer. He says it's real important."

Denise ran upstairs and picked up the phone. "Hello, this is Denise McBride," trying to catch her breath.

"Hi, Mrs. McBride, Umm, my name is Jacob Luke Withers and I am your husband's lawyer." Jacob said feeling somewhat out of place. "Ah, he asked me to call you and, well this is going to sound really unofficial, but what he wanted me to do is to tell you …" Jacob paused and breathed deeply to steady himself. "Sam said to tell you that he loves you, and that he's innocent. I know that doesn't sound very lawyerly." Jacob got up and paced the floor. "Look, I was wondering, Mrs. McBride, if you could possibly meet me at my office tomorrow. I've got some very important things to discuss with you, and it would be much better to do it in person." There was a slight hesitation on the other end of the line.

"Alright, Mr. Withers, but … I'm not sure how much of a help I can be to you. What time would you like me to be there? Oh, OK, hold on a second." Denise hurriedly searched through the junk drawer and grabbed a dry erase marker and then located a napkin and quickly wrote down the address. "OK, I'll see you at ten, Mr. Withers."

Later that evening after Denise said goodnight to Amanda, she lay down to sleep, but only tossed and turned in her bed. The winter wind screamed violently through the bedroom window. She was tormented by her worried thoughts, and as hard as she tried to shut them out, she was unsuccessful.

What did this attorney want her to do or say? How is Amanda handling all this?

When Denise finally did sleep, nightmares played on in her mind like an all night movie theater. First, she dreamed that she had lost everything she owned in bankruptcy court. Then she saw Amanda get busted for selling drugs and eventually wind up in foster care. A newscaster that had totally black eyes forecast that the sun would never shine again, all the while laughing hysterically. She twisted and turned trying to wake up.

Above her bed an ugly black twisted imp was floating at the ceiling while dripping an oily ointment on her forehead, causing the bad dreams.

In the next nightmare, Sam was sitting on the floor in the middle of the living room, drinking and laughing at her. "You're such a fool! I can't believe you fell for it again." The voice didn't sound like Sam's though. It was a deep sinister, raspy voice.

Denise woke up suddenly, and with a startled look she rubbed her forehead. An ominous voice whispered to her mind. "Cut your losses, Denise, and cut that bum loose. Look what he's done to your family. It's just going to get worse from here." She thought she heard someone in the room. She shivered and broke into a cold sweat as she looked around the room. The glowing green letters on the digital clock read only 3:30.

She sprang out of bed and went downstairs, trying to get away from the nightmares and that clinging feeling of dread.

She went to the refrigerator and made herself a good sized turkey and Swiss cheese sandwich, poured a glass of milk and sat down at the kitchen table. She grabbed the local *Hollywood Stars* magazine left there by Amanda and glanced through the pages.

From the corner of her eye, she saw Sam's Bible on the left corner of the table. *"Amanda must have been looking at that,"* she thought. She stared at it for a moment. Then at the magazine cover again. "Angels invade Detroit" was the headline with a picture of an air brushed woman in a white gown and obviously fake wings. She smirked and flipped the magazine over. She got up and went over to the edge of the table and picked up the Bible. Sitting back down, she slowly opened it to a random section. "So far so good," she said. "No lightning bolts," she joked, looking up in jest.

With her elbows on the table, she read the words on the page.

Even the darkness will not be dark to you; the night will shine like the day, for darkness is as light to you. For you created my inmost being; you knit me together in my mother's womb.

Denise got up to look at a picture of Amanda that she had put in a magnetic frame on the fridge. Her mind raced back 17 years to the time when she was pregnant, in happier, hopeful times. She and Sam were feeding the birds in the park as they watched kids playing on the merry-go-round and swing sets. They loved listening to the sounds of their laughter as they played.

"Do you feel that, Sam?" Sam placed his hand on her belly.

"It's moving!" he shouted. "The baby knows we're its parents." They had looked at each other with such love, such hope for the future.

Her mind rewound further. They were both on the patio in the back of her apartment. Sam wore blue jeans and a concert t-shirt and she had on her short shorts and a tube type tank top. She was lying back in a lawn chair. The Journey song *Faithfully* was playing on the radio. It was a hot, humid day in the low 90's.

"Hey! Turn that down for a second!" Sam said. Denise dialed down the volume while Sam reached behind the small garage door and pulled out an old beat up guitar that was missing a string. He attempted to play it while awkwardly singing his homemade song, "You are the only one for me. You are the girl of all my dreams." His singing was so terrible that she began to laugh hysterically. She turned over to hide her face.

"What are you laughing at? I wrote that for you." Sam said. She rolled back over and sat up.

"You wrote that for me? Really?" she asked playfully. "That is sweet, Sam. That's my nickname for you, Sweet Sam." She reached up, pulled him down to the chair, then kissed him softly on the mouth, then whispered, "I love you, Sam McBride."

"I love you too, 'Neesi," he said. What happened next made it one of the best memories of her life.

Suddenly, surprising her, Sam dropped to one knee. "Babe, I know I don't have a lot of money and all. And you could probably do a lot better than me. But when I'm around you my heart just ... man it explodes. It feels like everything's perfect. So, babe, if you'll have me, I'll ... I'll do my best to make you happy. I can't see myself ever being happy with anyone but you." Sam's look had grown increasingly more intense. "Denise, I'm in love with you."

Awestruck is the only word for the way Denise felt then. She had dreamed about that day for years. She remembered asking herself, *"Is this actually happening?"* staring at him awkwardly, almost as if everything was in slow motion. She saw the white picket fence, big house, big family, the whole nine yards. And then those special words just sprung out, "Denise Daniels, will you marry me?"

Speechless and dazed she simply studied him with her eyes for what seemed like minutes. Sam had become a little nervous and self-conscious to say the least. Finally he stammered, "Well, Denise?"

Abruptly she snapped out of it. "Yes, Yes," she exclaimed. "I'll marry you, you crazy man. I'll marry you! Yes! Oh Sam, yes."

But that was a long time ago, and things didn't work out the way she thought they would. She looked up at the clock, it was almost 4.00 a.m. now. She did reflect though, in all of Sam's mishaps and binges and all, he had never cheated on her; he never even looked at anyone else. And he never lied to her either. Denise looked down at the Bible again and continued to read softly, now out loud.

I praise You because I am fearfully and wonderfully made; your works are wonderful, I know that full well. My frame was not hidden from you when I was made in the secret place.

A tear ran down her cheek as she read intently; like she had just received a letter from a long lost friend. Her lip quivered, as she continued to read the words softly.

When I was woven together in the depths of the earth, your eyes saw my unformed body. All the days ordained for me were written in your book before one of them came to be.

"Wow!" she breathed deeply, folded her hands and rested her face softly on the top of Sam's Bible. She whispered, "You know me, don't You? You knew I would eventually need You. I do believe in You, don't I? I'm not sure, God, how or why, but I know You're there, and I don't want to give up, but I'm too tired to fight."

As she sat up and folded her hands together, her questions became her prayer. "God, please help me and my family, let me know this is all gonna turn out all right. Amen."

A single tear ran down her cheek. She quickly wiped it away, looking around to make sure no one saw it, even though it was four in the morning and she was alone. Denise McBride seldom cried.

Picking up Sam's Bible, she headed back upstairs and climbed into bed. She held the leather bound words close to her as she faded back to sleep. This time her rest was peaceful. There were a couple of angels with drawn swords having an angel food snack on the roof near Denise and Amanda's rooms. A dead deflated black demon body was dangling from a tree limb. The angels smiled at each other as it dissipated into the atmosphere.

In spite of the lack of a full night's sleep, Denise woke early. Feeling refreshed she fixed breakfast and prepared a school lunch for Amanda who was sitting at the table in her usual early morning teenage coma. There was a lingering silence between them and then finally, Amanda cleared the hair from her face, and blurted out, "Is that lawyer gonna get Dad out of jail?"

"He's gonna try, honey." Denise answered consolingly, her face looking out the window above the sink. She paused for a moment, then turned and faced her daughter. "How are you, Mandy? Are you doing OK?"

"I'm OK. Some people at school are harassing me, but I'll be all right. They're just idiots."

"OK, honey. You stay tough, OK? And if you need to talk, you let me know. I gotta get ready." Denise headed upstairs to get ready to meet with Mr. Withers. Learning about Amanda getting harassed at school stung her a bit and made her angry, and that made her much more eager to help Jacob achieve the task of getting Sam set free. *"They're messing with my kid now!"* she thought. *"No one messes with my kid."*

Denise ran to the upstairs bathroom and quickly put on her make-up and fixed her hair. She grabbed the directions, her purse and keys then jumped into her car and began the drive to Jacob Luke's office, debating with herself on the way.

"I don't know if I should be getting into this. What am I gonna say? But if I don't, I'll regret it. I don't know." Needing a distraction she turned on the radio and immediately recognized the classic Styx song, *Show me the way*. She turned the station and heard Journey's, *Wheel in the Sky* just ending and going into the Kansas song, *Hold On*. *"Huh?"* she asked herself. *"All classic, semi-spiritual ... what the heck?"* She turned the knob again only to hear *Bridge over Troubled Water*. She absolutely loved that song.

It was as if everything on the radio today was designed just for her. She had to try it one more time. She grabbed the radio dial and quickly turned it. Sure enough, it was the Doobie Brothers' hit *Jesus Is Just All Right With Me*. This made Denise laugh so much she stuck her head out the window looked up at the sky.

"OK! Are you trying to tell me something? I get it! I get it!"

And then the DJ cheerfully spouted, "Hits of yesterday and today and forever. Well folks, someone must be smiling down on us. The weather forecast says 60 and sunny; that's at least 25 degrees above the average. And now here's an old classic for you to bring back some memories. Barry Manilow with *Mandy*." Denise wore a permanent smile the rest of the way to Jacob's office.

In the quaint little town of Riverside Township, above a few antique and art shops, was Jacob's office. It was located on the second floor in a building that looked like it could have been an old mill at one time. The street was lined with Bradford pear trees. Denise couldn't believe such a neat town was so close and she'd never been here before

"I wouldn't mind living here someday," she thought.

She parked her car out front and scurried up the steps and came to a huge oak and iron-hinged door. Denise grabbed the iron knocker and pounded loudly.

Moments later the two hundred pound door squealed in protest as Jacob opened it, the chain was still on and peering out through the opening Jacob asked, "Denise McBride?"

"Yep, that's me." she replied smiling. She had on an old blue fabric button up coat that used to belong to her mother. It made her look older than she actually was, but she didn't care. She wore it when she felt insecure. Her mother had been the backbone of her family and this was one of the few things Denise had to remember her by.

"Please come in. Have a seat." Jacob spoke nervously as he moved some old law and fishing magazines off the couch. "Can I take your coat?" he asked.

"That's OK, I'll just keep it on if that's all right." She tried to avoid staring at the messy surroundings.

"Sorry about my place. I don't get to clean it much." Jacob smiled as he sat down in the old oak office chair. He extended a plate of cheese and crackers to her.

"No thanks," Denise replied. "I'd love some coffee though if you have some?"

"Yes, I was just thinking about that, too." Jacob quickly got up and headed for the kitchen talking the whole way. "OK, well as you know from our phone conversation, I've agreed to represent your husband. But what you may not know is why. You see, Mrs. McBride, to be totally honest with you, I haven't had a real case in years."

Denise leaned forward in the chair.

"Cream and sugar?" he shouted from the kitchen.

"Just black, thanks."

Jacob came back into the room and went on with his story as he handed Denise her coffee. "But just the other day I was sitting here watching the news about your husband on TV and something happened to me that has not happened in years. Well, actually it's never happened, not like this. Now you may find this hard to believe but ..."

Jacob proceeded to tell Denise about his conversation with God and how he was emotionally healed. "... and then, I don't have a better way to tell you this than to just say it ..." Jacob lifted his eyebrows, and with open arms and palms, exclaimed, "... the Lord told me to represent your husband." His look tempted her to laughter, but she decided against it.

"God told you to represent my husband?" She looked at the door as if she was contemplating making a run for it. She was still struggling with what she believed about everything that had happened.

Jacob paced for a moment. "Yes, I know, it sounds crazy, doesn't it? Even to me." He glanced over at the picture of his wife and daughter. "But it's the truth. If I told you anything else, I'd be a liar, and please, now if I may, let me tell you what Sam told me about the night of the accident." Denise nodded. For the time being, she was all ears.

Jacob proceeded to retell the story as best as he remembered it. Denise was amazed. Sure now that Sam never drank that night, her heart sank at the thought of the pain she had caused him, both physically and with her words. She would make it up to him at the right time, she thought. Now she had to help him get free.

"Sam saw an angel? Is this possible? You know Mr. Withers, if you would have told me all this a few days ago, I would have thought your elevator didn't stop at all the floors. But a lot has happened since then. And you know what? Even though I accused him of it, he has never really lied to me. I mean he's done a lot of dumb stuff, but he never was a liar or a cheat." Denise took a drink of coffee.

"Look I don't know what I believe as far as what he said he saw, but I had a real unusual night last night that is making me take a whole new look at things. And I definitely know something had changed in him. He was different, and I don't believe he could have just made all this up. There is something to all of this, there has to be. Anyway, here. I brought this for him, like you asked." She held out Sam's Bible to Jacob.

"Why don't you give it to him yourself?" Jacob asked.

"Oh I don't think he'll really want to see me. Not after everything I said to him."

"Are you kidding? The biggest thing he was concerned about was you! He wanted me to make sure you knew he didn't do it. He would love to see you, Mrs. McBride. Nothing would make him happier."

She hesitated looking down at her feet as she sometimes did when giving thought to something. She raised her head and with her cute crooked smile asked, "Are you going to see him today?"

"Yes, do you want to go?"

"Could I? Could I go with you? I'd want to talk to him alone for a minute if that would be all right. You understand, right?"

"Sure, of course. No problem. I'll let you two talk alone, and you can just let the guard know when you want me to come in." Jacob replied encouragingly.

They decided to go right away. As Jacob drove, Denise recounted things to him about Sam that he might need to know for Sam's defense. "He's never really held down too much of a job. He's not good at taking direction. I think it's because his old man was too harsh, you know? But this time, Mr. Withers, he was doing really well at the docks, 'til all of this happened."

Jacob pulled the car into the parking lot at the jail. They walked in together. At the desk they showed their identification as instructed and signed in. Separately they went through security.

"Excuse me, sir," Jacob said to the guard after they were cleared to enter the visiting area. "This is Sam McBride's wife. Could you just let it be a surprise for him?"

"Sure, no problem." the friendly guard said.

"I'll wait out here." Jacob said smiling at Denise. "Take as much time as you want."

The guard looked carefully through the Bible Denise brought and recorded it on his log, then allowed Denise to go in to the visiting area. Denise was a little intimidated by the whole jail atmosphere, but when she saw Sam, she forgot all about where she was and was filled with hope at the chance to make things right.

Sam was sitting at the table. When he looked up and saw Denise approaching, a huge smile came over his face. Sam got up and pulled the chair out for her. The guard lifted an eyebrow to warn Sam that he was being watched closely.

"Denise, you look beautiful. I'm so glad you came. I didn't know if you'd come."

"Sam, I'm sorry!" Denise's eyes pleaded for forgiveness.

"No, babe, I'm sorry I got us all mixed up in this. You've got nothing to be sorry about."

"Yes I do, Sam, please let me say my peace." Denise took a long deep breath and composed herself. "You tried to explain, and I wouldn't let you. I was so sure you were lying, and yet you never lied to me before. I mean you've done a lot of stupid things, but lying has never been one of them. I'm really sorry I didn't trust you, babe. And I'm so sorry for what I did to our pictures." At this Sam looked away trying not to show his emotion because he was still wounded from that. "We're going to have to renew our vows and get new pictures taken. We'll start again. OK, Sam?"

"You don't want a divorce?" he asked hopefully.

"No, Sam. I don't want a divorce. Listen, I woke up in the middle of the night last night. I remembered all the sweet things you've ever said or done, Sam, and I remembered when you proposed and you said that you couldn't be happy with anyone but me. You won my heart then. I can't see myself with anyone but you either, so for better or worse we're gonna fight this thing, baby." She took his hands in hers. "I love you, Sam McBride, the good, the bad and the ugly, you're my man and I love you. Let's fight this thing together, OK?"

"OK, 'Neesi. Wow! You are such a good woman." He lowered his head a bit and squeezed his lips together, bewildered at the miracle of her just being there. He looked up at her with such affection it made her blush. Sam could be really sweet when he wanted. Then he became serious.

"Is Mandy OK? Tell her I'm coming home, 'Neesi, OK? I'm innocent and I'm coming home." Denise was pleasantly surprised at his boldness. This was something she had seldom seen in him.

"I will. She's OK. She's been hanging with the wrong crowd though, and I think I'm gonna have to talk to her."

"I want you to bring her here, babe. I want to talk to her. She needs to hear from me that I'm innocent and that I'm coming home to her."

"I will, Sam. She misses you. Hey! You wouldn't believe what I did the other night!"

"What?" Sam asked.

"I read your Bible, or I mean some of it. It helped me, Sam. I know this might surprise you but I do believe in God, maybe not like you do right now, but I wanted you to know that."

"You going soft on me?" he joked with an ear to ear smile.

"Maybe a little," Denise smiled. "Is that OK?" Denise asked. She gave Sam that look that told him they were definitely back together. The same look she gave him on the night Amanda was conceived.

Sam was strengthened and relieved. "I can't wait to get home to you," Sam said, a recognizable twinkle in his eye and tiny beads of sweat forming on his forehead.

"Me too, babe." Denise said affectionately, blushing again. She knew she had to change the subject.

"Mr. Withers is waiting to see you, Sam. I'd like to stay and listen if that's OK? But before he comes in, I wanted to tell you, I do believe you're innocent, Sam. I don't know what you hit, but if you say you hit an angel, then I know that to you, it was just that. To me maybe it was an animal or something. But, I know you couldn't kill anything and then leave it or hide the body or whatever they're saying. So, I'm going to help Mr. Withers and we're going to get you out of here."

Denise turned around, motioned to the guard, and asked, "Could we let Mr. Withers in to join us now, please?"

The guard opened the door. Moments later Jacob walked in and came over to the table, shook hands with Sam and then sat down.

"Hi, Sam." He noticed Sam had a permanent smile on his face, and after seeing Denise and Sam look at each other Jacob blushed a little himself. "Well, I've found out a few things," Jacob said, opening his brown leather briefcase. He pulled out a manila file folder. "Sam, in the bar that night, was Roxanne wearing a white coat with feathers on it?"

"Yeah, I think she was, actually."

"Well, that may not be good news." Jacob drummed his fingers on the table with one hand while loosening his tie with the other. "In the grill of the car you were driving, they found a feather with blood on it, Sam."

Denise's face went bright white. She looked at Sam with a huge question mark in her eyes.

Sam looked at both of them, "Well, I don't know, it's got to be from the angel, right?"

"OK. Now you know I'm with you, Sam, but can you hear how that sounds?"

"He's right, honey. There's no way anyone is going to believe that ... unless ..." she thought for a second, "unless we find Roxanne."

"Or the angel shows up," Jacob joked. No one laughed.

Jacob stood and paced the floor. "They sent the feather and blood samples from the car and the road to the crime lab in Lansing. Now it could be up to two weeks to get the tests back. So we've got a little time. Sam, you're being prosecuted by the Wayne County Prosecutor, Brent Foster. And I have to tell you he's ... well, let's just say he's ruthless."

Sam was silent for a moment but then responded eagerly. "But I've got you, Jacob. And you're good, right? I mean we can do this. Can't we?" There was a hint of desperation in his voice.

Jacob hesitated.

"Mr. Withers, we can win this case, right?"

"To be honest, it's been a while since I've had a big case, but I'm not worried and I've been doing my homework. And I know that the Lord is on our side. Let's not worry, Sam," he said earnestly, "just pray, OK? We've only got one more day before your arraignment. Since they can't find a body, they've got the Wayne County Sheriff's Department and the local FBI assisting with the case. Now that might sound pretty heavy for you right now, but the FBI might actually help us if it turns out that Roxanne has left the state for some reason. They're well networked and could very well help us to get to the bottom of this."

Jacob looked towards Denise. "Did you tell Sam what you found out about Angelo Perello?"

"No, not yet. I wanted you to be here." She leaned in and looked at Sam intently and spoke softly, "I don't know anything for sure yet, but a friend of mine called me the other day and said that Angelo was known to be violent, and I was wondering if that might have something to do with Roxanne's disappearance?"

Jacob chimed in, "We could put Angelo through a deposition to find out what he knows. At least we'd get his testimony on tape so he wouldn't be able to change it later. All right, Sam, we'd better get going. I've got some things to check on and Denise rode with me. I'll leave you guys for a minute to say goodbye."

"Thank you again for everything, Mr. Withers." Sam extended his hand and Jacob Luke warmly shook it. Jacob smiled and nodded as he walked away. The second guard opened the door from the inside as Jacob neared. He turned. "Keep praying Sam, we're gonna win this." Sam waved as Jacob exited out the steel door.

Denise grabbed Sam's hands again. "I love you, baby. I'll see you in the courtroom in the morning. And I'm gonna try to bring Mandy after school tomorrow, OK?"

"OK! 'Neesi, I love you too." Denise kissed Sam on the lips as the guard came near. Motioning for Sam to stand up, the officer grabbed his arms, pulled them behind Sam's back, and placed chrome handcuffs on his wrists. The guard then escorted Denise toward the exit. He tapped on the door while showing his face at the wire mesh window so that the guard on the other side would open the door and escort Denise through.

Back in his cell, Sam eagerly opened his Bible, glad to have it again. He read from the Psalms:

You are my refuge and my shield; I have put my hope in your word.

He continued to read until he came upon a verse that became an inspiration to him:

Look upon my suffering and deliver me, for I have not forgotten your law.

Defend my cause and redeem me; preserve my life according to your promise.

Sam got down on his knees to pray. "You're my hope Lord. I'm sorry when I give in to doubt or when I'm afraid. You brought me my wife back today and thank you for Mandy and for Mr. Withers. Thank you for that church that's praying for me."

An echo of Sam's last words floated toward the heaven looking like a soft powder or smoke. It floated up into the heavens and formed into a solid piece of ancient looking paper. It landed in a golden bowl next to a man playing what looked like a 10-stringed guitar that had different colored gemstones inlaid in the surface. The man looked into the bowl, picked up the paper and rolled it into a scroll as he walked up to a building made out of crystal. It had columns made of various colored stones.

A hundred skylight-like portals were in the temple's roof. There were messengers of all sizes shapes and colors entering through them. As the man approached the building, a door just appeared in the wall. He passed through it and the place that he walked through closed up on itself like it was never there.

10
ANGELS AMONG US

"All rise." ordered Fred, a well built Indian-American deputy in a tan uniform, adorned with a gold badge. His deep baritone voice continued, "Court is now in session, Honorable Judge Steven P. Malkovich presiding."

The tall, white-haired, older man, who seemed more vibrant than his appearance suggested, walked up and seated himself behind the court's massive dark cherry, carved bench. Thirty years long he'd been with this court, and he had a reputation for shooting down any and all attorneys who ever dared raise their voices in his courtroom. Minutes passed by as the judge carefully put on his bifocals and looked over the charges under his prized gold-plated engraved lamp he had received from his staff as "thank-you-please-go-easy-on-us" gift.

Frightened by the judge's reputation and imposing presence, Sam waited and watched as the second hand of the clock marched slowly by. It was so quiet in the courtroom every single tick could be heard.

The judge's thick, curly white hair was reminiscent of George Washington to most that saw him. Jacob was terrified at the sight of this judge, and you could see it on his face. Sam was on his right. He looked over at Jacob for emotional support, but received none as Jacob's eyes remained fixed on the judge.

Denise sat in the back alone. Reporters across from her, in their designated section, looked over at her with curiosity. Many had been to her house and tried to get an interview or even a comment. But to no avail. They smiled her way, still hoping for that salary-increasing interview.

Up to this point, the judge had not allowed any cameras in the court, only handheld recorders. Many reporters were anxiously awaiting the beginning of the arraignment, others yawned with boredom at what they considered to be an open and shut case. Many were from out of town, and surprisingly, a few seemed to be from out of the country or at least had been hired by foreign news corporations. There was a lady with a burka who looked like she may have been from Iran or Iraq. Another man who held a notebook looked like he may have been from China. Denise was surprised by all the attention her husband's case was getting. It was unprecedented for this area, with the exception of the former mayor's arrest and the Big Three Bailouts. Apparently, this story had created a buzz around the world, mostly through the Internet she suspected, but now practically every form of media had picked up on it.

The judge read from his seat, after first clearing his throat, "The State of Michigan versus Samuel J. McBride. The defendant will rise please." He motioned with his hand for Sam to stand up. Sam stood slowly with a sour expression his face, looking as if he were putting his head in a noose. The judge continued, "Counselors, please stand and identify yourselves."

At that the prosecutor stood and smoothed his suit as he did. "Brent Foster, your honor, Prosecuting Attorney for the State of Michigan." He was so finely dressed and manicured, he looked like someone had put a coat of shellac on him. Jacob however was a different story.

Jacob, rising slowly muttered, "Jacob Luke Withers for the defense, Your Honor." Jacob wore a somewhat crumpled corduroy suit that looked like it was leftover from the sixties. His hair though fairly short, was in wild disarray due to the numerous times he had run his fingers through it as he had been waiting for the arraignment to begin. Jacob, who was black and silver-haired, had a prominent white spot in the front of his hair that he'd had all his life. His mom had called it an angel kiss. Denise had noticed it when she first met him. Also, he was noticeably thin, the result of his almost unending grief at the death of his wife and daughter.

"Mr. Samuel J. McBride, you stand accused in a Court of Law in the State of Michigan. The counts against you are as follows: Count one - leaving the scene of a personal injury automobile accident causing death. Count two - resisting arrest. Count three - second degree murder." Sam gasped and his jaw dropped at this news. At no time did he really believe they would try to charge him with murder. Even though Jacob had told him it was a possibility, Sam had never believed it could happen. Jacob remained relatively calm. He had expected it. Denise edged toward the front of the bench she sat on, longing to sit by her husband and offer him support.

"Mr. Withers, how does your client plead?" the judge asked.

"Not guilty on all counts, Your Honor."

"Mr. McBride, do you understand the charges that have been leveled against you in this court today?"

"Ummmm, yes sir," Sam said sheepishly. "But I didn't think I would really be charged with murder, sir. I didn't kill anyone."

"Humph!" Foster sighed, earning him a dirty look from the judge. The judge then turned his sights back on Sam.

"Mr. McBride. I will only say this once, and you can keep it with you for the remainder of our journey together in this courtroom. When I ask you a yes or no question, I only want you to answer yes or no. Do you understand?"

"Yes, sir." Sam meekly replied.

"Thank you. Now please let me try again." The judge grimaced. "Samuel J. McBride, do you understand the charges that have been made against you in this courtroom today?"

"Yes, sir."

"And you stand by your plea of not guilty?"

"Yes, sir."

Jacob whispered to Sam, "Call him, Your Honor."

"Mr. Withers!" the judge interrupted giving Jacob a disagreeable look. "Did I ask you to instruct your client how to address me?"

"No, Your Honor." Jacob simply looked down at his blank yellow legal pad, his hand visibly trembling. He clasped his hands together to try and hide his nervousness.

"I didn't think I did. Save your prep work for before or after the proceedings and please look at me when I address you."

Jacob looked up slowly.

The prosecutor was smiling now, snickering to himself. He savored the moment as he looked Jacob over, as if he were a prize buck, freshly wounded. His arrogance didn't escape the eyes of the judge however.

"Mr. Foster, is there something funny about me or the defense attorney or my courtroom that you think you'd like to share with the rest of us?"

"No, sir."

This time Jacob was tempted to laugh, but knew better.

"Good." The judge now looked again at Sam and calmed his tone.

"Mr. McBride, you may address me as 'Your Honor' or 'Sir' or you may answer my questions when asked with a simple yes or no, unless I ask you to elaborate further, do you understand?"

"Yes, Your Honor." Sam began to believe that even though this judge was tough, there was a certain kindness in his eyes.

As he was contemplating this, a soft voice whispered "I will never leave you, Sam." Sam was beginning to feel confident. *"This will all turn out in the end,"* he told himself.

The judge momentarily looked down at his papers. "Now I have carefully considered setting bail for you, Mr. McBride. However, I have one major obstacle to that endeavor, and that is the missing person, or body if you will, of Roxanne Perello."

"Counselor Foster, do you have any input in regards to setting the bond?"

"Yes I do, Your Honor. The State asks that no bail be set for Mr. McBride until said body is found. The State is concerned that the defendant, if released, may take steps to further hide or destroy evidence necessary for the prosecution of this case. Or, he may possibly be a flight risk."

"Mr. Withers what do you say?" the judge asked. Jacob had his eyes closed and appeared to be asleep. "Mr. Withers, are you sleeping?" the judge asked, irritated now and leaning forward he said louder, "Mr. Withers!" Again there was no reply. Judge Malkovich shouted now, "Jacob Luke Withers!" Still Jacob stood frozen. "Officer, please shake him." The court officer quickly walked over, grabbed Jacob by the shoulders and shook him with a fair amount of force. Gradually Jacob came to. His eyes slowly opened and he looked around the room as if he was not sure where he was. The prosecutor chuckled to himself. This time the judge didn't notice.

"Mr. Withers, are you drunk or something? Why are you sleeping in my courtroom?"

"Ahh, no, Your Honor." he paused. "I have a slight case of narcolepsy. I do apologize." Jacob rubbed his eyes looking down at the floor. "I take medicine for it, but I realized too late this morning that I had run out of it. I'm sorry." He looked up at the judge, his eyes pleading for understanding.

"Mr. Withers, I am ordering you to make sure that you have adequate medication for any such disease you may suffer during this arraignment, and any further proceedings, or you may be charged with contempt. Do you understand me?"

"Yes, Your Honor, I do apologize."

"Now, what do you say in regards to setting bail for your client? Prosecutor Foster asked that no bail be set. How do you see it, Mr. Withers?"

"Your Honor, my client has no criminal history. He is steadily employed and has family here. I don't believe he is a flight risk. And Your Honor, if I may, we contest that no serious crime has been committed at all. We thereby move that this case be dismissed, and if not Your Honor, that at least my client be granted bail on his own merit."

"Hmm. Arguable, Mr. Withers. However, I believe your client has made a confession that at the very least he left the scene and followed that up by resisting arrest." The judge paused and rubbed his chin as he contemplated the suggestion. "Well gentleman, it is a much simpler task to avoid breaking a fine piece of china than it is to try and restore it once it has been broken. Now, with that in mind, I am remanding Mr. McBride back into custody at least for now until this body or person is found, that being, Roxanne Perello."

"Pre-trial date will be set one week from today. That will be Monday, December sixth at nine o'clock sharp. I do not tolerate tardiness, gentleman. If you are not here on time, I will start without you."

"I see, Mr. Withers, that you are requesting a jury trial. We will begin jury selection on the same day one week later, Monday December thirteenth. One o'clock. We'll set the trial date during the pre-trial. That is unless you have any objection to those dates, gentlemen?"

Both Foster and Luke spoke simultaneously, "Fine, Your Honor."

"Prosecutor Foster, during this time I would encourage you and your team to diligently try to help find Mrs. Perello. These proceedings are now closed." The judge pounded the gavel, got up from his chair and entered his chamber directly behind the massive bench. The court officer handcuffed Sam and began to escort him back to the holding cell. Sam looked over his shoulder at Denise and mouthed the words, "I love you." She shouted out loud, "I love you, Sam McBride!" This gave the news hawks something to scribble about. Jacob walked in front of Sam and put a hand on his shoulder, "I'll come and see you tomorrow, Sam." Sam half-smiled back in reply. As hopeful as he felt about a good outcome right now, he didn't look forward to a hard bed and a 6 x 9 foot jail cell.

The famous bondo mobile was on the road again. This time Amanda was with her mom heading to see her dad at the Wayne County Jail. Amanda's mind raced with mixed feelings.

"I don't know what to say to him, Mom. I don't understand this whole thing."

"Mandy, do me a favor and just listen to what your father has to say."

Amanda gave her mom a rebellious look and stared out the window. She'd been taking a lot of grief at school from her classmates. It had become really hard to defend her dad when the story was 'so out there,' as Amanda would say.

They passed fresh snow drifts, as the area had received a whopping 9 inches of the white stuff the night before. There were children outside making snowmen and snow angels in the snow.

"How ironic," Denise thought, *"if only they were real."*

At the Wayne County Jail, they walked in, signed in and entered the checkpoint together. After going through the normal security procedures, Denise had Amanda go in to join her father while she waited back behind the security door.

Sam was overwhelmed with joy when he saw her. "Amanda!" He stood up and hugged her. She immediately stiffened.

"Hi, Dad." she replied woefully, looking around nervously like a cat in a room full of rocking chairs. Sam, sensing her fear, stepped back and spoke softly.

"You feel kind of uncomfortable here, don't you? I don't blame you." Amanda looked down, she shrugged and frowned.

"Mandy, I just wanted you to know I didn't do this, what they're saying. I know it's hard for everyone to believe, but the angel story is true. I've never lied to you, kiddo! Please just don't stop believing in me. You're one of my biggest fans and I can't lose you, Mandy. It's so important to me to have you by my side. You're still my little girl. "

Amanda relaxed some. She could see her dad was sincere.

"Look, Mandy," Sam said as they both sat down, "I've been wanting to talk to you. I should have told you a long time ago and, maybe now is not the best time either, but I wanted you to know, I'm sorry Amanda for all the times that I let you down. For all the drunk days and the things you shouldn't have had to go through.

I've had a lot of time to think about it. When you needed me, I wasn't there for you. I've been a terrible father." Sam's eyes were moistening now. He tried in vain to wipe the tears from his face, but they kept coming. The guard was getting misty-eyed too. "You deserve the best, honey, because you're the best kid a father could ever want; when I get out of here I'm gonna make it up to you. With God's help I will, 'cause I love you so much. You really are the very best."

Amanda, crying now, got up, came over and threw her arms around her father and both held on to each other for dear life.

"I miss you, Daddy." she whispered. "Come home. Come home to us. I do, I do believe you. It's just they tease me all the time at school and its hard, Dad." Sam rocked her in his arms.

"I know Amanda, I'm sorry." Sam cried.

"I won't give up, Daddy. I'll never give up on you. I love you too, and this whole angel thing does weird me out, but I know you wouldn't lie to me. I know you didn't do it. When you get out, I wanna'...I want to be a better daughter, too. I've been doing things that I know I shouldn't, Dad, and I'm sorry. I hope we all do better. I want to help get you out of here, Dad. What can I do?" Amanda sobbed.

Sam whispered, "Just do whatever your mother says, Mandy, and that would help me tremendously." Sam looked at the guard. "Could you let my wife in?"

Sam waved Denise over, who came and embraced them both. "Isn't she a great kid?" Sam said to Denise.

"Yeah, the best," Denise smiled lovingly at Amanda.

Amanda blushed, and with tears still in her eyes, she turned away giggling. "Stop you guys, you're embarrassing me."

"How you doing, babe?" Denise asked Sam.

"I'm on top of the world right now that my family's here." He hesitated, almost afraid to ruin the mood, but a certain question nagged at him incessantly. "Any news on Roxanne Perello?" he asked Denise, hopeful for a favorable response.

"No, not yet. No one's seen or heard anything, Sam. It's spooky. But wherever she is, or whatever happened to her, we'll find her.

There's a whole army of people searching and praying to find her." she said confidently as she took Sam's hand.

Sam looked at Denise lovingly, encouraged by her kindness. He thought, *"I don't know how or when, but she's changing. This is great. I want to go home and be with my new wife."*

Above the clouds and all the stars, a man with shoulder-length brown hair whistled a carefree tune while sitting on a tree stump in a field full of flowers. His face could not be seen as His hair blocked the view. He laughed heartily at Sam's' comments. He could hear them even when one else could. He, after all, was the King of Heaven and Earth. Around Him were birds and butterflies and horses. Tall cedars and massive redwoods bordered the field. Laying in the grass at His feet was a beautiful Irish setter named Ginger.

Looking down from a window in Heaven, the King watched as the McBride family embraced. Denise and Amanda were escorted out as Sam was led back to his cell. He was back in his cage now, yet about as free as a man could get, at least for the moment. There was a beautiful song in his heart. He was grateful.

Within the Kingdom, the voice of a little girl could be heard distinctly. The King now leaned forward and listened intently.

"Dear God, please don't let my mom and dad get divorced. I love both of them so much." The Lord leaned in further, gently taking hold of a tall wildflower, he brought it closer. Her voice seemed to be coming from the flower. "I don't know what I would do without either of them." The girl was Nadia Bingham. She was in her pajamas, supposed to be sleeping. It was ten o'clock at night where she lived. A lighthouse night light cast a soft glow in her room. Her mother was watching the news and didn't even know Nadia was still up. The girl was kneeling at her bed praying. She was going through what a four-year-old should never have to endure.

It's never night in Heaven though, and the King never sleeps. As he listened to her prayer a single tear fell from His eye and landed on His sandal. He looked up. "Go play," He said to His Irish Setter. She licked His face and ran off through the field near the tree line. The King walked into the bright crystalline palace. A door appeared and opened before him. Moments later, a trumpet sounded.

Many angels flew in through open sky portals and softly cascaded to the marble floor.

Coming out of an inside wall made of precious stones, a waterfall ran with sparkling, clear, pure water. Josag stopped for a quick drink and wiped his mouth with his wing. Josag was what you would call a rather stout messenger. It was never wise, however, to underestimate his speed because of his size. He was very fast. He was also very adept at hearing almost imperceivable sounds. Yet his best quality was his undying loyalty to his King.

Sam's guardian angel, Nathanael, walked in unpretentiously and knelt before the King. The Lord grabbed his shoulder and lifted him up.

Even though Nathanael had seen Him hundreds of times, he still stared with awe at the Light of the World. It was hard to escape the fact that He was the original, there from the very beginning.

"Nathanael," the King said;

"Yes, my Lord."

"We are sending you back on your mission, with help this time. Also, there is a strong church passionately praying. We have heard their prayers and are answering. You will go there and meet a man named Jacob Luke Withers. He may need a little encouraging. You will do what is needed to help him win his case, to free my friend and your charge, Samuel McBride." The Lord put His right hand on Nathaniel's shoulder. "We send you with extreme power and might as well as the support of your friends. You will have great victory and testify of Me. I am pleased with your service as I am with you, Nathanael. Be strong and courageous. I love you."

"And I, You, my Master." Nathanael said humbly, beaming with gratitude.

"Amoerus!" Messiah called. Amoerus stepped up. Nathanael then placed his hand on his shoulder.

"Keitsu." the King requested. Keitsu came forward. Amoerus likewise set his right hand upon his shoulder. As the Lord called out every name, each messenger did the same. Paz stepped up. "Arek!" The King called and Arek drew near. Satka, Josag, and Tro came forward as called. Then there was Mildheid, and finally Imperium. Now all the called had come forward. They were all somewhat nervous. It was hard not to be, in the presence of the Son. They all had their hands on each other's shoulders forming a circle.

"Faithful Light Bearers," the King made eye contact with each one as He spoke, "I call and anoint you for this great mission. You are My treasured messengers, My warriors. I love and I care for you, each one of you. Now be bold and be strong, for I Am with you. Be victorious."

"Josag?" Jesus looked to the left.

"Yes, my King?" Josag placed his closed hand over his heart, showing respect.

"On your visit I want you to take the band to Mount Rushmore. There you will see a little girl with her mother. Her name is Nadia. She will have a red hat on. I want you to tell her, I love her very much. Allow her, but her only, to see you there. Tell her we are doing every thing we can to answer her prayer. But we cannot force anyone against their choices. "

"Yes, my Lord." Josag replied.

One by one they put their hands together in the circle. Their light was emanating in all directions. Finally, the Lord placed His hand on top of theirs, completing the circle. The light became almost blinding. They all said together with a shout, "We are one!" The sound echoed loudly through the great chamber, out into the fields. The birds sang in response and shot into the air seeming to dance together as they turned and climbed in unison, upwards toward the clouds. The horses whinnied and reared up, even the wheat and the leaves on the trees seemed to sound back in celebration as the wind passed through them with a sudden gust.

Each messenger then took a step back, bowed one knee and proclaimed in harmony, "For the King and the Kingdom!" They arose, turned and walked toward the south wall. The whole wall before them miraculously opened as a great door. Nathanael, anxious to get the assignment completed, immediately took off running followed by Keitsu, and then Arek and the rest. Ten in all, the mightiest and the wisest. They all ran together in a flying V-formation.

All other messengers on the path and nearby, bowed their knees and prayed, then stood and saluted, closing their fists over their hearts. "Victory!" they all shouted. "For the King and the Kingdom!" Wings were raised in worship throughout the whole land.

Amoerus quickly passed Keitsu. He teased, "First you must have love, then comes joy," he quipped. Keitsu only laughed and ran harder trying to again gain his number two spot. They spread their wings ready for takeoff. Multi-colored leaves struggled to stay on the trees against their wake as they lifted off, the light of Heaven shimmered off their wings. They broke through the white, yellow and blue sky, past a rainbow and were soon in the outer layer.

Through the stars they traveled. Suddenly, they passed a space ship with an American flag painted on it's side. "Should we?" Keitsu, smiling, asked.

Imperium, big, bright white, and mostly serious answered, "We really should be getting to our destination."

"Ok then, just a quick laugh." Keitsu kidded as he darted to the window of the ship. He knocked three times on the window and then flew back to the group. They all laughed as they watched a few astronauts looking out the small oval window. Of course the angels were invisible to their eyes. The only exception to that rule was if the angels became wounded or chose to be visible for the sake of the Kingdom.

Valiantly, they escorted Nathanael through earth's atmosphere. Heat reflected off their wings and faces as they blazed through. They looked like ten balls of fire. They broke through the outer layer and into the blue. They were luminous through the power of the King and prayers of the saints.

A legion of the fallen approached two miles away and circled like a whirlwind. Rabbia, the demon warrior who was second in command, shouted, "Crush them!" He was considered tall for a Fallen. He was 5'9", and he was not quite as grotesque as the rest. He had black eyes and hair and his body was completely red. There was a sullen, sad look to him. Seeing him, a messenger might be tempted to pity him, that would be his last act of mercy however, as Rabbia would use that moment of hesitation to slaughter him.

"No, not yet" said Mefiance in a gruff tone. "They are too strong! Someone must be praying." Mefiance looked like a bloody ball of muscles with a head bulging in the middle. "Let us wait until the intercessors become distracted." The whirlwind of demons speedily hid themselves in a nearby dark cloud.

It was Sunday as Heaven's warriors descended softly on the courtroom steps. Huge marble pillars graced this magnificent courthouse. Quickly surveying the surrounding area and seeing it was clear of manifestations, Tro spoke, "We have to go now. It's time to visit the others." Tro was shorter than Josag and stocky, like a linebacker. He had a strong chin and piercing golden brown eyes.

He also was one of the few that carried a sling with him. King David was one of his heroes. For a human that is. His wings were a bit shorter than most, but he made up for that with his strength and speed. They all shot into the sky simultaneously.

Jacob was somewhat concerned but no longer as worried as he previously was. He woke up early to pray.

"Lord, you've gotten Daniel out of lions' den, and three men out of a fire. I'm just looking for one man to get out of a jail cell." There was only one day left until the pre-trial. Jacob arrived at church for the eleven o'clock worship service. The sun shone brightly through a large stained glass window as the church sang *In Your Presence*. It was a new song written by their worship leader, Tony Newman. Jacob remembered the previous week's service, how the presence of God just filled the place. Once again his eyes were drawn to the stained glass window.

He continued to worship and in his mind's eye he saw angels all over the building, their wings stretched toward the Heavens. He shook his head, laughing to himself at his overactive imagination. Yet he was flooded with joy at the thought of it. The worship continued; some people seemed to be singing in different languages, all unknown to Jacob. A hush came over the people. Many bowed down.

"The presence of the King is in this place," the pastor said.

A woman, weeping with joy, spoke loudly, "The Lord would say, I have found some faithful people to stand in the gap, and I am pleased. I will bring to pass that which I have begun, as I am the Author and Finisher of your faith. Continue to stand by the weak and I will show Myself strong. Do not let down your guard, but stay sober and vigilant. Do not be afraid, little ones, for I Am with you and you will be successful."

The pastor and another elder both said "Amen" to this utterance, signifying they believed it was a God-breathed prophecy.

At that, Jacob became very emotional. *That was meant for me,* he thought as he sat down in the pew, feeling as if his legs were going out from under him. A great peace came over him, and he just sat still and breathed it in and enjoyed it.

The service was nearing the end. The piano played softly as the pastor gave an alter call. "If there is anyone who would like to come up for prayer, please come up. The Lord knows your need. Now is the time." A young woman began to sing *How Great Thou Art*, her voice amazingly beautiful. Jacob didn't have to think twice, he was the first one up.

"What can I pray for you about today, my friend?" Pastor Dave asked, laying his hand on Jacob's shoulder.

"The pre-trial for Sam is tomorrow and I'll take all the prayer I can get."

"OK, yes. Hey, hold on a second, Jacob. Bryan, Bill, could you come here for a minute?" Bryan Reynolds and William Martin were elders of the church.

"Do you have that envelope, Bryan?"

Bryan Reynolds handed the pastor a manila envelope.

Pastor Dave then handed Jacob the envelope. "Jacob, the board of this church, after much prayer and discussion, has agreed to support you in representing Mr. McBride. There's three thousand dollars in there to cover your costs and immediate expenses. We don't want you to worry about anything except providing a great defense for Sam McBride. We would like to ask you to put together a budget as to your fees and other expenses in the future, just so we know what to plan for, and for good stewardship, you know. How does that sound, Jake?"

"How does that sound? That sounds great! So you believe him?" Jacob asked, a mile wide grin on his face.

"Jacob, we believe God told you to represent him. We believe that what he says happened is possible, extremely unusual yes, but possible. But the main thing for us is to obey the voice of God. And there are just certain things we may not know completely right now, but He is an amazing, wondrous God, so what more can I say. Let's pray."

The pastor anointed Jacob's forehead with oil and placed his hand there, the other elders placed their hands on Jacob's shoulders. A man with piercing blue eyes that Jacob didn't know and had never seen before also put his hand on Jacob's shoulder.

"Heavenly Father, please be with Jacob, anoint him for this task and help him in every way. Oh Lord, glorify Your name here. You are the same yesterday, today, and forever. Be glorified, O Lord." the pastor shook a little as he spoke, "in Jesus' name."

Everyone there agreed and said, "In Jesus' name. Amen."

"Thank you Pastor Dave, you don't know how much it means to me to have the church with me in this."

"You mean a great deal to us also, Jacob." The pastor was approached by a little girl who came up for prayer. Jacob made his way back to his pew.

"Excuse me." The blue-eyed man Jacob hadn't recognized was standing in front of him. He was dressed in a pair of knit slacks and a casual shirt. "Could I have a word with you?" The man walked towards an isolated pew in the back, away from the chattering crowd of people.

"Uh yeah, sure," Jacob replied as he followed. "Hmm … What's this all about?" Jacob wondered.

11
WATCHING OVER US

The unusual, tall stranger looked Jacob in the eye with a sincerity and authority that seemed unearthly, sending a shiver up Jacob's spine. Leaning in and looking Jacob in the eye, he spoke softly. "Don't be afraid Jacob. I am Sam's guardian, Nathanael. I have been sent by the Word to facilitate his freedom."

Jacob, speechless, was confounded by what he had just heard; he had trouble finding the right words in reply. "You mean, you're his guardian ... angel? Is that what you're telling me? Are you serious? Why should I believe that? I mean that's pretty out there, don't you think?" Jacob nervous, gulped repeatedly as he looked intently at this strange man.

In response and without blinking, Nathanael changed his eye color from blue to green to brown and then back to blue.

Jacob choked a little then smiled widely, not even trying to hide his amazement. "That was pretty good," he said shaking his head and nodding all at once. "All right, is that the best you can do though? Come on. Anyway, how did you do that? Who put you up to this?" He persisted, wondering if someone was playing an elaborate joke on him.

"Jacob, put your hand inside your jacket pocket." Nathanael said confidently.

Jacob did what Nathanael said.

"Now pull it out."

Jacob slowly pulled out his hand. It was white, cracked and blistered, like he had leprosy or some other terrible skin disease. Jacob's face turned white as a ghost. He immediately remembered reading about how this happened to Moses when he questioned God in the Old Testament.

"Heard of that one before?" Nathanael quickly asked, authority in his voice.

"Yes, sir." Jacob whispered, trembling. "OK, I'm sorry for not believing you. Please change it back?" His voice cracked with emotion as beads of sweat formed on his forehead.

"Jacob, put your hand back in your pocket and then take it out again."

Jacob did as he was told. When he pulled his hand out, it was restored exactly as before.

He exhaled. "Oh thank you! Thank you very much!" Jacob said, overwhelmingly relieved.

"No problem, you asked." Nathanael smiled, and then spoke calmly, "Listen, Jacob. I'm here to tell you to not be afraid, that the Lord is with you. Also, He said for you to put me on the witness list for the pre-trial."

Jacob thought about what he'd just been told, tilted his head slightly to the left a bit, and spoke nervously. "Sure Mr. Nathanael you got it, but I don't know how I'm supposed to call an angel to testify." Jacob paced the aisle. "They would want to validate your identity and all. Do you even have an address? A last name? Anything? And maybe you already know it, but we're up against one of the most ruthless prosecutors there is, Brent Foster. I don't even think he believes in God at all, so what makes you think he'll let you testify?"

"I reside in Heaven. My name is Nathanael of the Most High God." Nathanael proclaimed and leaned closer. "Jacob, do I look worried?"

"OK, well no," Jacob replied. "But how do I get a hold of you?" Jacob paced.

"Call the One you always call when you need help. He'll send me."

"Do you have a phone or something?"

Nathanael laughed "No, we're way too advanced for that. Look I'll be near, I've got to go now, but I'll see you at court, OK? Just put me down on the witness list and tell them that I'll testify as to my guardianship of Samuel McBride, that I was the one he hit with his car, and also that I will give testimony to the existence of the Most High God." Nathanael placed his fist over his heart when he mentioned the Lord.

Jacob grinned a little and thought about pinching himself to see if he was dreaming. "Won't that be a little too much? And what if they don't believe you? You don't have any kind of identification at all, do you?"

"Jacob, put your hand in your pocket." Nathanael said with a twinkle in his eye.

"No, never mind, I'll do what you say." Jacob trembled and looked at his hand to make sure it was still all right.

"Thank you." Nathanael said warmly as he quickly got up and walked out the front door of the church. In three steps he was semi-transparent. His clothes transformed back into his warrior outfit. Huge wings shot out as his bold walk turned into a sprint and he burst into the air.

Jacob, still perplexed, thought of another question. He quickly ran outside and tried to catch the messenger, but by the time he got to the door, he looked around and Nathanael was gone. Jacob ran and looked on every side of the church, but he was nowhere to be found.

"*He couldn't have left that fast.*" Jacob thought.

Jacob shook his head in wonder. *"Wow, what a day."* He pondered this day's events, a bit overwhelmed, but excited, even hopeful.

Jacob went home after that, and to celebrate made himself a huge roast beef and Swiss cheese sandwich and a glass of milk. Then full of food and deep satisfaction lay down for his usual Sunday afternoon nap.

Nathanael and the others, having a little free time on their hands, flew past wild geese and passenger planes on their way to visit Mt. Rushmore. There was a big, clear, blue sky as they made their way into South Dakota. They peered into the windows of a 747 as people were looking out the windows. In a fit of fun, the whole group then hitched a ride on top of the plane like they were surfing.

"Bet they wish they had wings," Satka laughed, referring to the passengers. He was the compassionate one of the group who wouldn't believe an evil thing about even the worst of humans, and he saw goodness in even the most hardened criminal. The King often used him in that regard. He often found himself behind prison bars, encouraging the desperate to hang on. He was bony, lean and long, with deep set eyes, stringy black and gray hair. He wasn't the sort of warrior that looked tough. But underestimating him would be a mistake. Although he was known for his gentleness, he was very loyal to protect the Kingdom; he was fast and especially skilled with a sword.

Arriving at their destination, they decided to have a little fun and took turns diving off the presidents' faces, drifting in the wind like hang gliders.

Josag kept a keen eye out for the little girl Nadia, and finally he saw her wearing her red hat as she came nearer to the mountain. She was dressed just as the King had described her. He thrust his wings in her direction landing gently beside her. He carefully knelt down so she could see him. Her mouth opened wide and her eyes grew large when she saw him. Josag leaned over and whispered in her ear. He then flew back and joined the others. Nadia's eyes lit up with hope, she smiled cheerfully, overjoyed at the message.

"Mommy, did you see that? That angel just came and told me God heard me, and that they're trying to keep you and daddy from getting divorced. Did you see him? Look! There he is!" Nadia pointed up toward the mountain. Her mother, instinctively turned but saw nothing.

"Mom, look! A bunch of them are flying by George Washington's face! Look!" The little girl giggled delightedly, pointing as Josag waved to her while he glided on the wind with the others. Nadia waved back.

"I don't see anything, honey." Nadia's mom, puzzled by what her daughter had told her, looked at her with compassion. "Let's have our lunch, honey," Nadia's mom suggested, wanting to cover her own emotions. They both sat down on a bench, her mother opened the back pack she brought and took out the peanut butter and jelly sandwiches prepared for the day. "You've got some kind of imagination on you, little girl," her mother said smiling. She opened a carton of chocolate milk and poured both of them a cup.

"I love you, Momma." Nadia said still watching the angels from the corner of her eye. Her mother smiled, tears welling in her eyes.

"I love you, too! I wish you didn't have to go through this, baby." Her look told her daughter all she needed to know. Mom would always be there. Nadia gave her mother a big hug and kiss, as her mom folded Nadia up in her arms.

Several hundred miles away, a blond haired young lady lay unconscious in a hospital bed. Next to the bed there was a pair of knee high brown boots. A large silver crucifix was nailed into the wall.

The woman had been beaten and was bruised almost beyond human recognition. No one knew her name, where she was from, or who she belonged to. Her hair was cut in ragged shards as the nuns had to scissor off pieces to get all the blood out. The woman had been found by a local farmer, Manuel Rodriguez.

He had been preparing to take his watermelons to market when he found her in a ditch alongside the road. He stayed at the hospital long enough to make sure she was all right.

Manuel was known in the area to be a good family man with a lovely Latina beauty of a wife, one young son, and seven beautiful pre-teen and teenage daughters. He constantly had to chase away the boys. He would not let anyone see his daughters unless it was when and how he said. He was a good father.

Manuel was a short man. He always wore a straw hat to protect his leathery skin that had been extremely darkened by the sun from days of farming. One distinguishing feature was his handlebar mustache, and he wore it with pride.

"¿Ella estará bien? " Manuel asked the sister nurse if the woman he found would be OK. He spoke the only language he knew, Spanish.

"Si, Manuel, but she needs rest. She's been beaten very badly."

"Por favor déjeme saber si hay cualquier cosa que puedo hacer para ayudar. " He said he wanted the nun to let him know if there was anything he could do.

"I will, Manuel, and you've been a prince. All we can do now is wait." Sister Rosaria Shalen was an extremely beautiful young nun that had been brought there as an orphan and raised her whole life by the sisters. The other nuns often had to ask her to run errands when men were around because she was unwittingly a distraction to most. Manuel however only looked at his wife that way and appreciated the sister's beauty in a much deeper, fatherly way.

"She almost died, you know." Sister Rosaria said. "You saved her life."

"El Jesucristo salva. Yo solamente ayudé. " (Jesus Christ saves. I only helped.) said Manuel.

Manuel took one last look at the stranger he had brought in. She had nothing with her when he found her, only the clothes on her back. And she had never regained consciousness. He made the sign of the cross, looking soberly down at the woman, wondering why he was the one chosen to find her.

"Someone's looking for her, Father. Help them find her." He prayed quietly in Spanish as he walked away. "She is somebody's daughter, like my own. Please help her," Manuel prayed, again crossing himself.

"All rise. Court is now in session, Honorable Judge Steven P. Malkovich presiding." The clock clicked to 9:00. It was Monday, December 13. It had been snowing all night in Detroit. The roads were treacherous, but both attorneys and Sam now stood at their perspective tables.

"Thank you, Officer. Well gentlemen, you've had some time to prepare your lists and motions. Mr. Foster, has your evidence arrived from Lansing yet?"

"No not yet Your Honor, but it should be here any day now. I am convinced of the strength of this case however, even in spite of the forensics."

"Yes, and …?" the judge asked, authoritatively, waving his hand for the prosecutor to continue.

"Your Honor, we have an eyewitness who saw a person in white get hit by the defendant's car. We have the defendant in the same location as the victim. We know she left the bar walking, wearing a white jacket with feathers on it. We have a white feather found in the grill of the vehicle at the scene." Foster took a deep breath and continued.

"We know through the bartender that Mrs. Perello and Sam McBride had words in the bar. The victim's husband Angelo Perello said the defendant was giving his wife hateful looks. We found blood at the scene, and the defendant admits to the accident, but claims it was an angel that he hit. Your Honor, we have no angel, just a missing lady." Foster again caught his breath and continued.

"Betty Steimer, the bartender, said she overheard Roxanne Perello tell Sam that, and I quote, 'Hey Sam, what are you doing here? I heard you quit the booze and got Jesus or something?' And then Betty heard Sam tell Roxanne to mind her own damn business."

"I object, Your Honor." Jacob spoke firmly. "My client did not say anything to Mrs. Perello in the bar, and hateful looks cannot be substantiated. There is no body and there is no proof that anyone at all was killed. Maybe it was an animal or maybe it was an angel. Who knows? My client is innocent until proven guilty, and since we have no body or evidence that any crime was committed, I move that this case be dismissed Your Honor, and all charges against my client dropped."

"Nice try again, Mr. Withers. You find me one Roxanne Perello alive and kicking, then I'll grant your request. Also in light of this angel story, I am ordering the defendant to undergo psychiatric testing to determine if he is mentally competent to stand trial.

"Your Honor," Jacob interjected, "I would like to request a Christian psychiatrist to examine my client."

"Explain, Mr. Withers." the judge raised an eyebrow.

"Your honor, many professionals in the medical and scientific field do not acknowledge the existence of God at all, and therefore wouldn't acknowledge the existence of His agents either. They might deem my client insane based only on their own understanding as to what they had formally seen or believed. On the contrary, a belief in angels to a Christian psychiatrist or psychologist would be an acceptable or even a perfectly normal thing.

"Good argument, Mr. Withers. Please first allow the State's psychiatrist to examine your client and if you are not satisfied with the results, you may have your own expert do the exam as well."

"Your Honor," Brent Foster spoke up, "with regards to this witness list, I have a question pertaining to a 'Nathanael of the Most High God'? What the heck does that mean, Mr. Withers? 'Of the Most High God?'" Foster spoke sourly, looking down his nose at Jacob. "What kind of title is that? And where is the contact number or address?"

The judge looked over his glasses at Jacob. "Well Mr. Withers, who is this and why is there no contact information?"

"Your Honor, to be honest, it's a, well …" Jacob knew this moment would come and stuttered a bit, "he said he was an angel, and I really don't think he lives here."

"Mr. Withers, should I order a psychiatric test for you also?"

"I know how it must sound, Your Honor, but he appeared to me at my church and said he was Sam McBride's guardian angel, the one that Sam hit with car. Then he …, Your Honor he … If I told you, you wouldn't believe me, but he asked to be on the list. So here we are." Jacob, aggravated that he couldn't tell the whole story for fear of ridicule or being held in contempt, shrugged his shoulders, a pleading look on his face.

"Mr. Withers, I hope you know what you are doing! I warn you, I will not permit you to make a charade of these proceedings. Do we understand each other?"

"Yes, sir," Jacob replied, sheepishly.

"Your Honor, the prosecution asks that this Nathanael, whoever he is, not be allowed to testify. As we do not allow angels, fairies, leprechauns, or any other such fabled characters credence in our courts. This is a court for humans, Your Honor."

"Mr. Foster, as unusual as Attorney Withers' request is. I have to remind you that our court system was actually modeled after Judeo-Christian principles, those in which angels just so happen to be a part of," the judge raised his eyebrows.

"Now if by some ever slight chance God did somehow decide to intervene in a human court, and sent a representative to speak here on someone's behalf, I personally would not wish to be the judge that stood in the Almighty's way. And one other thing to consider Mr. Foster, if we did not allow this person or angel or whatever he is to testify, the question would always hang in the air, what if? And then what? A mistrial? No, thanks. This possibly is some kind of hoax or trick or something, but we have to see it through."

The judge pointed his finger at Jacob, "And again, if it is a hoax, Mr. Withers, you better not have had anything to do with it or I'll have your law degree on my trophy wall, and also, Mr. Foster needs to be able to contact him, 'your Nathanael', so he can depose him if he so wishes." Jacob nodded in agreement to the judge.

"Your Honor?" Foster spoke again. "The prosecution then asks that tests be allowed to be done on this witness so that he might prove he is actually an angel, and if not, that he then be removed from the list."

"Tell you what. I'll meet you halfway Mr. Foster. Our system of justice is set up with the State having the burden of proof, so with that said," the judge leaned back in his chair, "I will allow you to test this Nathanael character, of course with his and the defense's permission, to see if you can prove that he is not who he says he is. And if so, I will grant your request, but if you cannot prove to this court beyond a shadow of a doubt that he is not who he says he is, then he will be allowed to testify."

Excited, Jacob breathed out a little "Yes!"

"Excuse me, Mr. Withers. Did you say something?" The judge gave Jacob his famous raised eye look.

"Ah no, Your Honor. Sorry."

"Now, how can Mr. Foster contact this witness?"

"Well, he could pray." Jacob suggested. "That's what we were doing when he showed up."

"Ha ha ha" the judge caught off guard, not being able to contain himself, let out a deep laugh with the rest of the people in court following.

"I object, Your Honor." Foster spewed. "I don't pray and I don't believe in angels, and I take that as a personal attack against myself and this courtroom. If the defense cannot supply reasonable contact information, I would ask again this witness be removed."

"I will decide if the courtroom is offended, Mr. Foster, and as far as a personal attack against yourself, Counsel, I would ask that you would lighten up a bit." The judged turned his stern eyes from Foster. "In regards to contact information, Mr. Withers, I am holding you responsible, especially in the area of making sure this witness shows up for any questions or deposition or whatever the prosecution requests. Do we understand each other?"

"Yes, Your Honor. Please leave my home office number and address as the contact for Nathanael. I will make sure he shows up at any tests or deposition you like." Jacob was feeling lightheaded, hoping he would be able to back up what he had just promised.

"Granted, and I will hold you to that, Mr. Withers. Also gentlemen," the judge continued, "in regards to the continuous amount of media attention we have been receiving, I have decided to allow one general video feed in the courtroom for this trial. Let's concentrate on having an honest and open trial with everything on the table. Mr. Foster, we could use some hard evidence here." He looked pointedly at the prosecutor. "I look forward to hearing a case based more on facts rather than 'he said, she said.' We'll set a trial date for December. 20 at 9:00 sharp, pending a successful jury selection, and evidentiary hearing. Court adjourned." The judge pounded the gavel once and then exited the courtroom into his chambers. He had a blue pillow shaped object in his hand. Jacob wondered what it was as he walked out the double doors of the courthouse.

Jacob quickly made his way down the cement steps and was flooded with reporters. "Mr. Withers?" Maria Espinosa asked, "What do you think about Judge Malkovich allowing cameras in the courtroom for the trial?"

"Well yes, I think it's a great idea. He said there will be one general video feed. It will help to guarantee my client a fair trial, knowing that the public is watching." Jacob continued briskly, trying to get to his car as quickly as possible. He wasn't particularly fond of being on television.

Maria followed him shoving the microphone in his face. "Your witness that was contested by the prosecutor ... you said he was an angel. Is that a joke, Mr. Withers? Do you really believe this guy's an angel?"

"I have no comment right now." Jacob turned from her, about to step into his car.

"Will Mr. McBride have to undergo a psychiatric examination?" she pressed.

This one stopped Jacob cold. He turned and looked her in the eye. "Yes, Mrs. Espinosa. And we gladly submit to the judge's ruling in that regard. Sam McBride is not crazy and looks forward to having that clarified by any means the court deems necessary."

"So you believe him, Mr. Withers? You believe his car struck an actual angel?"

"I didn't say that!" Jacob replied in a gruff tone.

"Well, it's either that or he's a crazy killer, or a liar or both, right?" she asked, more than a hint of sarcasm in her voice.

"Mrs. Espinosa, I believe that what my client said is possible, yes. Improbable, certainly, but angels have appeared many times throughout history, and this just maybe is one of those times." He moved quickly to the right and tried to walk around her, but she jumped in front of him again.

"How are you being supported, Mr. Withers? I've found out

through some acquaintances of yours that you haven't had a real case or a paying client in quite some time."

"God is supporting me, Mrs. Espinosa. Put that in your sound bite."

"Did I just say that? Man she's gonna have a field day with that," Jacob thought, angry at himself. He walked as fast as he could to get to his car.

"Oh I will, Mr. Withers!" she shouted at him. "Thank you!" Maria was quite the champion when it came to ruffling someone's feathers, especially an old bird like Jacob Luke Withers.

Jacob got in his car and drove off. Maria Espinosa walked back to the courthouse steps. "This just keeps getting better and better," she said as she looked up at the grey sky.

Sam was nervous as he waited in his jail cell. The day for his 'crazy test' had come and he had no idea what to expect. A woman officer led him in handcuffs and shackles to a white van with a cage inside. They drove for several minutes. Sam looked out the window, longing for his freedom. Arriving at a huge gray building, the officer beeped the horn until a mechanical door opened; she then drove the van inside. A man came out and accompanied her and Sam to the doctor's office where Sam was led though a white metal door that read "Dr. Henry Zingas."

She walked Sam over to a straight-backed leather chair in front of man in a white doctor's coat. He was sitting in a high backed leather chair, he was mostly bald with age spots on his head and curly white hair on the sides that kept springing out regardless of what product he used to try and keep them down.

The doctor looked up at the officer. "Please take off de handcuffs and shackles and wait outside." he said to the officer, who did exactly what the doctor had asked and left the room.

"Mr. McBride, tank you for coming today," the doctor said in a thick German accent.

"It's not like I had much of a choice," Sam muttered.

"Please sit down in da chair. May I call you Sam?" Sam nodded and sat. "You can call me Dr. Z," the doctor added, giving Sam a welcoming smile.

On the doctor's desk was a picture of his wife in a four-inch golden frame, some pens and notepads. And there was a paddle ball game, seeing that made Sam grin. "Maybe I'm gonna like this guy," he thought. Sam took in the rest of the room noticing beautiful paintings on the wall. One in particular stood out; it made Sam think of Amanda. It was a wood-framed scene of young children on a swing set on a bright summer day.

The doctor continued, "I vould like to ask you a few questions and please answer dem openly and honestly; dere is no bad answer." He pulled a silver clip board from his desk drawer and a pen from his pocket. "Sam, dey vant me to evaluate you to see if you are mentally competent to stand de trial, or as dey say, are crazy. I vant you to relax and know dat I mean you absolutely no harm, and I also vant to tell you dat ve are all, a little bit crazy, so don't vorry, I will be fair vit you." The doctor smiled. Sam was struggling hard to keep up with the doctor's broken English. But Dr. Z's smile and mannerisms made up for his poor speech patterns, putting Sam at ease.

"Now, da report here tells me dat you say dat you hit an angel vit your vehicle. Dis is correct, ja?"

"Yes, Dr Zinger."

"Again, please call me Dr. Z. Dat's vat zay all call me. Now is dis da first time you have seen de angel? Or do you see dem often, or sporadically? Please tell me."

"We'll sir, I've never seen one or even thought about them much until that night." Sam replayed the whole night for the doctor. "And then he just disappeared."

"And dat's ven dis lady, let's see now," the Doctor glanced at the police report, "Mrs. Lee, came out to talk vit you?"

"Well, she screamed at me. Yeah, I mean, yes sir, Dr. Z."

"Goot," Dr. Z added, leaning forward. "Now Sam, I vant to know some tings. I have to ask you some questions about dis Roxanne Perello, also about your vife and some tings in your history, for da record. But dat does not mean dat I do not believe da story, OK?"

"OK."

"Now I understand dat you lost your mama when you were a young lad. Yah?"

"Yeah," Sam replied quietly.

"How do you tink dis has affected you growing up, den as a young man and den now?"

"I, well, it sure hasn't been easy, that's for sure. It was like when I lost one parent, I lost both, 'cause my dad was never really like a dad after that. And my mom, boy, she was sure beautiful." Sam paused. "I have a picture of her hid away in a secret place in my dresser, but to be honest, I don't remember too much about her besides that, except that she could really make me and my dad laugh."

"Vould you say dat losing your mama made you angry, Sam?"

This doctor seems to really care," Sam thought. He relaxed a bit more and answered, "Yes, but not at her. She couldn't help what happened. I think I was angry at God for a long time, because, at the hospital my father, I remember him pleading, 'Please God, please God, don't take her from me.' But she died anyway. But, I don't think that you can blame God for that." Sam paused and shifted in his chair. "He told me it was man's desire for evil that brought sickness and death into the world."

"Who told you dat?" the doctor asked very calmly.

"God, when I was at the beach."

"God talks to you?"

"Well, yeah. He tries to talk to everybody, but not everyone's listening, I guess. You know," Sam spoke eagerly, "it's called a conscience. I didn't listen for a long time."

"Do you see him?"

Sam laughed. "What? Do you think I'm crazy or something?"

Doctor Z laughed and gave Sam a genuine grin and an affectionate, fatherly look. He liked Sam. He could tell, in spite of the very unusual and unlikely angel story, that Sam was somewhat well balanced. Proceeding with the testing, the doctor asked Sam various questions relating to the Mental Status Exam. It was a standard exam used by the State to determine levels of sanity.

"How do feel right now? Tink about an apple, a basketball, and a gray wig," the doctor asked. "Now repeat dese tings I tell you." Sam repeated the items.

The doctor then asked Sam to do some basic math problems, and after a few minutes asked Sam about the same items again. Again Sam repeated them back in order. He questioned Sam about some common phrases, then his drinking problems and finally, more family history. At three o'clock the doctor stood and shook Sam's hand and motioned for the officer to come into the room. They had been talking for an hour and a half.

In the meantime, two sets of wings circled the Empire State Building high above the New York City skyline.

"One of the busiest places on the planet," a strong looking chiseled chinned messenger named Mildheid said.

"See," the other replied in a Spanish accent, "a very industrious place it is, amigo. But this is one of the places the Lord wishes would pray more. Almost everyone follows New York in one way or another, but they are so self-reliant." Paz commented. Paz was gifted in helping to calm tensions, and was often used for peaceful negotiations between families, sometimes even countries.

As they descended onto Fifth Avenue, they watched a woman cross the street with her three-year-old boy. The light began to change. The 'Do Not Cross' sign was flashing. The mother hurried with her boy and almost reached the other side as a limousine darted suddenly around the corner. The driver, being pressured by her corporate client to rush to an appointment, didn't see the mother and child. The boy, for no known reason, broke away from his mother's grasp and shot off into the street. Breaks squealed, but it was too late. The boy was trapped under the limousine's front tire. The mother screamed frantically, "Gary Louis!" In a nanosecond, she grabbed the wheel well of the limo and with one hand raised the front tire six inches off the ground. With her other hand, she pulled the child out. No one could see Paz and Mildheid lifting the car with her. Paz appeared afterward, visible in a policeman's uniform. He lovingly touched the head of the child.

"Mi bebé," his mother whimpered in Spanish. She checked the child carefully, but miraculously he was not harmed. "Gloria a Jesucristo!" (Glory to Jesus Christ) she cried.

Paz whispered in her ear, "Sí, mi belleza. ¡Dios es bueno!" which is to say, "Yes, beautiful woman. God is good."

With that, Mildheid and Paz, back in angelic form, locked arms and spun in a circle like little kids do when they make themselves dizzy, creating a whirlwind with the leaves that had gathered in front of a storefront window. Nearby, a grandfather sitting on a bench with his granddaughter, pointed to the whirlwind.

"See Tina, when the wind spins the leaves in a circle like that, it means the angels are dancing!" The little girl smiled and gazed lovingly at her grandfather. Paz and Mildheid overhearing the conversation, laughed heartily at it as they spun up in the whirlwind, then off into the dim winter sky.

12
SEARCHING

The bondo mobile pulled up to a large structure with glass double doors and a white steeple on top. 'New Covenant Christian Church' was on the sign outside and on the glass doors.

"I'd be OK if I could get the Old Covenant on track." Denise thought as she tried to get up the nerve to go inside.

The sky was overcast. It was extremely frigid outside for December. She got out of the car and walked as quickly as possible to stave off the cold. She pulled open the door and stepped inside.

She was greeted warmly by a lady wearing a bright yellow-gold bow over her sunset orange shirt, with ruffles on the sleeves, her hair up in a bun. Denise just looked at her.

"Hi dear, how are you? I'm Mrs. Rumsy. He's waiting for you right in there," the lady behind the reception center said, pointing to an open door.

With the door closed behind her Denise said, "I'm Denise McBride." She was wearing her old blue coat.

"Would you like a cup of coffee, honey?" she asked Denise sweetly.

"That would be great, thank you Ma'am."

"You can just call me Darlene." Mrs. Rumsy told her.

She had been with the church ever since it's inception fifteen years ago.

She used to volunteer her time, but was blessed to get paid for her work now., although most knew she'd still do it for free if she were asked. She carried with her a tremendous sense of duty.

Denise wiped her feet on the rug by the door and walked slowly to the pastor's office. Stopping at the doorway she noticed there was a lamp on in the room on a small wooden table. It was the kind with a shade you'd find in a living room, not an office. The surroundings were pleasant, almost homey. Denise, although nervous at first, was letting down her guard.

Not having been in a church in so long she expected rules and wrath, but the atmosphere felt more like and love and fun and grace.

"Did you want anything in it?" Mrs. Rumsy asked from the reception area's coffee center.

"No thanks," replied Denise. She was soaking in the atmosphere. Down the hall was a foosball table in an open room with computers games and joysticks, with Christian rock band posters on the wall. Mrs. Rumsy handed her the mug.

"Thank you. Darlene, right? This place really has a lot of class. It's more like a restaurant or a recreation center, ya know." Mrs. Rumsy just smiled in reply.

"Come in, Mrs. McBride. I'm Pastor David Owen."

"It's nice to meet you, sir. I've heard a lot about you," she said, "ya' know from Jacob, I mean Mr. Withers, and just around, you know. I hear you guys help a lot of people." she said leaning against the door post, sipping her coffee.

"Thank you, Mrs. McBride. Please, sit down. What can I do for you today?"

She came over and slowly sat in a wing back chair with gold colored leaf designs on it. The pastor was sitting behind a fairly large oak desk. The wall behind him was a massive book shelf filled with various shapes, sizes and colors of books, tapes and other artifacts, from one end of the room to the other. There were various paintings and photos from the Upper Peninsula, as well as East Tawas, Oscoda and other scenic Michigan areas. There were photographs on the wall of his family and other weddings, and graduations.

"Hey, this place is super nice!" Denise smiled and looked around. The room was uncomfortably quiet for a moment. She hesitated trying to find the right words to say. "Jacob told me you're helping him help my husband Sam, and I really don't know what to say. I just wanted to thank you. I want to pay you back for everything."

"Wait, Mrs. McBride. Please. I really want to make it clear that we do what we do because God first gave to us. We don't expect anything in return, so thank you, but we simply ask that people would thank God for what He gives through us, and we pray that people would turn to Him, because He loves us all so much, that's all." Denise was awestruck.

"This man's sincere," she thought. She studied him carefully with her eyes.

She opened up a little. "To be honest with you, I've never really been close to Him, you know, or even saw much need for the whole thing, till now. Again, I'm just being honest."

She nervously chewed on her lip as she glimpsed the diplomas on the wall and then looked back to Pastor Dave.

"Something happened the other night and I think … and I don't say this lightly, it's like in my mind, ya' know, God told me He loved me. I don't know how to explain that." She looked down at her hands as she spoke now. "And the other thing is, I feel so bad about throwing Sam out that night. If I hadn't done that, none of this would be happening." Her face turned red from shame as she was speaking. "And I was so sure I was right, that he was drinking. But he wasn't." She wiped a tear from her eye. "And I threw him out! But I was wrong. And now I don't know what to do to make it right!"

Pastor Dave just smiled and listened patiently as she continued.

"What I wanted to say is thank you to you and all your people for prayin' for Sam. If you could pray that we'd find this Roxanne, that would be so great. And Pastor Dave, I don't know what to do, think or say from here to be honest. I never thought I'd believe in anything but what I could hold in my hand, but I found out I do believe, or at least, I want to believe. I want to help Sam too, but I don't even know how to really pray for him, or myself for that matter. Would it be too selfish to ask if you would pray for me too, ya' know, to know what to do?"

Pastor David smiled. "Of course I will, Mrs. McBride. I'd like to … ask you a personal question if that's alright with you?"

Denise nodded, and nervously pressed her lips together.

"Have you ever asked Jesus to be your Lord and Savior?"

There were a few seconds of silence, and then choosing her words thoughtfully she replied. "No, I haven't." She paused, "and to be upfront with you, I don't even know what that means. It's all really a little too much for me right now. But if you'd pray for me for now that would be great. I just need some time to think things through." She smiled.

"Sure, I understand." Pastor Dave replied. "But I want you to know the door is always open to you and your family. I was hoping you might come and visit us for service sometime. Jacob told me you have a daughter, her name is Amanda, right?"

"You sure do your homework." Denise said, sounding pleasantly surprised.

"It's my passion and my job, Mrs. McBride. We've been praying for your family. I once was looking for help and answers and God sent someone to lookout for me, but I just wanted you to know both you and Amanda would be welcome here, as well as Sam when he gets out."

"You do think Sam's coming home to us, right?" she asked with such love, yet fear in her eyes all at once.

"Yes, I do. All I can say for sure is, I really do believe the Lord wanted us to pray and help him, usually that means a successful end."

"Thank you, Pastor Dave." She stood, purse in hand. "I really appreciate your kindness. I better get goin' now. Mandy's home from school soon, plus I've got some calls to make."

The pastor got up and walked Denise out into the reception area.

"Mrs. McBride, we have a little something for you if you'll receive it," the church secretary handed the pastor an envelope. "We wanted to put a few dollars together for you. We know you've missed some work, trying to help Sam by finding this Roxanne lady, and we'd like you to have this." He extended the envelope to her.

Stunned, she looked at him with a big question mark in the middle of her face, unsure of what to make of this gesture. She'd always been so self-reliant. She slowly reached out and took the envelope.

"Thank you." she said humbly and put the envelope in her purse, retrieving her keys at the same time.

Mrs. Rumsy got out of her chair, came around and handed Denise a plastic plate full of brownies wrapped in cellophane. "I made these for your family. Can I give you a hug?" before Denise could reply, Darlene Rumsy wrapped her arms around her neck.

"Ya' know, I feel so good about all this. I mean, ya' know when I'm praying, I believe the Lord's gonna turn all this to His good, ya know. Keep your chin up, girl," she let go and touched Denise's face like a mother to a daughter. "And if you need a shoulder, I'm almost always here."

"Thank you," Denise replied, trembling a little now, touched deeply by both gestures. Both Pastor Dave and Mrs. Rumsy walked Denise to the door.

"Thanks again." As she turned to leave, she noticed a small stained glass cross ornament on the door, and in some odd way for a moment it seemed to speak to her: "I love you, Denise." A tear of gratitude ran down her cheek. She didn't wipe it away. She wanted to remember it.

"Thank you," she silently mouthed the words and looked up to the sky.

Back in the bondo mobile, she stopped at a red light and opened the envelope. Five one hundred dollar bills were in her hand. She looked at the money and then in the rear view mirror to make sure no one was looking, and shouted out the window, "Thank You, God!" Denise drove home full of hope praying, "Lord, please help me find this Roxanne Perello." She was more determined than ever.

Denise gasped as she turned the corner onto Johnson Street. News crews were parked in front of her house and up and down the whole block. There was a patrol car there just to help keep peace in the neighborhood. Maria Espinosa was there waving to Denise as she drove up.

"I have an idea," Denise thought as she rolled down the window.

"Oh Maria," she called to the gutsy reporter.

"Can I come up?" Maria asked excitedly.

"Yes, please, you want to come in and talk?"

"Are you serious?" Maria asked.

Denise nodded and then speedily pulled into her driveway. Maria and her cameraman approached as Denise got out of her car and they all walked towards the front door. Seeing this, all the other reporters then converged on the property. Denise quickly turned, stepped off the porch and barked, "Off my property!" They backed up a little.

"But what about them?" a man asked pointing to Maria and her cameraman.

"They were invited, you're not."

Denise walked into the house. "You can wait out here," she ordered the cameraman, pointing to the porch. Maria nodded her head in agreement. He stood on the porch for a second wondering what to do. A few seconds later, Denise opened the door and placed a chair out on the porch for him to sit on. Denise took off her coat, hung up her keys and pulled out a chair and sat down at the old Formica top 60's style table. "Sit down Maria, please?" She motioned her to sit in a ripped old red chair with the padding bursting out of it.

Maria was smiling like a Cheshire cat. She had not been able to get a single word out of Denise through phone calls, letters, face to face confrontations, nothing.

"And now I'm sitting at the McBride kitchen table," she was barely able to conceal her joy as she squirmed in her seat. Maria looked up to a beautiful tiffany lamp hanging over the table.

Denise answered what she knew Maria must have been thinking, "I know it doesn't fit in with everything else in here but my mother left it to me."

The McBride kitchen was very modest to put it lightly. Old wallpaper peeling from the walls in some areas, a hole in the ceiling in the dining room where a leak ruined the drywall and it had to be cut out to fix the leak. There was no money to replace it.

"We're gonna do better someday and that lamp reminds me of that."

Amanda walked into the room as Denise was talking. "Reporters in the house, you freaking out, Mom?"

Amanda went to the fridge to retrieve a soda.

"Can I ask Amanda a few questions?" Maria blurted out like Jack Russell Terrier on diet pills.

"No, absolutely not," she said sternly. "Please, leave my daughter out of this."

"Maria, I asked you to come in and talk to see if you could help me. Look, I just know this Roxanne Perello is out there somewhere and I think she's alive. I would be willing to let you interview me on camera, if we could put out a search for anyone who might have seen Roxanne, or knows anything about what happened to her."

"But we already did that, and the police got a few calls, but they were just a couple of crackpots looking for attention. Nothing came of it." Maria replied.

"I know, but maybe if it was me, pleading for my husband's freedom, it might stir up someone's memory or something."

"An exclusive, right? I can ask you other questions, too?"

"Yes, ma'am, but I have to warn you if you go too far, you may not like my response."

"OK, you've got a deal." Maria shook Denise's hand.

"Out here." Denise said as she walked out the back door.

"Just a second," Maria ran out the front door and whispered to the cameraman, "Don, go get the photo of Roxanne Perello and a light kit, then come through the house out the back door. We've got an exclusive!" She giggled like a school girl at her first prom.

Don was a tall mixed Chinese-American-looking man with dark hair and kind dark eyes. He left and returned quickly, entering through the front door with the camera in one hand and a manila envelope in the other.

The crowd of reporters moaned.

"Oh, come on," one reporter complained, frustrated.

In the back yard in front of the one car garage, with a rusty white door and broken window, Don set up the camera and one light and Maria went to work.

"This is Maria Espinosa with a Channel 3 News Exclusive. I'm standing with Denise McBride, the wife of Sam McBride who is in jail, now accused in the Hit & Run and murder of Roxanne Perello. Now, Denise, your husband actually claimed to have hit an angel in this accident, what can you tell us about that?" Maria asked.

"I really can't say much about it. Originally I thought it was crazy, impossible even. But see, Sam's done a lot of bad things in his life, and to be honest our marriage and family life have not been the greatest over the years, but one thing he's never done is lie to me. Now he says he hit an angel, so to him what he saw was an angel, and I'm sticking by my husband. That's why I'm here today. Please, if any of you know where this lady is … give me that picture." Maria, uncomfortably surrendering control, handed Roxanne's photo to Denise. Denise continued, "If anyone has seen this woman, please call me at 734-699-5483.

"How is your daughter handling all this, Mrs. McBride?

"I'm glad you asked, she has been approached by reporters, teased at school, and made to be an object of ridicule. Now let me tell you people, hell hath no fury like that of a mother whose daughter's privacy is being invaded and is being harassed. You school kids should be ashamed of yourselves, and to you moms and dads, would you want this to happen to your kids? And you reporters, I warn you, if you ever follow my daughter again, take pictures of her without my permission, I will come after you!" Denise said pointing her finger at the camera.

"Thank you, Mrs. McBride. That was an interesting interview to say the least. This has been a Maria Espinosa Channel 3 News Live Exclusive."

"You're welcome." Denise replied, smiling coyly.

13
IN THE NAME OF SCIENCE

Two-hundred and thirty-five feet up, on the 5th floor of the Wayne County Building, the greasy black hair of Angelo Perello could be clearly seen through the glass wall. He sat nervously thumping his fingers on the edge of a long wooden table. At the head of the table a steady red light at the end of a video camera focused on him with one of Detroit's finest officers behind it. Captain Franks was directly across from Jacob Luke, both of them three chairs away from Angelo who sat at the foot of the table.

"Mr. Perello," Ben Franks spoke up. "This is an official deposition that carries with it the same weight under the law as if your testimony were in a courtroom. Do you understand that you are being videotaped so that we have an accurate record of your testimony concerning the disappearance of your wife, Roxanne?"

"Yeah, OK." Angelo yawned, as if indifferent.

Captain Franks looked at Angelo, then at the camera. "I am Police Captain Benjamin Franks. I am here as an official witness of the court." Jacob Luke did the same.

"I am Attorney Jacob Luke Withers, I represent the defendant, Sam McBride." .

Captain Franks looked into the camera. "This is the Deposition of Angelo Perello. Today is December 14, 2011. Mr. Perello, do you promise to tell the truth, the whole truth, and nothing but the truth so help you God?"

"Sure, why not." he said with malice in his voice, squinting his eyes, glaring at Captain Franks.

Jacob stood and began to aggressively pace the old blue and white industrial carpet. He was certain Angelo had something do with Roxanne's disappearance. "So, Mr. Perello, would you say the last time you've seen or spoken to your wife was the night of December 2nd, the night that Sam McBride is accused of her murder?"

"Yeah, that's right."

"And you were inside the bar, and she what, she just left?" Jacob tilted his head to the left, looked at Angelo and anticipated his answer. It seemed to take Angelo forever to reply.

"She got mad about something, so I told her to go home." Angelo muttered defensively.

"What did she get mad about?"

"None of your damn business!" Angelo growled.

Ben Franks spoke. "Mr. Perello, if you don't answer the question, you will be charged with contempt of court and I will have to arrest you."

"She called me a pig. All right – pig!" he sneered at Captain Franks.

Irritated, the captain nevertheless just let the comment roll off his back.

"And why did she call you that?" Jacob asked.

With a sarcastic grin he replied, "I don't remember. I think I said something about her weight or something."

"So that was it. You stayed at the bar and she left, and that was the last time you've had any contact with her."

"Yeah, that was the last time, before your friend McBride ran into her so to speak. That dude's goin' up, man. And I got news for you!" Angelo's voice rose. "He's got an idiot for a lawyer, too!" Jacob stunned for a moment, just looked at him, opened his mouth as if to reply, then shook his head slightly and continued.

"And what time was that, when she left?"

Angelo replied, "I think about 6:30 or something."

"And what time did Sam McBride leave?"

"About 6:20, I guess. What are you getting at, Withers?"

"Just collecting facts." Jacob drew a breath and pressed on.

"When you spoke to the media, you said you believed that Sam killed your wife out of revenge. You called his wife that night and told her Sam was in the bar drinking. So, in essence you were instrumental in getting him thrown out of the house. Is that true?"

Angelo's eyes became slits, and his voice lowered menacingly. "Look, Jake, or whatever they call you, Denise is a cool lady and she deserves better than that bum and the way he treats her. If she threw him out he probably deserved it and that don't give him no right to go around running over people. Are we about done?"

"Mr. Perello." Jacob paused, turned his notes on the table and casually flipped through them, not speaking for about 30 seconds. Then, almost as if an afterthought, asked, "Have you ever hit your wife or abused her in any way that would cause her to leave you?"

Angelo leaned forward and screamed at him almost coming out of his chair, "No way man, what are you getting at?"

Captain Franks pushed his own chair back and stood up, ready to subdue him if necessary. At that, Angelo slowly leaned back, taunting the captain with another sneering smile.

"We love each other. Yeah we fight sometimes, but we always make up." Angelo stared maliciously at Ben Franks when he said this, then again leaned forward aggressively in Jacob's direction.

"Where's your wife at, dude? Did she leave you cause you hit her? Is she never coming back?" Angelo's taunts stung Jacob's heart.

"Could he somehow know about my wife," he pondered. Jacob's knees became weak, there was queasiness in his stomach, like he'd just been sucker punched. Trying his best to confine his emotions, he grabbed the edge of the table to steady himself. He couldn't see the gruesome, mocking spirit sitting on the floor whispering words to Angelo. He only could sense that Angelo had darkness, an evil aura surrounding him.

Breathing slowly, Jacob regained his composure. "Mr. Perello, if for some unknown reason Roxanne were to go somewhere, do you know where she might have gone?"

"Look, Jake." He snarled and pointed his finger. "Roxanne would never have left me, and she ain't got no family. I'm her family and she's my family, and that creep you're protecting took the only family I got from me, so why don't you just ask him."

Jacob remained calm. "Are you saying she never went anywhere to visit, not to a friends or anything?"

"Look, you want me to draw you a picture? What we did, we did together. I didn't like Roxanne to hang out with nobody, cause I'm her man. You understand that?"

"OK, Mr. Perello. That will be all for now." Jacob said.

At that Captain Franks opened the door. Angelo wasted no time leaving.

Later at Jacob's loft, he opened the bedroom window about three inches allowing an unusual warm breeze to flow in on what normally would be a cold December day. Jacob was on the phone. "Yes, 1:00 should be fine. I'll make sure he's there."

After putting down the receiver, Jacob sat down on his bed. He wondered how he was going to contact Nathanael.

Finally, he slipped to the floor and knelt down against the sofa. "Lord God, this prayer is a little weird, but I need a contact number for your angel, Nathanael. He's got to be at the county courthouse at 1:00 this Thursday. Thank you, Father, in Jesus' name, Amen."

"Hope that works," he thought.

Denise sat outside on the front porch step. She was enjoying the unusual December sunshine with temperatures in the upper 60's. She noticed all the snow had melted. Moments later her cell phone rang.

"Hello," Denise answered.

"Girl, you got some fierce love goin' on!" an unfamiliar voice said.

"Who is this? I mean, thank you I think. But, ah, who is this?"

"This is Large Marge. Now didn't Sam tell you about me?" Marge asked playfully.

"I like her already," Denise thought amused at the joyful voice on the other end. Sam had mentioned her.

Marge continued, "We were friends on Sam's bus ride home. I'm the one who told him to take you out to dinner."

"Yes," Denise shouted. She was so excited to hear from this stranger that she knew so much about, but had never met. "He did tell me about you. It's really good to hear from you. You must have heard what happened?"

"I sure did," Marge replied. "I watched you on the news and I've been prayin', and girl, I just wanted to encourage you that someone must know where this missin' lady is, and I'm prayin that they get a hold of you." Denise was walking up and down her driveway now. It looked like she was almost dancing, she was so happy to hear from this saint. She listened intently as Marge tried to lift her spirits. "Honey, I wanted to call you to let you know the Lord hears us, even when we don't say pretty words, even when we can only cry a little. He hears our tears, so don't be afraid, help is on the way."

A small tear of hope glistened in Denise's eye at the comforting words Marge spoke that, as far as Denise was concerned, seemed like they were from God Himself.

"Thank you, Marge. I'm so glad you called. I really hope to meet you someday."

"I think we will meet, Mrs. McBride. In the meantime, darlin', if you need me, you just call me and I'll be there."

"Thank you again, Marge. Thank you so much." She closed her phone and held it to her chest like it was a treasured keepsake. Hope shone in her eyes. She looked at her phone again. "Someone's going to call, someone's got to call." she said out loud. She heard a familiar song come on the radio. It was *Calling All Angels* by the band Train. Going into the house, she sensed the urge to pray.

Thursday afternoon found Jacob waiting nervously as he sat on the steps of the medical laboratory. *"Is this guy gonna show up?"* he said to himself.

Jacob was distracted, watching a squirrel look at him from a nearby chestnut tree, its mouth and cheeks full of nuts. "Hey friend, what are you doing?" Nathanael asked from behind him.

Jacob startled just about jumped out of his skin.

"Don't do that!" he said, turning around quickly. "Where did you come from? I didn't even hear you walk up. No, don't answer that, I don't want to know."

Jacob looked Nathanael over, head to toe. He was dressed in a flannel shirt, blue jeans, and wing tipped shoes. Jacob looked down at the shoes and then the rest of the outfit. "No fashion rules in Heaven, huh?"

Nathanael looked him in the eye. "Nice, right? I just got 'em."

"I was looking for you ... I wasn't sure, I didn't know if you'd come. You didn't give me any way to contact you." Jacob gently scolded, feeling vulnerable.

"You were looking for me in the chestnut tree? What, do you think I'm some kind of nut or something? Are you getting squirrelly on me?" Nathanael teased. Jacob didn't respond.

"I think you did okay. I'm here, right?" Nathanael said, more serious now, trying to ease Jacob's tension.

"Yes, you are." Jacob gave him a nervous grin, and then breathed deep and relaxed a little. "Are you ready?"

"Sure," Nathanael smiled. They walked in together to the east elevators and proceeded to room 103. A young lady who barely looked 18 greeted them from behind the nurse's desk. "Hello, gentlemen. May I help you?" she asked pleasantly as they approached. Jacob spoke to the nurse while Nathanael immediately turned around and walked back the way he had entered, turning sharply to the right he quickly pulled opened a steel door with a two-way mirrored window in it. There stood Prosecutor Foster, red as a beet, his hand on the door handle. He had been spying on them.

"You can come out now, Mr. Foster. I knew you were there." Nathanael smiled.

"How do you know who I am and how did you know I was there?"

"I know more about you than you think, and your curiosity has always gotten the best of you."

Foster puzzled and embarrassed replied, "Oh, OK. Well anyway, it's good you came, now maybe we can get this whole angel notion out of the way once and for all."

"That's right, you don't believe in angels, do you? Or even God for that matter."

"How did you know …? Never mind. Are you ready?" asked Foster.

"Sure," Nathanael replied.

Dr. Mathees came out. "Hello, gentleman." He nodded to each. "I'm Doctor Mathees. I will be performing the tests today. Are you …" he looked at Nathanael skeptically, "the angel character?"

"That's me. Yes sir, if you'd like to describe me that way." He bowed slightly. "Pleased to meet you." This gained nothing more than a suspicious look from the doctor. But it did win a little smile from Jacob Luke, who was getting used to Nathanael's dry sense of humor.

"And you must be Mr. Withers?" the doctor said, shaking Jacob's hand. He then turned to the prosecutor.

"Hello again, Brent." the doctor shook Foster's hand warmly, both his hands covering Brent's.

"Doc." Brent Foster smiled in return. "Good to see you."

They all walked together to the exam room where the doctor asked Nathanael to roll up his sleeve. While the nurse took his blood pressure, the doctor examined Nathanael's pupils, checked his throat and listened to his heart.

"Very good," he murmured with each step. "Now, I'd like to take a sample of your DNA through your saliva and also through your blood, if I may?"

"Sure, Doctor." Nathanael replied politely.

The doctor took a cotton swab and gently lifted saliva from the back of Nathanael's throat placing it in a test tube. He then removed a syringe from the drawer and took off the protective plastic seal. "Your arm, please?" the doctor held out his hand.

Nathanael raised his arm. The doctor found the vein quickly and methodically drew out the small portion of blood he needed.

"*Looks human to me,*" Foster thought to himself.

Nathanael leaned toward Foster and whispered, "Probably more so than yours," Nathanael replied as though Foster had spoken out loud.

All three men looked at Nathanael. Foster, eyes wide, began to sweat.

"*Who are you?*" Foster thought to himself. Nathanael just smiled with his eyes.

"Now gentleman, I'll have to ask you to leave the room for the next part of the examination to respect my patient's dignity as I must ask him to disrobe."

"No. I object," Foster said bluntly. "I want to be here for the whole process, besides he's not really your patient."

The doctor was agitated by his friend's arrogance.

"Tell it to the judge, Brent. He's in my care, and this is not a prison. Now please gentlemen, close the door on you way out." Jacob Luke stepped out. Foster hesitated for a moment trying to figure out an angle that could change the doctor's mind. You could almost hear the gears spinning in his head. Finally, not able to come up with anything legal, the doctor won the argument, and Foster reluctantly left the room.

The nurse asked Nathanael to take off his clothes and handed him a gown to put on then positioned him correctly behind the x-ray curtain.

"OK now, hold it," she said as she pressed the button on the machine. As she did, she saw what looked like white wing tips sticking out above the curtain. She rubbed her eyes, and gasped, "Doctor!"

He came out right away from the small office next to the X-ray room. "Yes, Victoria?"

She replied simply by pointing. "They … he had …" she stuttered. "There was …" she pointed once again, but there was nothing there except a view of the x-ray curtain and Nathanael's feet.

"He had what, Victoria? What are you carrying on about?"

"Doctor," she stuttered nervously, "you're going to think I'm crazy, but there were big white wings sticking out from behind that curtain!" The doctor walked behind the curtain. Nathanael waved, looking perfectly normal to the doctor.

"Hey! Do you mind?" Nathanael said, acting like he was embarrassed.

"OK Victoria, let's move on." The doctor sighed, frowning at her. She handed Nathanael a robe and gave him a look that said, "Don't mess with me, buddy."

They led Nathanael to a big machine, laid him flat, and gave him the final test, a CAT scan. When they were finished, the nurse escorted Nathanael back to the exam room and handed him his clothes.

Nathanael touched her hand slightly, sending shivers down her spine. Her eyes widened.

"You are loved," he said. "Don't ever doubt that."

"What?" she asked. Nathanael only nodded. She nervously, but happily, backed out of the room. Her husband had died earlier in the year and she lived all alone. She had prayed earlier in the week and told the Lord, "I don't feel like anyone cares about me. Help me to feel love again, Father." She had not told anyone at all about that prayer.

Minutes later, Nathanael, now fully dressed, sat on the exam bench looking around the office at the various charts and instruments. Outloud, he read the letters on the eye chart far across the room. Starting at the top "L-V-E-C-N-O," then all the way down to the smallest letters. The doctor, who had been listening outside of the door, walked in and acted like he hadn't heard Nathanael read the chart.

"Thank you, Mr. Nathanael. You've been an excellent subject. I believe we'll probably be seeing each other again."

"You mean in heaven, right?" Nathanael asked, half-joking.

"No. I mean in court." The doctor amused, laughed to himself. "Yes, maybe in heaven too." It had been one of the most exciting days he'd had in a while.

"You know, it's strange for me to even ask, but my nurse said she briefly saw ... well frankly, she said she saw wings sticking out when she took your X-ray. You didn't play ... some kind of trick on her, did you?"

"Doctor, I never joke about serious things, and I'm never serious when it's time to have fun. But to answer your question, no I didn't play a joke on her." A second of silence passed between them before the doctor spoke again.

"OK then, thank you, sir. Mr. Withers is waiting for you outside with Mr. Foster."

"Oh, is he still here?"

"You should know, right?" Now the doctor was having a little fun.

"You think I can see through walls, Doctor? Oh, by the way, do I get a manila folder, too?"

The doctor gave Nathanael a strange look, pondering how he possibly could have known he had just given both Jacob and Brent Foster folders with copies of acquisition forms for the tests he had performed.

Nathanael walked out, smiled at Brent Foster, and asked Jacob, "Are you ready?"

"Ahh, yeah," Jacob replied.

They walked out through the front door and down the steps.

"So Nathanael, please? How can I reach you? The court date is coming up and you have to be there."

"You reached me pretty easily this time." Nathanael threw his arm around Jacob. "I know the dates and times. But just to make you feel better, the date is December 20th, at 9:00. I'll see you there or even maybe before that. Maybe we'll get together for a coffee or some angel hair pasta or something," Nathanael grinned.

"You drink coffee?" Jacob asked, ignoring the angel hair pasta line.

"Yes, but none of that decaffeinated stuff. What were you people thinking? Gross! Hey Jacob, I'll see ya' later. We're going riding." Nathanael turned and began to walk away, then suddenly, right before Jacob's eyes, Nathanael's outfit changed into a leather jacket, boots and chaps. Jacob saw that the patch on his back read *Heaven's Angels*. Jacob laughed so hard he had to sit down. Nathanael walked around the corner leaving Jacob alone on the steps. Jacob heard a cooing and turned to see snow white doves in the same tree where he had seen the squirrel.

"I am not alone," he thought to himself. He felt the need to say a prayer right there.

"Thank You Lord, for today. Thank You for choosing me." In the middle of his prayer, the prosecutor walked out.

Hearing Jacob praying, he just shook his head, and muttered under his breath, "Idiot."

Jacob heard him. As Foster walked away, Jacob prayed, "Lord, I pray for Prosecutor Foster that he would know You too, in Jesus' name. Amen."

Meanwhile, the doctor walked back into the x-ray room. On the floor behind the curtain were two feathers. Doctor Mathees took off his glasses, cleaned them and put them back on. The feathers were still there. He opened a drawer, took out a plastic zip lock bag, and retrieved a pair of tweezers from an overhead cabinet. He walked over to the feathers, knelt down and using the tweezers, carefully picked them up and placed them in the bag. He filled out a request form and put the bag with the other items. He decided to leave early for the day and went to Mass.

14
HEAVEN'S ANGELS

"Park closed due to Government Shutdown," Nathanael read the sign in front of Michigan's Silver Lake State Park. He thought about what it meant for a second. Then he hopped on his bike, leading the others around the gate as they simply drove their bikes around the barricade and entered the park. Clouds of dust kicked up as the road turned to gravel getting closer to the water of Lake Michigan.

They all wore the red, gold, and white patch on their leather jackets that read *Heaven's Angels* across the top. The patches were all the same, an elaborate illustration of a muscle bike with an angel character riding on it, wings outstretched, riding into a magnificent orange sunset. Underneath the patch in white lettering was written, *There's no high like The Most High.*

The twelve pulled up to a path with a sign that read, *Little Sable Pointe Light House.* It had an arrow on it pointing west. They all parked their bikes and started walking in that direction. In a blink of an eye they transformed out of their bikers' outfits and were winged warriors again. They spread their wings and shot up to the tip of the lighthouse and flew over Lake Michigan.

"I bet these humans wish they could fly." Arek shouted as he soared into the sky nearing 70 miles per hour.

"We don't know," Josag replied following directly behind. "Maybe they will fly. After all, the Word says they'll be caught up in the clouds."

Arek did a backflip in the air and then a swan dive. He soared in the direction of Josag as if to hit him but just before smashing into him, he shot his wings out like a parachute, coming to a dead stop. Josag didn't even flinch.

With his hand, Arek playfully messed up Josag's hair. "That's it," Josag laughed as he gave chase. Easily out-flying Josag, Arek just continued to talk, "I know the Word says that, but that doesn't mean they will actually fly."

Tro flew over adding his two cents. "We know they'll have glorified bodies, so it would make sense to me."

A beautiful orange tint colored the clouds as the day was coming to an end.

"We'd better be getting back! It's getting late," Nathanael shouted to the others. Paz was swimming now. One of the humans fishing nearby thought a fish had jumped out of the water when he dove in. Nathanael was standing on the top of the lighthouse watching the light come on.

Keitsu joked, "What's the matter, Nate? Light getting dim again? Going for a recharge?"

Nathanael replied. "Hey, Keitsu, some things you just don't joke about." The teasing reminded Nathanael of the battle he had lost when first coming to help Sam that night, losing consciousness, seeing nothing, feeling nothing. Nathanael was still a little troubled from the memory. *"I won't lose this time,"* he thought. He was more focused than ever on accomplishing his mission. "Help me, Lord," he bowed his head and breathed a prayer as he thought about what lay ahead.

"Sorry, Nate. I didn't mean anything by it, sometimes I don't think before I speak."

"He can't help it, Nathanael." Satka said. "It's like he's got a wound up little kid in him."

With a bold leap, Nathanael shot into the air and turned a sharp left in front of the group. The others followed and joined him and flew back to the parking area. They landed at their bikes, instantly transforming back into their leather outfits. They quickly drove out of the park when moments later, they noticed a Michigan State Trooper car quickly approaching with its lights on and two officers inside.

"We weren't speeding or anything, were we?" Imperium asked Nathanael.

"I think Michigan has a helmet law, or it could be because the State Park was closed," Nathanael concluded.

"Maybe he saw us leave," Tro added as he pulled up next to Nathanael who was out in front with Amoerus riding on his right. "You ready to go?" Tro asked.

"Yeah, let's go." Nathanael said.

"To the sky!" Amoerus shouted as his words echoed through the area. With that, they all stood on their foot pegs and seats and shot into the sky with wings outstretched. They immediately transformed into their angelic forms again and in a flying V format, disappeared into the clouds. The motorcycles simply vanished into thin air.

The patrol car came to a sudden stop on the side of the road. "Did you just see what I saw?" Officer Cindy Travis asked her partner, Dave Stein, who sat staring at the empty road, his hands clutching the steering wheel.

"I didn't see a thing." His face was as white as a freshly bleached sheet.

"Me neither," Cindy murmured shaking her head.

After nearly a minute, Officer Stein drew a deep breath. "I think I need a day off," he said as he cautiously pulled the patrol car back on the road.

"Me too," Travis replied, her eyes searching the sky.

The freezing rain made a lonesome sound on the window beyond the bars of Sam's cell, making him remember how much he hated the cold Michigan winters. They were commonly gray days, often filled with cold wind, rain or snow or sleet, or some combination of all of those.

Now though, he thought, it wouldn't be that bad. He had a different mindset. He felt like he had something better with his family, any day could be a good day. He didn't feel like a worthless drunk anymore.

Sam's mind drifted back to when Mandy was a child, fresh snow had fallen, and it was the bright big-flaked, fluffy, good snowman making snow. On that day, the sun had come out and everything glistened and sparkled. Sam had thought, *"That's where they get the term 'Winter Wonderland.'"* Sam, Denise and Amanda McBride had the snowball battle of a lifetime. Sam, of course, had let the ladies win, pinning him to the ground so that he was finally forced to give up. The snow they had shoved down his jacket and shirt had given him a chill, and he'd called it quits. "I love you, guys," Sam had said as the family drove back home from the snow hill that day.

"We love you, Daddy." the then five-year-old Amanda had said sweetly. She was adorable, red-faced and dressed up in a new snow suit, knit hat and mittens. Denise had squeezed his hand and given him their secret smile. In a whisper she'd said, "Love you too, babe." It had been a perfect day.

The joy of the memory created a compelling urge in Sam to fight for what now, surprisingly seemed within reach, his family, their future. Even though he was in jail, he felt a flicker of hope burning even brighter now. Unknown to him, the church had started a prayer circle and had people praying for him around the clock. Marge, in Nebraska, also was praying for him and his family at that very moment.

Sam, not really knowing that he was in a sense joining them, felt the power of their prayers. He got down from his metal bed and sat on the floor and prayed, "I miss my family, Lord. Please get me out of here. Thank You for all that You've done for me. When I get out, I want to do things right, to put You first, and them. Please don't let me be selfish again, keep me from my own ways, Lord."

Prosecutor Foster stood over Nathanael who was sitting patiently at the foot of a long oak table in a side room at the Frank

Murphy Hall of Justice. Foster licked his lips, eager for the chance to 'de-feather this phony,' as Foster would put it.

The room was set up similar as it had been for the Angelo Perello deposition; a video camera was present to record the whole event. Captain Franks and Jacob were sitting next to each other on the east side of the table. This time a uniformed female officer was operating the camera from the head of the table.

Foster walked around the table opposite Nathanael and rested his palms on his chair.

"Mr. Nathanael, please state your full name for the record."

"I am Nathanael," replied God's messenger.

"You don't have a middle or last name?" asked Foster.

"No."

"Where were you born?"

"I wasn't born."

Skeptically, Foster raised an eyebrow but kept his voice professional. "Then how do you exist?"

"My Father made me."

"Who is your Father?"

"The Lord God Almighty."

"I don't believe that, I don't believe in God." Foster said.

"I know. You think we evolved from bacteria or something like that. Have you ever prayed to your bacteria God?" Jacob laughed at that. Foster ignored Nathanael's sardonic question and continued.

"Where are you from?"

"I am from Heaven."

"Are you an angel?"

Nathanael looked Foster in the eye and waited, surprising Foster and causing him a certain degree of apprehension. Nathanael gave him a heartfelt look of empathy, and slowly answered the question.

"Yes."

"Can you prove you are an angel?"

"Yes," Nathanael answered.

"OK, how?"

"I said I could prove it," he paused, "I didn't say that I *would* prove it."

"Why won't you prove it?" Foster asked, annoyed.

"Prove you are a human, Brent Foster." Nathanael's eyes were shining as he locked the prosecutor in his gaze.

Foster began to sweat, not from the answer, but from the fact that this man - creature – or whatever, seemed to be able to see directly into his soul.

Foster collected himself and asked, "What? What do you mean by that?"

"If you are a human, then you were made in His image, and if you were made in His image, you would love and respect Him. Yet you don't even give Him a moment's time. Rather, you mock and ridicule His existence, His people, and messengers. When you prove you are human, then you will know, I am who I said I am. "

Foster fought the urge to defend himself and an even stronger urge to call the whole thing off. Feeling like a little school kid outwitted by this 'Nathanael', he kept looking at the door, wishing he could he grab his marbles and go home.

"Why are you here, Nathanael?"

"To fulfill my assignment, to see God's child, Samuel McBride, set free."

"Aren't we all God's children? That's what I always heard."

"No, we all have the opportunity to be sons and daughters of God. Your Bible tells you that those who are led by the Spirit of God are the sons of God. Mr. Foster, you forsook your covenant with your family for one night's pleasure with a woman other than your wife." Nathanael then stood up, looked Foster in the eye, leaned in and boldly asked. "Do you think the Spirit of God led you to do that?"

Foster fell back violently at this, as though he had been shoved.

"So whose son do you think you are?" Nathanael pressed. "And what reward will you receive for your deeds?" Nathanael appeared to have some kind of light on his face as he continued. "You have the capacity to be His child. You have the image still of what was in the beginning. But consider your life carefully, Mr. Foster."

Ben Franks, Jacob, and the officer were awestruck!

Foster, confused, trembled and turned bright red. He hoped that no one could see how humiliated he felt. He raised his voice and pointed his finger at Nathanael.

"Hey! I'm asking the questions here! And you mind your own damn business! I don't know who you talked to, but if I find you've been meddling with my affairs, you will end up much worse than Samuel McBride."

Nathanael slowly sat down and replied, never taking his penetrating eyes off the prosecutor. "You asked me a question and I answered it. And how can you be so sure that you aren't my business?"

This guy's amazing," Captain Franks said to himself. He couldn't help but smile, trying to hide his amusement by covering his mouth with his hands as if he was yawning.

Foster changed the subject. "Where were you on the night of Friday, November nineteenth of this year?"

"I was in Heaven … and then I came to earth."

"OK sure," Foster said sarcastically, "and what were you doing in Heaven, and why exactly did you come to earth?"

"I received a scroll from the King telling me to come and bring comfort to Samuel. So I left for earth, and on my way here I was attacked and knocked unconscious. When I came to, I landed in front of the car Samuel was driving … and then he hit me."

"Who attacked you?"

"A demon prince."

"I don't believe that. I don't believe in angels, God or demons."

"I know." Nathanael looked at Foster somewhat quizzically, "but this isn't really about you, is it?"

"OK. And then what?" Foster sighed loudly.

"The accident had knocked me unconscious again. I was thrown against a tree by the force of the impact. I awoke, was healed and disappeared."

"You healed. What do you mean you healed?"

"We have an inner light given to us from the Light of the world. It heals us from the inside out."

"Of course it does." Foster agreed sarcastically. "What do you mean you disappeared?"

"I became other dimensional. Which, by the way, is why you normally cannot see or hear us, because you can only see certain dimensions. We exist in a state beyond your normal comprehension."

"Enough." Foster said, exhausted from the trying conversation. "That's it for today." He felt nauseous as if he was going to pass out.

Nathanael got up, ready to leave the room. As he did, he stopped and looked Prosecutor Foster in the eye, with great compassion emanating from him. Nathanael didn't open his mouth or move his lips, yet Foster heard his voice, *"If you would turn to Him, He would forgive you and restore you. He does love you."*

The door shut behind Nathanael as he exited with Jacob on his heels.

"Did you hear that?" Foster asked Captain Franks.

"Hear what?" Franks asked.

"Nothing. I just … never mind." Foster spoke quietly, like a man defeated.

Ben Franks labeled the video tape, recorded the times on a log, and handed the tape to Foster. "Don't lose that."

"I won't. Thank you, Captain Franks." Foster replied, shaking Ben's hand. They had known each other professionally for quite awhile.

"Are you going to be OK, Brent? You look a little shook up."

"Yeah, I'll be all right. I just can't quite figure this guy out. I know he's lying, but I just can't catch him. Can you put a tail on him?"

"With an official court order, sure."

"OK. Well, let me think about it. Thanks, Ben."

"Ya' know, Brent, I am a Christian," Ben began cautiously, "and I know you say you don't believe in God, the traditional one any way, but if you ever want to talk about it …. We could get a muffin and a coffee over at the Inner Peace Bakery – my treat."

"Thanks, Ben." Foster ran his fingers through his hair, and then pushed his hair down flat, clearly distracted by the afternoon's proceedings. "I'll keep that in mind. I'm going to go home and work there for a while, I think."

Foster grabbed up his brief case and left, calling over his shoulder, "Can you get the lights on your way out?"

"Sure Brent, get some rest, OK?"

Later, at home in his lavish living room, Foster turned on his gas fireplace, and made some green tea.

Taking the small video tape from his pocket, he plugged it into a digital video camera and hooked it up to his computer. He then recorded it to a DVD disc. Foster watched the last part of the deposition several times. "I swear I heard him say something," he muttered to himself.

"Maybe you did, Brent." a voice seemed to come from within, but he ignored it. A cold draft came in the window causing him to shiver suddenly. He went to make sure the window was shut. Then, trading the tea in for a scotch, he sat by the fire for a moment. Suddenly, he rose up and walked to the fireplace mantle to stare sorrowfully at a photo of his son. Finally, he set it down, turning the picture frame away from him. Filled with regret, and feeling alone, tears sneaked into his eyes. Even though no one else was in the room, he was embarrassed, and quickly wiped them from his face. He could leave no evidence that, behind this cold, calloused agnostic man was a real human being with feelings, a beating heart and all.

15
PROVIDENCE

Denise was putting away dishes, cooking sausage and eggs for breakfast, and waiting for Amanda to come down before school, when her cell phone rang. She quickly dried her hands on a dish towel.

"Hello, this is Denise." She listened for a moment and shouted, "You what?!!" Denise sat down to catch her breath, then immediately grabbed a pen and a notebook.

"Yep, that's what I said, I think I saw your missin' person. My name's Clara Biggs and I think I saw the person you're looking for. You were the one on the news, weren't ya?" Clara asked in a Texas accent.

"Yes, yes, thanks for calling. You're serious, right?" Denise asked overjoyed.

"Yes Ma'am, I wouldn't lie about something like that."

Clara, a dirty blond refugee from the 80's drug era, was a party girl who was now getting older. Her hard life left its mark like a wrinkled road map on her face. Her drinking and drugging days had taken a huge toll. Recently, she had begun to wish she'd taken a different path.

"Gotta do at least this one good thing," she had mumbled to herself before dialing the number she'd seen on the TV screen. *"Maybe,"* Clara thought, *"this is my way of turning over a new leaf; to help someone else, this woman, the lost woman."*

"I think the news said her name was Roxanne." Her voice was shaky. "Well anyways, if it was her she was with three guys in a black Monte Carlo with tinted windows. Those guys were really high. They wanted me to go with 'em. They said they were going to Mexico and I could do all the 'coke' I wanted, but they seemed super scary, ma'am, and I didn't feel right about it, so I didn't go."

"Clara, what made you think it was Roxanne?" Denise asked.

"Well, she looked liked the lady in the picture from the news, except she looked really tired, and she had a cut on her lip, and you could tell she was high. I hope she's all right 'cause these guys looked no good, ma'am. You ever know when someone just gives you the creeps? Well, these guys did me. Anyway, I just wanted to call you and try to help. I saw ya' on the news and you looked like a nice lady." She paused and wondered if she should ask, then curiosity got the best of her. "Hey, did your old man really hit an angel?"

"I'm not sure, honey. I think he might have." Denise answered. "Clara, where did all this happen?"

"It was at a little hole in the wall bar called *The Dungeon* off old Highway 59 just outside of Houston. I went outside with 'em for a minute 'cause they invited me to have a toke … that's between you and me, OK? But anyway, that's when I saw her in the car, and I thought right away that she looked like that girl on the news, but I didn't say nothin'. And then I forgot about it for a while, but it just kept naggin' at me so I called the news people and asked for your number and they gave me it to me. They wanted to talk to me but I told 'em I had to talk to you first."

"Thank you. Thank you, thank you so much for calling, Clara. I want to write down your phone number in case I need to get in touch with you. OK?"

"Yeah, no problem, it's my cell phone. I hope you find that lady soon 'cause, she didn't look too good."

"Well thanks, Clara. You did really great!"

Denise hit the off button on her phone and immediately called Maria Espinosa on her private cell line.

"Hello." Maria answered.

"Maria? This is Denise McBride. I need your help. I think Roxanne might be in Mexico and I'm not sure if she's dead or alive or hurt or what."

Denise proceeded to fill Maria in on all the details Clara had told her.

Colorful canopies blanketed the various shops at the Benito Juarez Market in Matamoros, Tamaulipas, Mexico. Manuel Rodriguez had brought his watermelons to the market simply known as El Mercado to the locals. El Mercado was a five block long conglomeration of shops selling all different kinds of clothes, foods, jewelry, you name it. In one of the shops he stopped at after selling his melons, Manuel listened to a TV broadcast. It was an English news channel coming in from Brownsville, Texas. Maria Espinosa was speaking, in English, but Spanish subtitles crossed the bottom of the sceen. Manuel gasped as he saw the photo of Roxanne Perello and quickly wrote down the phone number. He called the station right away.

"WKBD Channel 3 News!"

"Hola. Mi nombre es Manuel Rodriguez. ¿Puedo hablar con Maria Espinosa por favor?"

Manuel introduced himself, asking to speak to Maria.

"One moment, sir," the operator said, "let me get you someone who speaks Spanish." Seconds later a young lady, Elena, got on the phone.

"Hola. ¿De qué manera puedo ayudarle?" She asked if she could help him. Manuel again asked for Maria, and told the young lady that he thought he knew where to find Roxanne.

Elena screamed at the top of her lungs.

"¡Dios mio, hombre guapo!" That is to say, "Oh my God, you beautiful man!"

She continued to speak to him in Spanish.

"Maria se fue en una sesión de fotografía, pero la encontraré y pediré que ella le llame enseguida. ¿Cuál es su número de teléfono?"

Which translated means: Maria is out on a shoot, but I'll find her and have her call you right away, what is your phone number?

After Manuel gave Elena his cell phone number, she drove out to the shoot location and found Maria. Jumping up and down with excitement, she waved violently at Maria who was in the middle of a real estate interview with local brokers.

Maria, finishing the interview, turned to Elena, an eyebrow cocked quizzically, "What is it, Elena?"

"She's in Mexico. Roxanne Perello is in Mexico at a Mission Hospital. A man named Manuel called and told me. He just told me. Oh my gosh, like 5 minutes ago! Oh man, I'm gonna be famous."

"She's what? She's alive? She's alive?" Maria shouted, "Whoo Hoo!" and grabbed Elena's hands as both jumped up and down dancing in a circle with excitement. They looked like schoolgirls who had just found out they could go to their first prom.

"I've got to call Denise." Maria left Elena standing there as she got out her cell phone and called Denise.

"Hello, Maria," Denise answered, recognizing the number in her caller ID.

"Denise!" she practically shouted, "we're going to Mexico."

"Wait! What are you saying? Did someone find her?" Denise stammered.

"Yes, or at least I think it's her. If it is, she's been in a coma at the Refuge Mission Hospital in Matamoros, Mexico."

"I have the phone number of the person who brought her there. Can you come to the station? I'm going to have our affiliate in Texas try to get through to get more info, but I think we should go there right away. I'm going to try to get Channel 3 to pick up the trip if you'll let me go with you. But you need to come down here and help me talk to my boss. And Denise, you can't tell anyone until we know for sure, and if my boss pays for it, we get first air, OK?"

A sudden thought comes to Denise. "OK but hey, can we take my friend, Marge?"

"Maybe, I guess. How exactly does she fit into the picture?" Maria asked.

"She's Sam's friend he met on the bus. She kinda adopted him, like a disciple or something. I know that sounds weird but, she's really smart and she's tough. She might come in handy when it comes to dealing with strangers or talking to Roxanne. God, I hope it's really her down there." Denise paused for a second. "It has to be," she was thinking out loud, "it's the only lead we've got." She paced the kitchen floor. Lately she'd worn off most of the finish.

"I'll put in for a cameraman and for the three of us to go down there," Maria's voice was rising, "just cross your fingers that I get the approval," she said eagerly.

Elena then whispered in Maria's other ear while Maria was talking, "I want to go!"

Maria turned her back to get away from Elena, but Elena just came around again, and pointed to herself and mouthed the words, "I'm going with you."

Maria smiled at Elena's aggressiveness and then said to Denise, "I'll see you in about twenty minutes." she said, ending the call. She looked at Elena with a "go ahead and make your argument stare."

Elena quickly exclaimed, "My Spanish is way better than yours, and if someone needs to go into town for something I can speak the language. I can cook for you guys and ...." Maria stopped her and held her hand up.

"OK, OK, but you've gotta help me pitch it to the bosses, and when I tell you to … back off!"

"I know, I know. I am so invisible, you won't even know I'm there."

Comically, Elena stepped back and bowed her head like a quiet school child, did the 'lock my lip and toss the key' pantomime.

Maria laughed. "You are too much, Elena. OK, let's go sell this."

Denise prayed while pacing the floor. *"Oh God, let it be her, please God, let it be her. I have to call the police,"* she thought. She dialed the local number listed on the magnet on the fridge.

"Michigan State Police."

"I need to speak to the police captain." she told him.

"Can I help you with something?" the officer asked.

"No, this is Denise McBride and I need to talk to the captain right away. It's very important," she said boldly.

"Please hold." The extension was ringing.

"Captain Ben Franks here," said the voice on the other end.

"Captain, this is Denise McBride. I think we've found Roxanne Perello in a mission hospital in Mexico, and we're going to try to head out there today. If everything goes all right, we could be there by tomorrow evening or the following morning. But I can't be positive it's her, a Mexican farmer took someone there, and he said she was in a coma. Can you help me please, Captain? I know my husband's innocent." Denise pleaded.

"What do you want me to do for you, Mrs. McBride?"

"Can you call down there to check and help us get across the border and back?" she said almost out of breath.

"Well, Mrs. McBride, I do know some of the authorities in Brownsville, Texas. It borders Matamoros, and they have a good relationship with the police there. There's also an American Consulate there. Let me make some calls. And I'll let you know what I can find out and see if I can pull a few strings to help you. Can I reach you at this number?"

"Yes, yes you can. Thank you very much, and Captain? Please don't tell anyone about this until we're sure its her, and I promised Maria the story if they pay for everything."

At the Channel 3 news office, Maria and Elena were just coming out of the glass conference room. Elena laughed out loud in celebration. "We're going to Melhhhico!" she shouted gleefully with a contrived Spanish accent.

"Hey! Keep it professional, girlie." Maria grinned. Joking, she dialed Denise right away. "It's all set Denise. Yeah, get here as quick as you can. No, just bring clothes."

At home, Denise sat at her kitchen table rapidly penning a letter to Sam. Finishing, she put the letter together with a photo that they had had taken together. She addressed the envelope and put it in her purse, then grabbed a wheeled suitcase and headed out the door. Twenty minutes later, the bondo mobile exited the highway, stopped, and Denise dropped the letter off at the jail before going to meet Maria.

Three hours later, the news team's motor home was doing 75 mph down Interstate 94.

"Yeah, Marge, we'll be there in less than two hours." Denise spoke excitedly into her phone. "I can't wait to meet you either." Denise was exuberant. They were picking Marge up near Lincoln and from there they would drive straight through, and with Captain Franks help, enter Mexico through the border at Brownsville. They hoped to arrive in Matamoras between 6:00 and 8:00 pm the following day.

The wind had really kicked up while they'd been traveling. Keitsu and Paz were assigned to take turns outside keeping the motor home safe and steady on the road. Paz came in and rested and guarded the group of ladies and the cameraman, who now also had the title of driver. Kietsu kept watch outside.

Sam meanwhile, was in his prison cell praying. He was sitting on the floor with his Bible open. He really sensed the presence of God with him as he poured out his heart. Nathanael was in the room with him. Sam couldn't see him.

"Lord God Almighty, thank you for everything You're doing right now. I feel really good today. You put hope back in my heart. Please watch over my wife and my daughter. Thank You for sending me Jacob Luke. Thank you for ...." Sam hesitated for a moment sensing he wasn't alone. He turned to see the guard with a letter in his hand.

"Something for you, McBride. Sorry we had to open it, policy, you know. I think you're going to like this one though."

Grabbing the envelope and sitting on the bunk, Sam quickly read:

Dear Sam,

I've got really good news, possibly that is! We think we've found Roxanne and that she's in a coma at a mission hospital in Mexico. We're on our way there now to see if it's her and try and help her. Hopefully we'll be bringing her back. I wanted to tell you in person, but there just wasn't time. I tried to get through to Jacob but there was something wrong with his phone. I'll keep trying him though. I'll definitely let you all know as soon as we know if it's her. Maria said not to tell anyone but you and Jacob have to know.

Yours forever; stay strong. Gotta go, Love; your 'Neesi.

P.S. Amanda is staying with friends of Jacob's from his church. (Don't worry, I checked 'em out.) Did you know that the church gave us $500, Sam? And they're paying Jacob to represent you, too! Sam, things are looking up. Pray for us, OK? I mean it. I love you!

"Oh thank You, Lord. Let it be Roxanne and watch over my wife, please?" Sam lay back on the bunk, held the letter to his chest, and rested peacefully. Actually it was one of the best rests he'd had in a long time. He imagined getting all this over with.

At 3:00 that afternoon Sam was startled by two sets of footsteps.

"Someone to see you, McBride," the guard said.

"Hello, Sam," Jacob Luke said as the guard opened the sliding cell door.

"Hey, Jacob, it's good to see you." Sam stood quickly and greeted Jacob as the guard locked the cell door behind them. Sam straightened out the blanket on the bunk. "Sit down Jacob, how is everything?" Jacob noticed a picture of Denise and Amanda next to an envelope and a letter open on the bunk.

"Well, I'm afraid I've got some bad news, Sam. The DNA tests from the blood on the bumper of the car came back. They tested positive for Roxanne's blood."

"No way, that's impossible!" Sam insisted.

Jacob muttered and paced the small cell. "I don't understand it. Help me understand. Unless someone's playing an elaborate hoax on us, I met your angel, Nathanael, and he is very unusual, unearthly even. He did do things I can't even explain, like miracles, Sam." Jacob stared at the brick wall past the bars. "We've come up against a brick wall. How can this blood from the scene match Roxanne's if Nathanael is who he says he is?" Jacob looked Sam in the eye hoping for an answer. "It doesn't make any sense, Sam."

Sam thought carefully. "All I know, Jacob, is that it was not Roxanne I hit that night. It was an angel. He had wings. He had light coming from him and he definitely just disappeared. There must be a mix-up in the DNA or something."

"Sam, you know if we stick to this story we could wind up just looking like a couple of fools."

"I don't have a choice, Jacob. At least this time I'd look like a fool for the right reasons. I lived a lie all my life and now I'm standing with the truth, no matter what. Besides, didn't Denise call you?"

"I don't know, my phone's been having some trouble … she may have tried to call. I don't have a cell phone yet."

"Here, read this." Sam handed Denise's letter to Jacob.

Jacob took the letter from Sam and began to read.

Sam continued to talk while Jacob read. "They think Roxanne's in Mexico and they're gonna try and bring her back. Jacob, you've got to find out what went wrong with those tests. God wouldn't have brought us this far for nothing, right? We're going to win, Jacob, I just know it."

Jacob was unsure what to make of the potential Roxanne news, but he didn't want to discourage Sam.

Jacob gave Sam a surprised look. "You're doing well, aren't you?"

"Hope." Sam said, "I have it now, and I plan on keeping it."

"That's good to see, Sam. All right," he said, passing the letter back to Sam. "I'll talk to you soon. Keep praying. We go to trial in a couple days."

"Thank you, Jacob. We're going to win."

"Yes, Sam, I think you may be right. We're going to win." The two friends shook hands. Jacob signaled for the guard, he smiled, then turned and left.

It was Wednesday evening and the church was praying. Many were at the altar, some in pews with their heads bowed. Others burned a hole in the carpet, pacing the aisles with their hands raised, singing to God and crying out. Some prayed silently, but all seem to agree about what they were seeking.

One plea could be heard, "Be Glorified, Oh Lord, make your power known in this land. Pour on us Your new oil, Lord. Let people know Your love."

Some at the altar took prayer requests from a silver box on the second step. Each took a turn praying as they spoke each request to the Lord.

"Let this missing person be found, Lord, healthy and sound. Lord, we pray for Roxanne Perello. You know where she is, God, You know all things."

In his sleep that evening, Jacob had a dream about a feather coming through the window in a place he'd never seen. In his dream, he saw a man in a lab coat examining the feather, and also looking at what appeared to be blood in a microscope. Jacob sat up in bed in his flannel pajamas, took a pen and pad from his night stand, and scribbled a few notes. His brow wrinkled as he read what he had just written. Awestruck at the dream and what this meant to the case, he lifted his eyes to heaven.

"Thank You, Lord." he said solemnly. And then lay down and faded back to sleep.

16
THE WORD

The sound of keys rattling and approaching footsteps jolted Sam awake from his day dream. He stood up as the guard approached.

"Visitor for you, Sam. I told him we usually only let attorneys back in the cells, but sometimes we make exceptions for ministers, too." Captain Franks joked; Pastor Owen smiled.

"Hi Sam, I'm Pastor David Owen. I've heard a lot about you." The pastor shook Sam's hand as Ben Franks let him into Sam's cell.

"Hi, nice to meet you." Sam smiled then looked surprised over at the guard. "You're the police captain, Ben Franks, right? You do guard duty, too?"

"No, not usually. Pastor Dave and I are old friends, and when he said he was coming to see you, I thought that would be a good time to stop in and and visit you myself. You know, to see how you were? Besides, I've been meaning to stop by and see you since you got here. Unfortunately, I've been dealing with one emergency after another. So are you doing ok? Considering everything, of course?"

"Yeah, pretty good thanks," Sam replied nodding his head. "I'm doing better now. Have you heard they think they've found Roxanne Perello?"

"Yes, as a matter of fact Sam, we're helping to look into that. I've contacted some friends and connections to help your wife, Marge and the news team on their trip into Mexico."

"Marge is with them, too? You know Marge? Oh, that's great news, how did that all work out? My wife didn't say anything about Marge in her letter."

Pastor Dave looked at Ben Franks, also curious about this statement.

"Well, I hear your wife and Marge have become fast friends."

Captain Franks went on, "About a week ago, Marge called here at the front desk and wanted to know how we were treating you. She said she was praying for us to find the truth. Since my front desk guys know I'm a Christian, they put her through and we had an interesting talk. She's quite an interesting woman. And also I recently talked to your wife, and she asked me to help make some connections and get some information. As you must know, they're headed down there now."

"Yeah," Sam chimed in. "I've got the letter right here, except I didn't know Marge was going. Man," Sam shook his head grinning, "this just keeps getting better and better."

"I've been praying for you too, Mr. McBride." Franks said kindly. "Yours is an extraordinary story, yet, I know it's not impossible. I believe you really do believe it. And, forgive me, but I've overheard you praying in here, and I think I may be starting to believe it too. Anyway, I'll let you two talk." The captain smiled at Pastor Owen then turned to Sam again as he opened the cell and let the pastor in. "You take care, Sam McBride. It was nice to finally meet you." Captain Franks locked Pastor Dave and Sam in the cell and proceeded down the hall.

"Thanks for coming by, Captain, and thanks for your prayers, too." Sam called out as Ben faded out of sight.

"Pastor Owen, please sit down." Sam straightened out the blanket at the end of the bunk. "I'd offer you something but as you can see, we're not much for entertaining in here. I've heard a lot about you from Jacob. He told me you were supporting him in representing me, and then today my wife said you guys were helping her. I don't know how to begin to thank you. You have no idea what all that means to me." Sam got a little teary, which surprised Pastor Dave, who then got a little choked up himself.

"Sam, I don't know what to say except we prayed about it, and we really felt the Lord wanted us to help you. And like I told your wife when she came to see me, you don't owe us anything. We just hope that you give God the thanks, OK?"

Sam nodded. "So, Denise came to see you? Wow, that is amazing. So, do you believe it? Do believe everything? About the angel and all?"

"Well Sam, we know all things are possible with God, and it sure wouldn't be the first time He'd sent angels to interact with humans. He did it with Hagar in Genesis and in Acts 12 with Peter, and don't forget the Christmas story, when in Luke 2 after Jesus was born, it says there was a multitude of angels praising God. Do you know how much a multitude is?"

"No." Sam shook his head.

"Well neither do I exactly, but when Jesus fed the five thousand plus, the Bible said that was a multitude. Can you imagine 5000 angels appearing in the sky and singing to shepherds? Wow! Man, what a choir that must have been. I wonder if they had a good sound system. Heck Yeah! I guess the hills would have amplified the sound." Pastor Dave seemed to be answering his own questions as he asked them.

Sam laughed loudly and then quickly covered his mouth. "Sorry, you're just funny. I mean cool, in a dorky kind of way; you've got some life in you."

Pastor Dave replied smiling. "Thanks. I think. You know I wish more people knew, the joy the Lord desires for us is often right at our fingertips. No matter what we go through, if we give it all to Him, He'll turn it into something good in His time."

"I don't know too much about that. All I know is what happened to me was real." Sam looked at Pastor Dave sincerely. "Can you give me some of those scriptures to look up?"

Pastor Dave pulled a pen out of his Bible case. "Sure, and we could pray and read a few here if you like. But first I wanted to tell you what happened when your wife came to see me." The pastor lowered his voice.

"Sam, she feels so badly about not believing you. I could tell by our conversation that she loves you very much and she made it clear that she's unsure of where she's at with the Lord." The pastor paused for a moment. "For what it's worth Sam, I think she's very close to giving her life to Him, and maybe, just maybe you're the one who will lead her, Sam, and she could use Him right now, same as you, you know, for all you guys have been going through."

"I wouldn't know how to do that." Sam sputtered nervously. "I've never done anything like that before in my life."

"It's not really hard at all, Sam. It's done more with the heart than with the head. I mean sure, men have fashioned certain formulas over the years, but I don't think the Lord requires perfect words quite as much as He does a pure heart."

"The fact is Sam, you've probably heard it before, that all have sinned and need a Savior, a payment for the penalty all people face because of sin. And sin is simply breaking God's law. Jesus came to be that payment. He completely fulfilled God's law on our behalf. I'm sure you've heard John 3:16 before, but here, at the risk of being redundant, read this, OK?" Sam took the pastor's big Bible and read out loud.

"For God so loved the world, that He gave his only begotten Son, that whosoever believeth in Him should not perish, but have everlasting life. Yeah, I've heard that before," Sam added.

"You see Sam, many people misunderstand that passage, and think 'OK, I believe in Jesus. I'm good to go.' But it means so much more than what we often think *believe* means. What God is telling us is to trust in Him, trust the payment He's made, and then follow Him. The word *believe* when translated back from the Greek it was written in, Sam, means to trust."

"I always did wonder about that," Sam said, "it always seemed too easy before, now that verse makes a lot more sense."

"Yeah well, it means put all your eggs in His basket, so to speak. That's why Jesus said in John 14:6 ... well heck, go ahead and read that too, Sam. We're not in any hurry." Sam smiled, he was enjoying this. No one had ever really shown him things like this before, with the brief exception of Marge, of course. Sam looked like a kid in a candy store. Pastor Dave, from the look on his face was very glad he came. He smiled as Sam read the scripture,

Jesus said to him, I am the way, the truth, and the life: no man cometh unto the Father, but by me.

Sam looked up after reading. "But what about all the other ways and the people who follow them?" he asked.

"God sent one payment, for all time, so that when we receive Him, we welcome Him and are grateful for that gift, and we then stay with that gift. Other ways may kind of help you clean up on the outside, but there's only one way that makes you a brand new person. That's why Jesus said, 'you must be born again' in the 3rd chapter of John. It means being born from above. You have to be a new person to get into heaven. And Jesus is the only payment that God accepts, because in Him, God Himself has paid the price. All other ways are simply us as people trying to reach up, or work our way up. The real way, Sam, the only way that works, is Him reaching down and bringing us up by His power, not our own. It's a little hard to understand, I know. I don't know why I believed, but I believed and then the understanding came."

Sam just looked curious. "Hmmm." Sam handed the Bible back to him.

"But anyway Sam, in regards to Denise, here are some important guidelines if you sense the opportunity to pray with her." Pastor Dave pulled a packet of index cards from his pocket. "Here are some index cards with scriptures on them. They said I could leave these with you." The pastor read from the first card, "1 John 1:9 says, *If we confess our sins, He is faithful and just to forgive us our sins, and to cleanse us from all unrighteousness.*

Sam leaned back against the wall and breathed deep, "So part of salvation means admitting we're sick, so to speak, so He can heal us, right?" Sam said.

"Exactly." Pastor Dave replied and pulled out the next card, "OK, Acts 16:31 says, *if we believe on the Lord Jesus Christ, we and our households will be saved.* So again Sam, it's like trusting in what He's done, even for your family."

Pastor Dave handed the cards he'd read so far to Sam, who held them against his chest like a treasure.

"Another interesting verse," Pastor Dave concluded, "is John 1:12." Pastor Dave read from the card, *But as many as received him, to them gave he power to become the sons of God, even to them that believe on His name.*

"So, if we receive all He says, is and does, and we begin to walk in the new direction, we also receive the Holy Spirit when we ask, and are born again. You see Sam, it's a lot more than saying a few words. It's a life choice. Now if you pray and ask God to show you, I know He'll give you the wisdom to help your wife and, oh by the way, did you know your daughter said she was coming to our youth group?"

Sam's eyes grew really big, "Seriously? Man, miracles just keep coming today, don't they."

"Yeah, we invited Denise and asked her to bring Amanda. We really haven't seen them in church yet. I think that's partly because of Denise trying find Roxanne. But our youth leader called Amanda and she said she would come, and now she's staying with friends of mine from the church while your wife is in Mexico. And, she'll be coming to church with them."

"That is really good news, Pastor. I've been kinda worried about her through all this." Sam sighed deep in thought. "I sure miss her."

"Well Sam, it shouldn't be too long now, and you'll be home with her." the pastor said compassionately, "I want you to know the whole church is praying and believing for you."

"I know, and thanks again for all you've done for us. I'm gonna pay you back everything, I promise."

"You'd better not, Sam. We're doing what we're doing out of love. We don't want anything in return. You trying to spoil our blessing?"

A tear of gratitude slid out of Sam's eye. He tried to keep his composure and extended his hand. "Thank you. Thank you very much. I hope we can be good friends when I get out of here."

Pastor Dave replied, "What do you mean 'when you get out of here'? We can be good friends right now!" Both men laughed.

Pastor Dave stood up. "Well, I guess I'd better get going. My Laura's got some good cookin' going on and she doesn't like me to be late. I'll be in touch though. Guard!'" he called. A uniformed guard came and opened the cell door. Pastor Dave started down the hall. He turned a second later. "God bless you, my friend," he said.

"You too, sir. Thank you." Sam called out as he listened to the footsteps fade down the dim hall.

"Freedom. Thank you Lord, for freedom." He prayed in anticipation. He lay back in the bunk his Bible on his chest. He closed his eyes and dreamed of being free.

The giant red sun was setting on the group's trip to find Roxanne.

"I can't wait to get there and see her," Denise said.

"Less than a day away," Elena added.

"You know this is a long shot, you guys," Don, the cameraman, cautioned.

"What do you mean?" Denise asked, perturbed.

He responded, "People get all kinds of leads like this all the time on missing persons and most of them turn out to be nothing. I just don't want you to get your hopes up just to be disappointed."

"Girls, should we listen to this?" Marge asked.

"No." Maria said.

Denise and Elena shook their heads. "No way," they shouted at the same time.

Marge shouted up to the driver, "You're lucky that steering wheel is in your hands, Mister Cameraman, or my shoe might just find its way upside your head. Get behind me, satan," she shouted, smiling. All the girls laughed.

Don, realizing he was greatly outnumbered and not really meaning any harm, figured it would be better to change his tune. "I bet it's really her," he said. "Can't wait to get there."

At this everyone filled the motor home with the sound of laughter.

Marge suddenly began to belt out a bold rendition of *On Christ The Solid Rock I Stand* raising her hand high to shout, "All other ground is sinking sand, all other ground is sinking sand." The other ladies marveled at the depth of Marge's beautiful voice. They all clapped as Marge finished.

Denise thought for a second. Not knowing any church songs, she then led with the song *High Hopes*. Again they all broke into laughter and applause and then sang another verse.

Leaning against a wall at The Mexican Town restaurant in Detroit, Mildheid was undercover, awaiting instructions. He was dressed as a beggar in worn out human clothes, with fingerless gloves. He also was singing the *High Hopes* song.

Arek was high above the motor home which was now entering Tennessee. He was providing air cover for the protection of the group.

"You're not singing, Arek," Mildheid said from Detroit.

"I don't sing much, Mild One" (Mildheid's nickname).

"Here, how's this?" Arek asked. "Hmm hmm hmmm hmmm, hmmm hmmm, hmmm hmmm, hmmm hmmm." He hummed the tune.

"Better than nothing, I guess." Mildheid was asking strangers for pocket change. "Help the homeless, please?" A couple leaving the restaurant gave him 50 cents. "God bless you," he said to the well-dressed couple.

"God bless you, too! Merry Christmas," they called back to him as they walked on.

"You're not homeless," Arek said to him.

Always quick witted, Mildheid replied, "Does being a couple thousand miles away from home count?"

Arek laughed.

Back in the motor home, Elena was serving turkey and Swiss sandwiches and soda. Denise just about jumped out of her seat when her cell phone went off.

"Denise McBride?" an official sounding voice in broken English asked.

"Yes, this is Denise."

"This is Raymond Blair, from the Consulate in Matamoros, Mexico."

"Hey you guys, keep it down," Denise exclaimed. "It's the ambassador guy from Mexico!" All the ladies came over and tried to press their heads together to hear the conversation.

"Hello, Mrs. McBride, are you there?"

"Yes, I'm here. I'm sorry. Is it her? Did you find out?"

"We found out. Hrrmm," he cleared his throat. Denise grabbed Marge's hand and squeezed. "We found out, Mrs. McBride, that there is someone there and she is comatose. According to the nurses she had been beaten almost to death. We do not know for certain who she is Mrs. McBride, because she does not know who she is, or for that matter, what has happened to her. When she was brought in, she had no identification or money or anything. But she does somewhat fit the description of the photo that your police captain emailed to me. Although," he paused, "it is hard to say for certain because of the extent of the bruising that I saw on her face. She is in stable condition and healing well, but there is no guarantee as to her memory. That is really all I can tell you at this time."

"Oh thank you, Mr Blair! You've been very kind. Will you please call me if you find anything else out?"

"I certainly will, Ma'am.

Hope overflowed Denise's heart as she looked up at the others. Beginning with Marge, the women put their arms around her. Hot tears cascaded down her face as she experienced a deep love she'd not felt in a long time.

17
No Weapon Formed

December 17, 2011

"All rise." the court officer bellowed out. "Court is now in session. The State of Michigan versus Samuel J. McBride. The Honorable Judge Steven P. Malkovich presiding."

Judge Malkovich smiled and nodded to the court officer. The judge then carefully walked up and placed an ice pack on his chair. Unbeknownst to anyone, he had been suffering lately with a severe case of sciatica. *"If anyone said I was a cold judge, they wouldn't be lying,"* he thought, cringing as he sat. He turned on his favorite lamp as the court officer exclaimed, "You may be seated."

The courthouse was packed today. Downtown Detroit looked like a zoo. News crews from all over the country and every conceivable part of the world had converged on the area. They had come to report on the angel story. News had spread fast that the prosecution was not at all successful in eliminating the testimony of the supposed, self-proclaimed angel, Nathanael. Jury selection the previous week had been achieved without any major hiccups, and now the big day was at hand. Jacob Withers and Sam sat behind a long wooden table on the right front side of the courtroom. Prosecutor Foster and a young female intern/assistant sat directly next to them at the prosecution's table to the left.

"Samuel J. McBride, please rise." Sam looked sharp today, neatly dressed in a suit and tie. Sam and Jacob stood up together. The court was quiet; the air felt thin, as if everyone had taken in a deep breath at the same time. The judge looked at Sam. "Samuel J. McBride, you are being charged with murder in the Second Degree, which carries with it a potential life sentence. You are also charged with leaving the scene of a personal injury accident causing death, as well as resisting arrest. Do you understand the charges levied against you today?"

"Yes, Your Honor."

"How do you plead?"

"Not guilty Your Honor, except for resisting arrest, I did do that."

The judge smiled at Sam's seeming forthrightness. He noted his statement on a document in front of him as the stenographer typed rapidly. "Noted. I will enter into the record a not guilty plea on the second degree murder charge, as well as a not guilty plea for leaving the scene, and a guilty plea for resisting arrest. I take it, then, that the prosecution and defense have not been able to come to any plea agreement to keep us from proceeding today?" The judge looked over at Foster.

"Not even close, Your Honor." Foster said with determination written on his face.

Jacob and Sam shook their heads. "No, Your Honor," Jacob Withers said.

"In that case, " the judge intoned, "We will proceed with case #55131B."

"I would like to welcome the ladies and gentleman of the jury. Your instructions will be as follows: You will hear the complete case. The gravest charge is that of second degree murder, according to Act 328 of 1931 of the Michigan Penal Code. This charge does not require that the prosecution proves the murder was premeditated. The prosecution only needs to prove the defendant committed the crime purposefully, even if it was at the last minute in a moment of passion. If you do not understand any of these directions, please raise your hand." None of the twelve jurors did; the judge continued.

"In the second charge, leaving the scene of a personal automobile accident causing death, the prosecution is required to prove that the defendant left the scene of an accident he was involved in, and that death therefore resulted. He does not need to prove the defendant knew that the person died or would die. For the third charge, resisting arrest, the prosecution must prove that the defendant resisted a direct order of the police to cease escape, or to be taken into custody."

The judge took a breath.

Sam thought, *"This is real."*

The judge continued methodically, "I would also cautiously welcome the news media and advise you of the strict rules of this courtroom. You will at no time ask any witness or attorney, officer etc. directly or indirectly any question at all, in this courtroom. What you do outside of this courtroom is your business, with the exception of the jury, stay away from them. We will have no disorder here. You will have complete access to the stenographer's notes. And you may view the video feed also, if you miss anything. If I find that you have, in regards to asking verbal requests, passed notes or any such activity, not only you, but your network, paper, radio station, Internet company or any other entity I may have left out, will be ejected, and be barred from these proceedings. I am allowing you as a guest in my courtroom to report on these proceedings. Pencil and paper or personal recorders only will be permitted.

There will be one general news feed. Furthermore, any individual or their company that I find leaking information that has not yet been brought into testimony in this courtroom, thereby possibly tainting this jury, or causing other such possible harm..," he took another needed breath, "will be first banned from the courtroom permanently and second, charged with contempt and held without bail until these proceedings are fully completed. Please do not test me on this, people." He spoke boldly, looking carefully around the courtroom at the assembled media representatives. Then he shifted in his seat and adjusted his ice pack. "I only want to try this case once."

A heavy sigh and huff were heard following his statements in the courtroom. Judge Malkovich, known for his impeccable sense of hearing, glanced over at the reporters' section. "I'm sorry, did

I hear a complaint?" The reporters sat still, eyes wide, like a bunch of school children caught throwing spitballs in class. They shook their heads and looked at each other nervously.

"I didn't think so." the judge said firmly. "Ladies and gentleman, it is my hope, that we might possibly be finished with this matter before the first of the New Year. If not? That's OK. But I will not be tolerant of foolish attempts to purposely delay this trial. Is that understood …" he looked at Jacob Withers, "by the defense?"

"Acknowledged, Your Honor." Jacob replied.

The judge then looked over at Prosecutor Foster. "And by the prosecution?"

"Yes sir, Your Honor." Foster replied while fumbling through his notes on his yellow legal pad.

"Mr. Withers, do you have your medicine? " the judge asked Jacob in a fatherly way, looking down at him through his bifocal glasses.

"Yes, sir." Jacob responded, feeling a bit foolish.

Foster chuckled under his breath.

"Funny? Mr. Foster, you found something funny? Would you like to share it with the rest of the courtroom?"

"No, sir." Foster now humbled, timidly added, "No, Your Honor, I'm sorry."

"Your apology is accepted for now. I would like to remind you Prosecutor Foster, that you are a worker here, paid by the people of this great state to be professional at all times. Even though your position requires you to be aggressive, I expect you to be fair and just. I will not put up with arrogance and rudeness." The judge looked back to his notes.

Foster stood very still, looking like a deer caught in the headlamps. *"This judge has got it in for me. I don't know why."* he thought." He was, for the first time in his life it seemed, somewhat speechless.

Jacob thought to himself, *"At least he dishes it out evenly."* He almost expected the judge to have heard his thought.

Nathanael, who was sitting right behind him, stunned Jacob when he said. "I did hear it." Jacob turned and gave him a warning glance.

"This is Steven Hinter from Channel 3 News Live at the Wayne County Courthouse. The Angel Trial, as some have dubbed it, has become an international event. And it's about to get under way any minute now. The town is in gridlock with people coming from miles around to try and catch a glimpse of Nathanael, the alleged angel that has grown in popularity since one of the most notorious prosecutors, that being Brent Foster, has not been able to invalidate. We'll keep you posted as the trial unfolds. For now we're going back to the courtroom."

People from around the world had tuned in to this trial one way or another. A young man in Italy listened on a portable radio. In Russia, the prime minister, while drinking his evening tea, had the trial streaming on broadband Internet. The Prince of Wales watched with his family on the wide screen TV. It was the same in Israel, Spain, Jamaica, and countries all over the world. This story had overtaken the world like a firestorm. In Detroit all the highways were backed up. The sports bars, bowling alleys, and restaurants were all filled to capacity. Hundreds of people were packed in behind police barricades. One man had a sign "Free McBride. I hit an angel too! And it wasn't my fault either."

Prosecutor Foster's face was displayed on the TV set, arranging his paperwork and discussing the case with his assistant.

"That's your old man, isn't it, Bryan?" Russ Thomas said to Bryan Foster as they watched the prosecutor in court on the TV set in front of them.

"Sure, if you say so." Bryan responded resentfully.

"You ever talk to him?"

"No, and I don't plan on it. I swore I'd never speak to him again after he cheated on my ma and me. To be honest, man, I really don't want to talk about it."

"Oh, OK. Sure. Sorry." Russ replied uneasily, looking back at the television.

"This is so weird," Bryan thought, after seeing the judge reprimand his dad. *"I've never seen him so scared or unsure of himself."* Both teens continued to glue their eyes to the TV, hoping for a chance to see 'The Angel.'

Brent Foster was almost ready to give his opening statement.

"I would remind everyone that this is an extremely important case that affects the lives of many. The defendant, Samuel McBride, is considered innocent until proven guilty, and that the burden of proof rests on the state." the judge said. "Now to the jury, I would caution you that at this present time there is no body, but there is enough circumstantial evidence to continue. I will not tolerate public displays of emotion. In the unlikely case that anyone does not know how, or is unwilling to control their person in this court of law, they will be removed from the court." Again Judge Malkovich looked slowly around the courtroom before proceeding. "Prosecutor Foster, you may begin with your opening statement."

Foster stood unbuttoning a button on his exquisitely tailored suit and turned deliberately toward the jurors. He slowly made his way from his table to the jury box. "Ladies and gentleman of the jury, this case is not quite as unusual as it may seem. I believe it's as simple as Adam and Eve and an apple in the garden. Most of you here I'm sure, have heard that story. Whether or not you believe every word written in the Bible is not the issue here today. But, I'm sure we'd all agree, there are good moral stories written there about right and wrong. Adam and Eve, when questioned about eating the forbidden fruit …, well folks, they simply lied. All of creation may have turned out differently afterward, had they just told the truth. But, like the defendant, Sam McBride, they would not own up to what they had done."

Don and Linda Stimac sat in their living room watching on their new HDTV. "It's just like the devil to quote scripture," Linda blared out.

"Don't say that, honey. He's just a man and we have to pray for him, too." The Stimacs, a retired couple, had been active in praying for Sam and his family with the church prayer team.

Foster continued, "I am here to prove to you today that Sam McBride, the defendant, is just like Adam. He, quite simply, is unwilling to admit to what he did. And so he fabricated some cockamamie story about hitting some kind of angel to simply escape the consequences of his actions. And lo and behold, we have some man show up actually claiming to be that angel." Foster leaned in toward one of the juror's faces and smiled. "Now I ask you, in today's society, are we really surprised about that?"

The press and the jury began to look around the room, hoping to get a glimpse of Nathanael. A few pointed over near Jacob's area.

Foster crossed in front of the jury like a caged lion. "Now you may or may not believe in angels. If you do, you probably believe in the Biblical accounts like the Christmas story or Easter. However, it's highly unlikely that you, the rational, intelligent, responsible American citizens that you are, believe that angels go around getting hit by cars," Foster turned and pointed at Sam, "driven by irresponsible alcoholics that have just gotten thrown out of their houses for the umpteenth time!"

Jacob Luke Withers jumped up out of his seat. "I object your honor! Alcohol played no part in this case. Tests have shown my client did not have any alcohol in his blood whatsoever. And this man is using flattery to try and butter up the jury."

"Your first objection is sustained, Mr. Withers. Mr. Foster, you will not refer to the accused as an alcoholic. Jury, please disregard that statement. On your second objection? Nice try, Mr. Withers, but flattery is not prohibited, although as Antithenes said, 'It is better to fall among crows than flatterers; for those devour the dead only, these the living'. "

"I object to that, Your Honor," Foster said.

"Tough, Mr. Foster. Antithenes is dead so his words stand." A few people couldn't help but laugh at this.

The judge gave Foster a wave of the hand indicating he should carry on.

Bryan Foster, still watching at home, briefly laughed quietly as he saw the judge outwit his dad. He liked this judge, though he felt unsure what to make of the weakness he saw in his usually stone-strong father. He actually felt a little empathy for him. Puzzled and more fascinated than ever, he leaned closer toward the television set.

Foster continued. "I will also prove that this so called man, Sam McBride," again pointing his finger at Sam, "has a history of irresponsibility and that on the night of the murder, Sam McBride was at the very same bar as the missing person, Roxanne Perello. I will show you that he actually had words with her, that the blood found on the car of the accused was hers, and that a feather in the grill of that very same car came from her jacket. I will show you that she was out walking the very same night of the murder. Now this man, who by his own admission was not too long ago on an alcoholic binge, will tell you that he had a conversation with the Almighty Himself. And that his life was 'all of the sudden' all better because of a brief encounter with what he says was God. Now I believe maybe his conscience was tweaked a bit? When he ran out of money, maybe he got the shakes, had delusions. He came back to the source of his enabling, his wife, Denise McBride. Who by the way is not even here today at her own husband's trial. Doesn't that show you that probably, nothing has really changed for this man? He is a bum, ladies and gentlemen."

Jacob jumped up and shouted, "I object Your Honor! Denise McBride is out trying to find the missing person, Roxanne Perello, as we speak. There was a tip called in that Mrs. Perello might be in

Mexico, and I object to the repeated attacks on my client's character." You could hear all the rapid pencil scratches and papers shuffling from the media as Jacob let the secret out.

"No, I object, Your Honor, This poor excuse for a defense attorney used an objection to plant a thought in the mind of the jury that Roxanne Perello is alive somewhere, when there's not one shred of evidence to that supposition."

Bam! Bam! Bam! The judge slammed his gavel for the first time in this trial. "Mr. Foster you will not use insults, or in any way use your position to degrade people in my courtroom. I do not tolerate bullies. Do you understand me? This is your second and final warning!"

"Yes sir."

"Now apologize to Attorney Withers."

"But your Honor…" Foster whined.

"It was not a question, Mr. Foster."

"I'm sorry, Mr. Withers." Foster said, red faced, looking down so that the anger in his eyes could not be seen. Jacob graciously smiled in reply, assuring Foster he was forgiven.

"And Mr. Foster, you don't need to say Sam McBride's name every time you refer to him. Simply referring to him as 'the defendant' will do. We all know his name by now." Brent Foster nodded humbly to the judge in reply.

Bryan Foster, confused, still watching the trial, had an uncanny urge to help his dad whom he had such hatred for many years now.

"And now we'll take one objection at a time, gentlemen. The jury will disregard the remark made by the prosecutor as to the absence of Mrs. McBride in the courtroom. Furthermore, the jury will disregard the defense remarks about reports of Mrs. Perello being alive."

Jacob had a sparkle in his eye; he knew the jury would not be able to completely dismiss the fact that Roxanne might be alive.

Sam grinned as Jacob continued. He had worried a little at first about Jacob's abilities, but he could see plain as day that Jacob was on his game. Sam looked behind him at Nathanael, who just smiled knowingly.

Brent Foster continued. "And then they had to taser Sam McBride to stop him from running." Foster paced back and forth. "Does that sound like an innocent man to you? It doesn't to me. I intend to prove to you that Samuel McBride, in a fit of selfish, careless rage, out of revenge and anger at Angelo Perello for calling his wife Denise, thereby helping him to get thrown out of his house, I will prove that he purposely sped into Roxanne Perello causing her death. I will provide an eyewitness that saw the whole event and when she confronted Mr. McBride, he just sped off. Now, somehow Sam McBride, or if I may, 'the defendant,' got rid of the body which he must have put in his trunk, and then disposed of it before the police forcibly stopped him in a roadblock on I-94."

Foster quickly turned and looked each juror in the eye. "In spite of the fact that Roxanne Perello's body has not been found, ladies and gentlemen, I am fully convinced that when you see the enormity of the evidence against the defendant, and hear the witness' testimony, you will see beyond a shadow of a doubt that he is guilty. At the very least, you will be able to convict him of leaving the scene of an auto accident thereby causing death, and at the most, second degree murder."

Foster pointed directly at Nathanael, "I also intend to prove that this so called angel is a phony, and that this lame defense attorney has purposely orchestrated his participation to show doubt. I also intend to hold accountable any and all parties to this intended deception against this courtroom." With that last statement Foster shot a dirty look at Jacob Withers, then he slowly turned his head back toward the front of the courtroom and addressed the judge. "That would be all for now, Your Honor."

"No, that's not all, Mr. Foster. I am charging you with contempt of court. You have just libeled the defense attorney for the last time, and now, you sir, will be held accountable. I am charging you to remain in custody for 24 hours and pay a $1000 dollar fine. You may instruct your assistant to carry on for the rest of the day. If Mr. Withers is willing to forgive your slander and continue to try and work with you, you will have one more chance to operate in this court. But I will not have crimes committed in my courtroom by those who are entrusted to uphold the law. Officer, please take Prosecutor Foster into custody." All the air was sucked out of the court as everyone drew a breath, stunned by the judge's boldness.

"But! But I ..." Brent Foster could not find one word to say as he was escorted from the courtroom. "Come see me right after court, Sheila," he shouted to his assistant.

Bryan Foster asked, "Dad, what are you doing?" as he watched his dad become humiliated on national TV.

"Mr. Withers, are you prepared to give your opening statement?" Judge Malkovich asked.

"Yes, Your Honor. I am." Jacob Withers nodded to the judge and turned to the jury box.

"Ladies and gentlemen of the jury," Jacob looked at the assembled jurors, bowed his head toward them in a dignified manner. "Hello," he greeted the jury warmly. "My client has done many things he is not proud of. He has been an alcoholic. He has been a terrible husband and father. He has been irresponsible and unfaithful."

Sam McBride stood and shouted, "I object, Your Honor. I have never been unfaithful to my wife!" He looked at Jacob with surprise in his eyes.

"Sit down, Mr. McBride," the judge shouted. "You can't object to your own attorney. You can't object at all. Now sit down and be quiet." Sam meekly sat down. The judge shook his head in frustration, and then adjusted his ice pack.

"I do take that back though, and I apologize, Sam. What I meant to say, ladies and gentleman, is that he has not been faithful in providing for his family, in setting an example, in being the man of the house. On those points I think Sam would agree." Sam slightly nodded his head in agreement, somewhat relieved at the clarification.

A couple of the ladies on the jury give each other an approving look, clearly thinking about what Sam McBride had said in regards to his wife.

Jacob continued, "But there is one thing Sam McBride is not. He is not in any way a person who could kill someone, or anything for that matter, and then hide the body. Sam McBride, as you'll see for yourself, is a gentle soul. He has never hit his wife or his child. He has never even killed an animal. If Sam had actually hit even a small animal, much less a person, anyone that knows Sam knows that he would have stayed there to help. Now," Jacob looked and smiled at Sam, "he may have been found to be weak in many areas, but he has never been violent. I intend to prove to you that what Sam hit was not a human or an animal. I intend to show you that it was possibly exactly what he says, an angel. And, that no one was harmed, that there was no body there to take care of, or Sam would have stayed.

The beautiful thing about our criminal justice system is that a man is innocent until proven guilty. That is meant to assure that neither you or I will ever be found guilty and go to jail for something we did not do. That is what Sam holds on to, people of the jury. I'm very glad that Prosecutor Foster said he would prove that Sam is guilty and that Nathanael is a fraud because that's exactly what he has to do. He has to prove things. If there's even a shadow of a doubt, then you must find Sam McBride not guilty. Thank you, ladies and gentleman, and thank you, Your Honor." Jacob nodded to the judge that he was finished.

"Ladies and gentlemen," the judge intoned, "in light of the special circumstances involving the prosecution, court is now adjourned until 9:00 a.m. December 20th." As the judge got up to leave, applause erupted in the courtroom. Judge Malkovich turned around quickly and the applause ended just as quickly as it began. The judge picked up his gavel and ice pack, paused for a second, sighed and again, he just shook his head as he left the court for his quarters.

18
MEXICO

The motor home slowed for the stop sign, and about thirty screaming children ran up hands held out, begging for money. The sign in Spanish letters read "Alto." Denise and the news team had come into the town of Matamoros, Tamaulipas, Mexico. The children, many dirty and dishevlled-looking, smiled and cried out, "Americano, dinero, por favor." Watching out the window, Denise realized they were asking for money. They had probably been sent out to beg by their parents, if they were fortunate enough to have parents. This thought saddened Denise as she realized how good her life was in comparison.

"God, forgive me for ever complaining," she thought. Even though the McBrides had struggled in the past, they had never actually starved. Denise retrieved a U.S. $20 bill from her purse, opened the window, and handed it to a little girl about the age of five. "Gracias, mujer bonita, (Thank you, beautiful woman)," she said and smiled, a front tooth missing. She quickly ran with the money, causing some of the kids to take off after her. Others stayed, hands outstretched, voices raised, hoping there was more. But the motor home was moving again. The kids ran after it for about twenty feet until the next car pulled up at the stop sign, then they turned back.

Although the area was very tropical and lush in some areas, there were a lot of dilapitated homes, some were only shacks.

Denise had done a little research on the town as they traveled. The motor home was eqipped with satellite internet, as well just as just about every other electronic device necessary for a news crew. Denise had learned that in the year 1826, the governor had named the city Villa de Matamoros to honor the War of Independence hero, Don Mariano Matamoros. Years prior, however, in 1793, college missionaries from a Catholic order similar to the Fransiscan monks had named the area, Villa De Refugio (which means City of Refuge). When Denise told Marge this, Marge replied, "See honey, I don't thinks it's any accident she wound up here. The Lord is our refuge. I don't think we're ever going to forget this journey. Amen?"

"Amen!" Denise smiled comforted by Marge's faith. She was growing attached to Marge, so animated and full of life. She hoped they would be life-long friends.

Following the mission hospital signs, the coach pulled up at Santos Degollado Street and turned right. About 1½ miles down Stone Road, they pulled up slowly in front of what looked like an old Spanish fort surrounded by trees. A huge cornfield graced the left side of the mission. They parked off to the side of the road.

The cameraman, Don Rossellini, who was also now the driver, was affectionately referred to by Elena as "Don Won." Maria was certain Elena had a sparkle in her eye for him.

Don and Maria quickly readied the camera gear.

Marge, seeing their journalistic appetite for this story, walked over to Maria and Denise and politely asked, "Excuse me, I want to ask you and Denise a favor?"

With raised eyebrows and the brazenness Maria was famous for, she gave Marge a "what now?" look.

"Sure Marge, what is it?" Denise asked, giving Maria a harsh gaze, reminding her that this was her project. Maria looked away.

Marge answered, "From what we know from talking to the ambassador and all, this young lady doesn't even know who she is, where she's at, or anything." Marge paused. "And she's probably scared out of her mind. So please, before we all barge in there with these big cameras and microphones and questions and all, could I go in alone and just talk softly with her? Maybe say a prayer and ease her into all this?"

Denise agreed immediately, "I trust you, Marge. You let us know when you're ready and then we'll come in."

Elena, always the optimist, had a great idea. "Hey! We could take some shots of the building and trees and people and stuff for back story while Marge is in there with her."

"Don't get too ahead of yourself, Elena," Maria, tired from the long trip, warned her.

"Don, I want you to get some shots of the area, buildings, scenery etc ..."

"That's what I just ...."

Maria cut Elena off in mid-sentence. "Elena, come with me. We're going to use your Spanish to try and set up an interview with whoever is in charge of this place."

"That would be Mother Superior, Sister Mary Elizabeth," Elena said. "She said she'd help with whatever we need. "

"OK, Mary Poppins. Whatever. Let's go find her!" Maria strode away.

"OK." Elena responded, skipping along joyfully.

Maria rolled her eyes, already annoyed at Elena's "over the top" enthusiasm.

"I'm just going to stay here for a few minutes, OK?" Denise said. "I'll meet you guys inside."

"OK." Maria said looking over her shoulder. They walked into the hospital thirty feet behind Marge.

At the end of a long hallway, Marge was led to a room by Sister Anna. She took a moment to study the architecture and décor before going in. The cleanliness and old world beauty of this castle-like mission hospital was astonishing. Before entering the room of the person they hoped was Roxanne, Marge took a deep breath, and then slowly walked in. The air smelled of clean linen and held a light flowery fragrance she couldn't quite identify.

"I've done a great many things in the Lord's service," she thought, *"but this amnesia ministry thing is brand new to me."* She prayed softly, "Lord, please help me."

Inside the brightly sunlit room, Marge was further amazed by its simple beauty. A soft warm breeze blew lightly against the gold flecked sheer curtains. Cut flowers in a vase on a wrought iron, glass-topped table off to the side were beautifully displayed. Directly behind the table was a brilliantly colored renowned painting of Saint Francis of Assisi preaching to the ocean with fish jumping out of the water and tropical birds flying overhead to hear the message.

Near the bed stood a Victorian chair upholstered in gold with a luxuriously woven brown afghan draped on the back. It looked like it had been put there for visitors as well as for the nuns who often read to their patients. Marge took off her floppy purple hat and set it on the chair. The woman lying in the hospital bed had not moved or made a sound. Marge held in her hand a picture of Roxanne that Captain Franks had sent them in an email. Cautiously, she walked to the right side of the bed and breathed out a soft, "Hello." There was no response. Again she tried, "Hello."

Slowly a bruised eyelid opened and then the other eye…just a little. A blood-bruised, weak voice softly whispered back, "Hi." The woman licked her lips with the tip of her tongue, and then closed her eyes again.

Marge took another deep breath and hesitantly spoke again.

"Hi, umm, look. I know you're trying to rest and all, and really I'm sorry to bother you, but some friends of mine and myself … umm," now Marge licked her lips and hurried on, "we've come hundreds of miles to see you. You see, we think you're this person in this picture, Roxanne Perello. Does that mean anything to you?"

The woman on the bed had deep cuts on her lips and face; the skin on her face, neck and arms was deeply bruised. Some of her hair was missing. Slowly, painfully, she opened her swollen eyes again and looked up at Marge then smiled weakly. Suddenly her bruises didn't look quite as bad as they had moments before.

Her eyes lit up as she spoke. "The sisters here have been really good to me; they told me you were coming and that you guys thought I was some missing person or something…that you might take me back with you." She stopped; a painful and pleading look crossed her face before she continued. "To be honest with you, I can't remember anything except somebody hitting me and kicking me in my head … and me screaming and begging them to stop. But …" a sob escaped her throat, "they just kept beating me, and that's all I know." Her eyes filled with tears as she recounted that night. "The nuns told me someone found me in a ditch somewhere and brought me here. But I don't even remember that."

"You take it easy, honey. I'm here to help. If you are Roxanne Perello," Marge stated gently but firmly, "it's very important that we bring you back with us because there's a man there that is in court right now for your murder, and you're the only one who can save him."

"I wish I did know. I wish I could remember," she whispered.

"Can I show you this picture?" Marge held out the photo. The woman took it in her left hand with the IV tube hanging in the air as she did so.

"That person in the picture looks kinda like me, but she's much prettier. I'm so ugly. I don't even want to look at myself."

"You're not ugly, honey. You've just been through a lot. The sister said you should make a full recovery. Once you heal up, you'll be pretty again. Hey, can I ask you a favor?"

"All right," the patient replied.

Marge asked sweetly, "Could I pray for you?"

"OK." the young lady replied.

Marge slowly knelt down on the floor, grateful for her knees' sake that there was a big hand woven Spanish style rug beside the bed.

"Oh Lord, I think we've found your missing person, but I'm not positive. Either way Lord, this child needs you." Marge's words became lost in her tears as her heart went out toward this young lady. At this the young lady opened her left eye, then the right, and saw that Marge was weeping for her. She was touched deeply that a stranger could care about her that much. Marge continued. "Please Lord, touch this life, this soul, this body with your warm healin' love. Give her back her memory, show us all, what you want us to do. In Jesus name, Amen."

"That was nice," the patient gently replied. "I'm kinda tired now," she whispered, her voice fading.

"All right, child, we're gonna let you rest. I'll keep the wolves at bay and check in on ya in an hour or two."

"Wolves?" she asked.

"Just a figure of speech," Marge replied as she began to leave the room.

"Hey!" the young lady's weak voice cried out as she tried to sit up but couldn't. "What's your name?"

Marge, knowing she had already told her, realized that, for a while, she may have to tell her again and again. "Marguerite Marie Ashton is my name, but my friends call me Marge or large Marge. And I'd like to be your friend if that's all right?" She pulled out a pen and paper from her purse and added just a touch of her anointing oil. She wrote something down, walked back over and handed it to the woman.

"Sure." the young lady replied. "I could use a friend or two." She smiled a frail smile.

Marge handed her the paper, then left the room.

The woman held the paper in her hand for a second and looked at it carefully.

It read,

Sleep with the angels, child. I too am on your side. - your friend Marge.

Tears filled her eyes as she clutched the paper in her hand, and then, ever so slowly, and grimacing in pain, she put it up against her face. She felt its caress, and then she carefully rolled over on her left side and rested. Marge, who was watching just outside the doorway, quietly closed the door.

19
CAN I GET A WITNESS

December 20, 2011

A media cloud enveloped the court and the city like a tropical storm. All the world really was a stage for this court's cast of characters: Sam, Jacob Luke and Mr. Foster, not forgetting Nathanael and his mostly invisible friends. Sam prayed for Denise's safety. Denise and Marge still far away, prayed continually for Sam, and everyone was praying for Roxanne, except of course Mr. Foster, who didn't pray at all, but mostly complained. Yet unknown to him, some were praying on his behalf.

This case had drawn the interest of every type of person on the planet. There were angel enthusiasts bringing little statues and placing then on the courthouse steps and an angry lady carrying flowers and a large picture of Roxanne on a piece of cardboard with the caption, "Justice for Roxanne! Fry Sam McBride!" Then there were the atheists, some picketing the fact the court still used a Bible to swear on. "Bibles in court are unconstitutional," the sign said. Another read, "Creatures that don't exist shouldn't be allowed to testify," referring to the judge's decision to allow Nathanael's testimony. A few mocking youths wore the kind of angel wings one would find in a costume shop. But there were other youths there that were praying, kneeling on the court house steps.

The judge, not one for the spotlight, knew he'd have to endure it. He took the bench again, ice pack in hand, and there was the usual "please rise, please sit" fanfare. He didn't want to embarrass Prosecutor Foster any further, and decided not to mention the last time they were in court together. Peering over his spectacles, he greeted the attorneys with respect. "Mr. Foster, Mr. Withers, nice to see you today, gentleman. Is the prosecution prepared to call its first witness?"

"Yes, Your Honor. The state calls Mrs. Janine Lee. And Your Honor, I would like to ask that you and Mr. Withers and Mr. McBride," he paused and genuinely smiled, looking over at Jacob and Sam, "I ask that you would accept my apologies."

Bryan Foster who was watching the trial at home was mesmerized. "I've never seen him do that," he stated out loud, referring to his dad's apology.

"Thank you, Mr. Foster. Yes, now that is in the past. I have great hopes for the future, gentleman," the judge said. Jacob Luke and Sam smiled back at Foster. There was peace in the courtroom today, you could feel it. A couple angelic messengers were on the roof keeping watch.

Frail Mrs. Lee, leaning heavily on her cane, walked slowly up to the witness stand. She painfully lowered herself onto the chair. Breathing heavily, she took off her glasses and cleaned then with a tissue from her purse. The court officer held out a Bible and asked her, "Mrs. Lee, do you promise to tell the truth, and nothing but the truth, so help you God?"

"I do. And thank you for asking, young man," she added. The officer then took his usual position on the side of the bench.

Foster approached the witness, manila folder in hand. Opening it slowly, he glanced over at the jury and smiled. He hoped to win them over. He needed a quick victory, and wanted to impress them immediately.

"Hello Mrs. Lee, how are you today?"

"Good, Mr. Foster, it's nice to see you again, dear."

"And you as well, Mrs. Lee. You reside at 413 Bemis Road, Belleville, Michigan, is that correct?"

"Yes. Well mostly, sir," she replied sweetly, hands folded in her lap. "My home is actually in Van Buren Township, but it has a Belleville mailing address, and many people consider the whole area, the Belleville area." She smiled.

"Mrs. Lee, where were you on the night of Friday, November 19?"

"I was in my living room watching the television."

"And do you remember what you were watching?"

"Yes, I was watching *Jeopardy* with Alex Trebek. I like Alex, he's so sweet, don't you think?" she said smiling.

"I think we all do, Mrs. Lee. And what happened that night while you were watching TV?"

"Well, it was snowing and just terrible out. I was glad I didn't have to go anywhere. I was eating my dinner watching Alex. All of the sudden I heard the sound of brakes screeching, so I looked out the window and I saw this tan car just as it hit someone. So I got up and I got my cell phone that I always keep right beside me, and dialed 911. My son, Dean, got me the cell phone so that way if I ever got stranded or lost or someone tried to hurt me, or tried to break into the house, God forbid, I could call Dean right away."

"OK, yes, and then, Mrs. Lee?"

"Oh …Yes. I dialed 911 and went out the side door. I don't use the front, you know, because I try and keep the carpet nice. Carpet is so expensive these days and I'm on a fixed income, you know, since my husband died in …"

"Yes, Mrs. Lee." Foster interrupted, becoming frustrated. "What happened after you went out the side door?"

"Let's see. I went down the driveway still talking to a nice person at 911, telling them what just happened. And that man," she said pointing to Sam McBride, "he was standing outside of the car!" Her voice became shrill. "And when I said, 'you killed that man, where is he, what did you do with the body?' he said for me to mind my own business. He called me an old bat and he got into his car and drove off in such a hurry." She huffed, and turned back toward the prosecutor.

"Your Honor, please let the court enter into evidence that the witness identified the accused as the driver of the car."

"So entered," the judge nodded. You could hear the clicking of the keys as the stenographer typed rapidly.

"Now you just said 'that man'? Mrs. Lee, you told me in your deposition, you didn't know if it was a man or a woman that was hit by the car, isn't that correct?"

"Yes, that's right," she said pursing her lips in thought, then nodding her head. "Thank you for correcting me. From my house I couldn't tell if it was a man or a woman."

"And this person, Mrs. Lee, had on a long white coat and brown boots. Is that correct?"

"Objection your Honor, leading the witness." Jacob Withers cried out.

"I'll allow it for now Mr. Withers, if you find her present testimony different from that of her deposition, we'll strike it. You may answer the question, Mrs. Lee."

"Yes. It was definitely a long white coat, with feathers, I think and yes, brown boots."

"Did Mr. McBride tell you he hadn't hit a person, that it was an angel?" A mocking tone played in Foster's voice as he partially turned toward the jury box and lifted one eyebrow.

"Objection, Your Honor, again leading!"

"Objection sustained. Please, Mr. Foster, direct questions. Now rephrase your question."

"What did the defendant say, Mrs. Lee?"

"He just told me to mind my own business and then he drove off. You see, I think we all have a responsibility to look after each other and to obey the law, and my neighbor tells me to mind my own business too, when I try and keep his wife, Judy, informed about what's going on in the community. But I think we need to watch out for our community. Don't you?" She looked over at the jury for approval, and one of the jurors actually shook her head in agreement."Anyway, I think he was drinking and that's what caused it all."

"Did he say anything at all about an angel?"

"No, young man, he did not."

"Thank you, Mrs. Lee."

"It's well known that he's an alcoholic, you know." She sniffed the air and turned her whole body in her chair to face Sam, shooting him an accusing stare.

"That will be all. Thank you, Mrs. Lee!" Foster's voice rose as if to make her hear better. "Your Honor, no more questions for this witness at this time."

"Do you wish to cross, Mr. Withers?" Judge Malkovich asked.

"You bet, Your Honor, I mean yes, Your Honor." Jacob stood up and approached the witness stand to address Mrs. Lee. He stood on the right side of the witness box, facing the people and jury, so everyone could see both his and Mrs. Lee's faces during the questioning.

"Good morning, Mrs. Lee." Jacob smiled pleasantly. "How are you today?"

"Fine sir, thank you."

"Mrs. Lee, the glasses you're wearing, they are prescription, are they not?"

"No. They're just reading glasses. My eyes are fine, they're just old."

"And did you have your glasses on while you were watching TV?"

"No, I did not," she said with annoyance. "I don't use them to watch the TV."

"OK. Thank you. And the distance between your house and the edge of Bemis Road, would you say that was about twenty-five or thirty feet, maybe?"

"Yes, that sounds about right."

Foster quickly spoke up. "Objection Your Honor, leading the witness!"

"Sustained. Rephrase your question, Mr. Withers."

"Mrs. Lee, about how far would you say it was from your house to the edge of Bemis Road?"

"About 25 to 30 feet."

Jacob smiled over at Foster, turned and questioned Janine Lee again.

"Well actually Mrs. Lee, according to public records your house sits 80 feet from Bemis Road and your chair for television watching is right against your front window. Am I correct?"

"No, actually I keep it about three feet from the window to keep from getting a draft."

"And did you get up to see the accident, or did you see it from your chair?"

"I saw it from my chair." The lines in her face stiffened.

"So Mrs. Lee, would it be safe to say that since your house is eighty feet away from the road, and your chair is three feet away from the window, and having, as you say 'old eyes' and you were wearing no glasses," Jacob walked to the jury as he said this, "and it was a dark, snowy, drizzly, foggy night…would it be safe to say, that you're really not sure what you saw get hit?" Jacob was looking the jury in the eye as he said this.

"Well," she hesitated, "I'm pretty sure it was a person."

"And the coat, you said you were pretty sure that it had feathers on it when asked by Mr. Foster."

"Yes, it seemed like a feathery coat."

"Pretty sure? Please make a note of this ladies and gentleman of the jury, that we don't convict people of murder in this country on 'pretty sure' testimony."

"One last question, Mrs. Lee. It would be very much against my client's character to lie to anyone, and he's not known in the community as a rude man, but rather as a very polite man. It would be very unusual for him to tell someone to 'mind their own business.'" Are you sure he didn't say 'Ma'am, you don't understand. It wasn't a man. I didn't kill anyone.' Didn't he say something like that?"

"Objection, Your Honor, speculative and leading." Foster shouted. "The defendant's character has not been established."

"I'll leave it for now," the judge smiled down at Mrs. Lee. "Please answer the question, Mrs. Lee."

Shaking her finger in Jacob Luke's direction she blared out, "Are you calling me a liar, young man?"

"No Ma'am. I apologize if it sounded that way, but you already said your neighbor's husband often tells you to mind your own business, and I just thought, perhaps, you were confused as to what my client 'actually' said to you. Perhaps you'd gotten things misconstrued. As you did when you said it was 25 to 30 feet to the road when actually it was 83 feet. And also how you said you believed Sam McBride was drinking even though there wasn't a trace of alcohol in him, on him, or near him. I think possibly you've seen and heard things wrong Mrs. Lee, not necessarily on purpose."

"Oh, I don't know … I sometimes do get confused," she said, sounding more uncertain. Foster hung his head in defeat as Jacob appeared to have gutted his only eyewitness testimony.

"I guess he might have said what you said. But," she persisted, "if he's so innocent, why did he drive away?" She frowned, defensively folding her arms in front of her.

"Good question, Mrs. Lee. I'm glad you asked it." Jacob walked over to the jury. "Maybe he actually hit an angel and the angel disappeared and he knew no one would ever believe him. No further questions, Your Honor." Jacob sat down. Sam was intensely grateful for the job Jacob was doing, and he gave Jacob a reassuring smile that said just that.

Judge Malkovich looked over to Prosecutor Foster. "Your turn, Mr. Foster."

"Your Honor, the State calls Angelo Perello."

Angelo fully attired in his black leather, black boots, and fully greased black hair, took the stand.

Foster greeted him. "Good morning, Mr. Perello."

"Hi, how ya' doin'?" Angelo replied with his usual 'I could care less' attitude.

"I'm fine thank you," Foster replied. "Mr. Perello, on the night of Friday November 19, where were you?"

"I was at The Eagle's Nest bar with Roxanne having some drinks with the guys."

"And did you see the defendant, Sam McBride, there?"

"Yeah, he was at the bar having a drink, and me and Roxanne and the guys were over by the pool table putting some away, ya know, getting a little stoked, shootin' some pool."

"Is Sam McBride in the room, and if so could you please identify him?"

"Yeah, that's him over there sitting right by that lawyer Withers." Angelo pointed at Sam McBride.

"Let the record indicate Mr. Perello positively identified the defendant, Sam McBride, as being in the same bar as Roxanne on the night of the murder."

"So entered," the judge said.

"And did Roxanne or you have any conversation with the defendant?"

"Yeah, I saw Roxanne havin' a word with him on her way back from the head."

"From the head?" Foster asked.

"Yeah, the bathroom, you know the head, the john, the porcelain palace, the commode." Angelo placed his finger in his ear as though he might be searching for something. A few of the jury frowned in disgust. Angelo was never much for etiquette.

"And do you know what they talked about?" Foster asked.

"Objection Your Honor. Hearsay," Jacob said from his chair.

Angelo quickly spoke belligerently over Jacob's objection. "Yeah, I think he was tryin' to put the moves on her, and she backed him down."

"Again Your Honor, please, I object. We're not here for what he 'thinks' she said."

"Objection sustained. The jury will disregard Mr. Perello's last statement. Mr. Perello, if you don't know what she said, please, just say 'I don't know.'"

"I donno." Angelo said to the judge sarcastically.

"Please address the jury Mr. Perello, not me."

Angelo suddenly stood up, his face became red. "I don't know what they said to each other, all right?" He sat back down.

Taken aback, the judge gave a concerned look to the court officer, who smiled back slightly indicating he understood the unsaid command, he was to watch Angelo Perello closely.

"And afterward, when did Sam McBride leave the bar?" Foster continued.

"He left right after that." Angelo's tone calmed a little, though he gave a spiteful look to the court officer just for fun.

"And then what?"

"Well, I made a phone call to Denise McBride, cause she's a nice lady and I thought she should know her old man was in there drinking when he was supposed to be on the wagon. Ya know, I wanted to warn her – as a friend." He practically purred as he spoke of Denise.

"And then?" Foster asked.

"Then Roxanne made a wise crack. So out of respect for the patrons there at The Nest, we went outside to talk out our differences ... if ya know what I mean, and Roxanne decided she was gonna go home, and that's the last I'd seen her." Angelo cursed under his breath.

One of The Fallen, called Rage, was there enticing Angelo to anger, whispering evil thoughts in his ear, seeing this, Mildheld quickly drew his sword, ready to strike.

"No Mildheld, Rage is there by Angelo's own volition. If you take him out, you'll only be asking for more to come." Nathanael spoke without moving his lips. Mildheld sheathed his sword.

Angelo stood up giving in to Rage's enticement, "You're gonna pay, McBride. They're gonna fry you!" He sneered.

"Order, Mr. Perello!" Judge Malkovich shouted. "I am warning you! We don't tolerate outbursts like that in my courtroom! I will not tell you again. Now sit down!"

Angelo shot the judge an evil look.

"No further questions, Your Honor." Foster said anxiously.

"Your witness, Mr. Withers," the judge sighed.

Jacob slowly walked to the witness box.

"Good morning, Mr. Perello."

"Yeah? What's good about it?" Angelo replied, with his usual disgust for lawyers, and all authority for that matter. His face agreed with his tone, he had a snarled, sour look.

"So, Mr. Perello, please refresh my memory on the night of November 19, 2011, what time did you and Roxanne arrive at the bar?"

"I think about six o'clock."

"Now you said in your deposition statement that Sam McBride left that same bar at about 6:20. Correct?"

"Yeah, I think that's what I said."

"And that Roxanne left at 6:30, right?"

"Yeah, what about it? Look, we've been through this Jake, what are you getting at?"

"Your Honor, would you please instruct the witness to address me as Mr. Withers? There is only one person in my life I allow to address me as Jake. From anyone else I take it as a sign of disrespect." At this, Prosecutor Foster gave his famous sigh and roll of his eyes.

"Mr. Perello," the judge said. "You will address both counsels politely as sir or mister. Also you will only answer the questions, not ask them." Angelo merely stared at the judge, anger narrowing his eyes.

"Mr. Perello, have you ever struck your wife?" Jacob asked.

Foster spoke up. "Objection Your Honor, irrelevant. Mr. Perello is not on trial here!"

"Where are you headed with this, Mr. Withers?" the judge asked.

"Your Honor, I am trying to illustrate that Roxanne may have had good reasons to leave Mr. Perello, that she might possibly have been abused by him ... that she may be only missing, and not dead at all."

"Answer the question, Mr. Perello." Judge Malkovich ordered.

"Yeah, I mighta gave her some extra encouragement to be lady-like at times, 'cause she had a mouth on her, ya' know?" Angelo gritted his teeth and puffed out his cheeks.

"Does that mean you hit her?"

"I guess so. What do you think it means? That I bought her a present, a gift?"

"Mr. Perello," the judge warned.

"In the face? On the arm? Where did you hit her?" Jacob asked.

"I backhanded her a coupla times."

"And did she ever call the police?"

"Yeah, she called 'em once."

"Your Honor, I'd like to enter into evidence defense item 1- B, a police report dated July 7, 2008. The report states that police were called to the Perello home where Angelo Perello was arrested for domestic violence after he hit his wife in the face with his hands, causing a bloody lip and a small cut above her eye."

"So entered."

"She dropped the charges. Correct, Mr. Perello?"

"That's right," he answered callously.

"Why do you think that was, that she dropped the charges?"

"'Cause she loved me and wanted it to work."

"You didn't threaten to kill her if she pressed charges?"

"No way. Are you crazy? She's my girl; I could never really hurt her."

"Well, I have here a signed statement from Debra Rivers, the lady Roxanne called her adopted mother. Please enter into evidence Document 2. I am reading from line 7. 'Roxanne told me that Angelo said if she testified against him, it'd be the last time she'd ever testify against anyone.'"

"Did you tell Roxanne that, Mr. Perello?" The whole court seemed to be holding their breath, anticipating Angelo's reply.

"No, I never said that."

"Do I have to bring Mrs. Rivers in here to testify in person, Mr. Perello?"

"I don't care what you and that *#@* do. I ain't on @%# trial here."

Angelo spewed out a line of profanities that put the judge over the edge. He slammed his gavel down on the bench.

"Thirty days, Mr. Perello. Officer, you will take Mr. Perello immediately to the Wayne County Jail. I warned you, sir."

Jacob Withers was so happy at that, the old rock song, *Thirty Days in the Hole* was going through his mind. In his imagination, he was dancing to it.

The court officer quickly handcuffed Angelo. Infuriated, Angelo struggled shouting, "I'm warning you! You ain't no $ # @ judge! This is a kangaroo court. You're frickin Captain Kangaroo, you #

@ !" On that last note, the court officer strong armed him through a side door. The judge, sweating, wiped his brow. The media feed, broadcast across the nations, had many people all over the world, speculating about whether it was actually Angelo Perello who had killed his wife.

The jury and the media took notes on this latest twist in the case. Fortunately, the judge, fearing some kind of impassioned display, had hired a specialist for the media feed who bleeped out Angelo's expletives before they could be heard by the viewers.

This trial was becoming one of the most talked about news items around the world. With Angelo now viewed as a possible suspect, news anchors began to speculate with various guest experts as to what exactly had Sam McBride hit? Could it possibly have been an actual angel? The search for Roxanne grew stronger. There were new sightings and reports coming into the police station every day. Someone even said she had been spotted in Rome, Italy just walking down the street.

"I'm sorry to interrupt your cross, Mr. Withers, but this is a court of law, and I will have order in my court." Jacob merely smiled gratefully back at the judge.

A few of Heaven's Warriors on the courthouse roof high-fived each other as they saw Angelo escorted into a Wayne County Police van.

"We have to stop this," a large, grubby, bloodshot-eyed demon on a neighboring building said. "This has not turned in our favor at all. This will turn too many toward Him if we don't do something."

20
REJOICING IN HEAVEN

Pastor Dave had been leading the efforts to get all the churches across Metro Detroit praying for Sam and Roxanne. He seemed to have an understanding of the bigger picture regarding the trial and the publicity that came with it. He emailed every church he found in the phone book to ask for their prayers. His letter didn't dictate how to pray, but simply asked them to seek that God would be glorified through it all. An unusual unity amongst these diverse churches was forming. Most churches regardless of denominational affiliation began to share in prayer and worship.

The courtroom was peaceful now that Angelo Perello was gone.

"Call your next witness, Mr. Foster." the judge nodded to the prosecutor.

Foster stood. "The State calls forensic expert, Brian Anderson."

A bushy-bearded, rather disheveled looking young man dressed in blue jeans and a un-tucked blue striped button up shirt, casually made his way to the witness box.

The new court officer, a woman named Bethany, had temporarily replaced the officer in charge of escorting Angelo Perello from the courtroom. She asked Mr. Anderson, "Do you promise to tell the truth, the whole truth and nothing but the truth, so help you God?"

"I don't know about the help me God thing, but yes, I will tell the truth," he said, unwilling to put his hand on the Bible. The officer looked for approval from the judge and the judge nodded. Prosecutor Foster then walked up to the witness stand.

"Mr. Anderson, you are a specialist in DNA typing for the Lansing State Police. Is that correct?"

"Yes, that is correct." He said, stroking his beard.

"How long have you served in that capacity?"

"I've worked in Lansing for twelve years. But I taught at Boston University for five years, prior to my position with the crime lab here."

"Did you test the DNA from the blood that was found on the automobile bumper that Mr. McBride was driving on the night in question?"

"I did, yes."

"And you also tested the hair sample of Roxanne Perello that was provided by her husband Angelo. Is that correct?"

"Yes, that is correct."

"And what exactly were your findings, sir?"

"Using the standard formula that is used by the majority of laboratories in this country," Anderson then looked at the judge, "I found that all of the DNA markers found in the blood sample from the car are an exact match of the DNA sample taken from Roxanne Perello's hair."

"Awww," surprised onlookers gasped and all eyes focused on Sam McBride. "Did he do it?" was the question on everyone's mind.

"I have no further questions for this witness, Your Honor."

"Your witness, Mr. Withers."

Jacob carefully took his time. He looked down at the papers in his brief case. Nervously, he approached the witness box, running his fingers through his hair as he contemplated his next move, and then, he very confidently looked the witness in the eye.

"Mr. Anderson, isn't it true that there are a total of 112 total markers available for testing in every DNA strand?"

"Yes, that is true."

"And isn't it also true that current DNA tests only test for 23 markers?"

Foster gave Jacob a curious look wondering where he was going with his questioning.

"Yes, for the most part, that is also true," Anderson answered.

"Now, hypothetically, would it be possible that if God were to be tested for his DNA, Roxanne, being ultimately descended from God, would match His DNA?"

"I guess, yeah, if you believed in God, but I don't." Mr. Anderson replied.

"Frankly sir, that's your choice. But the question remains, if you took a, let's say hypothetical God, and he made men and women in His image, would they match his DNA?"

"Hypothetically, yes it would be likely that there would be a match, if you tested the full range of markers." he replied. Now the expert was curious and you could see it in his eyes.

Jacob continued. "Now again, hypothetically, if God made man, and God made angels, ultimately being the creator of both, do you think it would be possible that there would be some similarities in the DNA code?"

"Objection, Your Honor," Foster complained. "We're dealing in facts here, not fairy tales."

"Your honor," Jacob Withers responded passionately, "I'm just trying to show that there may be a different reason for the DNA from the car and hair to match. If this man is an angel," Jacob said as he pointed to Nathanael with every eye in the court following, "then we're dealing with a creature we've never really studied before, so we have to at least consider the possibility that his DNA would match hers on some level. Science would never have achieved anything had it not considered every angle, Your Honor. And if we only test 23 markers, out of a possible 112, maybe there's a chance the other 89 would tell us something that we're missing here."

"Good point, Mr. Withers. The witness will answer the question," the judge ordered.

"Hypothetically?" Anderson asked.

"Sure," Jacob smiled and nodded knowingly.

Anderson pulled at his beard again, "It could be possible, but I didn't think angels had blood or for that matter even physical bodies." he added.

Jacob smiled at the jury. "I didn't think you thought about angels at all, Mr. Anderson. As you've said, you don't believe in God. But for curiosity's sake, let's consider that the Bible, as well as other sacred writings, whether one believes in them or not, describes angels that appear in physical form. Now I doubt they have water for blood, but I could be wrong. Now in the Bible itself there are descriptions of different types of angels - some with six wings, some with two etc ... etc ... Sorry ladies," Jacob looked over at the jury and the crowd, "no cute little chubby baby angels, are really mentioned in the scriptures, although I know some of you like the paintings." He breathed deep and smiled. A few of the ladies and one man nodded. Nathanael laughed out loud, irritating the judge, who gave him a warning look.

"But at any rate," Jacob took his Bible off the table and opened it to a bookmarked page, "there is even a Bible passage that says, and I quote from the New International Version, Hebrews 13:2, 'Do not forget to entertain strangers, for by so doing some people have entertained angels without knowing it.' So, according to this passage, angels may appear to us as strangers, so by that we see they can show up in the form of, well, humans. Therefore, why wouldn't they have blood and physical bodies?" A few of the jurors, at this gave each other thoughtful looks.

"But, I don't have to prove that to you, Mr. Anderson, or ladies and gentleman of the jury. All I have to do is ..." Jacob abruptly stopped and closed his eyes. Total silence filled the courtroom. Everyone waited. Five seconds went by, then ten, and then twenty seconds passed. Finally the judge asked, "Mr. Withers?" and then again,"Mr. Withers!" He shouted and slammed the gavel after waiting a total of 30 seconds. Jacob still didn't budge. He looked like a mannequin, frozen in time.

Then the judge asked, "Officer, please shake Mr. Withers." Bethany grabbed Jacob by the shoulders and shook him quite aggressively. Slowly, he opened his eyes. There was a dumbfounded look on his face as he slowly peered up at the judge.

"Mr. Withers," the judge raised his voice, "I warned you about sleeping in my courtroom. Did you take your medication?"

"Yes, Your Honor, but it doesn't always work perfectly. I'm sorry." Jacob rubbed his chin. "Wha…, whe… where was I?" he stammered.

Nathanael spoke to him without moving his lips, "You were saying that you don't have to prove that angels or God exists, only reasonable doubt."

"Thank you, Nathanael." Jacob said. This prompted a few stares from the crowd, no one else heard Nathanael speak.

"As I was saying, and I do apologize for checking out on you for a moment …" He turned toward the jury and smiled. They smiled compassionately back at him. "I don't have to prove to you angels or God even exists. But if you think that there is a possibility that angels exist, and again if it's possible that God is real; then you have to consider the possibility that my client's story is true. And ladies and gentlemen, that would be reasonable doubt. Doubting that Sam McBride did not hit or kill anyone, you must set my client free." Jacob turned his eyes from the jury to the judge.

"Is that all for this witness, Mr. Withers?" asked the judge who by his tone and raised eyebrows, seemed to think Jacob had forgotten about Mr. Anderson still seated on the witness stand.

"No, that is not all, Your Honor." Jacob turned toward the witness. "There is one more thing. Mr. Anderson, did you compare the blood of the said angel, Nathanael," Jacob nodded in Nathanael's direction, "with the blood found at the scene of the crime to determine if his blood matched any of the blood found there?"

"No. I was never asked to. I was only asked to test the crime scene blood against the DNA of Roxanne Perello."

"And that was a match?"

"Yes."

"And was it human blood?"

"Yes."

"Have you ever tested angel blood?"

Anderson laughed, "Are you kidding? Yeah, sure all the time. No, of course not," he replied scowling.

"Then how can you know beyond a shadow of a doubt that they are not very similar?"

"I guess," he hesitated, "if there are such things as angels, I couldn't totally guarantee you that they would not be similar. I seriously doubt it though."

"Your Honor, I would ask that the blood of Nathanael be tested against the blood taken from the crime scene. I would further ask that all blood and hair samples would be tested for all the possible DNA markers to see if there is any difference in the three sets of samples."

"So ordered. Mr. Anderson," the judge looked over at the witness, "you will see to it." At that Anderson raised his eyebrows and slightly shook his head. The judge didn't see it though.

"One more question, Mr. Anderson." Anderson just stared, obviously irritated. "The feather that was found at the scene from the grill in the car, was it identified as an ostrich feather?"

"No it was not."

"Then, what was it identified as?" Jacob looked at the jury and smiled like a cat with a canary in its mouth.

"We sent the feather to a fish and wildlife expert. The report that we got back said the sample was unidentifiable." He mumbled the last word a bit, in obvious discomfort.

Jacob Withers continued, "Are there not some basic chemistry tests you can do to determine the basic make-ups of the feather, to at least determine if it is of a certain species, perhaps from a certain geographic area?"

"Yes, there are but that would take having to destroy a part of the sample to test for chemical compounds."

"Your Honor," Jacob looked intently at the judge, "I request these tests be done, and I further would like to enter the two feathers found in Dr. Mathees examination room into evidence and ask that they be tested against the feather found at the scene, to see if they are a match."

Foster, surprised that Jacob had these feathers, stood up like a rocket. "I object, Your Honor. Even though the feather from the car is not ostrich, there's a possibility the manufacturer mixed in other feathers into the feathers of the jacket Mrs. Perello was wearing that night. The defense is stalling for time. I move that we proceed without any further tests. And those feathers found in Dr. Mathees office may have been planted there by the angel thing, whatever." Beads of sweat gathered on Brent Foster's forehead.

"Objection denied. You will have the opportunity to examine all evidence, Mr. Foster." Foster, clearly frustrated, sat down. The judge asked, "How long will it take before all these tests can be completed, Mr. Anderson?"

"The chemical composition of the feathers, if done right away, could show us results in a few days to a week. But the further complex DNA sequencing would have to be sent to a special forensics lab in Florida and that could take from a few days up to a couple of weeks, depending on what their workload is."

"OK, well, please overnight these samples, Mr. Anderson, and I will get on the phone and see if there is a way to expedite these tests. See me after court and I'll sign the order."

"OK," Anderson replied meekly.

"Nicely done, Mr. Withers." the judge smiled at Jacob. "Will that be all for this witness?"

"Yes, thank you, Your Honor."

The judge's compliment caused an eyebrow raise from Foster.

"Let's call it a day, ladies and gentleman. Court will reconvene December 23rd at 9:00. And that will be our last day of court for the week until after Christmas. Ladies and gentlemen of the jury, I remind you that you are not to discuss this case with anyone on the outside, even though it is being broadcast. I don't want you influenced by outside sources. I am ordering you to refrain from news casts, interviews, talk shows, magazines, etc. Do I have your pledge on this?"

The people of the jury nodded in unison.

"Court adjourned. All rise." The judge left, and a general excitement broke out in the courtroom.

Overcome with gratitude at the job Jacob Withers was doing, Sam leaped up and embraced Jacob. "You are a Godsend. Thank you," Sam whispered in Jacob's ear. The officer then led Sam away. Jacob, more determined than ever, turned around to speak to Nathanael, but he was gone. No one had seen him leave.

A warm breeze carried the smell of wildflowers with it as Denise and Marge sat together on a worn farmer's bench placed under a tree behind the mission. The scenery was absolutely beautiful as sunlight cast shadows on the cornfields, trees and hills. Denise saw none of it really though; her heart only saw Sam in jail. She grew more nervous as they awaited approval for the amnesia victim they thought to be Roxanne to be released. "Do you think he's doing all right, Marge? I wish I was there, but I know his best hope is us getting her back there. I wish there was a way we could prove who she was by the phone or something."

"I didn't think it would take this long either," Marge replied, "but honey, we prayed and trusted the Lord this far, let's not give in to fear and doubt now, ok?"

Marge had a contemplative look on her face. "Hold on a minute; I gotta take care of something," she said excitedly as she walked into the motor home and then into the small bathroom. She took a debit/ credit card out of her wallet and held it up. "Lord, You know all I have is Yours, and if You're telling me to do what I think You are, let me know." A flood of joy and peace came over Marge as she put the card back in her purse, if only temporarily.

Marge ventured back out to where Denise was still sitting. Sheep grazed beyond a rusty wire fence east of the field. They belonged to the mission. As she walked back, she watched as a small lamb chased its mother for food. It reminded Marge of Denise. Marge was thrilled to see that she was beginning to pray, and knew that's why Denise had stayed behind earlier in the motor home. Marge breathed deep and walked up to Denise. "Hey girl," she spoke softly, "I think you should go home now, and trust me to bring this young lady back there to you when she's ready. And I will, just as soon as I can."

Denise had a curious look on her face. "But I don't have any way to get back there. It must be like 2000 miles, easy."

Marge pulled out her credit card. "The Lord will provide," Marge said, laughing with that huge white smile of hers.

"Marge, I couldn't ask you to do that! That would cost so much! I don't know when I could ever pay you back."

"Who said anything about paying back? I consider this an investment in a couple of God's beautiful children."

Denise's' eyes welled up with tears. "Are you serious?" she asked. Marge simply nodded. "Oh Marge, you've been just so great." Denise leaned over to give her a hug. Marge wrapped her big arms around Denise and cradled the back of her head like a mother would a child. Then she prayed, tears in her eyes. "Oh Lord, get this one back safe to her man. You've brought us all this far, You ain't' gonna quit us now, Lord." Denise felt the arms of her Heavenly Father through the arms of this robust, preaching, praying saint named Marge. Like sisters, they took each others' hands as Denise did her best to try and hold back the tears that had built up in her heart for so long.

"I'm gonna cook you one great big dinner when this is all over," Denise said, hope in her voice.

"And you know what?" Marge replied. "I'm gonna eat it too." Both ladies laughed heartily. Then Marge continued. "Now I know it's gonna be expensive, but I've got the money in there so don't worry about that. I think you should make some calls, get that young lady, Elena, to help you translate, and then I think it would be wise to take a taxi over the border and then book a flight from Brownsville back to Detroit."

"Okay." Denise nodded, smiling, "that's what I'll do. Thank you again Marge, thank you so much."

"Just thank the Lord girl, all good things come from Him." Full of joy, Denise looked up at the heavens and waved her hands in the air.

"Thank you Lord," she said looking at Marge again and laughing. And with that she swiftly went in to find Elena to help her make the plans.

As evening drew near, Marge made her way back to the hospital room to see how the patient was recovering.

She quietly sat in the Victorian chair and sang softly, "He carries me, when my burdens seem too heavy. He sets me free to fly into the heavens. His love is stronger than my pain. I know I'll never be the same, because He took away my shame. He carries me."

"Hi Marge," the young patient said and smiled, opening one eye.

"See, you remembered my name, girl! You are comin' along!"

"Wish I could remember my name. You sing good." She smiled weakly at Marge and then looked over at the fresh flowers the nuns had brought in.

"Oh, give it time, you will. We didn't come all this way for nothing. We care about Sam, sure, who definitely needs you. But I'll let you in on a little secret. God and all of us, we care about you, too. Now if you don't mind, I'm gonna call you Roxanne, cause I think you are her, and it won't be long till you're all healed up, and remembering things too. But God don't rush, and neither do we. He's right on time, so you rest honey, I mean, Roxanne. I'm gonna read you something, OK?" Marge began to read out loud to her from the Bible,

The Lord is my shepherd, I shall not want.
He maketh me to lie down in green pastures:
he leadeth me beside the still waters.
He restoreth my soul:
he leadeth me in the paths of righteousness for his name's sake.
Yea, though I walk through the valley of the shadow of death,
I will fear no evil: for thou art ..."

Marge was interrupted by the sound of loud footsteps out in

the hall. She stepped out and pulled the door shut behind her. Maria
and Don were standing there.

"Can we see her now?" Maria asked excitedly, like a kid on
Christmas morning.

"Maria please, just give me a little more time. She's healing up
good, but her memory isn't back yet. If we're patient she might
fully recover – not only her health, but her memory as well. But
she has to rest, dear, please?"

"Well, it sounded like you were doing her funeral in there to
me."

"Psalm 23? Are you kidding? Maria, that's about new life – not
death! Anyway, I want to get her back just as bad as you, but we
need her to be healthy enough to travel."

"All right," Maria grumbled, "but we can't stay here forever."

Maria and Don walked down the hall, Elena followed about 15
feet behind, just watching Don. It was clear that she had become
enamored. All three of the news team made their way back out to
the van. They'd already interviewed the head nun, the mayor and
shot all their extra town footage. Now they were going stir crazy.

Back inside the room, Marge had opened her Bible picking up
at:

> *I will fear no evil: for thou art with me;*
> *thy rod and thy staff they comfort me.*
> *Thou preparest a table before me in the presence of mine enemies:*
> *thou anointest my head with oil;*
> *my cup runneth over.*
> *Surely goodness and mercy shall follow me all the days of my life,*
> *and I will dwell in the house of the Lord forever.*

The young lady was fading back to sleep. Marge read on from
Matthew.

> *Come unto me, all ye that labour and are heavy laden and I will*
> *give you rest.*

Marge closed her eyes to rest too.

The next day was filled with phone calls and prayers. Marge and the team sent Denise on her way and, the patient was improving. Marge again came around back. Again there was the lamb drinking from her mother as if her life depended on it.

"Time for me to get back to my lamb," Marge thought as she went back in to sit with, read with, and pray with the woman whom she now called Roxanne.

The high pitch of the reverse engines filled Denise's ears as the tires finally hit the ground on the runway at the Detroit Metro Airport.

"I'm home! I'm home! I'm home!" She had a little party in her mind as the plane continued down the runway. At the baggage claim, Denise watched the bags go round and round.

"Denise? Is that you?"

She turned around and there was Mrs. Rumsy, hair in a bun and all. Denise had called her from Mexico to arrange a pick up.

"You're a sight for sore eyes," Denise said. "Thank you so much for agreeing to come and pick me up, Mrs. Rumsy." Denise tried to shake her hand, but Mrs. Rumsy gave her a firm embrace.

"I'm glad I could do it dear, it was good to get away from the desk for a while." Denise saw her bag and picked it up. As they began heading for the parking lot Mrs. Rumsy handed her a baggie of fresh oatmeal chocolate chip cookies. "Here, I brought you some cookies fresh from the oven. How did things go out there?"

"Not as good as I would have liked, not yet at least. The girl out there has amnesia and was beaten so bad there was no way to be sure whether it was Roxanne or not. And she's too frail to move, so until she heals up and or gets her memory back, we just have to wait."

Mrs. Rumsy clicked her tongue sympathetically. "So where do you want me to take you, dear?" she asked, ready to take care of business.

"I want to go and see Sam, but I can drive there. Could you just drop me downtown at Channel 3 News. I left my car in the parking lot."

"Wherever you want, dear." They both got into Mrs. Rumsy's Cadillac.

"Wow, nice car, Mrs. Rumsy."

"Thank you. My boys got it for my husband and me on our 50th Anniversary. I like it OK. It's just a little fancy for me." She smiled meekly.

"Well, if you ever want to downsize you can give it to me. Did I say that out loud? I didn't mean to say that." Denise blushed.

"It's OK dear, but you know the Lord does give people the desire of their hearts sometimes, and I know you've been through a rough patch. But if you stay close to Him, He will lead you to a better place, and if I ever do change cars, you'll be the first one I think of."

"Thank you." Denise said, still a little embarrassed. "Hey, how is Amanda doing?"

"She's doing really great, Denise. Mrs. Sederson, we call her Carly, her real name's is Carlita, she's so good with these girls. With all the activities she's been doing with Amanda and her daughter, Amanda hasn't had time to worry."

"Well, thanks so much for helping set all that up for me. I'll come and get her right after I see Sam."

Mrs. Rumsy dropped Denise off at her car by the Channel 3 WXTY sign in the parking lot.

Knowing Mandy was all right, she drove directly to the Wayne County Jail. She went through security and waited as Sam was led into the visiting room. He had no idea she was back and was coming to see him.

"Denise!" he shouted. "Oh, I can't believe it! You're back. Oh man, I missed you, baby." He held her closely. They embraced for what seemed like minutes.

"I missed you too, Sam." She slowly whispered in his ear while tears ran down her cheeks. Wiping at her face with her sleeve, she tried to hide them and regain her composure as he released her. They both sat down.

"Did you find her, 'Neesi? Did you bring her back?"

"Sam," she hesitated, trying to fine the right words, "we think we've found her, but she's been badly beaten and has amnesia. We had no prints or anything to go on except her picture. We think it's her but we aren't 100% positive. She's healing though," Denise looked at him hope shining in her eyes, "and we hope she gets her memory back." Denise took his hands in hers and brought them to her lips. "I just had to come and be with you, Sam. I couldn't let you go through all this alone. But Marge is with her, and she says not to worry, that the Lord wouldn't have gotten us this far to fail us now. Sam, … I love you. I … I've been praying. Can you believe that? It's like something is waking up inside of me, just like what happened to you, and I want it. I want it, too. I want to know Him. I want us to be together in this all the way!"

Sam, now getting misty-eyed, looked at Denise lovingly, longing to be home with her, now more than ever. He spoke slowly, "What you just said to me, makes me feel like the freest, happiest man in the world, even in here."

"Will you pray with me, Sam?"

"Really? What do you want me to pray?"

"I want Him to take over, Sam. I want what you've found. I just don't know how to ask Him."

Sam was trying hard to hold his emotions in, everything he thought he'd lost seemed to be returning to him. "It's gonna be different now, 'Neesi. It's gonna be better."

Sam bowed his head, Denise did the same. "Oh Lord God, thank You for my wife." Suddenly he wept profusely, his whole body shook. "Oh Lord, thank You for saving me. Thank You that we're gonna be free." She too wept freely now as their tears of joy and repentance mingled. "She wants to know You Lord, and that makes me the happiest man in the world." He laughed with joy, tears like a waterfall, fell washing his cheeks. "I've never prayed like this with anyone before Lord; please help me know what to say. I'm gonna try, 'Neesi. Pray what I pray." Sam felt an overwhelming power come over him.

"Heavenly Father."

Denise repeated, "Heavenly Father."

"Please forgive me for my sins."

Denise continued, "Please forgive me for my sins." Her lip quivered.

"Thank You for sending Your Son, Jesus, to die for me, paying the debt for my sins."

Denise, weeping openly, was shaking now. "Thank You for sending Your Son to die for me, paying the debt for my sins."

Sam went on, "Lord Jesus, come into my life and be my Savior."

Denise followed, "Lord Jesus, come into my life and be my Savior."

"And help me to follow You. Amen."

Denise repeated, "Help me to follow You. Amen."

He looked at her like he'd won the lottery. She returned the look, yet surprised Sam when she prayed, "And God, thank You for my husband. I know sometimes I've been mean and talked down to him, and I'm sorry. I'm sorry, Sam, when I made you feel small, cause you're one of the biggest men I know, to go through this and not be bitter, to forgive me after I accused you and you were innocent." She pleaded. "God, please help me to be a better wife."

"No, 'Neesi," Sam walked over to her, lifting her up, he embraced and consoled her. "You've been what's kept us together all this time, but now it's my turn to be strong." Affectionately he stroked her hair and locked his eyes on her. Her heart melted as she lost herself in his eyes. "And I'm gonna be strong, 'Neesi, by the grace of God. I'm gonna be a man this time." He looked up. "Oh Lord, help me be that man."

"Help us both then, Lord," Denise said as they both laughed and cried at the same time.

Sam kissed Denise on the mouth, both their lips quivering, he pressed his face into hers. "I'm comin' home, babe, I'm comin' home to you." He kissed her softly on each eye.

"I know you are, Sammy, and you're my man, and nothing's gonna separate us. Let's fight this thing together, OK?"

"We will babe, we'll fight and we'll win."

A tear fell from the eye of the Master who was looking down from Heaven through a portal.

Nathanael, invisible to Sam and Denise, was right there in the room, tears streaming down his eyes as well. He deeply treasured moments like this when he was blessed with the opportunity to witness godly human breakthroughs. He extended his wings and hands toward heaven and cried out in worship, a language that only heaven knew. The song echoed through the halls of the temple. Throughout the Kingdom, knees bowed and tears fell everywhere; there were thousands of angels and elders before the throne. A glorious light shot out and touched each one. They all cried out together,

"Blessing and Honor, and Glory and Power be unto Him who sits upon the throne and to the Lamb forever and ever."

21
MESSAGES FROM HEAVEN

December 23, 2011

The whirling blades of news helicopters could be heard as they circled above the courthouse trying to get video of any of the key players in the McBride trial. It seemed like every news channel, radio, newspaper, and Internet news service, was there. They were especially curious about Nathanael, yet so far he was able to elude the press. The best shot they had been able to get was the back of his head from the video feed.

Fred, the original court officer, was back now and bellowed out his usual, "All rise. Court is now in session. Judge Steven P. Malkovich presiding."

"I can't wait till I don't have to hear that anymore." Sam thought to himself.

Nathanael leaned slightly forward and whispered, "Me neither," he smiled mischievously.

Jacob turned around and gave Nathanael a look that said, "Behave yourself."

Judge Malkovich painfully took his seat, ice pack in hand. He turned on his lamp and peering through his bifocals addressed the crowd, "Welcome, everyone. Please be seated."

By this time, the amount of angel statues, letters, pictures and other memorabilia had so accumulated at the courthouse steps, the judge had to appoint an officer to clear it all off each day. The city stored the items in a Department of Public Works building until they could figure out what to do with it all.

The courtroom was filled to the rim with many new faces. The judge had to instruct a court officer to issue numbers to the first people in line early in the morning. Some folks had brought tents and portable heaters trying to camp out on the courthouse lawn and surrounding area, but they had been escorted away by the local police.

"Gentleman, we left off the other day on an important place in this trial in regards to the DNA evidence of three feathers and the blood sample of said angel, Nathanael. Mr. Foster, please update us on the status of our DNA tests."

Foster stood up. "Your Honor, all the tests are in."

After the last session the judge decided to fly Mr. Anderson to Florida to participate in the DNA testing of the blood and feathers.

"Thirty years on the bench does have its perks. I believe we left off with the defense, would you like to continue Mr. Withers?" the judge asked.

Jacob stood. "Your Honor, the defense again calls DNA expert, Mr. Anderson."

In his usual disheveled manner, Mr. Anderson slothfully took the witness stand.

"I remind you, sir, that you are still under oath." the judge said.

"Okay." Anderson replied.

Jacob walked directly up to Mr. Anderson, turning to smile at the jury.

"Mr. Anderson, in regards to the testing of the DNA samples taken from the three different sources, being Roxanne Perello, the scene of the accident, and said angel Nathanael. What are your conclusions?"

Unenthusiastically looking at the judge and then down at the floor, he said, "They all match." Whispers rose in the courtroom until the judge picked up his gavel and they immediately subsided.

"Are you saying" Jacob asked, "that blood sampled from said angel Nathanael who is sitting with us in this court today, matches the DNA of Roxanne Perello, and the DNA of the blood found on the scene."

"Yes, I don't quite understand it fully or know how to explain it, but yes."

"I object, Your Honor." Foster spoke up from his table, standing and raising his hand. "I ask that an independent laboratory be used to retest these samples."

The judged looked over at the witness. "Mr. Anderson. These samples were tested in your presence at the Federal Lab in Florida, were they not?"

"They were, Your Honor."

"Can't do much better than that, Mr. Foster, after all he's *your* witness, objection overruled. Continue, Mr. Withers."

"Was there anything else unique or interesting you found when comparing the blood tests, Mr. Anderson?" Jacob remembered the dream he had about the doctor looking through the microscope.

"Actually yes, the blood tested from Nathanael showed antibodies that seemed to have regenerative properties like a super-antibiotic or something. You might say this blood has high healing qualities. It also had an certain unique luminous quality that neither the lab technicians nor I could fully understand."

The jury's jaws dropped, as did those of everyone in the courtroom, all eyes focused on Nathanael.

"Who is this guy?" one man whispered.

"But yet, his blood had the same DNA markers as that at the scene of the said crime?"

"Yes, it's incomprehensible to me right now, but yes, all the markers matched those found at the scene."

"And the feathers that you tested, Mr. Anderson. What were the results of the chemical testing on that?" Jacob asked.

"To be honest, I am actually at a loss of words to describe the results of those tests." He cleared his throat and took a breath looking bewildered.

"Which were?" Jacob prompted.

He looked at Jacob, then the jury. "They were virtually indestructible." The jury leaned forward, all eyes on Nathanael, who simply kept his eyes straight ahead, and only showed a slight smile.

"Please explain." Jacob asked, sending a deliberate glance and grin to the jury.

"We could not cut them with the sharpest, hardest, cutting tools. We chemically tested one and could not dissolve it at all to determine any of its properties. It's waterproof and fireproof. To be totally honest with you all, I've never seen anything like it in my life. It's almost like an armor of some sort."

"Would you say it's possibly beyond our understanding, maybe from another place?" Jacob asked calmly, trying hard not to reveal his excitement at the way the trial was going. His foot was tapping on the carpet.

"I object, Your Honor, leading." Foster said fairly quietly this time, not even standing up.

"Overruled. Mr. Anderson, please answer the question," the judge replied.

Anderson replied. "I just don't know. I really just don't know what to say."

"Thank you, that'll be all, Mr. Anderson." Jacob said, practically skipping back to his seat.

"Mr. Foster, do you wish to cross?"

"No, Your Honor, not now. But I would like to reserve the right to look into the results of these tests and possibly revisit this."

"Very well. Your next witness, Mr. Foster." the judge said.

"Your Honor, I would like to call the one who goes by the name Nathanael to the stand."

Foster knew he was taking a chance, but it was the last one that he had. The court was completely silent in anticipation, all you could hear was the December wind blowing against the courthouse window as Nathanael slowly made his way to the front of the courtroom. He took his seat in the witness box.

"Do you swear to tell the truth, the whole truth, and nothing but the truth so help you God?"

With that, Nathanael clutched the Bible with both hands, embraced it against his heart and prayed, "So help me, God." He handed the Bible back to the clerk.

Brent Foster approached him slowly, the whole world was glued to their TV sets, streaming web video and radio broadcasts.

"What is your name, sir?" Foster asked in his most official voice.

"I am Nathanael." the messenger replied.

"And your last name?"

"I don't have a last name."

"Will you please state who you are and where you're from?"

"I am an angel sent down from Heaven." Nathanael stated calmly.

Denise was captivated, sitting behind the defense table, her husband within reaching distance. Her heart was beating wildly in her chest. Looking around the courtroom, she realized that this was one of the most exciting times she had ever had in her life. She was watching history in the making, and even though she faced the possibility of losing her husband, she thought to herself, *"I don't feel afraid. I'm not afraid."* Nathanael looked directly at her when she thought this and he smiled. *"Can he hear me?"* she asked herself.

"Did you think I was only Sam's guardian?" she heard his voice in her heart. She smiled, suddenly overcome with the feeling of being loved, to think that God had been watching over her and her family all this time, even through all her doubt, fear and unbelief. Hope sprang up in her heart like a Yellowstone geyser. She smiled her award-winning smile.

Foster placed his hands on the rails of the witness box. "You expect us to believe that you are a real angel sent down from Heaven?" he demanded.

"I have no expectations on you at all. I only expect that my King would be glorified here." Nathanael paused and seemed to peer inside Prosecutor Foster's soul. "And He will be."

Foster wiped a bead of sweat off his forehead. "If you are an angel, can you do a miracle or a trick or something to prove who you are?"

"I am. I could, but I won't." Nathanael was calm and collected, which just frustrated the prosecutor even more.

"Why not? Because you can't, because you're not an angel at all, are you? You're just playing a part. Ladies and Gentlemen of the jury, every angel I've heard of has had powers to appear and disappear or to do some sort of miracle, but this one can do nothing, because he's just a man." He leaned and looked Nathanael in the eye. "I'll give you one more chance to prove to this court who you are. One miracle, that's all I ask."

"It's not my mission to prove anything to you, Mr. Foster, except to give my testimony, to see Sam set free, and to help people believe in the One who sent me. I am not here to be a showman, except to show the One who really needs to be seen in your hearts and minds. He's at your door and if you open it, Mr. Foster, then you will have your miracle." Foster was becoming somewhat unraveled.

"What? Who hired you? Who told you to come here, sir?"

"The King of the Universe. The Most High God."

"And why …, why would you say He sent you?" Foster asked skeptically.

"He sent me to help His child, Sam McBride."

"You didn't do a very good job of that, did you?" Foster said mockingly. "According to that story, you were knocked unconscious by a demon?" Foster smirked looking over at the jury. "And then you were knocked to the ground when struck by a car. Do you expect us to believe that you are an angel with supernatural powers, yet you can't even help one man? And you don't know enough to stay out of the road in a snow storm?" There was muffled laughter in the courtroom at this. Nathanael looked vulnerable. That night was a low point in his service to the King. Yet he held his composure.

"I have no power except that which is given from above and that is largely dependent on the love and prayers of his children. Which concerning the initial group assigned to Sam was minimal and dispassionate at best." Nathanael looked directly at one of the visitors in the courtroom which happened to be a member of the church prayer team that night. "They chose to watch football instead." The man Nathanael stared at had a confused look on his face.

"I find that hard to believe. You say your power is dependent on the prayers of people?" Foster scoffed.

"You don't pray, right Mr. Foster? And how is your life going?" Nathanael taunted back.

Nathanael's comeback drew a perplexed look from Foster. He recovered quickly though, then asked, "So you're saying if I prayed, God would assign me an angel and His power would be dependent upon my prayers and/or the prayers of others?"

"To a certain degree, yes."

"Did Sam McBride pray?"

"Yes."

"And you are Sam's angel".

"Yes, he is under my guardianship."

"So why didn't you save him from all this?"

"Samuel made a decision to stop somewhere he shouldn't have. We can't interfere with human decision except in extremely rare cases. Mostly we warn and encourage people to make the right choices, which I tried to do."

"He didn't listen?"

"No, not right away, but he did eventually. By that time, the wheels of misfortune had already begun turning just by him being in the wrong place at the wrong time."

Foster tried to pitch Nathanael a curve ball. "When were you born?" Foster asked hurriedly.

"I wasn't born, I was created."

"How is that?" Foster queried.

"I was shaped by my Father's hands."

"And tell us, just who is your Father?"

"The almighty God, maker of Heaven and Earth."

"Well, how can you call him Father if He didn't actually father you, but rather made you?"

Nathanael now had a soft look of innocence to him like that of a small child. He spoke softly.

"He just created us in a different way is all. We're no less His children to Him. He loves us and loves to be called Father. He not only shows love, but is love. And He loves all of us, and all of you also." Nathanael looked at the people in the room and also into the TV camera, "even the worst in man's eyes has value in His eyes." Nathanael stared directly into Foster's eyes. "He cries when He loses one, even though they may not cry, He still does. Because being made in His image they still look like Him and He knew them once, even though they may have decided not to know Him, He knew them and loved them. It breaks His heart when they go dark, Mr. Foster." Nathanael had a single tear in his eye.

"What do you mean go dark?"

"It's a messenger term. It means to cross over from light to darkness."

Changing the focus, Foster paced in front of the witness stand. "Again, if you are an angel, why don't you give us a little miracle, so we can establish your identity?" Foster was out of ideas.

"I'm under strict guidelines, and can only do what my Lord has instructed."

"No, you just said 'Lord', but before you said God. Why?"

"Because I am under the authority of the Lord."

"You mean Jesus?" Foster asked.

"Oh sir, be careful. I didn't think you could say His name in court anymore."

"By Lord, do you mean Jesus, though?" Foster thought he was on to something.

"Yes." Nathanael's voice deepened as he stood up in honor of his King. He placed his closed fist over his heart and then lifted his hands toward the heavens. He spoke loudly, "Praise to the King of Glory, The Mighty God, The Prince of Peace, the Everlasting Father, El Gibor!"

"Sit down, Mr. Nathanael!" the judge ordered sharply.

"I will not sit down." Nathanael spoke boldly. He then looked up as if through the ceiling, being instructed from Heaven. "Ok, I will sit." He grinned.

Foster was getting impatient. "Which is it, is it God or Jesus?" Foster asked.

"Hear Oh Israel, the Lord our God is one Lord." Nathanael said in English, then in ancient Hebrew. Then in Russian, "Hear

Oh Russia, the Lord is one," then in Chinese, "Hear Oh China, the Lord is one." Then is Spanish, "Hear…"

"Please stop that." Foster interrupted. "Now, what do you mean? Who do you serve?"

"I will not divide God for you, Mr. Foster. I am a servant of the King."

"Your Honor, I am just trying to establish this person's identity, to find out whether he is telling the truth or not."

"Please answer the question, Mr. Nathanael." the judge said.

"You want to know His name, yet you use it for a curse word. One day you'll wish you hadn't." Nathanael spoke passionately, "There is time for repentance now though. Your own Bible tells you who He is and how we should respond to Him," Nathanael stood up again arms outstretched. His voice became deep and bold as he quoted Philippians 2:9-11 from memory:

Wherefore God also hath highly exalted him,
and given him a name which is above every name:
That at the name of Jesus every knee should bow,
of things in heaven, and things in earth,
and things under the earth;
And that every tongue should confess that Jesus Christ is Lord,
to the glory of God the Father.

"I serve the Lord God Almighty, the maker of heaven and earth. The One that came to save you, your knees will bow," he paused momentarily and looked around the room. "Your eyes will see, don't wait until it's too late, people of the earth. Bow your knees now, to the King of Glory!" he pleaded. "Open your heart now. His kingdom is coming. Choose to live in truth and love now, while there is yet time to choose. You make so much of me with your cameras and your crowds, yet I am just a messenger. He is your God and lives among you every day and you often just ignore Him." Tears were streaming down his cheeks.

Nathanael looked over at the judge, who this time patiently gave a humble smile and waved his hand calmly in a gesture for Nathanael to sit down.

"Thank you, Your Honor." Nathanael smiled and sat.

Foster visibly shaken and frustrated also sat down. "I have no further questions for this witness at this time, Your Honor."

"Your witness, Mr. Withers."

Jacob approached the bench. "Hi, Nathanael."

"Hi, Jake," This won a squinty-eyed stare and a slight frown from Jacob, but he decided to let it go.

"Nathanael, when did I first meet you?"

"In your church." Nathanael replied.

"And what did you say to me? And what did you tell me to say to Sam?"

"I told you to not be afraid, to put me on the witness list, and that I would testify about that night, and about the Lord. That I was the one Sam hit. I told you to tell Sam McBride we would never leave him or forsake him." He paused and looked over at Sam with integrity and loyalty shining in his eyes. "And we won't, Sam. We will be victorious."

Sam smiled and nodded his appreciation.

"And what did you do to my hand, to show me that you really were an angel."

"You tell me, Mr. Withers." Nathanael smiled lightheartedly.

Jacob looked at the jury and spoke, "He changed his eye color while I was looking at him. I was looking him right in the eye, and when I thought that was a trick, he made my hand turn leprous, like God did to Moses in the Old Testament."

"I object, Your Honor." Foster spoke. "The defense attorney is not called to testify."

"I'll allow it for now." The judge himself was curious.

"Can you do something like that now" Jacob asked, "for the benefit of the jury?"

"I could, but I won't."

"Why not? For me you can." Jacob said, now himself slightly irritated.

"Because as I said, I am under certain instructions. Why are you people of earth are always looking for signs." He surveyed the room as he spoke. "You already have so many. God sent you a star when the Christ was coming, but so few of you rarely think of it. When that time of celebration comes, you'd rather frustrate yourselves financially, forgetting the true riches, that He gave His all for you Himself.

Some say there is no God, yet every day birds sing out His praises; the leaves of the trees, they dance for Him. The sun rises and sets at His command. Yet people boast in their own temporary achievements." Nathanael cocked his head to the left contemplating. "You invent gadgets like video games, and talk on cellular phones in your cars to someone who is not near you, while your own children sit next to you and would love for a few minutes of your time." A concerned look was increasingly evident on his face.

"You want me to show you a sign, so you can make a big deal out of me, but God doesn't want you to make a big deal out of His messengers at all. We are around you all the time, thousands of us, and yet you don't see us, or recognize us. Why? Because, it's about Him, and you. You are the big deal." Nathanael looked around the room. "God loved you so much that He sent His Son to pay your way into the greatest dwelling in the universe. An eternal, joy-filled kingdom. He split open time, showed signs and did miracles. He healed. He commanded nature to obey Him. But the greatest miracle He did was to walk with you, eat and laugh with you, to show you, what love really is. He showed you who He really is.

"These statues that you bring and pictures and costumes and everything? You really don't understand, do you? Why worship dead things when your God, who is life, is willing to live right inside your heart?"

Mr. Foster's son, Bryan and his friend were at home watching.

"Is this guy for real?" Bryan's friend said.

"Shhh!" Bryan replied. "I'm trying to listen."

Nathanael's face began to glow as he continued, "You truly are," he paused, "the miracles. I am still amazed when I see someone go under the cleansing water and come up as a new creation."

"He's talking about baptism." a Chinese man told his wife as they were watching the television.

"I know, shhh," she replied.

Nathanael looked over at the jury. "I bring Him your tears and prayers and carry back to you His love. I see a changed heart that's being molded to be just like the Father's heart, and I wonder why sometimes you don't see that you already have all that you need." He looked into the television camera. "You ask for healing, but then wound your brother with your words. Some of you wanted to hurt Sam McBride and judge him because your hearts are empty and wounded. The Lord wants you to have healing but first you must use what you have. Don't kill your brother with your words, speak healing and love and faith to each other, and your Father will speak faith and love and healing to you. It's not really that complicated. If you admit when you're wrong and ask Him for help, He will help you. Just like Jesus said when He walked with you, how He said to be like little children."

High above in the Holy place, watching through the portal, behind the curtain the One on the throne looked at His Son, both standing just out of focus. "I remember that day, Son. That was a very good day."

The messenger continued. "You already have His words, and He would speak more, but you have to hear what you've already been told first."

"Your Honor, I object," Foster stood up. "What has any of this to do with this case? We don't need a scolding from this imposter!"

"I'm not so sure. Sit down, Mr. Foster." the judge ordered. "Continue, Mr. Nathanael." The judge seemed to be intrigued with the dialogue.

Foster, frustrated, laid his head in his arms on top of the desk.

Nathanael's face was glowing with joy and strength as he looked into the camera. "But there are also many who have found the true riches in the secret place, and the fellowship of sharing in His suffering. There are some who have refused to cause division, and have blessed even when being cursed. Know that He sees your tears. Oh barren lands, you will bear fruit, trees of His planting. Please don't give up; don't let your love grow cold." Nathanael was weeping. "He is just and He will reward according to what He has said. Those who truly follow Him will not be disappointed."

Foster bravely stood up again. "Please, Your Honor, I beg you, this is very pretty sounding and all, but what does this have to do with the case?"

"Mr. Withers, do you have any further questions for your witness that are related to this case?"

"Yes, indeed." Jacob turned from the judge and faced Nathanael. "Nathanael, you are legitimately an angel from Heaven, is that correct?"

"That is correct, my friend. As you say here on earth, I am too legit to quit." Nathanael smiled jokingly.

Jacob smiled at being called a friend and the angel's earthly humor. "On the night of November 19, you were coming to help Sam McBride and ..."

"Objection, Your Honor," Foster stated, "the defense is leading the witness."

"Sustained." the judge said. "Mr. Withers, you will ask direct, but not leading questions."

"Yes, Your Honor. On the night of November 19th, please, Nathanael, tell us what happened."

"I was in Heaven when I received instructions on a scroll, and was on my way to encourage Sam McBride, who was in my charge. I learned he had been thrown out of his house and falsely accused of returning to drinking alcohol. I was instructed to comfort him and give him strength.

"I was on my way, soaring through the atmosphere, when I was attacked by Sorcers, a dark angel who specializes in sowing confusion and is well equipped for battle. I noticed that I was low on power, yet I tried my best to break through his attack and get to Sam on time. Unfortunately, Sorcers landed a blow that wounded me deeply. I went blank, but the Lord heard me cry out when I was wounded, and He brought me back to consciousness. I came to, right before the impact. That's when Sam McBride hit me with his car. Knocking me unconscious again, I was thrown into a tree."

"Then what happened?" Jacob asked.

"Then I came to. I healed up and disappeared."

"No further questions, Your Honor."

"Mr. Foster, your witness."

"The Prosecution calls no further witnesses at this time, Your Honor." Foster said.

Surprised he didn't re-cross Nathanael, Jacob gave Foster a curious look.

"Mr. Withers?" the judge asked. "Would you like to call another witness?"

"Your Honor, I call Doctor Zingas to the stand."

Unbeknownst to anyone in this courtroom, the news team was on its way home now. The bus was making its way through Toledo, Ohio. Marge placed a call to the court.

"The court is in session," the court clerk said. "They can't be interrupted unless it's a matter of life and death."

"But it's very important," Marge said, "I have to talk to the judge right away. Tell him that …"

Don was watching in the rear view mirror as Marge continued her conversation. He couldn't hear her but noticed she was sweating profusely.

"… and that we're on our way." Marge concluded.

"OK ma'am, I'll give them your message. I have to take another call now, goodbye."

"Ummmmmm," the dial tone filled Marge's ear.

"Put the pedal to the medal there, Don Won." Marge told the driver. Once again she tried to dial Denise.

"We're sorry, your call did not go through, please check the number and dial again." Frustrated, Marge bowed her head and prayed.

Two warriors were flying high overhead keeping watch.

The clerk handed the note to the officer who then passed it to the judge. He looked at it, raised an eyebrow, then folded it and put it by his lamp.

"Dr Zingas, good day, sir." Jacob greeted the doctor politely.

"Good day to you, Mr. Withers. Please call me Dr Z." He replied in his usual broken English.

"Thank you sir, I will. Now you examined Sam McBride to see if he was mentally able to stand trial, is that correct?"

"Dat ees correct."

"What were your findings, sir?"

"I found dat Mr. McBride ees fully as sane as any of us are."

"Do you believe that he actually saw and hit an angel?"

"I object, Your Honor," Foster barked. "This isn't about what the doctor believes or doesn't believe, this is about whether Sam McBride is sane or not, and the doctor has already stated that he is. Is any more testimony from this man even necessary?"

"Where are you going with this, Mr. Withers?" the judge asked.

"Your Honor, I'm just trying to find out if the doctor believes that Sam really thinks he hit an angel, or if he thinks Sam is lying. He's the State's professional, Your Honor."

"Then rephrase the question, Mr. Withers."

"Dr. Z, in your professional opinion, do you believe Sam McBride truly believes that he hit an angel?"

"Yes, I believe dat he believes everything he is saying."

"No further questions for this witness, Your Honor."

"Your witness, Mr. Foster." the judge said.

Foster got up, straightened his tie and slacks and stepped up to the witness stand.

"Dr Zingas, your report indicates, as well as your recent testimony, that you consider Sam McBride sane, as do I. I just believe he may be lying to try and save his own skin. Now you just said that he believes that he saw what he saw. How did you determine that? Did you give him a lie detector test?"

"No. When I say I believe dat he believes vat he'ez saying, I say dat only as my opinion, from dealing vit many patients and studying deir body movements over the years. Mr. McBride looked me right in de eye ven we talked. He was very direct and not over-talkative, and was even somewhat humorous, indicating a lack of nervousness. All dese are usually signs that someone is telling the trut, or at least vat dey know to be da trut."

Denise left the courtroom to try and call Maria. There had been no word since she left Mexico and she was a little concerned.

"We're sorry, but the person you're trying to reach is currently unavailable."

"Damn!" Denise said as she hit the stop button. "Oh sorry, Lord." She looked up. Denise was making a worthy attempt to change her bad language habits.

She watched for a minute out in the hall through a TV on a stand coming out of the ceiling. The court was at overflow capacity. Some of the spectators and media had to sit on extras chairs in the hall to watch.

"Is it possible, Dr. Zingas, that Mr. McBride was coached into believing that what he said was true, by his attorney or possibly someone else?"

"Objection, Your Honor.." Jacob protested loudly. "The Prosecutor is really reaching here."

"I'll allow it for now, Mr. Withers. I really don't think you have too much to worry about here."

"Please, answer the question, Dr. Z. "

"In my professional opinion, I don't think anyone, short of an expert CIA operative, has the skills to coach someone to the degree of believability that Sam McBride has shown."

The judge then asked, "For the record, Mr. Withers, you're not with the CIA, right?" making light of Foster's questioning. No one laughed, of course. Especially not Prosecutor Foster.

"Any further questions for the doctor, Mr. Foster?" the judge asked.

"No, sir." Foster whispered dejectedly.

"Re-cross, Mr. Withers?"

"No, Your Honor." Jacob replied, smiling brazenly.

Bryan Foster had never seen his dad looking so defeated. His heart toward his dad was softening a little.

"Your witness, Mr. Withers?"

"Your Honor, I call Sam McBride."

22
MIRACLES

Sam stood slowly. He turned and reached out to Denise. She held his hand as long as she could before he gently pulled away and walked toward the witness box. He gave her a reassuring smile. The ladies on the jury, watching their affection for each other, seemed moved. Sam looked really sharp. He was dressed in dark slacks and a pale blue shirt Denise had bought for him from money the church had given her.

After Sam was sworn in, Jacob approached and greeted him.

"Mr. McBride, how are you today, sir?"

"I'm doing really good, Jacob." Sam said confidently.

"Yes, really, and why is that?"

"Because I have hope now like I've never had before. My wife is here and Jacob, you may not have heard about it yet, but Denise gave her heart to the Lord and was saved when she visited me at the jail."

"Your Honor, must we really?" Foster begged sitting in his chair.

"Mr. Withers, let's stay focused here," the judge warned.

Jacob smiled at the judge. "Sam McBride, on the night of November 19, did you, with the car you were driving, hit and kill Roxanne Perello?"

"No, I did not."

"Then what was it exactly, that you hit?"

"It was an angel."

"Is that angel in the courtroom with us today?"

"Yes, that's him right there." Sam McBride pointed to Nathanael who was sitting on Sam's left, 20 feet from the jury. Nathanael gave Sam a smile and a wave of his hand.

"Sam, do you love your wife and daughter?" Jacob asked.

"More than anything is this world." Sam looked at Denise, affection evident in his eyes.

"Would you ever do anything to jeopardize that love?"

"Never, no, not on purpose."

"Have you ever cheated on your wife, Sam?"

"No, never."

"Have you ever lied to your wife?"

"No, sir." The jury was watching Sam closely. They noticed Sam and Denise could barely take their eyes off of each other.

"No further questions, Your Honor."

"Mr. Foster, do you wish to cross?"

"Yes, Your Honor." Foster answered. He hesitated as he approached, looked down at the floor, then after a moment began.

"Mr. McBride, I wanted to tell you, and I hope that you understand I don't wish you any ill will at all …" Foster paced in front of Sam like a giraffe looking for some forage.

Sam squinted his eyes, more than a bit suspicious at Foster's comment.

"… but I have a job to do." Foster continued. "I am responsible to answer to the people of this fine state. So forgive me, Mr. McBride, if I don't give you the benefit of the doubt on this whole angel story." Foster was dressed in black today.

"He looks like an undertaker." Sam thought.

"Do you honestly expect me, the jury, and this courtroom to believe that after living irresponsibly as an alcoholic all these years, neglecting family and work responsibilities that you suddenly had a little talk with God and turned over a new leaf? Then you just happened to wander into the Eagle's Nest bar, where you were seen talking to the victim? Then you say you left the bar, had a fight with your wife, who kicked you out of your house, so you went and struck an angel with your car, fled the scene of the crime, and then your angel comes to court to testify on your behalf? Can you see how unbelievable this all sounds, Mr. McBride?"

Foster took a breath, then looked up and rolled his eyes for effect, making sure the jury could see him.

"I've heard more believable alien abduction stories," he said. "So I'm asking you, for the sake of being able to live with yourself, to cause no further injury to your family and friends, not to mention all the time and money and costs to this court and the jury. Please Mr. McBride, for once in your life show some accountability. Tell us what really happened."

"OK." Sam said. "I'm going to be totally straight forward and accountable here."

"Good." Foster said. "Go ahead."

"I am guilty of being a lousy husband and a miserable father. I've been an emotional cripple, a lazy bum, and an overall poor excuse for a man. But you know, that's all over now because I really did meet God that day on the beach. And He really did take away my desire to drink. And He gave me hope. He also put people in my path and spoke through them that if I would humble myself before my wife and family He would restore things. And He did, and is.

"Then one night I made a really dumb decision and I almost threw it all away. I almost took that drink. But you know, at the last minute, I made the right decision and walked out of that bar. But it was too late, or so it seemed, 'cause the devil called my wife and planted the lie in her mind that I was drinking. And with the information she had, she did what was right. She threw me out. But Heaven heard my cry and sent me an angel to comfort me. But the enemy wasn't going to give in that soon. That's when I hit my angel with my car." Sam looked over at Nathanael. "Sorry, Nathanael."

Nathanael smiled back and said, "No problem, Sam."

"Now, that is the whole truth. I did not hit or kill any person, I just ran into my angel. And he doesn't seem to want to press charges."

Some in the audience and jury began to applaud.

Bang! Bang! The judge hit his gavel twice. "Excuse me folks, this isn't the *Tonight Show*." he scolded.

Denise gave Sam a proud smile.

"Umm, thank you, Mr. McBride, no further questions, Your Honor." Foster seemed almost touched for a second by the confidence and sincerity of Sam's testimony. He was confused, at a loss for words even.

"You're going soft, Foster," a sinister voice spoke in his head. *"Can't you see through this clown's lies?"*

"Your witness, Mr. Withers," the judge called.

"Your Honor, the defense calls ..."

Suddenly the doors at the back of the courthouse opened. All eyes turned and watched as first Elena and then Don walked in, then Maria, and then a court officer and Marge, one on each side, helping to hold up this little young blonde lady walking slowly with a cane. Marge looked to Denise and pointed, mouthing the words, *"It's her!"*

Jacob seeing this shouted out over the commotion, "Your Honor! The defense calls Roxanne Perello." Everyone in the courtroom gasped, staring fixatedly at this new person in court.

"Is it her? It doesn't look like her picture," a lady jurist remarked.

"I bet this is some kind of put on," a man in the crowd scowled.

"Order!" the judge pounded the gavel.

Foster stood up, and opened his mouth, and looked at the judge. Then he closed his mouth and sat back down. *"I better wait,"* he thought.

Bruises and stitches were noticeable as this young lady slowly made her way to the witness box.

Angelo, who was still in custody in his cell, had been allowed to watch the trial on TV. He stood as he saw her.

"Son of a %&*. I can't believe it."

Some people scooted in to make way for Maria and the news crew to sit down.

Still bruised and struggling to walk, with Marge's help she made her way up to the witness box; the judge then leaned over to her and asked. "Young lady, are you really Roxanne Perello?"

"Yes sir, I am," she said weakly as she sat, and before the officer could even ask her she continued, "and I promise to tell the truth, the whole truth and nothing but the truth so help me God," she then put her hand on the Bible in front of her.

The officer just shrugged his shoulders and walked away.

Jacob Luke approached her. He was speechless for a moment.

"How are you feeling, Mrs. Perello?" He looked her over like a doctor would a patient. He could tell she was still in bad shape.

"I've felt better, but I'll be alright," she said.

"You're somewhat of a miracle to us, Mrs. Perello. I'm sure you must be aware that we've been having your murder trial?"

Her blue bruised eyes wrinkled a little as she forced a smile.

"Yeah, well I'm not dead, so I think it's a little premature." People in the courtroom laughed at this.

Foster stood up. "Objection Your Honor, how do we really know this is the victim and not just another of the defense's tricks?"

"Mr. Foster, I know of no tricks the defense has played so far. Do you really wish to go there again?" Foster shook his head and sat down. "No, Your Honor."

"Young lady, do you have any proof of who you are?" the judge asked kindly.

"Yes, sir. That's my stepmom right there, Debra Rivers." Roxanne pointed to a middle-aged brunette lady sitting by Marge. "She's got all kinds of pictures of me, graduation stuff and all."

"Please stand up, Mrs. Reames. Is this true, you can provide evidence to this courtroom?"

"Yes Your Honor," as she stood. "I have her school yearbook and photos right here," she said, holding them up. The judge motioned for her to come forward, so she brought several items to the front and showed them to the judge.

"Please continue, Mr. Withers."

"So Roxanne," Jacob continued, "if I may call you by your first name?"

Roxanne smiled and nodded.

"Where have you been all this time, and what happened to you?" Jacob stepped back and leaned against the defense table.

"Well," Roxanne's voice was soft, "believe it or not, I've just recently begun remembering things. The night I left Michigan, the night you say that Sam McBride killed me, I was at the bar with my idiot, soon-to-be-ex-husband, Angelo."

Angelo still watching from the jail just frowned.

"And he was flirting with someone on the phone and I overheard him. So I called him a pig. So he grabbed me and pulled me outside and split my lip open for me. And that's when I decided that was it. I was leaving. I told Angelo before that if he ever hit me again I would leave. Because he's put his hands on me before, Your Honor," she said looking at the judge. "Well, he told me if I ever left him, it would be the last thing I'd ever do. So I knew I had to get far away." Roxanne paused to catch her breath.

"So I started hitching west. I made it as far as Illinois when I got picked up by these three guys. They said they were going to Texas and asked, 'did I want to go?' Well I didn't have no money or nothin' and they said they had some dope so I figured, what the heck, I didn't have anything to lose. We partied the whole way there. No one even slept.

"Everything was cool for a while, they even tried to get another girl to go, but for some reason she wouldn't get in the car. It was getting late and we were all stoned. Then the two guys in the back tried to put some moves on me. I tried to stop them but one wouldn't take no for an answer. He was trying to kiss me and he put his hand where he shouldn't have. So I bit him on his cheek, hard and it bled. He didn't like that at all, so he beat me real bad. I tried to jump out but they wouldn't let me. They laughed at me. They pulled the car over and raped me and beat me up real bad. I blacked out. The next thing I knew I was in a hospital bed with a nun looking down on me talking some foreign language, which I now know was Spanish.

"The nuns put ointments and ice packs on me and sewed me up and all. For a long time I didn't remember anything. I didn't know who I was or where I was, nothing. One of them that talked English told me some farmer found me and that I was in Mexico. I was in lot of pain and confused. I slept a lot.

"And then one day this beautiful angel named Marge came walking in." Roxanne smiled at Marge. Marge returned the gesture.

"She stayed by my side the whole time. Love you, Marge," Roxanne said from the witness box. The judge cleared his throat.

"She prayed for me and sang to me and read from the Bible and all. And then I finally remembered what happened when I blacked out. I thought it was a dream at first." Roxanne's forehead creased, she turned her head away as if she was seeing what happened for the first time, her eyes closed and lips locked together as she remembered, tears streaming down her face. "They left me for dead like I was a piece of trash or somethin'." Roxanne was sobbing now as were half the people in the courtroom. Denise was especially touched. Gathering her strength, Roxanne continued. "But Marge came and was right there holding me and praying for me almost like she was my mother." Again, now with mascara-streaked cheeks, she looked affectionately over Marge's way.

"Finally, the nuns said I was well enough to travel." Roxanne looked tired and a little embarrassed as she looked around the courtroom with so many strangers hearing her story. "And here I am, still alive." She laughed with a nervous laughter and wiped her eyes and looked thoughtfully over at Sam at the defense table. "I'm sorry, Mr. McBride. I'm sorry for all you went through, but I know they're gonna let you go home now, and I'm glad for ya'. I don't know what I'm gonna do, but I'll be alright. I know I ain't gonna let nobody put their hands on me again."

Angelo in the jail looked down in shame.

Households throughout the world were quiet, eyes fixed on their television sets.

"Your Honor, in light of present circumstances," Jacob Withers stepped forward, "I ask that all charges against my client be dismissed."

The judge looked over at the jury, and then he carefully examined the yearbook and photos of Roxanne.

Seconds passed.

Denise bit her lip.

Jacob ran his fingers through his hair.

Foster, with a hanky, wiped a scuff off his shoes.

The world was on the edge of their seats.

A few whispers could be heard in the jury box.

"Ladies and gentleman of the jury, and all concerned parties," the planet seemed to stop for a moment, holding its breath, "in light of the healthy recovery of said victim, Roxanne Perello, this court offers its sincere apologies to the falsely accused, Mr. Samuel McBride and his family, for the injustice they have endured and we ask for your forgiveness. This case is now dismissed."

The judge banged his gavel and said, "Mr. McBride, you are a free man."

Everyone rose to their feet, the courtroom erupted in applause.

Sam came over and hugged Denise.

A warm breeze that seemed to come from nowhere in particular ruffled the hair and clothes of all the people in the courtroom.

"Did you feel that?" a man asked.

"Heck yeah, where'd it come from?" a lady in a green dress replied.

They both looked around.

All at once a handful of some of the spectators in the court seemed to take on a strange glow. In the blink of an eye their clothes changed from grays and browns to white and gold. They're shoes turned into boots. Shiny swords appeared at their side as their wings spread out and then lifted to the sky. Other messengers, not previously in the courtroom, just appeared out of thin air. Nathanael, now in his angelic form, began to sing with a strong deep voice. As he did, those in the courtroom that could see and hear him were speechless. The ones who couldn't see were confounded.

"Great and marvelous are your deeds, Lord God Almighty.

Just and true are your ways, King of the ages." the other messengers joined in.

"Who will not fear you, O Lord,
and bring glory to your name?
For you alone are holy.

All nations will come
and worship before you,
for your righteous acts have been revealed."

Now, of the handful of people who could see and hear this phenomenon, one responded with laughter, another with tears, others just had a look of awe. Some actually had gotten down on their knees and prayed. One lady lifted her hands.

A few had a look of confusion on their face, wondering why the others who could see the angels were acting so funny. Some people in the courtroom applauded even more loudly. The judge was about to call for order with his gavel in hand but decided against it, and just smiled and shook his head in amazement.

Sam looked over at one of the angels who looked a lot like Officer Steve, who he'd met on Holiday Beach, but only with longer hair and a beard. Sam curiously looked him over, he returned Sam's look and gave him a big bright smile, then a wink. Surprise and unbelievable joy washed over Sam.

"What is it?" Denise asked Sam, noticing the astonished look on his face.

"That's him, the police officer from the beach," Sam said.

The angel waved at Sam and Denise, and then simply vanished before their eyes. Sam and Denise just looked at each other, amazed.

Through the corner of his eye, Sam saw a lady he'd not yet met, Mrs. Rumsy, come in with Pastor Dave and with them was...

"Amanda!" Sam shouted, and quickly walked over and grabbed up his daughter, lifting her off the ground. "I'm comin' home, baby."

"I know, Daddy, I'm so glad." She looked at him, tears of relief and joy filled both their eyes. They held on to each other like life depended on it.

"I've got my family back." Sam said outloud.

Finally Sam let go of Amanda for a moment and gave Jacob a bear hug, and then another for Marge. "Thank you, Thank you,

Oh thank you all so much for not giving up," he laughed and cried, tears of joy running down his cheeks. "I love you guys."

Denise looked at Marge and took her hands, "You are a life saver, Marge."

"No, not me," Marge smiled, looking up as if to Heaven. They both smiled and shook their heads in agreement.

Everyone in the courtroom was shaking hands and exchanging embraces.

Roxanne sat down with her foster mom, who had always been good to Roxanne, never really affectionate though. Roxanne looked at Sam with his family and friends embracing, laughing, and carrying on. She secretly longed for that kind of love in her life.

"Where is Nathanael?" Sam looked around for him. He couldn't see him anywhere, nor Prosecutor Foster for that matter. Sam made a mention of that to Jacob Luke.

"No, I haven't seen them either. Not since the case was dismissed." Jacob said, now looking, curious also.

Sam, Jacob, Denise and Marge all made their way out of the courtroom. Following closely behind them was Roxanne and her foster mom, Debra. Video cameras and microphones were held up and cameras clicked as they walked down the steps onto the sidewalk.

The media had been roped off with the rest of the public. The judge ordered the police that no one was to go through the boundary without explicit permission from the McBride family. The Wayne County Sheriff Deputies saw to that. Denise had already promised Maria an exclusive afterwards, so they were basically uninterested in any thing more than that as far as interviews went. They just wanted to get home.

On the courthouse steps, a man in the crowd shouted out "Sam McBride, where's your angel?"

A reporter moved toward them. He shoved his way through as he tried to wave down one of the group. "Can I just ask a few questions, please?"

But Sam and his family and friends just humbly waved and continued walking.

Denise leaned over and whispered in Sam's ear. Sam gave her back an inquisitive look; he cocked his head slightly sideways thinking, then after a few seconds he said "OK, let's do it."

Denise turned to look at Roxanne who was only three feet behind her with her foster mom. Denise stopped, turned and gave Roxanne a hug. "I wanted to tell you thank you, Roxanne," Denise said. "Thank you for being so brave. I'm so sorry about all you've been through …. You know, Sam and I were wondering …" Just as Denise was speaking, the sun suddenly broke through the gray clouds so brightly that it startled both Denise and Roxanne.

"Wow," Denise said as she and Roxanne both looked at the glaring sun, "maybe we could call that a sun-sign." Both ladies laughed. "Because Roxanne, Sam, Amanda and I … you know, we have an extra room, and we wanted to know if you might be interested in coming to stay with us for a while, like part of our family? You know you could take your time and sort things out and what not, for as long as you wanted. That is…" Denise looked respectfully at Debra, "if you don't already have plans, of course."

Roxanne was speechless. Her eyes welled up with tears. She nervously fumbled with her purse, looked down at the ground and asked, "Really? You're serious?"

"Yes, we're serious." Denise replied lovingly.

"OK! Yes, thanks. You mean right now, right away? I get to stay with the famous angel family?" Roxanne asked filled with anticipation at a new start.

Denise replied, "Whenever you're ready. You can come right now and we'll have some lunch, and get your things later if you want?" Roxanne looked at Debra, who returned a reassuring smile and gave Roxanne a handshake. No words had to be said.

The McBride's with Roxanne climbed into the bondo mobile to head for home. Sam sat in back so Roxanne could sit up front with Denise. Amanda scooted into her dad's arms, and with a nice backfire and puff of black smoke from the tail pipe, they were on their way home.

The end of this ordeal had turned out much better than any of them could have imagined.

Denise didn't have a new car yet, but she seemed to appreciate the old one more.

Mandy would have a new friend with Roxanne being around, who was much more hip, and somewhat younger than her mom.

Sam had a new chance, a third chance, and he was ready to make the most of it. So what could have been a terrible end, wound up to be brand new beginning.

Blowing somewhere in the wind, the question still loomed. Whatever happened to Nathanael and the prosecutor?

"So, hey God! That was You back there? I can't even believe all that. Angels that get beat up; runaway victims. What is this – some kind of joke?" Prosecutor Foster was speeding on his way home. Furious, hurt and disappointed, a wide range of emotions funneled through his mind.

"What did I ever do to You?" he shouted at the still bright sky. "If this was really You, and if You're so good and real and all, how about one little miracle for Brent Foster? If You gave me one little bonafide miracle, I'd serve You, too. Oh, but not me. You've got it in for me, don't you? But yeah, one sure thing, even a little one, and then I'd do whatever you said. Yeah, we'll see how real You are, here I am waiting!"

The Three which are One peered through a portal. An angel took notes on a scroll and then took the file in to the great wall that had millions, maybe even billions of names written on it. Each name had a box behind it filled with scrolls, every word, ever spoken about God, or to God, from the beginning of time was stored here. He spread his wings and flew up about 5000 feet. Finding the box that read 'Brent Foster' he deposited the scroll.

At the court, Judge Malkovich had been finalizing paperwork concerning the trial. "Fred," he called the officer who came right over, "bring me all the evidence; I've got a courier coming to take everything to storage within the hour." The officer went to the evidence table and picked up the sealed packages and brought them to the judge. The judge broke the seals to make quick checks of the contents before sending them off. Inside a glass beaker was a hair sample labeled 'Roxanne Perello.' There was also a blotter with a blood sample that read 'Crime scene, auto.' But the blotter that had Nathanael's name on it was crystal clear, as if it had never been used.

The clear bags that were labeled 'Feathers' were there, but the feathers were gone. The X-ray envelope was there but when the judge looked inside there was no x-ray, only a blank film.

"What the heck," the judge asked, looking at Officer Fred.

"I don't know, Your Honor, that stuff hasn't been touched by anyone." Fred said. The judge was perplexed. He walked over to the table and began looking around.

Brent Foster pulled into his driveway. Finding his way into his office, he saw he'd left his oil-filled heater on while at court. Breaking a sweat, he cracked the window to cool down the room.

He poured himself a scotch and sat at his desk and for a moment hung his head, then he looked up at the picture of his son, when just then, right before his eyes, a white foot-long feather landed on his desk in front of his son's picture. He picked the feather up and looked at it closely.

"What in the world?"

Foster, amazed, stared at the feather in his hand. Then the phone rang. He picked up the receiver and slowly answered, still distracted by the feather.

"Hello."

"Hi, … Dad?"

"Bryan? Is that you?" Foster asked excitedly, he set the feather on the desk.

"Yeah, Dad, it's me."

"Are you OK? You're not hurt or anything, are you?" Brent Foster asked.

"No Dad, I'm OK."

"I thought I'd never hear from you again, I mean I'm glad you called, but that's what you told me, you said you never wanted to talk to me again." Brent's voice dropped low almost to a whisper, overcome with emotion.

"I know, Dad." Bryan paused. "I've been thinking. You know it still hurts what you did to ma and me. I didn't think I could ever forgive you. But, umm, I was watching the trial, and I saw how hurt you looked there, you know. And I realized, I do miss you. And even though I'm still mad at you …" There was a longer pause this time. "I love you, Dad. I'm mad at you, but I love you, and I don't know what to do with that." Tears filled Bryan's voice. "Maybe you could help me figure it out, maybe we could talk, and maybe even be father and son again. I don't know, but if we don't talk about it, we'll never know, will we?" Bryan waited nervously, not knowing what to expect. There was a long silence on the other end.

"Oh son," Brent Foster cried, "I didn't think this day would ever come. I'm sorry, I'm sorry I hurt you and your mom." His heart of stone had somehow become soft, and the dam finally broke. "I've wanted to tell you that for a long time, but I guess I haven't had the guts. I've missed you so much." Brent wiped the tears from his face and looked at his wet hand, amazed. He hadn't seen his own tears in years. An unusually warm breeze blew in from the partly open window blowing some papers off of the credenza nearby.

"Son, can you excuse me for just a second?" He went to close the window. He heard a still calm voice call to him, *"What do you think, Brent? We kept our end of the bargain."*

Foster jerked open the window, "OK!" he shouted to the sky, "OK, I believe! You win! Whatever You want, I'm Yours!" Suddenly another stronger wind came in and blew through the room, sweeping the feather off the desk and up into the air. Foster saw it lift out the window and tried, but couldn't catch it. It went up past the old oak tree that bordered his yard until it drifted out of sight, and then, he could've sworn he heard Nathanael's voice that now seemed to come from inside him, *"Feels good, doesn't it Brent, being human?"*

Slowly a smile spread over his face.

Foster walked back over to the desk and picked up the phone.

"Son, I think I just got my miracle."

"What do you mean, Dad?"

"You son, you're my miracle. Can we get together?"

The End.

Or maybe? The beginning.

Also from Energion Publications

Prayer Trilogy is a story to remind us all that
... PRAYER is the key. ... Thumbs up!

— Doreen Ingram, author
My Sanctuary: A Place Called Home
series

You feel a need. You hear God
calling. What do you do now?

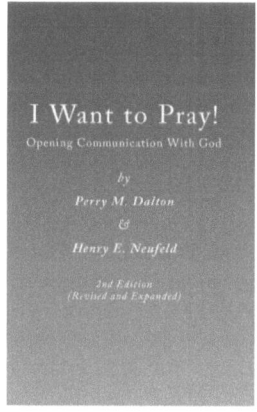

More from Energion Publications

Personal Study

The Jesus Paradigm	David Alan Black	$17.99
Finding My Way in Christianity	Herold Weiss	$16.99
When People Speak for God	Henry Neufeld	$17.99
Holy Smoke, Unholy Fire	Bob McKibben	$14.99
Not Ashamed of the Gospel	Henry Neufeld	$12.99
Evidence for the Bible	Elgin Hushbeck, Jr.	$16.99
Christianity and Secularism	Elgin Hushbeck, Jr.	$16.99
The Messiah and His Kingdom to Come	Bob Makar	$19.99 (B&W)

Christian Living

The Sacred Journey	Chris Surber	$11.99
Directed Paths	Myrtle Neufeld	$7.99
Grief: Finding the Candle of Light	Jody Neufeld	$8.99
Soup Kitchen for the Soul	Renee Crosby	$12.99
Will You Join the Cause of Global Missions?	David Alan Black	$4.99
I Want to Pray!	Perry Dalton	$7.99
Disciples: Jesus With Us	Riley Richardson	$7.99

Bible Study

"In the Original Text It Says"	Ben Baxter	$9.99
Learning and Living Scripture	Geoffrey Lentz	$12.99
The Gospel According to St. Luke: A Participatory Study Guide	Geoffrey Lentz	$8.99
Why Four Gospels?	David Alan Black	$11.99
Philippians: A Participatory Study Guide	Bruce Epperly	$9.99
Ephesians: A Participatory Study Guide	Bob Cornwall	$9.99

Theology

Christian Archy	David Alan Black	$9.99
God's Desire for the Nations	Philip O. Hopkins	$18.99
Ultimate Allegiance	Bob Cornwall	$9.99
History and Christian Faith	Edward W. H. Vick	$9.99
The Adventists' Dilemma	Edward W. H. Vick	$14.99
From Inspiration to Understanding	Edward W. H. Vick	$24.99
Out of This World	Darren McClellan	$24.99
The Questioning God	Ant Greenham	$9.99

Energion Publications — P.O. Box 841
Gonzalez, FL 32560
Website: http://energionpubs.com
Phone: (850) 525-3916